SWEET SURRENDER

Hungrily Jonah pressed his lips to hers. As if they had been separated a lifetime, they savored the luscious kiss. Her fingers knocked his hat to the floor of the buggy as K.T. put her arms around him to feel the strength of his body overwhelming her. The howl of the wind vanished as he leaned her back against the narrow seat.

A fervent sigh of longing drifted from her lips as his fingers gently sought the buttons of her shirtwaist. Knowing she should halt him, she did not want to do anything to cause him to take his hand from her. Deep inside her, she felt an emptiness she longed for him to fill with his warmth.

His mouth seemed determined not to miss a single inch of her skin. Each time she started to protest when he undid another button, he silenced her with a heated kiss that burned to her very center, releasing a sweetness that flowed outward to urge her closer to him.

When he pulled apart her gaping blouse, she did not feel any cold, for he bent to taste the flavors of the skin she had allowed no other man to touch. Her fingers twisted in his hair to keep him close to her when the stroke of his tongue sought beneath the lace of her chemise to tease her sensitive skin.

"K.T.," he whispered, "I have missed you so deeply the past two days. Come home with me tonight."

UNDER THE OUTLAW MOON

JOANN FERGUSON

To Mary,
Best wishes!
Hope you enjoy this!
JoAnn Ferguson

TUDOR PUBLISHING, INC.
NEW YORK CITY

Dedication:
Kate, Jeanette, Allison, Sandra . . . and Ron
     Thank you

Acknowledgments:
Many thanks to the Montana Travel Promotion board. Also, thanks to Mary Murphy, director of the Butte-Silver Bow Public Archives, and her staff, for their assistance and suggestions.

A TUDOR BOOK

December 1989

Published by

Tudor Publishing, Inc.
276 Fifth Avenue
New York, NY 10001

CHAPTER ONE

The whistle screamed through the valley before ricocheting off the Montana mountains. Passengers clung to their seats as the train fought its own inertia to stop before reaching the flames on the tracks. The flare of light cut through the darkness of the forested night.

Curses echoed from the engine through the full length of the train. Freight slid across the cars, careening off walls with a thunderous crash. People bounced forward, unable to stop as quickly as the train. Shrieks announced the pained impact of bodies against the unyielding seats.

As the cowcatcher halted less than a yard from the conflagration feeding on tar-covered ties beneath the tracks, the engineer slumped weakly against his speed lever. His forehead shone with perspiration. He had not been sure they could stop in time.

1

"Hands in sight, please."

The engineer did not show any astonishment at the voice sounding from beyond the cab. He slowly lifted his hands away from the throttle. Standing next to him, the fireman dropped his coal shovel to the floor. Its heavy iron scoop clanged in the fearful silence. He glanced with open fear at the window and raised his arms over his head hastily.

The rifle sticking through the glassless window withdrew long enough for a man to swing up into the small compartment. A dusty navy kerchief obscured the lower half of his face. The part visible was shadowed by the brim of his too-large hat. Keeping the weapon pointed at the silent men, he shouted what was clearly a signal to his cohorts.

To the trainmen, he said quietly, "A short delay only, gentlemen. The business will be done with proper haste. Then you may clear the tracks." He chuckled as his two captives exchanged a wary glance.

Farther back along the train, another form emerged from the shadows to enter the car he had been watching intently from the top of the grade. His pistol rested easily in his hand as he adjusted a handkerchief over his nose. Sapphire eyes twinkled with malicious glee. For more than twenty years, he had waited for this moment.

Deciding on a dramatic entrance, he kicked open the unlocked door. The lone man within saw the gun and froze. In a voice warm with amusement, the masked intruder ordered, "Unhook your gunbelt. Kick it over here."

The man in a beige shirt emblazoned "Flynn's Copper Mining Company" followed the order. To be defiant might save his employer's payroll, but it could cost him his life. He was not loyal enough to that old cutthroat to trade his life for money that did not belong to him. The leather gunbelt clunked dully on the dusty wood boards. With the tip of his boot, he pushed it toward the interloper.

The robber bent cautiously, never removing his eyes from the guard. He placed the belt over his left arm and signaled with his right. The gun made his point without words. The tan-shirted man walked swiftly to a safe in the corner, never taking his gaze from the blue eyes showcasing the criminal's delight. Bending, the guard twirled the dials to the proper combination. The small vault opened with a satisfying click.

As if he were royalty accepting his due, the thief took the gray cloth bag marked with the name on the man's shirt. Flynn's Copper Mining Company would pay its employees late this month. He hefted it, although there was no way to determine the exact amount in the bag without opening it. That detail did not matter to him, for he knew to the penny what should be in this sack. Flynn ordered the same amount from his bank in Butte every month.

"I thank you, sir, for your compliance. Express to your boss my gratitude for this generous gift." He laughed. "Tell Flynn this will not be the last time he suffers before we are done with him."

"And thank you, sir, for saving me the trouble

of having to ask this gentleman to retrieve the money for me."

The thief would have twirled at the sound of the light voice behind him, but the steel finger of a gun barrel in his lower back urged him to resist the impulse. Instead he glared at the guard. He had banked on the rich man's miserly reputation to post only one man on the train to guard the company payroll. He should have expected Flynn to be wiser than that. When he noted that the expression on the guard's face was not one of relief, he wondered what the guard was able to see that he could not.

"The money satchel, sir," said the still pleasant voice behind him. "But first, your gunbelts. On the floor. Both of them."

Knowing better than to spit out the curses racing through his head, he echoed the guard's degrading motions of loosening his gunbelt and letting it drop to the floor. The barrel in his back moved only slightly as his captor stretched to kick the weapons aside.

"Now the gun you are holding. Place it in my hand."

He regarded the slender fingers edging around his waist. A right hand. The scoundrel behind him must be left-handed. When he moved as if to grab the hand, he heard the distinctive click of a trigger. He spat an obscenity as he reluctantly obeyed the order.

"Now, now, sir. No hard feelings about this, right? I am sorry I have interrupted your plans, but, you see, this was my train tonight." The easy humor in the voice faded as it demanded, "The money sack. Now!"

As soon as he put the bag into the second thief's hands, he felt the gun leave the middle of his back. He whirled, but his fingers grasped nothing but air. The lyrical laugh, which enraged him, vanished as he saw a shadow moving beyond the door. He raced to it, the guard close behind him.

An exultant shout sounded through the night. Four riders' flight could be seen in the dust raised by their mounts climbing the grade. For a moment they were silhouetted against the starlit sky. With a distant whoop, they disappeared into the next valley.

The sound reminded the first thief of his perilous situation. He might not have garnered the prize, but he had attempted this robbery. Before the dazed guard could move, he leapt across the narrow room, grabbed his gunbelt, and fled through the door.

"Well, I'll be," murmured the man in the beige shirt. He wondered who would believe his tale of being held up by one thief, only to be witness to a second robbery of the same bag. As long as Mr. Flynn believed him, he would be all right. He did not want to lose more than his job as a result of tonight's experience. In spite of his dim future, he chuckled as he thought of the shock on the first thief's face when the second one pushed a gun in his back. That one must be a cocky young thing to steal money from a man nearly twice his size. The story would be worth many drinks by the time they reached Copper Peak.

He did not stir from the door as he saw another group of riders climbing the rock-covered ridge. That would be the first man's gang. He doubted if they would find the successful thieves. As composed as the young scamp had been, the guard was sure the youngster's gang would have been swallowed by the night.

The leader of the pursuing riders decided the same thing quickly. As they reached the crest, nothing could be seen moving in any direction. Only the swish of the wind through the stands of pine broke the midnight thick silence. He grumbled before rising to stand in his stirrups.

"You'll pay for this, you bastard!" he shouted into the night. The imagined sound of superior laughter taunted him. He did not like to think of the amusement he had heard in the other bandit's voice.

"Easy, Jonah," urged one of his companions. "You did what you wanted. You hurt Flynn."

"*I* didn't! It was that undersized bastard who—"

"Who had the guts to best you!" Laughter brightened the other men's spirits. Their only regret, other than losing what they would have been paid for their escapade tonight, was not being able to repeat the tale of the little thief who topped Jonah Bancroft at his own sport.

Their leader snapped, "How did they get past us? Didn't you keep a lookout?"

The men glanced guiltily at each other. One offered, "Jonah, we were busy. We—"

"Never mind. Let's go home." Jonah glared over his shoulder once more before he followed his own command. He would get that youngster. No one must halt his revenge against Lyndon Flynn.

No one.

On the far side of the ridge, the four riders slowed their pace. They shoved their kerchiefs down to their necks as they celebrated their coup. After an afternoon of watching the other gang build the pyre on the tracks and planning their attack, they had succeeded far better than they had hoped. All of the money from Flynn's payroll was theirs.

"I wish I could have seen the expression on his face," chortled the shortest one, who continued to hold one hand on the money satchel slung over the saddle horn. "I could see Meyer's face. He will have to think of a good one to tell Flynn how he allowed himself to be robbed twice tonight!"

"K.T., let's go into town and celebrate." The man on a black horse clapped his hands together in anticipation. "We sure can have fun with the amount of money in that bag."

"No," came back the quick answer. "Give them a day or two to cool off, Les. Flynn will have his new sheriff hot on our trail. We have to make sure he does not find us. Once things are calm again, then we can heat the town back up a little."

"Dammit, K.T., I—"

"Hush! I think I hear something."

A distant shout resounded over the valley. It silenced them as they tried to discern the words. When they understood the anger in the deep voice, laughter bubbled quietly from their lips.

The leader of the riders leapt to the ground and hefted the canvas bag from the saddle. K.T. pulled the broad-brimmed hat off to reveal a cascade of dark hair. She shook it back over her shoulders, glad it no longer pressed down on the top of her head. Swinging the hat in the air, she vowed, "You will have your chance, mister! You keep trying to rob our trains, and you will meet the Forresters again. I can promise you that!"

The three men standing near her echoed her words. This was Forrester territory. Other thieves should know better than to enter this section of Montana with larceny on their minds. She hoped the tale of the duping of those fools who worked so hard all day in the sun would convince competitors to stay away from Copper Peak and the region the Forrester gang called their own.

She grabbed the reins of her bay and motioned with her head for the others to follow her. They did not have far to go to the shack they lived in temporarily. Once she paid off Les Proulx and Jimmy Schurman, she and Ethan could deal with the rest of their good fortune.

The night welcomed them as they followed the rushing stream bed on its meandering journey. Others had lived here long ago, before the white settlers arrived and the ancient people were shoved aside to seek other fertile lands. High mountain pine and wolves called this desolate region home now. The creatures of the wilderness shared it with the Forrester gang, once led by Elijah Forrester. After his untimely death at the end of a hangman's rope, the leadership fell to the next elder Forrester. The rest of the quartet called her simply K.T.

A skip lightened her step as she led the way along the valley. Although she had been involved in other heists, never had she orchestrated anything this daring. She could not keep from smiling as she recalled the rage in the other thief's voice. Her decision not to let him see her directly had been a wise one. She doubted if he would have been as willing to cooperate if he had known he stood a head taller than she. His strong hands could have broken her, if the broad shoulders in front of her nose had been any indication of his strength.

She concentrated on her footing as she climbed the path that led to their aerie perched precariously on the ridge. It was not easy to get to, but it was simple to protect. Only one approach led to the place, so no one could attack them unseen. Eli had chosen it after careful consideration. Her older brother always thought everything through before he made a decision. That habit had kept him alive far longer than the average man in his trade.

K.T. pushed the thought of danger from her mind. Tonight she wanted only to celebrate their good fortune. It would allow them to survive until the next robbery.

Tossing the reins of her horse to Jimmy, she carried the bag into the tumbledown hut. Automatically, she tugged on the cloth nailed over the single window before she lit the lantern. She did not think the other gang would pursue them into the forested maze, but she had no intentions of letting a vagrant light betray them.

She hung the lantern on a hook pounded into

9

the rafters. The light revealed the few pieces of furniture in the room. A stove best known for its failure to heat the shack took half of the floor. A set of bunkbeds leaned against the wall. Behind them stood a changing screen made from feed-sack remnants and branches still covered with peeling bark.

She dropped the valuable bag onto the rickety table and pulled off her coat. Dust and pine needles billowed from the wool as she dropped it on the lower bunk. Her hat was flung on top of it. She slapped her denim trousers to loosen the dirt from them.

While she waited for her partners, she braided her hair to keep it from her eyes. The dark strands resisted every attempt she had ever made to control it into a bun. She found it easiest to contain it in the braids she had worn from her childhood. That time seemed an eternity ago, when her days were filled with luxury and she went to sleep each night to the velvet tones of a lullaby. Certainly, in the sweet security of her past, she never would have imagined she would be living this type of life.

By the time the three men came into the small cabin, she sat impatiently in the sole chair. All thoughts of the years gone by had vanished as she itched to see what they had garnered to-night. She said nothing as she stood and ripped open the buckles on the bag. With a victorious shout, she tipped it upside down. Clumps of greenbacks poured onto the table.

K.T. watched as the two taller men ran their fingers through it as eagerly as they caressed the bar harlots in town. Only Ethan held back in silence. She smiled when she shoved their hands away. They grumbled, but no one contradicted her leadership, although each man had to look down to meet her stern gaze.

"If you can stop acting like crazed fools, we can count this out and you'll get your share."

"Let us enjoy this a little, K.T.," muttered Les. He ran a hand through sparse hair spread across his surprisingly pale head. The line where his hat usually sat on his forehead made a sharp delineation between tanned skin and his cadaverously white scalp.

She slapped away his wide-knuckled fingers. "Celebrate later. This is business. Business I want done right, so none of you buzzards can accuse me of cheating you."

"We trust you, K.T.!"

Her face softened as she looked at Ethan. To anyone else, her younger brother would seem a liability, but she refused to let him be left behind when they did their work. He was too gentle and too kind, which was surprising because he had been raised to this life after their mother's death. He could not remember the other times when she and Eli had lived in the warmth of familial love. She wanted Ethan to learn to be strong, to be able to replace her as the leader of the Forrester gang. If something happened to her, Les and Jimmy would drop him instantly. He had to be able to take care of himself. That was a tall order for a boy just turned sixteen, but K.T. had found the world a rough place not willing to help anyone.

11

"I will count it with you watching," she said, flashing a smile in his direction. His brown hair was the color all the Forresters shared. Dark eyes so like hers must one day be as hard as the glittering eyes of a rattler hypnotizing its prey. She would teach him. Turning, she glared at the other men, who stayed with her only because they did not have the brains to find their own opportunities for profit. "Then you two can get out of here."

Silence filled the cabin as she sorted the bound packets of money. She knew how much should be in the bag. Flynn never varied his order to the bank. His parsimonious ways were well known. Men had worked for him for years without a raise.

A murmur of appreciation filled the room as she finished the count. Deftly she divided it into the shares they had agreed on while waiting for the night train. Handing Les and Jimmy their spoils, she motioned toward the door with her head.

"Find a hole somewhere for about a week. Don't come out and certainly don't start dropping big piles of money in town. If you want to hit big again, we must not let it be known that we were the ones who ended up with Flynn's money."

"Ah, K.T., what is the point of—"

She rose and confronted Jimmy. His bulbous nose had been broken in too many saloon fights. It lay defeated against his sallow cheeks. No matter how much they stole and how well they ate, Jimmy always looked half-starved. He lowered his pale eyes before her glare.

"What is the point of having money if you can't spend it? Is that what you were going to say?" she demanded. Her hands fisted on her hips as she wished she could find some brains for these men whose burly muscles were necessary to her. "Think about this. What is the point of having money if you are swinging at the end of a rope? Be free with that cash, and Flynn's new sheriff will haul you in quicker than you can blink. We may have had Clapton fooled, but this new one might be smarter."

"K.T.," he began in a petulant tone.

She grasped two handfuls of his dirty shirt and stuck her nose directly beneath his. "Listen, you fool! I do not intend to swing for your idiocy. Betray us by being unable to wait a measly week to spend your money on cheap whiskey and cheap women and I will never let you work with us again."

As he did every time she forced the issue of her leadership in the gang, he backed down. He could have crushed her arm with the grip of a single hand, but he feared her intelligence too much to harm her. Even Elijah Forrester had not had her natural knack of finding prey. When she confronted him, Jimmy forgot she was a woman and saw only her rage.

"All right," he grumbled. "One week."

"Seven nights!"

"I ain't stupid!"

"Prove it to me," she snapped, releasing his shirt. She wiped her hands on her trousers. A glare in Les's direction told her he would accept her restrictions as well, since he was acting uncharacteristically cooperative. She motioned toward the door. "Get out of here. I'll send for you if I need you."

"Soon?" asked Les greedily.

"As soon as I hear when Flynn arranges for the shipment to replace this one. He will learn we aren't finished with him yet." Abruptly she frowned as she heard similar words repeated in her memory. She had not spoken them. The tall man who first robbed Flynn's guard had said them. Her soft "Damn" was swallowed by the closing of the door as her partners left.

It had been fun to show up that other gang tonight, but it was not something she wanted to make a practice of. For one thing, there had been five of the others. Being outnumbered could lead to defeat quicker than anything else. She trusted the trueness of her eye and the swiftness of her trigger finger, but she could not best too many at once. Neither did she want to be in competition for what she considered *her* prey. Having the law on their trail was bad enough. They did not need vengeance-seeking competitors trying to destroy them.

She sighed and went to the tattered screen on the far side of the bunks. Her clothes were filthy and stiff with perspiration from the hours of lying on the hilltop and watching the others lay kindling on the tracks.

"K.T., I'm going out for some water," called her brother.

"Make sure you clean the green scum off the cistern. Last time you forgot, we got sick."

"I remember. There isn't much water left."

"I know." She smiled as she peeked around the edge of the screen. When she winked at him, the years of rough living fell from her face. Her slender features glowed with a happiness she felt too seldom. "Another stroke of luck like tonight and we can be done with this. I like to think of Flynn paying for our tickets to a better life."

Ethan chuckled as he went out into the yard. Too often lately he had heard K.T. musing aloud of another life far from the ridges overlooking the rails in southwestern Montana. It brought the old, unanswered questions to the forefront of his mind.

She had told him very little about their family. Eli had said nothing. In spite of their reticence, he suspected that the Forrester family once had made their living in a way that did not include holding up mail and payroll trains. K.T. never said exactly what she wanted to do when they left, but he was sure it would be in a place where she could luxuriate in the lush life she craved.

He leaned over the cistern. High on the cliff, they had found it impossible to sink a well. Instead they relied on the rains to provide them with the water they needed. It had been too long since the last rainfall. If rain did not come soon, they would be desperate for water.

The bucket crashed against the stones at the bottom at the same time it splashed into the water. Ethan frowned. In the starlight, he could not see any reflection in the cistern. They might be in worse straits than he had thought. He must let K.T. know. She would have a plan to deal with this. She always did manage something.

Leaning over the stones, trying to discern the water remaining, he did not see the form moving behind him. Pain flashed through his head to leave him in darkness. Only a hand clutching the back of his shirt kept him from pitching head first into the cistern. He moaned once more as he was dropped to the cold ground, then was silent.

In the cabin, K.T. began to wonder what was taking her brother so long. She hoped he had not gone down to the river to get water. Any pursuit would come that way. He should know that, but he did not share her natural affinity for this job.

She kicked aside her filthy clothes. Tomorrow, if it dawned sunny, she had to do laundry. She must have her single frock cleaned and freshly pressed before she and Ethan went into Copper Peak to spend some of their share of the money for supplies. The cupboards over the stove were nearly as empty as the cistern in the yard.

When the door opened slowly, she started to speak. Some sense she could not name kept her silent. It was not Ethan entering the cabin. He never came in without calling a greeting, even when he had been only as far as the stable.

Slowly she squatted so her eye was even with one of the rents in the changing screen. She scowled, but was not surprised to see a man's hand reaching for the packets that held the Forresters' share of the money stolen tonight. Moving cautiously, she hoped the sound of her silken undergarments would not betray her. Her hand slipped to her right calf. A smile settled on her lips as she touched the weapon secured there. Easily she withdrew the knife.

"Back so soon?"

Her words startled the man into dropping his loot. He stared at her in terror. His eyes riveted on the knife in her hand visible around the edge of the screen. When he started to back away, her smile broadened. In a fluid motion so fast he could not follow it, she sent her weapon speeding toward him.

The knife thudded into the wall, pinning his sleeve to the wood. She whipped her wrapper around her, buttoning it into place as she emerged from behind the screen. In her hand was her pistol. Her eyes flashed ebony fire as she crossed the narrow room. Before the man could speak, she reached up and plucked her knife from his sleeve.

"Out, Les. Out, and don't come back again. You got your share. I'll be damned to hell before I let you have mine and Ethan's."

He pressed his hand over his bleeding arm. That she had only nicked his skin was her choice. He knew that if she wanted, she could have killed him with ease. Snarling, he threatened, "You will be sorry, K.T. Forrester. If Eli was alive—"

"He would shoot you." She smiled grimly as her thumb rested lightly on the hammer of the gun. "But aren't you lucky that I am more forgiving?" With her head, she motioned toward the door. She wiped her knife on the skirt of her

17

dressing gown. Her smile never faltered as she said almost conversationally, "If I were you, Les, I would leave. I can feel my compassion for you fading very, very fast."

"K.T., I—"

Her eyes narrowed as she interrupted him. "I said very, very fast, Les."

Knowing better than to argue, he whirled and ran out of the door. He collided with Ethan, but simply pushed the slighter man out of his way. Shouting a question after Les, Ethan looked at his sister in confusion. When he saw the pistol in her hand, he frowned. Instantly he understood it must have been their partner who had knocked him aside the head.

K.T. pulled her eyes from the man riding away on his horse. She felt some regret at losing Les. He was a good strong-arm man. The rebellion had been building for the past six months since she assumed leadership of the Forrester gang. Tightening the neckline of her well-worn robe, she murmured, "We don't need any snakes anyhow."

"K.T.?"

"He tried to rob us," she said without emotion. When she heard his sharp intake of breath, she laughed. The cold sound filled the small room. "What's wrong, Ethan?"

He rubbed the back of his head, but said nothing. K.T. had enough to think about without bothering with his headache. "Nothing," he mumbled.

"You have to stop judging everyone else by your standards," she admonished. "Did you think he was so honest he would never do anything to us?"

"You would not steal from him."

She shrugged. "And maybe that is my short-coming." She sighed and stepped aside to let him in the cabin. "How about a late supper? What do we have?"

"Bread, beans, salt pork. Maybe a bit of flour for flapjacks."

"Whatever you want to make, Ethan."

She paid no attention to him as she scooped the rest of the money into the bag. If she kept her ear to the ground, she would be able to discover when Flynn was shipping his next payroll. Then it would be split only three ways. Two for the Forresters and one for Jimmy. She forced a tired smile onto her lips.

This life might lack easy comforts, but it was extremely profitable. It would buy K.T. Forrester her dreams, and that was all that mattered.

CHAPTER TWO

K.T. adjusted her bonnet as she drove with her brother into Copper Peak in the wagon they had found broken near the riverbed. With his mechanical ability, which enabled him to take anything apart or put it back together with a minimum of tools, Ethan had repaired it. They normally kept the wagon hidden beneath a bower of pine branches half a mile from their cabin.

With his arms resting lightly on his knees, Ethan held the reins loosely. As his sister did, he studied the street. It had become habitual with both of them to check out every new scene before lowering their guard. Today they must stay alert all the time they were in the village.

Copper Peak was not much of a settlement. It clung to the hills overlooking the massive mine that had eaten into the valley. The smelter just beyond the town spat its noxious fumes into the air, destroying the fresh scent of the pines. This was the first of the many sites now owned by Flynn's Copper Mining Company. The success Lyndon Flynn had had here enabled him to buy up other useless silver claims and profit from finding the copper the previous prospectors had ignored.

Slowly Ethan drove along the single business street. The houses of Flynn's employees ran in rows perpendicular to the street. They were tarpaper and board shacks not much better than the cabin where the Forresters lived overlooking their deserted riverbed. K.T. always refused to look at the cluster of houses. She did not want to think of the horrid lives of those who called them home. Flynn's employees were slaves, tied to him through subtle economic controls and the lack of other jobs in the valley.

Ethan stopped the wagon in front of the mercantile store, the only one in Copper Peak. He leapt from the high seat. After tying the horses to the hitching pole, he came around to help K.T. He smiled at her impatience. She felt more comfortable in her denims, riding astride on her horse through the open areas of the forest. As he did every time she made this transformation, he admired her ability to play the role of a lady accustomed to wearing only gingham and calico.

Smoothing her thick layers of skirts, K.T. examined the many people on the street. She frowned in the shade of her poke bonnet. It was not a holiday by her calculation. There must be some other explanation for the crowds loitering on the rutted, dirt road.

"Ethan, what do you think is going on?"

21

"I'll listen about. Do you want me to go to the saloon?"

She smiled at his distaste. Her brother belonged in a fine Eastern home instead of being caught in this rough world. Not that he was unwilling to fight when necessary. It was simply that he avoided any confrontation. In that way he was the opposite of her. She delighted in any chance to face her problems head-on.

"No, not yet." She tucked the strings of her bag over her arm. More money than she normally carried had been stuck in it before they left home. She did not trust Les not to come back to the cabin and rob them while they were in Copper Peak. "Let's go in the store. Maybe we can do our shopping and get out of here before whatever is supposed to happen happens."

He nodded. He could sense eager anticipation flitting from one person to another like a message bouncing along a telegraph wire. When he saw the disquiet on his sister's face, he knew he had a reason to worry. He trusted her intuition. If she wanted to hurry, he would do all he could to get them out of town before . . . whatever.

Inside, they found the cluttered store rumbling with conversation. K.T. had to remember her image as a gentlewoman coming to do her shopping. Flynn was glad to have the outlying ranchers and few prospectors come into Copper Peak to buy their supplies. When they first arrived here, Eli had intimated that they owned a sheep ranch higher in the mountains. That would explain why they came into town so seldom. So far the story had served them well.

She gave her brother a silent order. Instantly he moved away from her to wander about the room as if interested in the products on the overburdened shelves. Instead he was listening to the various conversations to learn what he could of incidents in town, and possibly even the valuable information as to when Flynn promised his employees they would be paid. From that they could calculate when the next shipment of money would be on the westbound train.

Feigning a similar interest in the multitude of items, K.T. felt her mouth tighten. Flynn did not offer all these wares for the sake of his employees. Few could afford to buy the luxuries in plain view, but simply by signing a promissory note, the fantasies could belong to them—at least until they fell behind in the payments. Then Flynn repossessed, and added a hefty interest charge to their debts.

She stopped at the counter. "Good day, Mr. Barlow," she said to the man on the other side.

He grinned broadly. As assistant to the store manager, he took orders from the customers. Dark hair that looked as if it had not seen a brush in weeks drooped over his indolent eyes. A wrinkled shirt smoothed as he leaned forward to rest his elbows on the waist-high counter.

"It's been a long time, honey."

"Yes, we have been busy," she answered noncommittally.

"I don't understand why a pretty gal like you wants to be living up on a high reaches ranch with her brothers. Why don't you come to town? I could show you how to kick up your heels."

With a smile, she said, "I'm sure you could, Mr. Barlow. Unfortunately the ewes don't understand when I want to take a day off." She held out a slip of paper. "If you would have this order filled, I would appreciate it very much."

"How much?"

"Very much." She pretended she did not see his lecherous wink.

Turning her back on him, she watched Ethan walking about the room. No one near her seemed to be interested in what might be going on outside. She scowled. Foolish females! All that mattered to them was if the shipment of new fabrics had arrived. She wondered what they would do if they had to earn the money they wasted on the overpriced items at Flynn's store.

Her forehead threaded with concern as she saw her brother surreptitiously signaling for her attention. She crossed the room to stand by one of the two plate glass windows flanking the door. When he put his hand on her shoulder, she tilted her head toward him. Her eyes noted the concern on his face, gray beneath his permanent tan. Suddenly she did not want to hear what he had to say.

Perversely she heard herself asking, "What is it, Ethan? What have you heard?"

"K.T., they are going to hang Jimmy."

"What?" she gasped. She spun to see the crowd gathering on the street. It continued to amaze her that professed God-fearing, honest folk delighted in such executions. Children ran among the adults, playing games as if a carnival or a snake oil salesman had come to town.

24

Drawing her brother to one side of the store, she asked, "What are they hanging him for?"

"He tried to rob the bank."

"He what?" She lowered her voice, which had risen on the two words. The curse she whispered would have shocked the other women in the store. "How could he be so stupid?"

Ethan shrugged with the eloquence of his bony shoulders and too-large hands. "Don't know. Guess the temptation of all that money was too much to be denied. Caught him last week."

"Last week, was it?" The rage that had daunted men twice K.T.'s size silenced her brother. After Jimmy had promised her he would lay low, he ran immediately for Copper Peak. The lure of fast women and smooth whiskey had proven too much for him. She looked across the street to the single saloon, owned as everything else was in Copper Peak by Lyndon Flynn. One of the dance hall girls must be enjoying the money K.T. had risked her life to steal from that train.

As suddenly as it had flared, her fury vanished. This was not the time to be angry about Jimmy's betrayal. Compared to what Les had done, this was nothing. She sighed. Jimmy would die at the age of twenty-two.

Ethan whispered the details of the bank robbery. It had been little more than a drunken carousal, but Flynn's new sheriff competently had matched Jimmy's name and description to a yellowing wanted poster in his office.

"Wanted poster? His own? Not one for the Forrester gang?" She did not want their names to be brought to the forefront in the aftermath of the train robbery. She did not need some sheriff anxious to impress Flynn hot on their trail.

"Seems he was involved in some bank hold-ups in Texas before he attached himself to Eli."

"So they decided to hang him so quickly?"

"He shot five people in Texas, K.T."

His words deflated her totally. Gentle Jimmy did not seem the type to pull the trigger of his gun randomly. She could imagine Les slaying someone simply for the excitement. Often she had seen Les cleaning his gun, rubbing it for hours with an expression of pure delight on his face. Les could slay a man easily, but not her other partner.

"I felt the same," Ethan added softly when he saw her expression. It was odd for K.T. to reveal her feelings this way. He knew how upset she must be.

When she stepped purposefully toward the door, he caught her arm. He pulled his fingers away at her glare. Her features softened when she took his arm and placed her fingers on it.

"I'm going out there."

"Are you sure, K.T.?"

"Someone who cares for him should be with him when he dies." She reached up and tapped the brim of his hat. "Keep this low. We don't want anyone having any suspicions we are any different from these vultures who delight in lawful murder."

K.T. pulled on the wide front of her bonnet. She could not allow anyone to recognize her.

Not that many here would. Only the few guards they had confronted on various trains might have seen her wide, nearly black eyes and guessed her to be the slight robber who stole what they had been paid to protect.

The street had become a human river. She wondered if the copper mines had been closed so the miners could rejoice in this due process carried out by the judge Flynn had chosen to preside over his city. Only that would explain the mass of people crowding to find a vantage point to watch the execution.

Using her elbows, she fought her way toward the front. Ethan followed in her wake, tipping his hat to the disgruntled ladies his sister had shoved aside. They stopped about fifteen feet back from the scaffolding. She did not want to be closer. Although she tried to tell herself it was because she did not want to risk being seen, she wondered more honestly if she could halt herself from racing up to prevent her friend from being killed.

Jimmy had been with them only a year when Eli died after the botched holdup six months before. She remembered him refusing to let the Forresters watch Eli's hanging. Perhaps he had been right, although she had stamped in fury around the cave they were hiding in. As weak as she felt today with a stomach that threatened to erupt at any second, she could imagine how much worse it would have been to see her adored brother executed by a vengeful public.

She scowled as she saw the man she knew was Lyndon Flynn step up on the gallows. Trust the braggart to use this opportunity to show how he controlled the town! He never missed any chance to parade his superiority before those who depended on him for their livelihood.

The sun glistened off the sweat beaded like a string of obscene jewels on his wide forehead. He had fought his way up from being as poor as his employees to owning Flynn's Copper Mining Company and the town of Copper Peak. Every scar of that scraping path to the top showed on his features. He tried to hide his low-class background with expensive silk suits and the flash of gold on his fingers and in the pocketwatch at his waist. He opened it as if time were more important than a man's life.

K.T. wanted to scream out her revulsion as Flynn waved in a startlingly suggestive motion to a woman standing not far from her. His libertine tastes were well known throughout the valley, but men who wanted to keep their jobs soon found it wise to relinquish their daughters and wives temporarily to their employer. K.T. allowed a smile to play about her lips as she imagined how she would introduce him to the most trusted friend she always wore strapped to her calf. Her knife would teach him how foolish he was to try to seduce her against her will.

A low murmur ran through the crowd when the new sheriff appeared next to his employer. K.T. keenly appraised the man. If Flynn hoped to find another lackey like Clapton, he appeared to have failed. This handsome man who held the eye of every woman on the street did not look the type to bow to Flynn's superiority. As her eyes wandered from his smile sparkling beneath his auburn mustache to the breadth of his shoulders garbed in dark flannel, she felt sure that this man had earned the right to wear the silver star pinned to his chest. His pistols were slung at exactly the right height to enable him to pull them with ease.

She wondered if Flynn would have this man riding shotgun on the payroll. Her tongue dampened her suddenly dry lips. If she met this new sheriff on the train, she was not sure which one of them would be the victor. She listened to the twittering from two women in front of her. It would seem the sheriff had been victorious in a few social confrontations already, although he had not proven his lawkeeping ability until he captured Jimmy.

A shout resounded along the street. K.T. forgot everything but the fact that her friend was going to die within minutes. She clenched her teeth in rage as she saw the deputy push the convicted man ahead of him. Jimmy's hands were tied behind his back, and his scrawny legs kept tripping in his boots, which seemed too big. She wanted to scream out that someone had stolen the fine leather boots he was so proud of.

She heard Ethan's muffled sniffle next to her. Patting her brother's hand, she offered him a comfort she could not feel. Her gaze did not waver from Jimmy's uneven steps climbing the stairs to the waiting noose.

"Oh, Jimmy," she whispered, "how could you be so stupid?"

She felt Ethan put his arm around her trembling

29

shoulders as Jimmy was propelled forward to stand beneath the rope. Wanting to close her eyes, but fearing she would imagine worse than the reality if she did, she stared unblinkingly at her friend. That he saw them standing near the front of the crowd she knew by his quick smile in their direction. It was as if he wanted to console them.

Flynn demanded, "Any last words, Schurman?"

"Just a few." Jimmy retained an odd dignity as the rope wider than K.T.'s largest finger was slipped over his head. "I want to say I have had a damn good life with good friends, good times, and a hell of a lot of fun with your money, Flynn."

Choleric color emphasized the scars on Flynn's face. He spat, "Tell us the ones who helped you, Schurman, and we will—"

"No," the condemned man said without hesitation. His gaze went to K.T. and quickly away. "I won't betray my friends. They are all halfway to California by this time anyhow."

K.T. did not see the signal Flynn made. Later she guessed it was the sheriff who had gestured to the hangman. The trap door vanished beneath Jimmy. Within seconds, he was no more than a corpse swinging with the motion of the twisted rope.

Biting her lip, she took a handkerchief from her bag and pretended to wipe dust from her face. Instead she used it to blot the wetness clouding her eyes. She had not cried when Eli was captured and suffered this fate, but now it seemed she would not be able to control the floodtide rising behind her eyelashes.

"Are you all right?"

She nodded silently to her brother. "Let's go. Our order should be ready by now. I have had enough of Copper Peak."

"Yes, K.T.," he replied meekly. He rubbed his nose against his sleeve as he watched her adjust her bonnet. Although she must feel the same nauseous weight in her stomach he was suffering after seeing their friend killed so heartlessly, she acted as if the hanging had been no more than an unavoidable delay in getting out of town.

She led the way through the clumps of conversation to the general store. Once she had determined their order was complete, Ethan would bring the wagon around to be loaded. She could return to the privacy of her home and the muffling thickness of her pillow. Until then, she would allow no one to guess at the pain within her.

As she stepped onto the boardwalk in front of the store, she paused. The crowd had begun to drift away. A familiar voice caught K.T.'s keen ear.

"That is one less of those bastards to prey on our town."

She whirled. Her mouth became an "O" to match her wide eyes. Ready to point out to her brother that she had heard the man she had tricked on the night train, she found she was looking at a man who could not be the same one she had duped so deftly. This man wore a silver star over his heart.

The sheriff was leaning on a hitching bar in front of his office next to the mercantile. His blue eyes crinkled with good humor as he spoke to another man. Broad shoulders strained his shirt as he flung out his hands to accent his words spoken in a warm drawl. He slapped a third man companionably on the back as the newcomer joined the conversation.

K.T. clutched onto the porch upright and wondered if she had gone mad. When the sheriff turned his back to her to laugh with his friends, she could not doubt that he was the man she had stolen Flynn's payroll from. The same lithe line of his hips with a gunbelt drooping across them had been directly in front of her when she demanded the money satchel from him.

"K.T.?"

She swallowed, and Ethan stared at her surprisingly pale features. He could not remember the last time he had seen her frightened, but he was sure she was terrified now.

"Who is that?" she whispered, pointing a trembling finger toward the threesome just beyond earshot of her soft voice.

"The sheriff. I think the other two are—"

"Never mind them!" Frustration sharpened her voice. "I mean, what is his name? The sheriff's!"

He shrugged. "Who knows? Flynn hired him on about a month ago, from what I heard before . . ." He glanced guiltily at the gibbet, unable to speak of the execution. Clearing his throat, he said, "Just steer clear of him, K.T. He is a sharp one, from everything I have heard."

"He must be," she mused. When Ethan asked her what she meant, she did not reply. A slow smile crossed her face. She had to admire a man who hid his larcenous activities behind the guise of a lawman. It was a ploy worthy of the Forrester gang at their finest.

She hurried into the store before the sheriff could look her way and suspect what she did. If he discovered her identity, she would die, even if he was not the thief she had stolen from. As a peace officer, he must be anxious to rid the region of the remnants of the Forrester gang. As a bandit, he would want to rid himself of his competition.

Mr. Haggerty greeted all his many customers with a smile. Although he was paid a straight salary like the rest of those living in Copper Peak, the store manager was pleased with the turnout for the hanging. The more things he sold for Mr. Flynn, the less he would risk losing his job. He had been here only a year and did not want to suffer the dismissal his predecessor had.

"Yes, miss," he said quickly when she asked if her order was ready.

"Good. My brother is bringing our wagon around. I will be happy to be on the road early. I don't like returning to the ranch after dark."

He nodded. "That is wise. Young things like you two should not be out on the trail by yourselves. Never can tell who might be ready to rob you. You should have your older brother with you."

"My other brother is competent with a rifle, Mr. Haggerty." She smiled with what she hoped was a convincing expression. "He has to be. Wolves don't give us much warning when they sneak up on the flock. How much?"

When he named a figure, she was pleased she had guessed what it would be. She did not want anyone to see how much money she had in her bag. She withdrew the small roll of bills and handed them to him. Watching him count, she said softly, "I hope that is enough. Money is not something I am good at handling."

The storekeeper handed her back a five-dollar bill. "Here you go, miss. You are lucky you have brothers to take care of you. Get yourself a husband, and you will never have to worry your head with such details."

"Isn't that the truth?" She widened her eyes in an insipid look she found worked best on these fools. As if she wanted a man to run her life! She could do quite well by herself. Putting the extra money in her bag, she added, "I trust I will see you again soon, Mr. Haggerty. At least before the snow flies."

"Have a good journey!" he called to her back.

She turned and waved lightly before going out of the store. One thing she admired about Haggerty. He might be flirtatious, but he was honest. She did not have to check to be sure that everything she ordered would be loaded into the wagon. That was especially important today when she wanted to put the false fronts of the buildings of Copper Peak far behind them.

She watched Ethan help Barlow put the wrapped packages in the back of the wagon. She was glad they had the money to buy a few extras. Living had been lean for the past months. If things went as she hoped, better times were ahead for them.

"Good afternoon, ma'am."

K.T. glanced over her shoulder to see the sheriff leaning against a pole. Only the sternest discipline kept her terrified reaction from her face. The chances of his recognizing her in her calico gown·and poke bonnet were minuscule, but still her heart raced with fear as she coolly replied, "Good afternoon, sheriff."

"In town for the hanging?" he asked as he stepped toward her. She kept her eyes on the silver clasp closing the string tie at his throat. By looking at that, she did not need to meet his eyes, which might discover the truth.

"Why do you ask?"

He smiled with a warmth as thick as the Southern slur on his words. "I don't remember seeing you before. I was sure I would have met every pretty lady in Copper Peak by this time."

"It seems you were wrong."

"It seems I was." He looked up at the wagon in front of her. His keen eyes narrowed when they met Ethan's instantly guilty expression. Glancing from the lad to the woman who clearly had been waiting for this·ride, he wondered what the young man was afraid of. Every lad had done something he'd hope the town law officer would never learn about. A borrowed horse returned exhausted to its owner, or a bottle of whiskey stolen from behind the saloon and taken to a distant hillside to enjoy with comrades. Such escapades appealed to boys about this one's age.

He released the lad from scrutiny and returned his gaze to the woman quite willingly. Although he had spoken the words in an easy compliment, he was eager to learn why he had not

35

seen this pretty lady in Copper Peak before today. His eyes moved along the bright yellow of
her gown and appraised the beauty of her slender form. Other women he had met in town had
been awed by his title as sheriff or overly anxious to consider him for a husband. This one
regarded him with a coolness he seldom saw.

"May I help you up, miss?" he asked when he
realized he was being impolite for staring so
steadily at her.

"That isn't necessary. I can manage."

He grinned. "I'm sure you can. Just wanted to
be neighborly."

K.T. debated internally. She must remember
to think like a lady shepherd, not like a female
train robber confronting the man who would
kill her if he knew her identity. Letting a smile
drift across her lips, she resorted to the tactics
she had used with Haggerty and his assistants.
From the corner of her eye, she saw Ethan rest
his hand on the rifle that leaned on the seat
between them. If she did not end this unfortunate meeting soon, she feared her brother might
panic.

In a gentle voice unlike her usually forthright
tones, she purred, "Why, sheriff, that would be
so kind of you. I just did not want to keep you
from your important work."

"No need to worry." His gaze moved along
her body admiringly again as he held out his
wide hand. "I'm taking a break after stretching
the neck of that murderous thief. No need to
chase after shadows that I may never catch. I
figure his partners are halfway to California by
now as he said."

"Did he say that?"

When his eyes narrowed to sapphire slits, she was afraid she had made a horrible error. All he said was, "I would have thought you could hear well where you were standing in the crowd. You and your friend were quite close to the gallows."

Putting her hand to the lacy bodice of her gown, she murmured, "Oh, sheriff, that horrendous sight so upset me, I don't think I can recall a single word anyone said. Such a terrible way to end, don't you think?"

"A fate all such skunks deserve."

"Yes, I suppose you are right." She placed her hand on the palm still waiting for it. It did not surprise her that the skin was as harsh as the rock outcroppings edging the valley.

He drew her closer to help her climb around the wheel. "Left-handed, are you?"

In shock, she halted with her feet balanced on the running board. It brought her face to a level with his. When she saw other questions blossoming in his eyes, she knew she must get out of Copper Peak before this too intuitive man discerned other clues about her that had to be kept hidden.

"Why, yes. Is that suddenly a crime?" She laughed lightly. She was pleased when he showed the same puzzlement she had felt when she discovered the sheriff of Copper Peak might be a bandit. It meant he could not believe that this quiet-speaking, ladylike creature was the one who had pressed a gun to his back and stolen the payroll from him.

"Of course not." He assisted her to the high bench at the front of the wagon. "Good day, ma'am." Stepping back onto the boardwalk, he tipped his hat to her.

Ethan needed no order from his sister to slap the reins on the backs of the horses. He was careful not to show the urgency he felt as he drove the wagon south. When he started to turn on the seat, he felt K.T.'s hand on his arm.

"Don't look back!" she hissed. "He is watching us."

"He can't know. K.T., you must be wrong. The sheriff can't be the same man you robbed on the train."

"I know what I know." Bitterly she said, "He is the same man. If he recognized me, he would have wasted no time setting us to swing next to Jimmy."

"So what do we do?"

A smile teased her lips. "We teach him how stupid it is to try to inveigle his way into Forrester territory. Even lawmen can make mistakes. He made his when he tried to rob our train. If he has not learned that, he will." She relaxed as she grinned more broadly. "I promise you that, Ethan. He will learn how big a mistake that was."

CHAPTER THREE

With a nod, K.T. signaled to Ethan. He caught
the flash of her gun, although darkness hung
around them like a black fog. As one, they
shouted to their horses and rode full speed down
the ridge. She easily held to the saddle as the
back hooves of her horse slid on the steep slope.
The screech of the train whistle hurt her head,
but it was the best sign of victory. The train
must stop. Then the payroll would be theirs again.

The news of this shipment from Flynn's bank
had reached them just yesterday when Ethan
rode into Copper Peak to listen to the gossip at
the saloon. They had had little time to plan.
When they reconnoitered the area earlier in the
day, they had not been surprised to see that
someone had been there before them. Rocks piled
on the tracks would halt the train. She guessed
it was the handiwork of the bogus sheriff and
his gang.

Her eyes glittered as brightly as the stars overhead. She enjoyed the added excitement of the chance to beat the tall man once again. She watched the train come to a sudden halt, the cars bumping into each other. Sparks leapt from the wheels as the brakes locked, and cries of terror rose from the passengers.

When they reached the train, K.T. motioned to Ethan to take his usual position as a lookout. If trouble came, he would let her know by firing his rifle into the air. He had tried to convince her to allow him to take over Les's job of guarding her path of retreat. Only her insistence that he was of greater help watching for the law or the other gang made him grudgingly agree.

K.T. left her horse in the shadows of the vanguard trees along the hillside. She drew her pistol as she heard the shouts from the front of the train. The gun's grip felt cool in her hand, but warmed quickly. The days when she had been uncomfortable holding the weapon were so far in the past that she could not recall them. She had come to be most at ease when the shiny gun protected her from any surprises. By honing her skills through hours of practice, she knew she could beat anyone to the draw.

Stealthily she edged toward the mail car where she knew the payroll would be carried. She swung with ease onto the platform at the back. A frown ruffled her forehead when she realized the car must be empty, for no one challenged her. Then she shook her head in denial. Someone must be in this car, for Flynn always shipped his payroll with the mail.

She took a deep breath as she pulled her handkerchief tighter over her nose and prepared to stalk her prey. Adrenalin seared through her, and a smile came to her lips. Others might like the rewards of a successful heist. They bragged of the wealth garnered. To her, the money was secondary, although she wanted the easy life it could bring her. This was what she adored. To watch a man blanch before her and to know, for one moment, that she controlled his life gave her the excitement she craved. More than the possession of the finest jewel, she savored this enthralling experience.

Her eyes glittered with anticipation as she reached for the doorknob. In her other hand, she held her pistol. With cautious swiftness, she opened the door.

"Don't move!" she shouted as she leapt forward.

No reaction came to her words. In shock, she looked about the room. Her gun lowered slightly as she relaxed from her aggressive stance.

It was exactly the same as the last time. The small coal stove clung to its corner where the stovepipe climbed a crooked path to the ceiling. Opposite, a small table had a single chair pushed beneath it. Piles of mailbags were jumbled haphazardly to one side, but it was to the small safe her eyes went.

"Damn," she whispered. The open door and the empty interior were enough to tell her she had not been the first one here tonight. The tall man who might be the sheriff must have beaten her. "Damn," she repeated, hoping the curse would ease her frustration.

A moan interrupted her as she was turning to leave, and she tensed instantly, bringing her gun to the ready. When the sound came again, she looked for its source. With care, she crept toward the mailbags. She lost all ability to move when she saw what waited there.

She had seen death of all kinds, but even the recent execution of Jimmy had not sickened her as much as what lay on the floor. The guard's tan shirt had darkened with the stream of blood cascading from the slit in his throat. She wanted to help him, but knew there was no way to ease his pain. His eyes had rolled into his head as he breathed his last, agonizing breaths.

She wished she could flee, but her feet were as useless as the guard's attempts to live. She watched in silent sympathy while his chest quivered with his efforts. Her own breast ached as she wanted to help push air back into his lungs.

The sound of a rifle shot outside brought her sharply back to her own predicament. The rifle fired again. She could sense Ethan's urgency to warn her before he fled as they had planned. She turned to run, but it was too late. A moonlit shadow crawled along the platform at the back of the car, announcing the oncoming man.

She was too far from the other end of the car to escape in that direction, so her only choice was to conceal herself. She crouched behind a pile of mailbags. As the door opened wider, she tried not to breathe. It did not surprise her when the man she had bested in their last attempt to rob Flynn cautiously entered the small room. He shouted for the guard to surrender, as she had. Closing her eyes, she prayed as she had not in years. It surprised her she remembered how.

More quickly than she had, he noted the empty safe. When he spoke, she quivered with fear. His words told her she could expect no mercy if he discovered her in the dusky corner.

"So that little bastard beat me again," he growled. "How? How can they know?"

When he moved to search the room, K.T. began to edge toward the door. She had to flee while he was involved with the dead man, which was sure to keep him busy for the few seconds she needed to escape. His curse announced his discovery of the blood-covered corpse.

Her boots slid along the floor as she remained close to the walls. The edge of a blackboard cut into her ribs, but she swallowed the gasp of pain. Never did her eyes leave the broad back of her enemy. Only her right hand feeling for the frame of the door told her when she had reached it. She whirled to flee.

"Hey!" came the shout from behind her. "Stop!"

She did not have to look to know he was aiming at the center of her back. A prickling of fear and a sense she could not define warned her. Twirling to face him, she raised her own pistol in a reflex action. The gun came alive in her hand as she pulled the trigger. For some reason she did not understand, she aimed high. The man dropped to the floor as splinters rained from the ceiling.

Leaping from the car, she ran toward the place where her horse was hidden. She heard shouts behind her. The scream of a bullet past her head ended in a dull thud against a nearby tree. Without slowing her pace, she fired over her shoulders, but she was not aiming at anyone. Her mind was concerned with nothing but flight.

Even before she was in the saddle, she ordered the horse to go. She had trained it for an emergency such as this. The horse responded instantly. The pounding of its hoofbeats as they climbed the ridge did not mask the sounds of the horses in pursuit. The tall man did not intend to lose her again. He thought she had the money and planned to make her pay for beating him to the cache.

She leaned forward against the neck of the horse. Few men were capable of hitting a low, quick-moving target. She steered the horse in a zigzag course up the hill. The stands of trees offered the only screen from the men following her. She gasped as the horse jumped over a low rock and her nose bumped the hard bone beneath its mane. Tears surged into her eyes, but she ignored them.

At the crest, she whispered to the horse to go faster. The twitch of its ears was the only indication that it had heard her before it rushed forward. The rough terrain was not safe at this speed, but she had the choice between risking her life this way or dying to appease the pride of the man behind her.

Tree branches threatened to sweep her from the saddle as they continued at their breakneck pace. With her knees clenched against the horse's side, she let the creature select its own path. As long as it led away from the train and the other gang, she did not care where she went. She knew these hills well. If she became lost tonight, she would find her way home in the morning light.

She ducked as she heard a gun fire through the night. Whispering a curse, she reached for her own weapon. Cautiously she turned in the saddle to look over her shoulder. Moonlight glinted for a second off metal on a harness. Sighting on that spot, she raised her gun. She compensated for the motion of the horse and squeezed the trigger. The firing at her ceased as she heard voices calling a warning.

"Let's go," she urged the horse.

As if it understood her words, she felt it increase its speed. She kept her gun at the ready to fire if the men behind her decided to shoot again. The minutes passed, and she began to allow herself to relax. The last time they had met, the other gang had not followed them far. It appeared their leader might have made the same decision this time.

She slowed her horse to allow it to rest. The movement of its straining sides pressed against her legs as she turned it on a parallel course with the river. Somewhere in the next few miles, she had to find her way down to the river, because there was no path from the top of the cliff to her home. Her ears remained alert for every sound. Nothing came but the clomp of the horse's hoofs and the pounding of her heartbeat.

Tonight had been a disaster from the beginning. She wondered who had taken the money and killed the guard. Her stomach lurched at the memory. Eli had been as adamant as she against killing except in self-defense. The posture of the man sprawled on the floor told her that was not what had happened. Whoever killed him had stood behind the guard as he opened the safe. When the door clicked open, the knife had been drawn across the man's throat.

She shivered. If such a maniacal killer was loose along the river valley, no one was safe. It might not have been the money the thief wanted as much as the thrill of slaughtering an unsuspecting man. She had heard of such men, but hoped never to meet one.

Quickly she calculated how much money was left from the earlier robbery. Flynn had taken two weeks to get the money on the train this time. If he waited another two weeks, a double payroll would be coming through the valley. She smiled. They had enough supplies to survive until that jackpot became available.

The whisper of a branch snapping back in place broke her reverie. She glanced in every direction. Cursing at the darkness which was her bane and her salvation, she urged the tired horse to a quicker pace.

Suddenly the silence of the night was severed. A gun fired directly behind her. K.T. screamed as pain exploded through her left shoulder. The concussion knocked her forward into the neck of her horse. Her own weapon dropped from her hand as she fought to stay in the saddle. She forced her left hand to cling to the horse's mane. Her right hand reached across her chest to the searing agony. Stickiness met her fingers. Looking at her hand in the moonlight, she saw the blackness dripping from it.

Blood! She had been shot.

Without conscious thought, she knew what she had to do. Ethan already would be well on his way to their hideout by the alternate route they had plotted earlier. She had to hide from her pursuers until they gave up the search for her. Then she could return to the cabin and have Ethan bandage her shoulder.

She knew that, but the words would not form in her mouth to urge the bay to hurry. Mumbles of pained phrases oozed from her lips. She tried to push herself up to sit in the saddle. She succeeded, but swayed so sharply she had to grasp the reins with both hands. An involuntary moan sounded too loud in her ears fuzzy with some internal noise. Wetness flowed along her left arm making a silvery river in the moonlight.

Exactly when she fell off the horse, she did not know. Her fingers remained curled as if holding the reins, but the animal had rushed on riderless. Digging her nails into the earth covered with pine needles, she tried to pull herself behind some bushes. Anything to hide.

Her head dropped to the earth damp with her own blood. She could not force it to rise. Blinking did not clear the fog before her eyes. She vowed to survive, but her body refused to answer her commands. Even the beat of several horses' hoofs striking the ground failed to pump strength into her. She sagged against the ground, her right hand outstretched in a final attempt to flee.

"Here he is!" crowed a voice she did not recognize. "Shall I finish him off, Jonah?"

"Not yet." She tried to open her eyes to see the face matching the voice she had heard too often. She wanted to know if the leader of this gang and the sheriff of Copper Peak were indeed the same man. Curiosity taunted her, but she lay motionless in the dirt.

The thump of boots came close to her head, but she could not move away. When a hand grasped her to roll her on her back, she groaned with the anguish increasing at every second. Her stomach churned with nausea. She was weak from losing blood in a steady pulse through the hole in her shoulder.

A movement of air told her a man had squatted next to her. She could not react when she heard the leader say, "I want to see who the bastard is before we put him out of his misery."

The handkerchief was jerked from her face, taking with it the strands of hair tied into the knot. Broad fingers tilted her head so the moonlight streamed on it. She thought she heard a gasp, but the sound came from too far away. Her mind drifted into a realm free of the pain inflicted on her. Even her own screams when he touched her again did not penetrate the pleasant blackness of oblivion.

Sunlight streamed through a window brightened by chintz curtains. K.T. blinked as she tried to guess where she was. She was lying in a bed with a canopy of crocheted netting over it. She put out her hand and stroked the top of an appliquéd quilt. When she tried to sit up, she moaned with the pain she had been oblivious to since . . . how long had it been?

She had no time to think of that now. She had to get away from whatever pretty prison this might be. Pressing her right hand to the mattress, she managed to pull herself up into a sitting position. Her eyes blurred, and the room telescoped into blackness. By sitting quietly against the spindles of the headboard until the gray edges of her vision unraveled to reveal reality, she kept from fainting again.

She looked about the room for possible ways to escape. There was only one door, and the window with the chintz curtains. She knew that someone would be guarding the door. The window was her only escape.

She stood on rubbery knees and forced her feet the few steps to the window. In shock, she suddenly noticed that she was dressed in what appeared to be a man's nightshirt. It was far too long and pooled in a cream circle at her feet.

Fright surged through her as she reached gingerly for the pain at the top of her left arm. Someone had bandaged her shoulder. That same person must have dressed her in this nightshirt. She feared she was being treated this well only so she could be finished off in a more diabolical manner and be the next one scheduled to hang in the middle of the main street of Copper Peak.

The sickening thought gave her the strength to reach up for the window. It would not be easy to open with only one hand, but she had to try. Intent on her task, she did not hear the door open.

"So you are up? I'm not surprised that you are so stupid as to try to escape, but I suggest you get back in that bed before your wound starts to leak again."

She turned quickly to face the speaker. As she had half expected, a silver star was pinned to the tall man's chamois shirt. With her hands on the windowsill to help her keep her precarious balance, she regarded him with what dredges of defiance she could muster.

"I would guess that any sheriff who engages in the nocturnal activities you favor, sir, would find nothing surprising."

His mouth twisted beneath his auburn mustache. Crossing the room, he grasped her right arm and swung her toward the bed. When she tripped on the uneven floorboards, he scooped her up and deposited her with a bounce on the rumpled covers. She started to sit up. Pulling his gun from his holster, he pointed it coldly at her. The expression on his furious face did not alter. She did not doubt he would pull the trigger to complete what he or one of his men had done to her the previous night.

His deep voice rumbled in her ears. "You would be wise to follow orders, honey. Otherwise you might find yourself trying to stave off gangrene in that wound while you wait in the town jail for your hanging."

"Not mine alone," she retorted, but did not move. Her chest rose and fell rapidly as she fought to regain her breath. The simple act of walking across the floor had taken more out of her than she would have guessed.

He chuckled. "Who would believe you? A train robber and a murderer."

"No!" she cried. Her face paled. "I didn't kill anyone. The man was dead when I entered the car. I don't know who killed him." Regaining her composure slightly, she added in a calmer, more derisive tone, "I may be a thief, sheriff, but I don't murder people. If I wanted to do that, I could have chosen to do something foolish like robbing stages or banks. There are always innocent people there to shoot."

"So you have morals?"

"A few." She winced. "May I move? Lying like this hurts."

Motioning permission with his gun, Jonah watched as she propped herself against the pillows. He reached forward to toss the covers over her. It would be easier to conduct this interrogation if she did not look so winsomely pretty in his nightshirt.

After the initial shock of learning that his competitor for Flynn's money was female, he knew they could not shoot her. Like his prisoner, he might have few morals, but some residual training from his childhood kept him from killing a wounded woman. He had been relieved to discover that his partners felt the same. They had brought her here before returning to their own lives. What they would have done with her, he could only guess, but he suspected he would find a way to deal with this lovely lady.

Lovely was the exact word for her. Although

her skin was too deeply tanned for a pampered Eastern beauty, the curves of her trim form caught a man's eye. He had had a chance during the night to examine that slender body closely. Some other vestigial sense of courtesy had kept him from doing anything but tend to her wound and clothe her in his nightshirt. Her own things had been so blood-soaked that he threw them in the stove in the front room.

He looked at her tightly controlled face. If she was terrified, as she had every right to be, she concealed it well. He wondered if he would be so self-assured if the circumstances were reversed. His brow furrowed as he wondered, as he had so often since he had put her senseless in his bed, where he had seen her before. The diminutive thief had faced him last night with a bandana over her face. Yet he could swear those dark eyes had regarded him this icily before in the daylight.

"It seems we have a stalemate," he said quietly as he leaned on the upright of the bed. "If I put you in jail as you so clearly deserve, you will squawk and cause some folks to start asking questions I don't want asked. If I let you go, you will just stir up more trouble."

"You could shoot me."

He started at her forthright suggestion. Blue sparks flashed from his eyes as he stated, "You are either very brave or very stupid, honey."

"Neither." She grimaced as she tried to reposition her bandaged shoulder to make herself more comfortable. "If you were planning to kill me, you would have done so last night. You certainly had ample opportunity. I assume you didn't allow me to live simply because you couldn't fight your gentlemanly inclinations."

"What's your name?"

"What's yours?" she retorted.

"Jonah Bancroft, sheriff of Copper Peak." He grinned as he added, "And a comparatively incompetent train robber. Now, your name, honey." When she did not answer, he held the gun so the steel barrel touched her nose. "I said I wanted to know your name, honey."

Dampening her lips, she wondered how far she could push him. Until she knew, she could not guess if he would kill her so openly. Her voice trembled despite her efforts to make it steady.

"My name is K.T."

"Katie?"

She shook her head. "No, not Katie as in Katharine. Those are my initials."

"And?" he persisted. His thumb reached for the hammer of the gun, and she gasped. He smiled when she looked at him with the first open expression of horror he had seen on her face. It pleased him to break down that thick wall of resistance. "I'm still waiting, honey."

"Karleen Tamara." She wet her lips again and swallowed harshly before continuing, "Karleen Tamara Forrester."

"Forrester? Oh, ho!" he hooted as he removed the gun from the end of her nose. "Now it all comes together." He leaned one hand on the headboard behind her. Her gaze remained on the pistol in his other hand. "I remember where

I saw you before. At the hanging of that scum who tried to rob the bank. He admitted he had been with the so-called Forrester gang, but refused to give us any information as to your whereabouts. Seems like you didn't go to California as he wanted us to believe. Maybe you *are* stupid, if you came into town when every lawman in the territory is looking for you."

There was no reason to lie. She had never discovered any comfort in falsehood. Eli always had found her out if she tried to lie her way out of a predicament. His warning to tell the truth when necessary and lie only when nothing would betray her sounded through her head. She would save her falsehoods for when they would do the most good.

"Jimmy Schurman was my friend, Sheriff Bancroft, although he wouldn't listen to me when I told him to lay low after the robbery." There was no need either to lie about what he must know concerning the attack on the first train. She moaned as she inadvertently moved her shoulder. "I happened to be in town the day you prescribed your questionable form of justice, sheriff. I couldn't let him die alone."

If she had expected him to laugh at her weakness for her friends, she was disappointed. Instead he holstered his weapon and reached for the collar of the too-large nightshirt. She started to reach out her hand to block his presumptuous motion, then halted. If she had awakened in this strange bed, which she suspected was his, someone must have put her in it. She did not doubt it was this man. He would not have dared to let anyone else overhear what she might say in her delirium.

"You were with a young man that day."

"Was I?" She looked at the far wall, fighting her unease as this stranger touched her too intimately while readjusting the bandaging over her shoulder. In spite of their rough living conditions, her brothers and partners had known that she expected privacy behind her screen when she changed or bathed.

"Yes." He felt some perverse satisfaction as she gasped when her abused shoulder reacted to his examination. When he had removed the bullet fired from his gun, he had been glad she did not awaken from her stupor. Taking her chin in his palm, he forced her to look at him. "Who is he?"

"I don't know what you are talking about, Sheriff Bancroft."

"Young boy, man high, hair and coloring like yours." He frowned. "A Forrester I would guess. I watched when they hanged Elijah Forrester in Butte. You three all look alike. Where is he, honey?"

"I don't know what you are talking about," she repeated. If he thought she would betray her brother, he was indulging in wishful thinking. By now, Ethan would be certain something had happened to her. Her horse must have returned before daylight. He knew what he must do. Eli had taught this lesson over and over. If one of them was captured, the others were to leave the area for at least three months. They had done that after Eli was hanged. Ethan must hide alone this time.

He shrugged. "Be uncooperative if you want, but you will find that I can be much more pleasant if you do as I tell you."

"Sheriff," she retorted with a scowl, "I have absolutely no interest in having you be pleasant to me."

"Maybe I would like to treat you really nice, honey."

K.T. cowered away from him and the lust glowing in his eyes. She clutched close the night-shirt collar.

"Your predilection for criminal acts in all varieties continues to amaze me." Her words were spoken with more calm than she felt.

He chuckled with easy amusement and turned to complete the task of checking her shoulder. Her right hand clutched the sheets as his fingers gently touched the bandages tinted scarlet with her blood. The virulent pain of the seconds after the bullet had struck her returned. She moaned. Her head spun as the room vanished.

When her eyes opened some indeterminable time later, she was staring at the canopy again. Baffled, she looked at the man sitting on the edge of the bed and smiling at her. As she had been on the day of Jimmy's hanging, she was astonished to notice what a fine-looking man he was. Reddish hair, lightened by the harsh sun, twisted across his bronzed forehead. The thick mustache hiding his upper lip tilted in a smile as he saw she had regained consciousness.

"I hope that convinces you to be smart and stay in bed for a few days."

"Then what?" she whispered.

"Then we'll decide." He stood slowly so the bed did not move to hurt her shoulder more. "You are right, Miss Forrester. If I had wanted to kill you, you would have been dead last night. Let me get you some soup. It'll help revitalize you."

She relaxed into the pillows after he left the room. She refused to surrender her will to him, although she feared that was inevitable. All the advantages were his except for her knowledge of his nocturnal activities. That in itself might be more dangerous than valuable.

Sheriff Bancroft was correct. She must rest in order to recover. As she had no alternatives, she would have to accept his hospitality until she was well enough to plan her escape. Then she would find Ethan, and they would leave this river valley to find another where the line between the law and criminals had not blurred.

Too soon the door reopened. When she heard a bolt slide in the seconds before the sheriff entered, she knew she had guessed correctly. The door offered no escape.

As if she were a precious friend instead of an avowed enemy, he brought the tray and placed it on the dresser. He plumped pillows and helped her sit up. The hands that had been so cruel could be as tender as a beloved parent's. She watched him closely as he took a bowl of soup from the tray. When her hands shook as she raised them to take it, he shook his head.

"I don't want my bed covered with spots of

57

soup." He dipped the spoon in the bowl. "Open up," he ordered.

"I'm not a child."

"Honey, you don't have to tell me that." He laughed when she blushed. "Eat, so you can have that pretty color in your cheeks all the time."

She acquiesced. She was hungry, and the only way she would heal was to eat. Steam rose from the bowl to strike her face. "It's too hot."

"Then blow on it. Not too hard," he warned. "I don't want soup all over me." When he saw her teeter as she tried to sit forward, he put his arm around her carefully. She did not pull away from him. He glanced at her face so close to him and noted the sickly paleness beneath her tan. K.T. Forrester must be hurting far more than she allowed him to see. He tried to keep his voice light as he continued, "I'm not the best cook, but I have survived on this soup. You will too." He held his hand under her chin to catch the drip of soup falling from the spoon.

She swallowed the broth gratefully. It was warm and tasted wonderful. She did not bother to tell him she could not cook at all. If it were not for Ethan, they would have starved months ago.

"Thank you," she murmured as she watched him collect more soup into the wooden spoon.

"Don't be too grateful."

K.T. stared at him. His face had frozen into its unforgiving lines again. "And what does that mean?"

"This is not out of generosity. You are going to repay me for this doctoring."

"How?" She wanted to tell him she did not want his help, but she was dependent on him. This hateful situation would not last forever. If she knew what he intended to do with her, she could work to prevent it.

Jonah Bancroft smiled and watched the fear return to his captive's ebony eyes. "I don't know yet what this is going to cost you, K.T., but I can assure you that when I do decide, you will do as I tell you or you will die."

CHAPTER FOUR

In spite of her distrust of the man who held her prisoner, K.T. did not fight the restrictions he put on her. Not that she would have been able to wrestle a particle of dust, for she had never felt so weak. Infection attacked her. Her escape from her pursuers by crawling across the mountainside had packed the wound with dirt. Although Sheriff Bancroft had done his best to wash it, some filth must have remained in the cleansed wound.

The second night she was incarcerated in his bedroom, Jonah came home to find her thrashing with fever. He had made it a practice to tie her right arm to the spindles of the headboard while he was at his office. He had to be sure he appeared there often enough so that no one, including his thick-headed deputy Peabody, would question why he suddenly had changed his schedule. Although he hated to leave K.T.

sick and bound to the bed, he had no other choice. Her left hand remained useless in the sling he had rigged for her, but he did not want her sneaking out of his house and collapsing on the street.

Normally she greeted him with a snarled insult when he entered the bedroom. When only silence responded to his call, he eased into the room cautiously. He did not trust her, for she would use any ploy to escape. All his attempts to keep her leashed and away from anything she could use as a weapon might not be enough to restrain that quick mind she possessed. She was like a mountain wolf. Swift, cunning, and loyal to her allies with what was close to obsession.

He hurried to the bed where she fought the fever that burned his hand when he touched her forehead. Unintelligible phrases bubbled from her lips. It took all his strength to hold her shivering body still long enough to check her wound.

He cursed when he saw the angry red lines radiating from beneath the blood-encrusted bandage. If he called in the doctor, it would be just a matter of time before everyone in town learned that Sheriff Bancroft was hiding a woman in his house. A woman suffering from a gunshot wound. There would be questions asked that would wreck everything he had worked for in Copper Peak.

Jonah sighed. He could not let K.T. die just to keep himself from the gallows. If he met her again across firing guns, he could accept killing the woman. But to let her suffer like this was something he could not do. When he heard her moan with the agony threatening to destroy her, he made his decision, which had been inevitable from the beginning.

Dousing the candle burned nearly to a stub on the dresser, he went to the door. "I'll be right back," he called, although he knew she was not cognizant of anything.

He pulled his hat off the peg by the door and jammed it on his head. The door slammed behind him as he stepped out onto the boardwalk. He nodded an absent greeting to a fellow resident as he strode along the street to the doctor's office. It was only a few storefronts away from the house that had been provided for his use while he wore a badge in Copper Peak. Lyndon Flynn liked keeping all his key people under his eye.

Looking up at the huge white house perched on a hill, Jonah wondered who else had a vendetta against Flynn. If K.T. had not murdered the guard, and he believed her, for she had not had the money with her, then someone else was interested in the payroll. Perhaps the faceless murderer only wanted to profit, but he suspected it was a more intricate plot than that. Too many robbers suddenly had developed an interest in the trains rolling into this valley.

He pushed open the etched-glass door gilded with the doctor's name, nodded to the people in the waiting room, and walked into the examination room. Without pausing to give the busy doctor a chance to greet him, he said in a subdued tone, "Doc, I have to speak to you. Right away."

Dr. Havering glanced up and smiled grimly. "As soon as I finish with this lad." He looked back at the boy staring wide-eyed at the sheriff. "Open your mouth, son. Good boy." Mumbling something to himself, he pulled down a bottle and poured a white powder into a paper packet. "Take a spoonful of this in hot water every morning and every night until all the powder is gone. That should cure that throat. Understand?"

"Yes, doc." The boy hopped down from the ripped upholstery of the table and pulled on his shirt. With an excited grin in the direction of the silent sheriff, he raced out the room. His sore throat was forgotten as he hurried to tell his friends how Sheriff Bancroft had come in while Dr. Havering was checking him. Surely that meant something was happening to bring more excitement to the village. Perhaps even another hanging like the one a few weeks ago.

"What is it, Jonah?"

"I need some medicine and no questions." Bancroft came across the room lined with shelves containing bottles of multicolored powders to enter the pool of light near the doctor's table. Flynn allowed none of his employees much money for things like candles or keroscne. Although the copper from the mine on the far side of town went East to make wires for the new electric lamps, the miserly Flynn had not bothered to have Copper Peak wired for such luxuries. On another table to one side of the cool glow of the lamp was the paraphernalia used to create tablets and fill capsules. Various medical books sat on the desk by the single window. A skeleton leered its macabre empty-eyed smile in a far corner.

The doctor ran his fingers through his mop of graying hair before rubbing his bright blue eyes ringed with creases of fatigue. As he sat at the desk cluttered with a landscape of half-answered letters and opened books, his deep voice rumbled, "What is wrong with your friend? From your tone, I trust I won't be seeing this patient personally."

"No questions, doc. I can tell you the problem." Jonah hesitated as he wondered if he could think of another reason why K.T. suffered. There was nothing he could use but the truth. "Gunshot wound."

Dr. Havering sat up, instantly alert. "Jonah, that's not something to play with. Bring your friend in. I won't let Flynn know that I tended to someone not connected with the mines. If you want, I can go to see him where he is now, but it is hard for me to make a house call when there are so many eyes about, ready to report any indiscretion to Flynn."

Jonah sat on the chair the doctor used for dentistry. The plush fabric threatened to swallow him in its lushness. Few came for dental work, for it was more painful to have a tooth extracted than suffer a few days of discomfort. As his fingers created patterns in velvet on the chair's arm, he said, "Flynn is not the problem, but I can't bring my friend here. Will you help me, doc? This person is going to die without treatment."

For a long minute the doctor did not answer.

Without seeing the wound, he did not know what to suggest. A wrong guess could bring death as quickly as the power of an infection. He asked a few questions to determine exactly what the wound looked like. When he heard the patient was delirious, he shook his head.

"Dammit, Jonah, you should have brought him in right away. These wounds fester, and the poison goes directly to the brain. It may be too late."

"If it isn't, what should I try?" Bancroft asked stubbornly. For a reason he could not fathom, he did not want the woman to die. It would be simpler if she did. He could devise a tale of finding her dead on the trail and arrange a nameless grave for her. That way he would be guaranteed that she did not betray him, but the easy way did not appeal to him in this case.

The doctor sighed again. "All right, if you insist on being stubborn and risking your friend's life, the best I can tell you is to wash the wound with carbolic acid. A very weak solution of not much more than ten drops to a pint of water." He reached for a bottle on a shelf and held it out to the sheriff. As Jonah took it, he cautioned, "Keep the wound and surrounding area extremely clean. I'll give you some powders to lessen the pain, but if it becomes gangrenous, the limb must come off."

"It's in the shoulder." He pointed to a spot just below and to the left of the curve of his collar. "Right here."

Dr. Havering shook his head. "You should have brought him to me right away. Jonah, he is wounded so close to the vital organs and has an infection, and you expect him to live? Why don't you go down to the store and buy a headstone from Haggerty now? He's going to die."

"No," retorted Jonah. "This time Death has met his match. I won't let him win this battle." Standing, he went to the door. "Thanks, doc."

Jonah's unformed hopes that K.T. would be better when he got back were forgotten as soon as he entered the darkened bedroom to find her writhing in delirium. He had no time to waste.

Following the doctor's instructions, he bathed the wound with the carbolic acid solution. Hours passed with tormenting slowness as she came in and out of consciousness. He kept water warm on the hearth, so he could place damp cloths on her head to halt the fever from rising to bring on brain vapors.

K.T.'s moans of pain cut through Jonah. He could not help recalling her taunting laugh, so full of life, as she raced away from him the first time they met. That life might be snuffed out by his too-quick reaction. At the time, as he drew his gun to sight on the form fleeing through the night, he had thought only of stopping a murderer and the one who had shown him up once again. He had not thought beyond that moment.

"Ethan?"

He was shocked to hear the word come clearly from her cracked lips. Although he was not sure who she called, he answered, "What is it, K.T.?"

"They caught Eli. Lord, they caught him. He —he delayed for me. My horse went down. He gave

66

me his horse. They—they caught him." Her voice rose into a shriek over past pain. "It should have been me! Not him!"

"Hush," Jonah whispered as he replaced the damp cloth on her forehead. He guessed Ethan was the young man she had been with when he saw her in town. "It's all right, K.T. Just relax. It's all right."

He doubted if she heard him, for the mumbles from her lips had become unintelligible again. Smoothing the creases of pain from her forehead, he realized she must have been talking about Elijah Forrester's capture half a year before. As fiercely loyal as K.T. seemed to be to her allies and they to her, it should not surprise him that her brother had sacrificed his life to save her.

Yet he was astonished. Never had he thought of criminals as having families or ties of any kind other than the brief alliances they formed to prey on the lawful. He wondered who might be mourning for K.T., believing she was dead.

The tender feelings of compassion within him astounded him further. He shook his head to clear his mind of the images of K.T.'s friends. If he started feeling more for her than he would for a sick beast, he might find himself doing something foolish, such as easing his guard over her. She would take his sympathy for weakness and prey on it to make her escape as soon as she was well.

Jonah jolted awake at the sound of a woman speaking. He nearly slipped onto the floor before he remembered he was not in his own bed, but propped between two chairs. As her light laugh sang through the dust motes dancing on the first gleams of the sunrise, he forced his weary body from the uncomfortable perch.

"K.T.?" he managed to croak. His throat felt as dry as the grasslands to the east. "K.T., are you awake?" he asked as he entered the bedroom.

"Isn't it a wonderful day?" came the barely audible reply in a tone unlike any he had heard her use. The strident assertiveness had vanished. "And a rainbow. Who would have guessed there would be rainbows here, too?"

Puzzled, he glanced over his shoulder out the window. Even if an arc had crossed the sky, she would not be able to see it from where she was lying. He knelt by the side of the bed and picked up her limp fingers.

That he had not answered did not seem to interest her. Her voice grew softer and gentler as she opened her eyes. He nearly smiled as he hoped the fever had released her. Then he saw the glazed blindness as she looked past him to someone visible only to her. When she spoke, there was a childish lilt to her words.

"Mama! Look, Mama, I caught a butterfly." He watched as her hand rose to offer the nonexistent insect to an imaginary parent.

Rising, he paced across the room, too upset to sit still any longer. He had to face the fact that he was losing her. She was sinking deeper into her past. He had seen this before, and knew that, as the pain increased, the injured person sought farther and farther back into time to find a safer place, a place free from the agony of the present. K.T. had reached the early years of her childhood and might never return.

A twinge of pain seared through him at the thought. With a vicious curse, he whirled to pick up the bowl with the carbolic acid solution and went to bathe the wound again.

He had vowed that Death would not win. The battle was not yet over, and Jonah Bancroft intended to be the victor.

Jonah used the excuse he was busy with an investigation to stay away from his office for the hours he sat each day by K.T.'s bed, wondering how that slight form could continue to fight the deadly forces within her. He had bound her arm to her chest to keep her from waving it about and reinjuring the shoulder. Although he had learned little about this woman who led the Forrester gang, he knew he had never met anyone with her determination to live.

"Thirsty," came a gasp from the bed.

Leaning forward to look at her face in the dim light from the stars, he saw that her eyes were open and not blurred with the fever. He cautiously touched her forehead, not wanting to give her more pain. Less heat burned there than before, and he saw her gaze focus for a brief moment on him.

He reached for a cup and slid an arm beneath her, carefully avoiding her wounded shoulder. With difficulty, he balanced her and held the cup to her lips. Although she drank little more than a swallow, it was the most he had gotten past her lips in days.

As tenderly as if she were made of the starglow flowing through the windows, he lowered her back onto the pillows. He saw her lips move, but could not understand what she said until he put his ear close to them. The barely perceptible breeze of her breath warmed his ear as he understood her trying to thank him.

"You are very welcome, K.T." He smiled and added, "Why don't you close your eyes and sleep, honey? You have a long recovery ahead of you."

He sat on the side of the bed and watched as she obeyed. A soft chuckle escaped from his lips. She may not have heard what he suggested, for she had been sinking back into sleep even as he spoke. It would be more like K.T. Forrester to balk at any command he made, even when it was meant to help her.

This period of recuperation might prove interesting. He stifled an involuntary yawn and wondered if there were fewer hours of sleep ahead of him. Once she was better, she would attempt to flee. Then he would have to guard her far more closely.

Moving back to his makeshift bed, he sat and put his feet on the opposite chair. The patched blanket covered his knees as he leaned back on the awkwardly balanced pillow. Sleep was the prescription for both of them, for when she awoke again, the real battle would be just beginning.

K.T. scowled as her eyes opened to the light. Instantly her forehead smoothed as she realized that something as simple as opening her eyes caused pain. She wondered what was wrong. She felt as if she had been struck by a fast-moving train. If she was a drinker, she would have guessed she had gotten some bad whiskey. Every muscle of her body ached.

The bed sucked her down into an indentation in the mattress, as if she had been lying in one position too long. She tried to move and cried out involuntarily. Pain severed her into a thousand pieces, each one a separate torment.

"Take it easy, K.T."

She looked up at the deep voice. Memory rushed back to flood her with myriad impressions of fear and a gnawing pain from a piece of lead cutting through her skin. All of the scenes in her head added up to one thing. This man named Sheriff Bancroft had shot her and wanted to get her well so he could use her in some way.

The panic tangling her in its clammy strands was a strange emotion. In all the times she had been involved in robbery, she had never reacted like this. She clawed at the sheets to pull away from the broad hand reaching out to her. When it took her hand, she wanted to scream. All that came from her throat was a dried croak.

"Hush, K.T. You are fine. Lie still."

Jonah looked down into wide, dark eyes broadcasting her terror. He took a cloth from the bowl by the bed. Watching her relax into the pillows as he put the warm dampness on her sweaty forehead, he smiled. That she was frightened of him meant she had left her crazed world of delirium.

71

"I'm not going to hurt you," he murmured. When he saw her expression of disbelief, he added, "Not again. You have been very sick. If I'd wanted you dead, I could have had my wish any time in the past week. All I had to do was walk out of the house and leave you to the mercy of the infection."

She saw that his face was dark with rust whiskers. When she first opened her eyes, she had thought they were simply shadows. If he had not shaved long enough to grow this brush on his face, he might be telling the truth. She certainly felt as if she had fought the devil himself.

"Do you think you can eat something?"

"I—I—" She swallowed past the thickness in her throat and began again. Her cracking voice was unrecognizable in her ears. "I think so."

"Good. Let me get some soup." He smiled with gentle compassion. "Don't run away while I'm in the other room."

K.T. was shocked to find her lips tilting to respond to his humor. When he removed the damp cloth from her forehead and stroked her head as tenderly as if she were his child, she closed her eyes to savor the touch. For days, she had been lost in a nether world. She longed now for any sensation to tell her she had regained her hold on reality where memories of the past and fears of the future did not juxtapose to create a kaleidoscope of horror.

"Will you be all right for a few minutes?"

Opening her eyes again, she saw the concern on his surprisingly honest face. She started to nod, but the pain careened through her head again. Her right hand gripped the headboard to keep her from sliding into torturous oblivion once more. She did not want to return to that misty place of constant pain.

"K.T.? K.T., honey, are you all right?"

His voice drew her back from the slippery edge of unconsciousness. She bit her bottom lip and gazed with entreaty at him. Until he lifted her hand to sandwich it between his two larger ones, she did not realize she had been clutching onto his fingers. "It hurts so damn bad," she murmured.

Jonah started at her words. He had spent the last week listening to her speak in jumbled phrases that suggested a life totally different from the rough one she lived in Montana territory. Her uncultured answer sounded so strange in his ears accustomed to that lyrical voice. His jaw clenched as he reminded himself that K.T. Forrester was a train robber. She might resemble a porcelain doll when she rested on the cream of his pillow, but she could become a spitting cat in a second.

Gruffly he said, "What do you expect? You did get shot, after all."

The sharpness of his words severed her fantasy that he might have sympathy for her. She jerked her hand away from him. "You don't have to look so proud of yourself. It was a lucky shot." Her vindictive smile warned him he would have more problems as soon as she was better. "If I had known then that you would follow me up the ridge, I would have unloaded my pistol into you on the train."

"You missed."

"On purpose. I aimed high." She chuckled darkly. "I hit what I aim at, sheriff. If you doubt me, give me a gun."

In spite of his intentions to treat her as a despised prisoner, he laughed. Her wits had not been dulled by her wound. He must find a way to use her in his plans for Copper Peak. Otherwise he had no choice but to send her to hang, and that, he decided, would be a terrible waste.

"I'm not the one who has been suffering with an addled brain," he retorted. "I know better than to give you a gun. Maybe we will have a shooting contest one of these days. For now, you're going to have something to eat."

"Yes," she agreed with sudden fervor. Until this moment, she had not realized how starved she was. She tried to watch him leave the room, but her eyes ached with the crust clinging to the corners.

That he left the door open behind him told her how little he trusted her, although she was completely confined to the bed. Simply to raise her hand to run it through her dirty hair took more energy than she possessed.

K.T. thought of what he had said about her having an addled brain. She prayed she had not spoken aloud during her delirium, but it seemed she must have. Because he did not taunt her with anything she might have divulged, she sank back into the pillow with a sigh. Sheriff Bancroft was not likely to keep such information secret long and would want to interrogate her more while she was weak.

Whether he was gone only a second or an hour, she had no idea. The sound of his returning footsteps and the door closing roused her from a dream of riding free along the ridges as the wind blew her hat back from her head. The scents of the pine and the sensation of the breeze ruffling her hair urged her to set the bay horse to its top speed, but the magnificent vistas vanished to be replaced by the simple walls of her prison. She wanted to sob out her frustration when she discovered her captivity was the reality.

Jonah did not ask her if she needed help to sit. She gasped when he simply pulled back the blankets and put his arms around her waist. As if she weighed no more than the pillows behind her, he propped her against them. Her outrage disappeared when her shoulder announced its agony.

"K.T.!" The sound of his voice was her lifeline to hold onto consciousness. She clung to it and forced her vision to right itself. When he asked if she was all right, she nodded carefully. Any sudden motion threatened to send her head careening off across the room.

"I don't think I can manage to eat alone." She admitted her weakness reluctantly, for it galled her to be unable to handle a spoon. Beneath the covers, she flexed her left hand and fought the pain rutting her forehead. Her fingers were stiff, and she faced long hours of practice before she could regain the lightning-quick draw that had been her pride.

"I didn't expect you would." Jonah sat on the edge of the bed and placed the bowl on the table. Tucking a washrag beneath her chin as if she were a baby, he grinned at her shock. "This service I have given very few train robbers."

"Then I should be honored." She swallowed the soup gratefully and wondered if she had ever tasted anything as delicious as this plain chicken broth.

He said in a strange tone, "Yes, you should be honored."

K.T. glanced up at him to see an expression unlike any she had seen before on his face. Uneasily, she watched as his eyes moved along her body. Within her oozed a warmth she was sure had nothing to do with the fever that had sapped her for days.

"Thank you." Her laugh was a shadow of its previous exuberance. "If 'thank you' is the right thing to say to the person who shot you."

"You're welcome. Here, eat." He dabbed a spot of broth from her chin and started to do the same with some that had dripped onto the nightshirt she wore. Instantly he halted his hand inches from the white muslin. For the past week, she had been his patient, the wager he was determined to win from death, a body burning with fever. That had now changed.

Jonah held up the spoon and saw her eyes watching him warily. If they had been yellowish-green instead of the brown of pine bark, it could have been a cornered mountain lion regarding him with caution but no sign of fear. She had not missed his aborted action, and understood exactly how the relationship between them had changed to enmity the second she had roused from her delirium.

"Eat!" he repeated tersely.

She did not answer but did as he commanded. The subtle hint of a scowl warned her to remember what he had told her the first morning she awoke in this room. He intended to use her in some way to repay him for saving the life he nearly had stolen from her. From the expression on his cold features, she was sure the price would be far higher than she was willing to pay.

CHAPTER FIVE

"**W**hy are you doing that?"

"Why am I doing what?" Jonah turned from the mirror to glance at his prized prisoner. He no longer had to pretend to note improvement in K.T.'s condition. Today she had managed to prop herself against the pillows before he came into the room with her breakfast. She must have been awakened by his footsteps in the front room where he slept since she gained consciousness and did not need or want him by her bedside. When he saw her smile at his face half covered with soap, he said, "You must have seen a man shave before."

"Yes, many times," K.T. said with a laugh as he turned back to the small mirror barely large enough to show him his face, "but I have never seen a man make as many strange faces as you do."

He chuckled as he tilted his chin upward to

scrape the straightedge razor along his skin. "You would make odd faces too if you wanted to avoid cutting a hole in your throat." When he saw her amusement vanish from her face, he said, "I'm sorry, K.T. I didn't mean to remind you of Meyer's murder."

"Did you find out who—?" She could not bring herself to speak of the sight that haunted her dreams. Seeing Flynn's guard on the train gasping for his last breaths as he lay in his own blood was a scene she doubted she would ever forget. She had never been squeamish, but such cruel, useless carnage continued to sicken her.

"No, I have no idea who killed him." Wiping his cheeks on a damp towel, he walked to the bed. He sat on the edge and watched as she pulled her feet away from him. No matter what he did, he could not break through the wall she hid behind. He could not blame her for not trusting him even though he saved her life, for he did not trust her either. "To tell you the truth, K.T., I've been too busy caring for you to look for Meyer's murderer. Worse than that, I've been too busy caring for you even to halt the train for the double payroll."

She pushed herself up higher against the pillows. Ignoring the pain screeching through her head like an eagle circling for its prey, she gasped, "That has come already?"

"You have been here over two weeks. Even Flynn can't keep his employees without wages for more than a month."

"It arrived without mishap?"

He watched her face intently as he asked,

"Why? Did you think your little brother Ethan would have gotten together the rest of your gang to rob the train without you?"

K.T. cried, "How do you know his name?" She clamped her lips as she realized she had said too much already. With her eyes on her right hand twisting mounds in the nap of the blanket, she knew she must have spoken of her brother while mad with fever. She wondered what else she had mentioned that the sheriff could use.

In a steadier voice, she said, "I didn't think Ethan would rob the train without me, but you cannot continue to ignore the facts, sheriff. I was too late to get the last payroll. You didn't get it either, I would guess."

"No," he admitted with reluctance.

"Then someone else did."

"Who?"

"That is the mystery, isn't it? This is Forrester territory. Other gangs have respected that for the past year. We don't intrude on the Black Flats gang or any others. You were the ones who invaded our territory." She smiled as she added with a condescending tone, "But I guess with you being lawmen and such law-abiding folks, you didn't know the rules, did you?"

He smiled as he dropped the towel into a bowl on the dresser. "I didn't suspect there was much honor among thieves in Montana territory."

"There isn't, but lately, with all the money coming in and out of Butte, there has been enough for everyone. It takes time to learn our business, sheriff."

Clasping his hands around his knee, he regarded her sitting so ladylike against his pillows. It was not easy for him to remember that this delicate woman was the same person who had pressed a gun barrel into his spine and coldbloodedly robbed him. "I'm aware of that now. You made it seem so simple."

"Did I?" K.T. asked, astounded at the compliment.

"You certainly never seemed frightened."

With a secretive smile, she said, "I never am frightened when I'm involved in the actual work. It's too much fun."

"Fun?" He could not hide his amazement as he regarded the woman who clearly was enjoying her fond memories of the crimes she had boldly committed. "You find robbing trains fun?"

K.T. did not hesitate as she asked, "Didn't you? Didn't you enjoy the thrill of the blood coursing through your head as you faced your foe and knew you could have whatever you wanted from him? From the sound of your voice, I would have guessed you enjoyed every second. Until I arrived, of course," she finished with a sly chuckle.

"I did enjoy it . . . until you arrived, of course." When she laughed heartily, he allowed himself to laugh with her. She was charming, despite her rough manners and outspokenness. If she had planned to use the money she garnered to buy her way into society as many thieves did, he did not doubt she could have managed to convince everyone she had spent all her life as a fine lady instead of as a bandit in a hovel in the mountains.

Jonah let her continue to joke with him as his thoughts followed a sudden trail of inspiration. His smile grew wider. The answer of what to do with K.T. Forrester had been before him from the first time he saw her pretty face in Copper Peak. Whether she would agree with the plan he would put forth as soon as she was well, he did not let concern him. She already had learned that her life belonged to him from the moment it had become entangled in his.

Revenge would be his, and K.T. Forrester would be the way he obtained it.

The days passed in an unchanging pattern of mutual distrust. Jonah returned to his office intermittently. By being there to give his deputy trivial tasks to do, he knew he could keep Peabody from becoming suspicious of the sheriff's new schedule.

K.T. concentrated on her recovery. Each day she tried to bring herself closer to her goal of escaping from the house before the sheriff put into motion whatever plan made his eyes glow with malicious delight each time he looked at her. Under his guard, she rebuilt her endurance as she struggled a bit farther every evening until she could walk across the small room and back alone.

By herself, during the hours he spent at his office, she practiced the motion necessary to whip her pistol quickly from the holster she would wear once again on her hip. Tears of pain distorted her vision when she forced her aching arm to meet her demands, but she did not stop. Her life would depend on this. When the time came to put this prison behind her, her left arm must be ready to pull her gun on her command.

She did not worry about the sheriff having her weapons. Others could be purchased easily at one of the small towns beyond Copper Peak. Then she could return to her free life in the mountains without this hypocritical sheriff and his threats.

Jonah knew exactly what she had planned, although he had never seen her practicing. One day when he deemed she was well enough, he ordered her to join him in the front room of the house. With a tight smile, he watched as she emerged from the bedroom into the room she had seen only through the narrow doorway.

"Why don't you sit on the sofa, K.T.?" he offered.

She nodded, wondering if she could manage to walk that far. In the confines of the small bedchamber, she had become overconfident of her limited abilities. How far she still must work to be totally recovered she discovered as she moved stiffly toward the gray settee. She ignored the other chairs and the table next to the stove in the tiny kitchen. All of her attention centered on her goal of reaching that sofa shadowed by the drapes pulled tight over the two windows.

Her toe stubbed an uneven floorboard hidden beneath the rug. Gratefully she held onto Sheriff Bancroft as he assisted her the last few steps.

She dropped onto the unyielding cushions and drew the nightshirt around her when a shiver raced along her spine.

"Cold?" he asked.

"Yes." K.T. did not tell him she was lying. The tremors were from fear of what the future offered, for she had not realized how weak she remained. She wanted to cry, but she did not dare to let her uneven emotions betray her further to her captor.

From a chair, he pulled a blanket. He tucked it around her as she put her feet on the small stool. Closing her eyes, she savored the warmth of the fire on the raised hearth. Such luxury this was! A real house with furniture not made of castoff crates and broken planks. She wondered when she would be able to enjoy such an easy life again.

"It's time to talk, K.T."

She blinked at the serious tone of Jonah's voice. Turning slightly so she could see him as he sat next to her on the sofa, she asked, "About what, sheriff?"

"About what to do with you." He watched her face grow blank. In the days she had been in his care, he had learned to recognize her determination to show no fear. That she hid it so well had become a sign to him of how frightened she truly was. "I have an offer to make you."

"I'm listening." She folded her hands in her lap, regarding him steadily. He would have to say the words that would doom them both, for she refused to beg for her life. She also had no intention of swinging alone at the gallows.

"Why did you rob the train?"

His question caught her off guard. She sputtered several times before she managed to say, "The money, of course. Why else?"

With a tight laugh, he agreed, "Why else, indeed?" He leaned forward, his gaze holding her captive. A malicious grin crossed his face, transforming it from the kind man who had tended her so carefully. "Do you want to know why I was there?"

"I'm curious why a lawman suddenly decides to hold up trains."

"Revenge, K.T. Pure and simple revenge."

"Against Flynn? What did he do to you?" Her eyes widened in shock that Sheriff Bancroft would be so daring as to collect his pay from his employer and try to steal from him at the same time.

"You're quick." Reluctant admiration filled his voice. "And you're right. I want Flynn to suffer. Why is none of your business. All that matters to you is that you can save your life by cooperating."

"How?"

He removed one of his pistols from the holster and cracked it open. She swallowed harshly as she watched him shake the bullets into his hand. His action was calculated to show her who was in charge. Although one gun was broken down, he could reach the other in a second if she gave him cause.

"Twenty years ago, the Union Army occupied New Orleans." When she gave him a blank stare, he scowled. He knew she was not stupid. "The

War Between the States, K.T. You must have heard about it."

"I have!" she snapped. "Are you telling me you are after Flynn because of something that happened two decades ago?"

"Listen." He did not like her deprecation of his ideals. Since before his tenth birthday, he had waited for this opportunity. Her entrance into his life proved a fortuitous turn of events once he thought of a way to include her in his revenge. "Flynn served as an aide to an officer with General Benjamin Butler, the military commander of the city. Flynn had as his mistress a woman named Eugenie St. Pierre. During the more than six months he lived in the city, she shared his bed."

"So?"

"So I want you to convince Flynn you are the child of that liaison."

"You must be crazy! Me? A mealymouthed Eastern gal?" She laughed lightly. "Who would believe that?"

"I believed you were a train robber."

"I am."

He shook his head, but did not look at her as he polished the gun barrel with a greased cloth. "No, honey, you are something else entirely. I haven't figured you out yet, but I will. Karleen Tamara Forrester wasn't meant to be a bandit in the Montana hills. Where were you born?"

"I don't know. All I know is the date when I was inflicted on the world."

His wide hand gripped her right arm as he tugged her closer to him. When she gasped, he disregarded the pain that contorted her soft lips. He shook her, then shoved her against the back of the sofa. "Cooperate, K.T.!"

"I am." She reached across her body to grasp his wrist. Steadily her nails bit into his skin. When he yelped and pulled away, she smiled. "Where I was born and who I was before our unfortunate meeting is none of your business." She watched him from beneath flirtatiously lowered lashes as she added, "Just as you told me it's none of my business to know why you are so interested in Flynn's relationship with some harlot in New Orleans."

Rage discolored his face. His eyebrows crowded the center of his forehead as he scowled at her. Instantly K.T. comprehended what he did not say. This Eugenie St. Pierre must be more to him than a casual acquaintance. A sister, a cousin, perhaps even his mother forced to share the bed of an enemy. Why he wanted her to pretend to be Flynn's bastard child, she did not know, but she remembered his threat. If she did not do as he wished, he would kill her. She did not doubt him.

More gently she asked, "How do you intend to convince Flynn I'm his daughter?"

"I will deal with that." He shoved the bullets back into the chambers and spun the cylinder experimentally. "Will you do it?"

"Do I have any choice?" she asked quietly as she watched him check the sight on the pistol.

"No." He grinned at her as he brought the gun about to point at her. "None at all."

*　　*　　*

The next day began the interminable round of lessons about things the daughter of Eugenie St. Pierre and Lyndon Flynn would know. Jonah selected the name Katharine for her. "Then you can be called Katie. It's close enough to what you are accustomed to so you will answer to it readily."

He drilled her on the geography of New Orleans until she was sure she would recognize each quarter if she ever visited the city. His descriptions of the lush flowers heavy with scent on a sultry afternoon were so complete they evoked images in her mind. She listened, enthralled, when he described the sights of the city, and forced herself to remember all the details. He quizzed her again and again until she could describe the iron gates in front of the massive stone walls of the Ursuline Convent or the shape of the fountain at a specific address in the French Quarter.

He told her little of what had happened to this Eugenie St. Pierre who was her supposed mother. Each time she queried him on that subject, he brushed it aside by snapping a question about the city. If she delayed in answering, he made her work at repeating her lessons until she struggled to keep her weary eyes open.

One night she rose from the table where they had been having supper and stamped to the sofa. Angrily she sat and snapped, "I'm tired of this. I know more about this Katharine St. Pierre's life than I do about my own. I think it's time to talk about other things."

"Such as?" He put his coffee cup down. His fierce eyes remained on her as he sat next to her.

"Such as what's my reward for this?" she asked as she regarded him steadily.

"Will money suffice?"

"It's a beginning." She refolded her hands in her lap. Her motion pulled up the hem of her odd outfit, offering him an enticing view of her slender ankles. She had not become accustomed to these clothes, even after the weeks of alternating her wardrobe between his two nightshirts.

Feeling his eyes on her, K.T. jerked the fullness of the nightshirt around her feet. She stepped on the hem to hide her toes. Again the warmth rose on her skin. Her face tinted in the glow of the setting sunshine golden off the plastered walls.

His smile was surprisingly gentle as he asked, "And what is money the beginning of for you, K.T.?"

"Life." Her voice melted into her dreams. She relaxed back against the cushions. Gazing at the ceiling, she spoke of what she wanted. "Like it was before. Velvet portieres, silk settees, hushed-footed servants."

"A bordello?"

She grinned. His teasing would not tarnish her precious, half-formed memories from a time so distant she often wondered if it were simply a dream. "To tell you the truth, I have thought of opening a bawdyhouse, sheriff. It would be far easier to rob men with a softly curved woman than with a hard-barreled gun."

"You would make a charming madam."

"I thank you for your compliment." Her eyes grew nugget hard. "It's an expensive proposal to start such a business. I trust you will remember that during our negotiations."

He rose and removed the kettle from the stove. Refilling the two cups, he brought them to the sofa. "I'll make you an offer, K.T., and you will accept it."

"Not necessarily."

"What do you mean?"

She laughed. "I'm not the only one in trouble, sheriff. Lest we forget, you too can have your neck stretched at the end of a noose. I suggest you make this worth my while and the risk, or a word whispered in the wrong ear . . ."

"Twenty-five thousand dollars."

K.T. stared at him as if he were mad. When he chuckled and repeated the amount, she whispered, "For me?"

"For you and whomever you want to divide it with."

She whistled, at a loss for words. If he realized she had been willing to settle for a mere five thousand, he would renege on his offer. Before he could do that, she held out her hand.

"It's a deal, sheriff."

"I thought it would be." He shook her hand gravely. "You are a smart woman, honey. Let me know when you open that business. I might want to pay you a call."

Her eyes sparkled with eager greed. "Why would I want to take your money then? I'll have enough to live well the rest of my life."

"So you shall." He leaned back on the sofa.

"Tomorrow we shall start this masquerade. I think you have learned all you can of what I have to teach you. You are well enough to manage the life of a lady."

"A lady?" Ruefully she added as she looked at the nightshirt, "You expect Flynn to welcome his daughter when she is dressed like this?"

He smiled mysteriously. "Don't worry about that, honey. All those details will be taken care of before you are welcomed home by your loving father. I've tended to that. All you must do is remember the reasons why you must not betray me."

K.T. nodded, for she had no idea how to respond to this enemy whose ally she had become in the past week. Then she smiled. This plan offered her the chance to escape from this arrogant man. Once she entered Flynn's house, she could flee at her leisure, and her life would be hers again.

"I will remember all the reasons not to betray you, sheriff," she vowed quietly. To herself she added that she would be the one to have the final power when he saw his plot crumble around him and leave him bare to his enemy. Lifting her cup to his, she clinked it to seal the bargain. She lowered her eyes as she saw the sudden confusion in his. That pleased her, for she had to keep him off-balance as long as possible to facilitate her flight. "To success!" she added to break the silence.

"To success," he repeated, but his enthusiasm had dimmed slightly. She guessed he rued bringing her deeper into his deception, but the game had begun. Only she knew that the prank would be turned about to ruin the prankster.

Jonah recalled K.T.'s expression as he made the preparations for the beginning of the masquerade. His other allies played their parts to perfection, and he had learned he could depend on them. The woman was another matter. She would be happy to betray him on a whim. Knowing that, he had been determined to offer her so much money that even Flynn would not be able to top it and buy her loyalty.

Despite his qualms, he continued with his plans. It was too late, he had invested too many years to stop at this point. This serendipitous chance never would come again, so he had to snatch at it while he could.

Going to his office, he sent Peabody on an errand. He could not tolerate the inept deputy who preferred to spend his time at the saloon with his over-aged dancehall girl who was glad to listen to his whining in exchange for his gold. If Peabody had been more interested in his job, Jonah's efforts to keep him from being suspicious about the sheriff's sometimes odd activities might have been more difficult. Jonah had learned that a simple hint of upcoming work, especially if it required Peabody to draw his gun or be shot at, sent the deputy scurrying to find a place to hide.

After the deputy had been dealt with, Jonah put his hat on the peg behind his desk. He started to pace the short distance between the door and the single jail cell, which was currently empty.

Occasionally a few miners were put in there to sober up after spending their paychecks at the saloon, but the cell seldom held any real criminals. Those who were placed in there, like Jimmy Schurman, were quickly hanged.

He sighed as he sat at the sagging desk. Everything in the office looked as if it had been brought to Copper Peak on the underside of a Conestoga. He glared at the wall of "Wanted" posters. That was where he had discovered that Schurman's crimes went further than a drunken spree at the bank. In the months he had been in Flynn's city, he had come to hate everything about this dirty office and the buildings surrounding it.

A familiar carriage stopping before the office interrupted his thoughts. He quickly scanned the room to be sure that nothing was amiss. Everything was ready for the drama to begin. He smiled as he bent to pretend to be working industriously at some papers before him. It was starting . . . finally!

Jonah glanced up as the door crashed open. He kept a smile from his face when he looked at the clock above the window. Flynn was within fifteen minutes of the time he had expected him. Silently he thanked Duncan. He should have guessed the telegraph operator would be sure this particular wire was delivered posthaste to Flynn. All of them would profit if they were able to hoodwink the powerful owner of Flynn's Copper Mining Company.

He rose and allowed his professional expression of welcome to settle on his face. Never could he allow his true emotions to show before the man he had despised for more years than he could remember. He recalled the day he first rode into Copper Peak with his lies prepared. Duncan had informed him that Flynn was anxious to find a new sheriff to replace his incompetent one. The raids by the Forrester gang and others had enraged Flynn. Clapton, the sheriff, was flummoxed by the lightning-quick robberies. When Elijah Forrester was captured by another law officer, Flynn was outraged. He had wanted the pleasure of seeing his enemy hang in the middle of the main street of Copper Peak.

Going to the massive house on the hill overlooking the village and the copper mines, Jonah had spoken to Flynn face-to-face for the first time. He had not been disappointed by the unchanged appearance of the man he considered as evil as Lucifer. After an interview during which he agreed outwardly with everything Flynn suggested, he had found himself the new sheriff of Copper Peak. It was the perfect position for what he wanted to do. He took perverse pleasure out of collecting his pay from Flynn while working to ruin him.

As he greeted his employer, he savored the thoughts of that moment when he could unveil who he was in truth. "Why, hello, Mr. Flynn. I didn't expect you here at this time of day."

"Bancroft, read this!" Flynn wasted no time on pleasantries. Pulling a piece of paper from beneath his morning coat, he tossed the page onto the desk.

Jonah picked it up and pretended to peruse it.

He mumbled the words aloud. Duncan had changed a few things and made it more realistic. He was a good ally.

"'Lyndon Flynn, Flynn's Copper Mining Company, Copper Peak, Montana Territory. Daughter named Katharine St. Pierre will arrive September 9, 1888, on Northern Pacific train from Bozeman. Born May 5, 1863, child of Eugenie St. Pierre. Mother dead.'" He looked up with the proper expression of disbelief. "Your daughter? I did not know you had a child living back East, Mr. Flynn."

Storming about the room like a corraled bull, Flynn muttered, "Neither did I." He whirled and pointed at the younger man. "Take my advice, Bancroft. Don't do something now that can come back to haunt you in the years to come." He pounded his fist on the desktop until the bottle of ink danced in a strange pattern across the blotter. "Damn Eugenie! I should have known she would send the girl on to me like this. She—" He interrupted himself when he realized these were secrets of the past he did not want to share with anyone.

"So what are you going to do?"

"If she's my daughter, and I stress *if*, then I will have to see to her future. She has to prove to me that she is who she says she is and not some tramp eager to steal my money." He chuckled with sudden good humor. "In the market for a wife, sheriff? I can make it worth your while to take this one off my hands."

Jonah sat on the edge of his desk and folded his arms over the star on his chest. His long legs stretched far out into the middle of the dirty floor. Crossing his ankles, he appeared to be gazing at the engraving on his leather boots. He wanted to be sure Flynn did not see his amusement.

"Do I get a chance to see this daughter of yours first? I never have made it a practice to buy things sight unseen."

"She'll be lovely." Flynn turned to look at the board covered with wanted posters. His voice became distant as he went on, "If she looks anything like her mother, she will be a delight to the eyes. Slender, blonde hair, and eyes as dark as the night. How that one tempted me! Then she pretended she did not want to be mine because of the uniform I wore." His jaw tightened as he spat, "This must be Eugenie's final curse on me. She could have borne me a son to give the mines to, but no, she inflicts this girl-child on me."

"Not exactly a child." Jonah pretended to be checking the date. "She's over twenty-five."

He snapped, "What am I going to do with a twenty-five-year-old spinster? She should have been married by now, unless there's something wrong with her." With a bitten-off obscenity, he mumbled, "Probably squinty-eyed or simple-minded."

"You just said she would be beautiful."

"Why does she have to come now?" Flynn continued as if his sheriff had not spoken. "Dammit, both Clark and Daly are on me to sell the company to them."

Jonah asked lightly, "Why don't you? They

are both rich enough to pay you a healthy price for it." The term *rich* paled next to the incredible wealth and power amassed by the two premier Copper Kings. William Clark and Marcus Daly had been the first to discover the copper beneath Butte's "richest hill in the world," as they possessively called it. From the beginning the two men hated each other, and each worked to put his rival out of business. The attempt to buy out the smaller, but profitable, Flynn's Copper Mining Company was simply an effort by one to succeed over the other.

Those facts everyone in Montana territory knew. Jonah did not pause to think of it as he added, "Perhaps it might be a good idea. What with the union-forming activities at the smelter and mine, you could let someone else handle those problems."

"Problems? Those uneducated troublemakers?" Flynn snorted with his characteristic crudeness. "I don't know who you have been listening to, sheriff, but we are having no problems at the company. If you could handle this rash of train robberies as easily as I deal with rabblerousers, you might find me far more appreciative of your work."

Deciding they had dealt with side issues long enough, Bancroft turned the conversation adroitly back to the topic that irritated Flynn most. "I'm glad you have everything under control at the mine, because you're going to have to decide what to do with this surprise visitor."

"Damn daughter! Showing up like this without so much as a letter asking for permission to come first."

Jonah said nothing as the man raved on and on. He had never seen Flynn so agitated. It was difficult not to smile. This was going to be delightful, and the fun had only begun. By the time Flynn met K.T. in her role as his daughter, he would be totally incapable of dealing with the situation logically and might forget the questions he should ask to make sure that Katharine St. Pierre was actually his daughter.

When Flynn finally ran out of bluster, he stormed from the office without the courtesy of a farewell. Even from his desk, Jonah could hear him shouting at his carriage driver to hurry them home and get them out of the rain.

Leaning back in his chair, he wondered if the beginning could have gone better. Flynn was totally incoherent with rage and a surprisingly large load of guilt, which would continue to grow in the days before K.T. arrived. He spun at the sound of footsteps pausing before the door. When he determined it was not Flynn, he picked up the newspaper as if it interested him.

Paddy Duncan eased into the room. He smiled as he saw the booted feet on the desk. Jonah could hide behind the newspaper and pretend to be indifferent to the situation that was growing rapidly more complicated. But none of his allies believed this pose.

Walking to the desk, Duncan shoved the dusty boots to the floor. Jonah folded the paper and dropped it on the desk. His friend, with his unruly shock of startling red hair, leaned on the cluttered desktop. His cotton shirt was spotted with the rain splattering on the dirty windows.

"Well?" Duncan demanded.

"He's a walking case of nerves. The telegram has upset him so much he doesn't know what to think."

The telegram operator regarded his friend's broad smile. "He believes she's his daughter."

"He believes it's possible." Jonah stood up with a laugh. Slapping his shorter friend companionably on the back, he crossed the small room to the wall covered with wanted posters. He ripped one from among the dozen waiting there. When he tossed it to Duncan, the red-haired man caught it with ease.

He read it quickly. There was no smile on his full lips as he looked up from the yellowed page announcing the reward for the leader of the Forrester gang wanted for train robbery and other unspecified crimes. It did not mention that the leader was a female, although it described her size and coloring accurately.

"Will she cooperate?"

"Yes." Jonah added nothing else as he looked out the window at the empty street. The cold rain kept everyone inside. A flash of lightning seared his eyes.

"Are you so sure?"

"Everything is arranged. She will be under surveillance until she goes to Flynn's house. I have alerted Lenny, so he will make sure she arrives on time. If she tries to betray us, she knows she risks her life."

"But after—"

A tight smile crossed his lips. "Money's the only way I can control her. She wants what I have offered as her share of ruining Flynn. Dammit! I wish I could find the kid who was with her the day we hanged Schurman. The kid's her brother. With that Forrester behind bars, she would do everything exactly as I tell her."

"Arrange it."

"What?"

Duncan smiled. "You are good friends with the U.S. Marshall in Butte. I am sure you two can work out some way to handle one young train robber named—"

"Ethan Forrester." He grinned with sudden vindictiveness. "She made the mistake of telling me that one day. One of the few she has made." Sitting on the radiator beneath the window, he leaned against the cool glass. A smile flirted with the hard expression in his eyes. K.T. Forrester would be glad to see Jonah Bancroft hang for halting her crimes. He needed something to hold over her head. Something more than the promise of money, and this could be it. Glancing at his friend, he added, "You are diabolical, Duncan."

"Learned it from the master," he said, doffing his hat in the sheriff's direction.

"And well, I would say." He grabbed his own hat and pointed to the door. "Let's go to the telegraph office and see what we can arrange for Mr. Ethan Forrester."

K.T. sat up alertly as she heard the front door open. She winced. Never would she become accustomed to being leashed like a beast in a pen.

Her nearly healed shoulder burned with renewed pain as she pulled against the ropes binding her hands to the headboard. She had wondered if Sheriff Bancroft would ever return today. Never had he been gone so long. Her whole body ached from sitting in one position for half a day.

The footsteps she would recognize the rest of her life walked directly to her door. Her forehead rutted in bafflement. She was filled with disquiet at the sudden change in his routine. Usually the sheriff paused in the other room to remove his coat and taunt her into wondering if he would refuse to release her that night. When the door opened, she met his shadowed face without speaking.

Twilight was forced back as he lit the lamp on the dresser. She gasped as she saw the downward tilt of his mustache. Something horrible had happened. What it was she could not guess. She did not want to guess.

"K.T., I . . ."

"What's wrong?" she cried, straining forward as far as the ropes allowed.

He did not answer as he reached for the knife on his belt. Instead of untying the ropes as he normally did, he sliced easily through them. His gaze noted her deepening shock. For a moment, a twinge of guilt seared through him. He was astonished how much he wanted to take her in his arms and smooth the fear from her features. Shaking off that urge, he watched as she flexed her cramped arms. She rolled the too-big sleeves back to her elbows and straightened the vee neckline so it did not reveal the lace at the top of her chemise.

Silently he held out the slip of paper darkened by raindrops. She did not raise her hand to take it. Taking her wrist still wearing the rope manacle, he pressed the page into her palm. He sat next to her so he could watch her read it.

K.T. looked from his unsmiling face to the piece of paper. She did not have to unfold it to know it was a telegram. Suddenly she relaxed. Sheriff Bancroft had told her he was going to send Flynn a message supposedly from New Orleans via the telegraph. This must be a copy of that.

"Did he believe you?" she asked.

"Later, K.T. Read this."

She placed it on the bed covers. Drawing her knees up to her chest, she folded her arms on top of them. She put her chin on her arms and grinned. "Tell me what happened. Did he believe it? What did he say? Am I going to have to pretend to be Eugenie St. Pierre's daughter?"

"K.T., read the telegram first." He picked it up and held it out to her again.

Wanting to ask why he did not regale her with the beginning of his plan to ruin Flynn, she took the wrinkled page. The only way she would hear what took place in the office across the street was to do as he wanted. Quickly she scanned the page.

Horror spread through her as she made out the dim handwriting on the splotched page. The instant Ethan's name caught her eyes, she knew that something terrible had happened to her beloved brother.

"No!" she screamed. She surged from the bed in a blind path to the door. When hands caught her, she struck out at the one who dared to halt her from going to help Ethan.

"K.T.! K.T.!" Jonah had not expected such a violent reaction from her. He ducked as her fist nearly hit his nose. Not wanting to hurt her, but having no desire to feel her rage bruise him, he flipped her over his shoulder. As he had the first morning she woke in his bed, he dropped her onto the covers.

She rolled to leap off the bed. The pain in her shoulder she disregarded. No one was going to keep her in Copper Peak when her baby brother risked dying in Butte. She had no idea how she would get to the city forty miles away, but somehow she would.

Heavy hands pressed her back into the mattress. She kicked out her feet. Crying "Ouch!" when her bare toes struck a hard body, she heard her captor's grunt of pain. She reached out to scratch at his face. No one would stop her from helping Ethan.

Her wrists were pinned to the covers as his solid form kept her from moving. The red-tinted madness dissolved to show her Sheriff Bancroft's face directly above hers. Through clenched teeth, she commanded, "Let me go! I'll come back to help you against Flynn! I promise. Just please let me go and rescue Ethan."

"How?"

At the one-word question, she felt her strength

drain from her. Tears blossomed in her eyes to glitter like dark jewels. She gazed up at the face so close to hers. The lantern light deepened the angles of his face, turned down in surprising sympathy.

"Help me, sheriff! Help me free Ethan. I'll take no money for helping you to ruin Flynn." Her voice broke as she begged, "Just don't let them hang my brother. He's the only one I have left."

Jonah gazed down at her vulnerable face. He had not expected her to react like this to the news of her brother's capture. Anger. Frustration, perhaps, but not this insane desire to trade anything for his release. He knew he could force her to do whatever he wished to save Forrester.

Whatever he wished . . . Suddenly he became aware of her slender form so intimately close to him. He had tended this slight body during her sickness, but had never felt an inkling of desire swelling through him as he did now. His eyes left her face to move along her body in a slow, luxurious caress. The nightshirt clung to her curves revealingly. Waves of dark hair flowed across the cream covers. He raised his gaze to her face once more. It did not surprise him that she had been aware of his scrutiny.

K.T. wondered if she could breathe as she sensed the change in the man lying over her. Moments before, he had been interested only in subduing her with his superior strength. His hands loosened on her wrists to stroke the sensitive skin along her inner arms. Although he explored no farther than the angle of her elbow where the sleeves of his nightshirt bunched, she could see his yearning to touch her far more sensuously.

When she spoke, she saw his eyes widen with astonishment. She did not care if she surprised him with her forthright words. All she wanted was to do what she must to save Ethan. If this was what he wanted, the quicker he began, the quicker the horror would be over.

"Is that the cost of letting me help Ethan?" Her fingers slid out from beneath his hands to reach for the buttons at the collar of the long nightshirt.

"No!" he commanded. He moved hastily away from her and the shocked expression in her eyes. Without speaking, he watched her sit up on the bed. He noticed the strips of rope still hanging on her arms as she redid the loosened nightshirt. His heart pounded as he thought how luscious it would be to hold her more sweetly in his bed. Nothing had warned him that K.T. would feel so wonderful beneath him.

"I'm going to Butte." Her voice left no room for argument. "If you want, I will come back to help you. Otherwise, I can agree to repay you as you wish before I go. Anything, sheriff, for I won't let Ethan die."

"He won't die in Butte." He picked up the page from the floor. Stepping toward her, he placed it in her lap. "You didn't give me a chance to explain, K.T. I sent a telegram back to the marshall, who is a friend of mine. Ethan Forrester will be held in the Butte jail indefinitely."

Her shoulders drooped as she understood what

he meant. "He will be kept from the gallows as long as I do as you wish?"

"Yes."

"And you will arrange for him to go free when we are done here?"

"Yes, I have dealt with that already. When you have completed your role as Katharine St. Pierre, the marshall will arrange for your brother to escape."

She nodded slowly. Wiping her damp face with the too-wide sleeves, she whispered, "Then I will pose as Flynn's daughter. I will convince him I'm Katharine St. Pierre." She rose to her knees as she added, "I will do the best I can. I promise you that, sheriff."

Jonah took her hand in his. "I know you will, K.T." Abruptly he felt nothing but remorse. He knew he had had no choice. If he had not followed Duncan's suggestion, he would have had no way to keep K.T. from betraying him at the earliest time. Yet he felt no sense of victory to see her hurt.

CHAPTER SIX

K.T. adjusted her flowered shawl as the train slowed to a stop. She had not enjoyed her first experience on a train that was actually moving. Too nervous to think of anything but the coming meeting, she imagined all the things that could go wrong. There were so many. All of which would guarantee her death at the end of a rope.

More than once, she had asked herself why she did not simply stay on the train until the next stop. She could get out there and find her way to Butte. There she would discover where Ethan was held and determine some way to release him. With her brother, she could leave this region and begin anew elsewhere.

"Miss St. Pierre?"

When she did not react to the voice, fingers settled on her shoulder. Her left hand reached automatically for the pistol that should have been resting on her hip. She touched only heavy wool as she looked up at the conductor. "Yes?" she whispered.

"Miss St. Pierre," he repeated, emphasizing the name with a satisfied smile, "we're at your stop. I'm sure you wouldn't want to miss disembarking at Copper Peak."

Her breath caught in her throat as she recognized the voice. This was the man who had suggested they kill her when she lay on the side of the mountain, bleeding from her wound. She wondered if he had been averse to forcing her to play this role, or if he delighted in her horrible situation as Sheriff Bancroft did. Her fingers itched to feel the familiar blade of her knife against her palm. Then she would teach this man the cost of laughing at her.

She had to hide those rebellious thoughts. Ethan's life depended on her compliance with their orders. Somehow she murmured, "Thank you, sir. This is Copper Peak so soon?"

"Yes, miss. This is Copper Peak." He winked broadly at her before he continued along the aisle.

She watched him progress between the rows of seats, often stopping to talk lightheartedly to the other passengers. More than once, he glanced in her direction. Her unformed plan of continuing on to the next junction faded. He would make sure she left the train before the wheels rolled again. With a sigh, she stood to retrieve the hatbox that Sheriff Bancroft had shoved in her hands before she boarded.

As her hands reached for the bandbox, she

recalled the final instructions the sheriff had given her at the town nearly fifteen miles to the east of Copper Peak. He had woken her in the quiet, early hours of the morning before the sun rose, so they could have enough time to make the long journey. They had said little as they drove through the incredible vistas of rugged mountains caressing the purple blanket of the dawn sky.

He had been as silent as those stone megaliths when he helped her down from the buggy at the strange train platform. Tying the reins to a hitching post next to the street, he took her hand and twirled her slowly about to be sure she fit his image of the daughter of Lyndon Flynn and Eugenie St. Pierre. The full skirts of her dark gray traveling suit sang a hushed melody of wool as it brushed the ground.

"Sheriff!" she had gasped as he reached for the lapels of her jacket.

"Hush, K.T.," he had ordered as he straightened the wool coat decorated with crimson braid. "I'm just trying to make you look presentable."

"I think I can dress myself!"

She had pulled away from him and readjusted her clothes until they were comfortable again. With her face averted, he could not see her cheeks matched the color of the braid. She did not want him to guess at the odd weakness that swept through her each time he touched her, for he would capitalize on it to bind her more tightly to his will.

Where Sheriff Bancroft had purchased the lovely gowns she had watched him pack in a large trunk before they left Copper Peak, she could not guess. For an unmarried man to make such a large and extravagant purchase should have drawn the storekeeper's attention immediately. She tried to guess the lies he had told Haggerty to allay his suspicions, but could not imagine any that would suffice unless the town's storekeeper . . .

K.T. froze in the aisle of the train. The telegraph operator, the train conductor, the town sheriff, *and* the storekeeper must make up four of the five gang members who had worked to stop the train. She did not dare to think who might be the fifth man. The only one she was sure was not the final mysterious bandit was Lyndon Flynn.

"Allow me, miss."

She emerged from her horrible thoughts to see a young man tipping his silk hat to her. His too-fancy clothes immediately labeled him as an Eastern import. He easily lifted the gaily decorated box with its velvet ribbon handle from the shelf over the seats. With a smile, he placed it in her hands.

"Thank you," she whispered.

"My pleasure, Miss—?"

Her breath caught in her throat as she nearly replied with her true name. She could not believe that this man with innocent brown eyes that reminded her so much of Ethan's was the last of the gang led by Jonah Bancroft. Then she reminded herself of the sheriff's twisted mind. He would be quite apt to place this man on the train to test her. If she failed, her brother would pay the price.

Bringing to mind the memories she had tried to seal away into the forgotten pain of the past, she raised her chin as she recalled women did in the Southern city where Katharine St. Pierre had been born. A nearly forgotten slur returned to her voice. How long had it been since she had heard her words soften with the same rhythm as Sheriff Bancroft's speech! She smiled as she imagined how he would react to this shocking transformation of K.T. Forrester into the incredibly feminine Katharine St. Pierre.

She steeled herself to speak calmly. "I am Miss St. Pierre, sir." Her eyes widened as she saw the effect of her husky whisper on him. After years of spending most of her time in trousers and tattered flannel, she had forgotten that women had ways other than using pistols of bringing men to heel. "Are you stopping in Copper Peak, sir?"

"Yes. Oh, I am Coleman Brown. It's my good fortune that Mr. Flynn has hired me to be his new bookkeeper. I am pleased to make your acquaintance, Miss St. Pierre." He smiled, suddenly looking as unsophisticated as his words. "Perhaps I might have the honor of calling on you when you are settled in Copper Peak. We can share tales of our arduous journey west."

"I'm unsure, for I must check with my father before I receive any callers at our home."

"And where does Mr. St. Pierre reside?" he persisted, unwilling to let her leave the train before he could gain permission to see her again. He had been watching her since he awoke this morning and spent the last few miles of the trip trying to guess how he could have missed her elegance before.

"My father's name is Lyndon Flynn." She spoke the lie uneasily. Noting the shock on his face, she realized that she must accustom herself to being someone of import in this small town. She was beginning to see how complicated her role would be in the small town of Copper Peak.

"The Lyndon Flynn of Flynn's Copper Mining Company?" He gulped loudly as he tried to recall if he had said anything negative about his new employer to Flynn's daughter.

"Yes, he's my father. Good day, sir," she said hastily. She was unsure how long she could continue the charade with this obviously harmless man. Her gloved hands clenched on the ribbon at the top of the bandbox to keep them from shaking with her growing terror. The few moments of pretending to be someone she was not showed her how difficult it was.

She hurried toward the door at the front of the car. Without looking back, she knew that the startled young man was watching her. Suddenly she smiled as she recalled the fear on his face when she announced her identity. Her new life as Katharine St. Pierre would not be easy, but it might have some advantages she had not considered at the outset. Power was an awesome tool, and her "father" wielded ultimate power in Copper Peak. Some of that was sure to reflect on her, and would enable her to do things she could not do as K.T. Forrester.

Her grin faded as she saw the conductor waiting by the steps from the car. When he tipped the well-polished brim of his cap toward her, she wanted to spit out recriminations. "Finish her off" had been what he would have done if Sheriff Bancroft had not halted him. Instead of saying the insults in her mind, she assumed her new role.

"Thank you, sir, for my ride in your charmingly primitive vehicle," she gushed. "La! If I ever get the dirt from my clothes, I swear they will be fit only for the church charity box." She delighted in the tightening of his professional smile and knew she had struck him in a tender spot. From the small experience she had had with rail employees, she had found them to be a loyal lot, fiercely devoted to and proud of their iron chargers.

"You are welcome, Miss St. Pierre. I do hope you will be traveling with us again soon."

She did not smile as she answered with cold hauteur, "If I do, it shan't be in such a cluttered coach. Good-bye."

What he muttered at her back she could not understand, but she had no time to think of it as she stepped onto the platform, and into the beginning of a new life she expected to despise. It was not necessary to pretend fright. Every inch of her body trembled in a way she had never suffered even when robbing trains.

"Miss St. Pierre?"

She turned to see a man step from the shadows beneath the canopy protecting half of the platform in front of the squat building marked "Copper Peak." He was a slender man in a dirty shirt and trousers covered with debris from the

113

mines. The color of his hair matched the sable shadows of the mountains rising in the distance.

"Yes?" she asked, recalling her role. From this point until Sheriff Bancroft got whatever he wanted in revenge, she must never forget she was no longer K.T. Forrester. She was Katharine St. Pierre, but she would allow her dearest friends to call her Katie. In her mind sounded an endless litany of the orders and the facts she must remember.

"I'm Max, Miss St. Pierre. Mr. Flynn asked me to bring you up to the house."

With distaste, she eyed his dirty clothes. "Sir, I'm not accustomed to riding with roustabouts. I will wait here while my father sends a suitable conveyance for me."

"Miss, I—I—"

"Sir, you are simply delaying the time when I shall meet my father." Rubbing her gray-gloved hands together, she looked at the buildings around her and scowled. "This is worse than I expected." She turned again to the disconcerted man and asked, "La, sir, why do you dawdle here? I thought I had made myself quite clear."

"Problem, Max?"

K.T. kept her face in a frustrated expression as she turned slowly. She could not let the sheriff's astonishing presence at this moment fluster her. He must have driven at top speed to be back in Copper Peak before the train. If he was testing her, she wanted him to be pleased with her. To fail would cost her more than she was willing to sacrifice.

"Sheriff?" She shifted her box to her other

hand as she peered at him as if in confusion. "I trust that is what that piece of misshapen tin on your chest means, Sheriff—?"

He tipped his hat to her. "Bancroft, ma'am. Jonah Bancroft." He did not comment on her derogatory words, but she saw fury flash in his eyes. That pleased her. She wanted him to realize how important she was to this escapade. No longer his captive, she had regained some control of her own life.

"I am Miss St. Pierre. My father is Lyndon Flynn. This fool insists that I travel to meet my father in that." Her finger pointed at the cart where her luggage was being loaded by two chattering lads. "I'm sure there has been some sort of mistake, but he refuses to listen to reason."

Max's lips became a straight line. With her French name and her citified manners, she acted as if he had no worth. Just like her father she was. Everyone had shared Flynn's dubiety about the validity of this woman's claim of being his daughter, but Max was sure that would change when the townspeople met Miss La-di-da St. Pierre. Her lack of manners convinced him she must be the old bastard's illegitimate daughter. Remembering he had to be polite if he did not want to lose his job, he said quickly, "Sheriff, Mr. Flynn told me—"

Smoothly Jonah said, "I'm sure this is all nothing more than a simple misunderstanding. Miss St. Pierre, my buggy is over here. I can take you to your father's house, if you wish."

She looked past him and sniffed in derision. 'In that? It's dusty, sir. I look wrinkled enough after the horrendously long journey from my beloved New Orleans. You will understand I don't want to meet my father filthy as well."

"It is a short drive to Mr. Flynn's house."

"Very well." She sighed as she turned to the infuriated Max. "Please bring my bags to the house."

Both men watched as she flowed smoothly across the dirt-covered planks of the platform. When she waited with obvious impatience to be handed into the carriage, Jonah shared a wry expression of disgust with Max. Miss St. Pierre made it clear very quickly that she expected Eastern courtesies in this rough town.

Jonah went to her and offered her his hand. When she placed her extended fingers delicately on his palm, her "Thank you" spoken in a hushed voice earned his admiration. He could not believe how swiftly she had acquired an accent that sounded authentic to his ears, which had been longing for the sound of voices from home.

He shook his head to clear away nostalgic thoughts and leapt into the other side of the carriage. Picking up the reins, he slapped them on the back of the horse.

"Sir, don't beat that poor creature. I swear he looks worn near to the death by your ill treatment." She met his angry gaze evenly. "Is horse-flesh of so little value in Montana that you can abuse the creatures that way?"

"Don't carry this deception too far," he warned her quietly. He understood her anger with him for making sure personally that she acted as he had ordered. If she had expected him to think she'd do as told without being watched, she must be less intelligent than he thought. "I didn't want to get involved yet."

"Yet?" She laughed with an iciness meant to freeze the public smile from his face. "It would seem to me, sheriff, that you were involved in this affair long before I was. If you want me to be this St. Pierre woman, you have to let me play the role as you gave it to me. I cannot imagine Katharine St. Pierre riding in that dogcart."

"Where did you learn to talk like that?"

She turned to look at the curious people pausing on the street to watch the buggy pass. All of them must have heard of the arrival of a secret that Lyndon Flynn had hoped would be kept hidden forever. They regarded her with tense looks that revealed their wonder about what changes she would bring to Copper Peak. When Sheriff Bancroft repeated his question in a sharper tone, she sighed.

"As it comes so easily to me after all these years, I suspect I learned this accent in the same place you did, sheriff."

"In New Orleans?"

A shrug of her shoulders brought a grimace of pain to her face. She could not forget how tender her left shoulder remained, although most of the pain had faded with the passing of the days. In a strained voice, she answered, "Perhaps. To tell you the truth, I don't know. Wherever it was, we left it before I realized it needed a name other than Home."

"Your older brother must have known."

"It appears it is too late to ask him." She tightened her shawl around her shoulders as she met his eyes squarely. "You lawmen made sure of that, didn't you?"

As the horse plodded along the street, he covertly viewed her. Dressed like a proper lady, she was prettier than he had guessed she would be. The month of being housebound had lessened the sun-darkened hue of her skin, but the natural blush remained in her cheeks. With Haggerty's wife's assistance, he had purchased the appropriate clothing for an impoverished lady from New Orleans. It pleased him to see the results of his work.

K.T. felt his eyes on her, but refused to acknowledge him. With her gaze on the road directly in front of them, she rehearsed what she had planned for her meeting with Lyndon Flynn. She must take the offensive as her creation of Katharine St. Pierre would do, so she could keep Flynn off-balance. If he had a chance to ask questions she could not answer, the plot might be finished before it began.

Her eyes widened as the buggy climbed the hill toward the wrought-iron gates in the stone wall that separated Flynn's house from the lowly residences of his employees. At either side of the gate, twin posts nearly eight feet tall of the same native stone as the wall were topped with formidable-looking pyramids. No one entered the sanctum inside without the proper measure of awe.

Up the curving driveway they drove, to stop before the house decorated with a profusion of gingerbread trimmings on the porches and eaves. To the right a round tower rose the full three stories of the house to a roof capped in brilliant red tiles.

Jonah halted the buggy, fixed the brake, and leapt to the gravel road. He walked around to the opposite side and held up his hands to his passenger.

When she started to put her own hands on his shoulders so he could lift her down, she realized that Katharine St. Pierre would allow no strange man to treat her so familiarly. She smiled with cool disdain as she placed her fingers on one upraised palm. Stepping from the carriage, she said with perfect correctness, "Thank you, sheriff."

"You are welcome, Miss St. Pierre."

He watched as she moved toward the house. For a moment, he was tempted to let her meet the devil in his lair by herself, but then he followed. Not out of sympathy, but simply because he did not trust her.

K.T. paused as she reached for the railing by the steps. Her fingers recoiled from the wood. Some premonition she could not name warned her of the danger waiting for her in the house, a danger more deadly than anything Sheriff Bancroft had suggested might live within this beautiful home. Once she stepped through that door, her life would never be the same again. Everything she had been would be stripped away to leave her bare and vulnerable to the whims of those around her.

The presence of the unseen threat breathed like a beast of prey sneaking up to pounce on her, raising the small hairs at the back of her neck. She fought the pressure of its mighty weight grinding down on her. Over and over, she reminded herself she was once again in control of her life. When she entered Flynn's house, she would be the one to determine how the rest of the masquerade went. Her life and her brother's life depended on her ability to convince the man waiting impatiently inside that she was the daughter of a woman he had abused and abandoned.

That thought strengthened her. No crimes she had committed compared with the atrocities that Sheriff Bancroft hinted Flynn had perpetrated. She had stolen money and threatened the lives of those who guarded what she wanted, but she had never robbed another of precious dreams. Flynn deserved everything they would do to him, and she would be richly rewarded. It was worth the risk.

"Scared?"

She turned to look over her shoulder at the blue eyes regarding her with a surprising lack of irony. Occasionally she saw kindness in those compelling eyes, but so seldom that it always surprised her. Her gaze dropped to the perfectly tied dark string tie contrasting with the tan of his shirt which followed the lithe lines of his strong body. As always, the silver star rested over his heart.

Dampening her lips, she answered simply. "Yes, sheriff, I'm scared. I would be foolish not to be."

"Yes, you would." He motioned toward the door. "Shall we?"

Although she yearned to race in any direction but up the steps, she preceded him toward the door. That they had been watched she knew when the door opened just as she reached it. A tall man in a spotless black suit bowed his head as she entered. "Good afternoon, miss, sheriff."

"Miss St. Pierre, this is Taylor, the butler for Mr. Flynn." He gauged the white-haired man's reaction as he continued, "Taylor, Miss Katharine St. Pierre, Mr. Flynn's daughter recently arrived from New Orleans." It amused him that, other than a flicker of astonishment at the young woman's lovely appearance, which bore no resemblance to Flynn's gross features, the butler showed no emotion.

Speaking a greeting, she looked about the lush interior. In spite of her best efforts, K.T. could not keep from gawking at the well-polished furniture and crystal chandeliers brightening the foyer. A subtle elbow in her ribs warned her to close her gaping mouth. She feared that he may have expected too much of her. She had never seen anything like this house. If she was this overawed by the entrance hall, she began to doubt she could convince anyone that she had been surrounded by such luxury all her life.

"Follow me, please," said Taylor.

Taking her elbow, Jonah steered her across the floor and whispered a warning in her ear. But she did not hear what he said. At this moment, when she stood literally on the threshold of this adventure, her instincts had taken over. So often she had had to trust her instincts to guide her through the treacherous life she lived, and she had come to know that she could depend on them totally.

As soon as Taylor opened the door, K.T. left the sheriff standing in the doorway and crossed the large room to the imposing figure standing by his mahogany desk.

"Mr. Flynn?" she said coolly, extending her hand. "I am Katharine St. Pierre."

The broad man did nothing but regard her in shock. Papers he had been holding in order to confront her with facts she must confirm dropped unnoticed to the floor. His mouth moved, but no words emerged while he viewed her in an unblinking stare. Slowly his hand rose to take hers.

"I didn't believe it possible," he gasped, "but it's true! You are Eugenie's image except . . ."

Katie could not pull away quickly enough as his snake-thick fingers rudely pushed the bonnet from her head. Loosened strands of hair puffed into the air. He touched the silken ebony. A half-swallowed word was unintelligible as he held up the tresses. The color was nearly identical to his own thinning hair.

"Sir, if you please!"

He flinched at her quiet protest. Releasing her hair, he glanced at the silent man by the door. Bancroft was being uncharacteristically reticent. Flynn scowled. Perhaps the sheriff enjoyed watching Flynn make a fool of himself after the scene in town earlier in the week.

"Do you want something, sheriff?" he asked gruffly.

Flynn could not keep his eyes from straying to the woman redoing her hair before a gilded mirror. Even her lithe movements brought to mind Eugenie St. Pierre. If only she were not his daughter . . . He swallowed harshly. He had been guilty of many crimes as he clawed his way to wealth, but he could not conceive the perversion of taking his own daughter to his bed.

"I escorted your daughter here, Mr. Flynn. There seems to have been some sort of misunderstanding. Max was there with unsuitable transportation for Miss St. Pierre. I thought it best if I escorted her home myself." He put only the slightest emphasis on the word "home."

This complete acceptance of K.T. by Flynn was something Jonah could not have foreseen. If the rest of the masquerade went as smoothly, he would have his revenge before winter. His gaze settled on K.T. He had to admit she was intriguing, and undeniably accurate in her portrayal of a beleaguered Southern lady who finds herself transported to the strange world of Montana territory.

"Good of you, sheriff. Can't trust those in town not to be upset to see her arrive."

"Why?" asked K.T. as she turned from the mirror, her hair perfectly groomed again. She drew off her gloves as she walked toward them. "Why would anyone be upset about anything in this stupid little town?" Jonah was once again impressed at her skill in creating Katharine St. Pierre.

"Don't worry yourself about that, my dear," urged Flynn. "You will become accustomed to the fools who live in Copper Peak. We don't need to talk about this now. You have had a long journey. You must be exhausted."

She did not pause as she walked to the windows draped in forest-green velvet. Her fingers reached out to touch the golden fringe. With her face turned toward the window, neither of the men could see her awe at the plushness surrounding her. This was the room she held in her dreams. The room she had spoken of to the sheriff when they negotiated the price of her cooperation.

"Yes, Mr. Flynn, I am tired. I was up early this morning on that uncomfortable train." She shuddered with patrician disgust. "My friend Mary Sue went on and on about her trip on the train to New York. La! I don't know why she raved about it. Surely it must be the most horrible thing I ever have suffered, save for Mama's death."

Her eyes grew hard in an expression that Jonah recognized. He could not help being awed by the vast repertoire of emotions she could project as Katharine St. Pierre. If he had not known the truth, he would never have suspected she was anyone but the woman he had invented. He asked himself how a tattered, train-robbing urchin could know all she seemed to about being a fine lady from New Orleans. The information he had given her had not been enough to teach her all this.

Katie looked directly at the disconcerted man who was supposedly her father. "Of course, I doubt that Mama's demise bothered you much, Mr. Flynn. In the years since you left New Orleans, you never once contacted us. Therefore you do not know how Mama mourned for you."

124

"Eugenie mourned for me?" He dropped, thunderstruck, in the chair behind him. After his heartless treatment of the woman, after she had cursed him to suffer the most painful scourges known to man, he found it incredulous that she had longed for him to return.

"Oh, yes." She flashed Jonah a superior smile. His obvious discomfort at her improvisation pleased her. Although he had not seen fit to tell her exactly what he had planned, she knew he wanted to hurt Flynn. She had her own ideas of how to do that quickly so she could collect her twenty-five thousand dollars and free Ethan. "Can we discuss this at another time, Mr. Flynn? This isn't the proper topic to be spoken of before outsiders."

The man leapt to his feet like a puppy longing to please its master. He took her hands in his. When she pulled them away with a shocked gasp, he apologized quickly. He added, "You must call me Father."

"I think it's a bit late for that, sir."

"Then, at least Lyndon, and I will call you Katie, if I may."

Bright tears suddenly filled her large eyes. When the man in front of her looked to the sheriff to gain his help in understanding the mercurial moods of his newly discovered daughter, she whispered, "That is what Mama called me. Will you excuse me before I embarrass myself before you?"

Flynn motioned to the servant waiting silently in the doorway. "Go with Mrs. Grodin. She will take you to your room. We dine at seven."

She nodded, gulping as she tried to hold back the tears. So quietly they had difficulty discerning her words, she said, "And thank you, Sheriff Bancroft, for seeing me to my new home. I trust I will see you again about town."

"Yes, Miss St. Pierre."

Jonah watched as she was led from the room by the housekeeper. Silently he thanked Duncan for his wonderful idea of showing K.T. that her success in this masquerade was the only way she could keep her brother from hanging. But a doubt arose in him too: If she could assume this character so perfectly, how would he be able to tell whether she spoke the truth at any other time?

She paused on the steps, her slim fingers pale against the dark wood banister. When she winked at him boldly, Jonah choked back a laugh. In spite of her early trepidation, it seemed that she intended to enjoy this new life she had been given. So far she had been superb.

Pulling his gaze away from the vanishing hem of her traveling suit, he turned to Flynn. She had done her part. Now he must do his to be sure they continued to delude Flynn.

As if the idea had just popped into his mind, Jonah said in a reflective tone, "In answer to your question of the other day, Mr. Flynn, I must say I wouldn't mind considering it."

The harried man scowled. "Considering what?"

"Taking her off your hands. If not marrying, at least courting your pretty daughter. I trust I might call on her."

"You trust wrong." He flung out a wide hand

and pointed to the door. "My daughter isn't going to lower herself to wedding some half-witted law officer. You saw. She's a lady. A real lady, not some whore like those down in the town. She doesn't want to be bothered by someone like you."

"Would you care to make a wager on that?"

Flynn's eyes narrowed, but a smile twisted his lips. "Bet that she will accept your attentions? I find it unseemly to bet on what my daughter will do."

With his shoulder against the door frame, Jonah asked in a quiet challenge, "So afraid I will prove you wrong?" He shrugged. "Have it your way."

Carefully he watched his enemy's reaction. If Flynn had been the high-class gentleman he wished everyone to believe he was, he would have tossed out any man who suggested such a wager. Jonah intended to remind the owner of the copper mines exactly how plebeian his beginnings were. With a bogus Katharine St. Pierre to assist him, he should be able to do everything he had hoped.

"Don't suggest more than you can afford to lose, sheriff," Flynn said slowly. He could not resist the offer to show his sheriff his subservient position in Copper Peak. "She will cut you down so quickly when you make any move toward her that you won't have time to bleed from your wounds." Buffing his coarse nails on his silk coat, he said, "Shall we say one month of your wages? Fifty dollars too rich for you, Bancroft?"

"Why not?"

"Indeed. All right. I will wager fifty dollars that Katharine St. Pierre will not accept your invitation to the Copper King's ball in Butte in six weeks."

Jonah frowned. "Why should she? The likes of me are not invited to such elegant affairs. She will know that."

"I will arrange for you to be invited, Bancroft. Or is this your way of backing out of a bet?"

"All right. I will bet fifty dollars that I can convince her to let me escort her to the Copper King's ball."

Flynn guffawed. "Good. It will be the easiest fifty dollars I have ever earned. Now get out of here."

With a tip of his hat to his employer, Jonah went into the hallway. He glanced involuntarily up the stairs. He was sure K.T. would make herself right at home. A smile tilted his mustache. Fortunately Flynn would allow him to call on her, so he could keep an eye on what she did. As he nodded to the butler holding the door, he told himself that was the only reason he wanted to come to visit her. He refused to admit that he dreaded the emptiness of his house without her sharp wit in it.

CHAPTER SEVEN

"If you will follow me, Miss St. Pierre," Mrs. Grodin said quietly. She had frowned when she heard the lilt in Mr. Flynn's voice as he addressed his daughter.

Daughter! The housekeeper had not believed such nonsense when Mr. Flynn had come home two weeks ago raving about some child he had begat with a New Orleans woman. That Mr. Flynn accepted this Miss St. Pierre so quickly must mean he truly believed her to be his child. Mrs. Grodin sneaked a glance at the young woman and wondered if Mr. Flynn simply had had his head turned at the sight of such a lovely woman, daughter or no daughter.

Daughter! She nearly snorted her disgust. As if they needed another one like Mr. Flynn in Copper Peak! Listening by the doorway, she had heard the high-and-mighty way this Miss St. Pierre spoke to Mr. Flynn. If she treated her father so coldly, what could be in store for the rest of them?

Mrs. Grodin let none of her distress show as she led the way up the dark walnut stairs. She did not pause to allow K.T. to admire the huge stained-glass window that brought light into the foyer.

K.T. decided it was just as well, for she was too nervous to appreciate the design. Her ears remained intent on gauging the reaction of the men after she had left, but the thick walls of the house prevented her from learning whether she had revealed the truth about herself in any unconscious error.

The housekeeper opened a door close to the stairs. Although Flynn had had little time to prepare for her, he had set his staff to creating a suite of rooms that rivaled her fantasies. New pink paint glistened on the walls of the sitting room, interrupted by ceiling high-windows with drapes in a darker pink. Gaslights shone throughout the room. Its soft glow brought out the newness of the furniture arranged comfortably on a pale rug. Through other doors she could see a bedroom and a strange compartment.

Her brow furrowing, she walked to the door of the curious room, and gasped when she saw what lay within. The housekeeper moved to stand behind her and turn up the gaslight.

Mrs. Grodin asked, "Is something wrong with the bathroom, Miss St. Pierre?"

"No, no, nothing at all." She had heard of such luxurious rooms created simply to tend to the body's needs, but had never expected to see

130

one. Remembering her role, she added in the condescending tone that had worked so well with Flynn, "This is very nice. Thank you." K.T. tried to act naturally, but the quiet reserve of the housekeeper disconcerted her. She did not like lying to this woman, who no doubt had as much right to despise Flynn as the rest of them.

"Shall I have a tray sent up to you? You must be famished after your long trip."

"Tea and toast will be sufficient." As the woman turned to leave, K.T. added, "I'm sorry if I'm causing you trouble. I certainly had no intention to be a bother."

Mrs. Grodin glanced at the young woman. Slowly she smiled. "You are no trouble. Just a surprise."

"I know I am quite unexpected."

"Miss St. Pierre, unexpected is not exactly the word I would have used. Mr. Flynn has been acting like a total fool for the past week." She pressed her hand over her mouth. If Miss St. Pierre told her father what the housekeeper had just said, Mrs. Grodin could be without a job in a town where Mr. Flynn controlled everything.

K.T. placed her hat and bag on the closest table. Drawing off her gloves, she said, "Don't worry, Mrs. Grodin. As I am sure you know about the circumstances that have brought me to Copper Peak, you will not be surprised that there is no familial affection between your employer and me." She hesitated, for she had to devise her tale as she went along. As she unbuttoned her jacket, she said, "I have not decided if I will stay long. This is the only place I had to come to after Mama died and left me in ... uncomfortable circumstances."

Mrs. Grodin understood immediately what a lady should not say, even by a subtle reference. "I'm sorry, Miss St. Pierre."

"It is all right, Mrs. Grodin. Mama died nearly three months ago." She smiled gently as if strengthening herself to bear past grief. "I would appreciate it if you called me by my given name. I will be staying for a while at least."

"Of course. Whatever you wish, Miss Katharine."

Unsure if she would remember to answer to that strange name, K.T. urged, "I would prefer if you call me 'Katie.' "

Mrs. Grodin's smile widened. This young lady seemed totally without pretensions. Though she was the prettiest lady ever to enter Copper Peak in Mrs. Grodin's long memory, she acted as if her beauty were of no importance. Such a difference from the simpering females who paraded through Mr. Flynn's rooms hoping to gain prestige and wealth in exchange for their favors. She wondered if Mr. Flynn would cease those activities when his own daughter slept under the roof of his home. It might not be so horrible to have Katie St. Pierre here.

"Let me have Betsey bring up your tray, Miss Katie. Mr. Flynn is an early riser, but our cook, Mrs. Howard, will be pleased to prepare breakfast for you in the informal dining room whenever you wish it. As you heard, we normally dine at seven, but you will find there is no set timetable during the day. Mr. Flynn spends most

132

of his day at the mines, so we adjust to his schedule." As she opened the door, she added, "I took the liberty of unpacking for you. When do you expect your other things?"

Katie smiled, pleased that Mrs. Grodin had decided to be friendly. "Someone called Max said he would deliver it."

"I will check on it. That young fool doesn't remember from one minute to the next what he is supposed to do. Make yourself comfortable, Miss Katie."

Katie thanked the housekeeper. When the other woman was gone, she released the breath tight in her chest. She wondered if she had been holding it ever since Sheriff Bancroft assisted her from the carriage. The idea of living this charade day after day daunted the vestiges of her courage. Her one consolation was that there was no one in Copper Peak ready to reveal her true identity as K.T. Forrester. With Jimmy dead and Ethan in jail, only Les Proulx was free to betray her. She guessed he had fled far from Copper Peak as soon as he heard Ethan had been captured.

Deciding she must do something or she would start to imagine all kinds of evil happenings in her future, she began to explore her new home. Her eyes grew wide as she entered the bedroom. A canopy bed had been set on a platform. A satin cover of pale brown matched the curtains hanging from the bed's high tester poles. She touched the velvet fabric on the pair of chairs by the hearth. On the opposite side of the room near a window waited a dressing table.

Her imagination had not painted Flynn's home like this—neither its majesty nor its reclusive site high on a hill that effectively shut out the world. In this strange room in the strange house, she was far from the beloved familiarity of her own shack on the ridge overlooking the gushing river. Here she was distant from the comforting sound of the wind singing through the clefts in the mountains and the symphony of the storms. A bottomless silence seemed to entomb the huge house.

Suddenly she smiled. Dropping into one of the velvet chairs, she put her feet up on the other. In her normal voice, she crowed, "Dammit, K.T., you have landed on your feet this time! Who would believe you're getting paid for living so well?"

When a knock sounded on the door, she jumped, startled at the intrusion of sound into the elegant room. She hoped her voice had not carried past the walls to betray her. Automatically her hand went for her pistol as she skulked across the room. She whispered a curse when she remembered how weaponless, how nakedly vulnerable she was. Somehow she would have to remedy that soon. The sheriff had her guns, so she must find some other way to defend herself.

She opened the door to find a serving maid in her early teens. As Mrs. Grodin had been, the girl was dressed in unrelieved gray. Even her apron took on that dull color, for the thin linen captured the darkness of the material beneath it. With a smile that did not hide her curiosity, the maid placed the tray on a table and dipped in a brief curtsy before leaving.

Katie stared at the abundance of food. There was enough for three on the tray. Many nights she could remember having less than this for all of the Forresters to eat, and she wondered what her brothers would think of such waste. Pouring herself a cup of tea, she put marmalade on a piece of still-warm toast. She relaxed against the back of the settee. After her long day, which was far from over, she was happy just to sit on something stationary.

Her eyes glinted as she picked up the knife again. But she dropped it onto the tray in disgust. A butter knife, good only for spreading jelly. She needed a weapon that could deter anyone who wanted to keep her in this house longer than she wished.

With effort, she took a calm sip of the tea. She had just arrived, so she had time to gather the tools she needed. Reaching for another piece of toast, she decided she might as well enjoy this luxury while she could. Sheriff Bancroft did not seem the type to delay when he was so close to his goal.

A short while later, Katie lay down on the luscious comfort of the huge bed, but sleep evaded her. Every sound in the house demanded to be identified. Most she dismissed quickly as sounds of the staff working in the many rooms of the house or out on the grounds. Each quarter-hour was pronounced with stately decorum by the grandfather clock in the foyer. She listened to its periodic chime until it told her it was time she must prepare for dinner.

Taking her dressing gown and clean linen, she

went into the bathroom and examined the strange fixtures. She laughed with childish glee as she twisted the faucet handles of the claw-footed tub. Both cold and hot water poured forth to dance on her skin with sparkling droplets. In a few seconds, she had the temperature adjusted as she wished.

She frowned when the water did not stay in the tub but ran down a hole. A plug hung from a chain from a metal circle between the faucets. Realizing what it was for, she placed the stopper in the drain.

"How wonderful!" she breathed when she considered the luxury of being able simply to pull the stopper to release the water. She had always hated the task of emptying her tub, especially on a cold night when she did not want to lose the warmth from her long soak.

It did not take her long to strip off her clothes. She threw them into a crumpled heap on the floor as she searched for a towel. She found several as well as jasmine-scented soap in a cupboard near a washbasin equipped like the tub with faucets and pipes.

Her eyes closed in sybaritic delight as she sank into the steaming water. The porcelain above the water line was a cold shock, but she slid down until only her head was above the water.

Too soon she had to rise from the water, but promised herself this luxury again soon. While the water gurgled away, she drew her lovely wrapper around her. She hummed a song as she went into the sitting room. Only her years of being prepared for any emergency kept her from screaming when she saw who stood in the hall door.

"Mr. Flynn!" she gasped. She clasped the wrapper around her as the burly man walked toward her.

He pointed to a chair and raised his brows in question. She nodded her permission mutely. He settled himself into it. Pudgy hands bright with gems and gold pyramided before his face. She continued to regard him without speaking. If she said the wrong thing, she might divulge the whole plot to Flynn. He would delight in seeing her suffer.

"Miss St. Pierre . . ." He cleared his throat and continued, "Because of our relationship, I shall call you Katie. You will call me Fa—"

"No!" she said emphatically. "Only my dire circumstances have reduced me to seeking your charity, sir. I told you earlier that I don't plan to pretend a daughterly fealty to you that does not exist."

His eyes nearly disappeared into the deepening folds of his wide face. Shoving aside his nonchalant pose, he snarled, "And what dire circumstances did you suffer that sent you to the shelter of your father's house after twenty-five years?"

Katie did not dare to hesitate. Neither she nor Sheriff Bancroft had thought to give her alter ego much of a past other than being Lyndon Flynn's New Orleans-born daughter. Rising, she went to the dressing table and toyed with the bottles there.

"I told you earlier that Mama died."

"Yes?" he said, and waited for more.

She swallowed. With sudden inspiration, she knew she must not hide her distress. Her only chance was to convince him there was good reason for her nervous reaction to his question.

"There are few things a single woman can do when she is left alone in the world." She turned to face the man who was watching her with the intensity of a cat regarding the mouse it was about to devour. "I did not like any of the offers I received."

"Marriage would be good for you, Katie. A husband to take care of you, a home to oversee, and children to raise."

"What made you think anyone offered me marriage?"

Leaping to his feet, he roared, "Are you telling me that the daughter of Lyndon Flynn, owner of the Flynn's Copper Mining Company, was not good enough—?"

"*Illegitimate* daughter," she corrected. She watched as the bluster vanished and his face lost its choleric color. Looking down at her slender fingers, she added, "Few men wished to tarnish their family lines by marrying a woman known to be a bastard and without the promise of a fine inheritance to ease the shame of her birth. So you see, sir, your name brought me nothing but the chance to share the life my mother had. That I will not do."

"Eugenie became a—?" He could not bring himself to say the word before his elegant daughter. As he watched her move with her mother's grace, he wondered if anything of him had been bred into her.

Katie sat in a velvet chair. She made the movement seem normal, but her knees were shaking like an aspen in the wind. Shaking her head, she said, "Not what you are thinking. When Mama—when she came home, her family was determined no one would know what had happened with you. They married her to Elwood McGwein."

"Then your name is rightfully—"

"No!" she cried. "Mr. McGwein never accepted me as his child. Until I was born, Mama never . . ." She lowered her eyes modestly to emphasize the delicacy of the subject. Hastily she continued, "Anyhow, he made it clear to everyone that I was not his child. He did make sure Mama bore him more children who called him 'Father.' He insisted I always call him 'Mr. McGwein,' which satisfied me, for I wanted nothing to do with that boor. Once I was delivered safely to everyone's regret, he took Mama to his plantation upriver. Only when Grandmère died and I had no one else to go to did he allow me to come to live with them.

"I was eleven and discovered a family I did not know I had. Especially an uncle named André." She shivered with emoted distaste as she gauged his reaction to her lies.

"Did he touch you, child?"

At the sympathy in his voice, she whirled to glare at him. "Why else do you think I would come to this godforsaken place?" She lowered her eyes to look at her hands. It was easier to spin her tale when she did not have to meet the challenge on his face. "After Mama died, we buried her next to Mr. McGwein. The immediate question was what to do with Katie who was simply a burden on the McGwein family. Uncle André had a unique answer. He wasn't related by blood to me. He was inheriting the plantation and needed a wife, but until an appropriate one could be found, he would be glad to have me sleep with him. Our bastard children would provide badly needed laborers for the plantation."

Her eyebrows arched as she asked, "Now, Mr. Flynn, do you understand why I came all the way here? Surely nothing can be worse than being forced to sleep with a fat toad you despise."

He mumbled something she could not understand. Katie watched him and wondered how a man who was so wise about other things could not see through the falsehoods making up her story. It was as filled with holes as a sieve. She wondered if it was guilt that blinded him to the truth. Her story could have been Eugenie St. Pierre's, except that Katie St. Pierre supposedly had escaped from the man who longed to prostitute her.

When Mr. Flynn turned to her suddenly, she was unprepared for the rage on his full-jowled face. She started to cower away, then remembered she must show only dislike for this man. His hand raised, but he simply patted her with surprising tenderness on the shoulder.

"Dinner is in half an hour, Katie. I trust you will be finished dressing by then. If you have any problems, ring for Mrs. Grodin. Tomorrow I

will see about hiring you a lady's maid. Someone in Butte must be willing to part with one.
Certainly there is no one around here capable of
such work."

Katie nodded. Softly she said, "I will be ready,
Mr. Flynn."

"Lyndon, at least," he corrected.

"Very well, Lyndon."

When the door closed behind him, she hid her
face in her hands and let her body tremble as it
insisted. She had created a tale that he believed,
but she feared she would forget some facet of it.
Over and over she retold to herself the history
she had created for Katie St. Pierre. She added
a few pertinent details to fill it out as much as
she could and decided the empty spots would be
explained as too painful to repeat or lost in the
simple forgetfulness of youth.

She rose and walked stiffly into her bedroom.
Opening the closet, she stared at the unfamiliar
clothes hanging in a neat row. She ran her fingers across the velvets, the satins, and the silks
as she longed for the comforting coarseness of a
flannel shirt dyed dark to hide in the night shadows when they rode to watch the trains cutting
through the mountains.

"Do you need help, Miss Katie?"

With a gasp, she turned to see Mrs. Grodin
standing in the doorway. "I—I—I did not hear
you come in," she stammered.

"I didn't mean to startle you." Chuckling, the
housekeeper pointed to her heavy shoes. "I'm
accustomed to the household maids who have
learned to listen for my steps so I do not find

141

them idle. Perhaps these large feet have learned to be too silent.''

Katie smiled weakly. She had to stop expecting everyone in this house to be eager to unmask her. With Mr. Flynn, or Lyndon as he insisted she call him, accepting her irrefutably, nobody in the house would question her identity. If she continued to wait for them to pounce on her, sooner or later she would make the mistake she dreaded. She must relax and continue to improvise as she went.

"I'm just not sure exactly how formal Lyndon wishes dinner to be."

The housekeeper reached past her to draw out a cranberry velvet dress trimmed with swags of ecru lace. "This will do fine, Miss Katie. I'm glad you have some dresses suitable for this cooler climate, but you must speak to Mr. Flynn about some clothing for the winter."

"Winter?"

"I noticed when I unpacked for you, there was nothing heavier than this and only a single light cloak."

Ignoring the housekeeper's baffled expression, Katie grumbled internally. Sheriff Bancroft could have informed her of this when he let her on her own to deal with this strange new life. Perhaps he had thought she would guess that a woman from New Orleans who was running away from her future would not have anything appropriate for a Montana winter. If the next winter was like the last . . .

Katie shivered as she recalled the horrendous cold and blizzards of the previous winter. Even those who had been in the territory more years than she had lived were awed by the frigid blasts from the Arctic. She and her brothers had huddled close to their stove and prayed spring would come before their meager supplies ran out.

Her gaze swept the room. If this game continued more than a few weeks, she would not have to worry about that this year, for these luxurious quarters must stay comfortable all year.

The triumphant smile returned to her lips as she allowed the housekeeper to help her dress and hook the myriad closures on the back of the gown. With the broad straps of her chemise covering her shoulders in lace, she did not have to worry about the scars from the bullet's passage being noticed and creating a curiosity she could not satisfy.

Instead of waiting for the housekeeper to ask her about things she did not know, a few subtle questions garnered Katie a treasurehold of information as Mrs. Grodin chatted openly about the man who owned this house and the staff working for him. Looking into the mirror as she adjusted the gown, Katie reminded herself to think of this as an adventure which should prove profitable for both her and Ethan.

In the foyer, the clock continued its steady pronouncement of the passage of time as Katie descended the stairs with forced grace. She needed to remind herself she was a lady, not a hellion riding wild through the trees.

"Good evening, Taylor," she said with perfect aplomb when the butler appeared exactly as she stepped down from the bottommost stair.

"May I show you to the dining room, Miss St. Pierre?"

"Yes, you may, if," she smiled as she added, "you call me 'Miss Katie' as Mrs. Grodin does."

He inclined his white-topped head and stated in his well-modulated voice, "It will be my pleasure, Miss Katie," He gestured toward the hallway leading away on the opposite side of the staircase from the drawing room where she had first met Lyndon. "This way."

Katie exerted all her self-will not to gape at the lovely artwork on the walls. Even the wall-covering itself was a masterpiece of silk dyed in colors she could not name. Just as she had decided the hallway was the purple-gray of the sky just before dawn, they paused before a wide pair of pocket doors slid open to reveal a formal dining room.

Despite her best efforts, "Oh, my!" escaped from her lips. Boundless in its ostentation, the room mirrored the new wealth of the man who owned this house. Gas whispered in the chandelier centered on the middle of the table, which was more than twelve feet long. Sparkling crystal matched the beauty of the drops on the light overhead, which was reflected in the well-polished top of the cherry table. Blue china edged in gold had a lacy garland design about its rim. Only when she stepped closer could she see a fleur-de-lis design in the center of each plate.

Although she had thought her gown overly elaborate, she felt impoverished in comparison with the wealth gaudily displayed in the room. The walls were covered with paintings placed too close together to be enjoyed. Some were lit enough so she could see they were portraits or landscapes, while others hid in the shadows of their heavy frames.

"A drink before dinner, Miss Katie?" Taylor asked.

"No, no, thank you," she said hastily. The brandy that could soothe her unease might lure her into speaking before she thought through each word carefully. "Where should I sit?"

"This way, miss."

Katie thanked him again when he seated her graciously at one of the two places set close to each other at the far end of the long table. Flashing him a shortlived smile, she tried to imagine how she would manage to eat with her stomach twisted in spasms.

At the sharp sound of unapologetic footsteps, she looked up to see Lyndon entering the room. His dark evening suit did not lessen his image as the laborer he had been. The fullness of his choleric face narrowed only slightly into the thick neck squeezed into the prison of the tight stand-up collar and tie. Gems flashed on his fingers as he greeted her.

"Good evening, my dear. Didn't Taylor offer you a drink?" He walked purposefully to the sideboard. "Sometimes that fool—"

"He offered, but I refused, Lyndon," she defended the butler hastily. Taylor and Mrs. Grodin had been so kind to her that she did not want to see them reprimanded because of her.

"Are you sure? This is a lovely brandy. I have it shipped all the way from San Francisco. If those fools who stole the payroll had not taken the last shipment—"

"They took the brandy, too?" When his eyes focused on her to determine what she knew of events that had taken place before she started toward Copper Peak, she explained, "Mrs. Grodin was telling me about the trouble the town had been having with thieves."

Bringing his drink and the decanter to the table, he sat opposite her. He took a deep draught of the jeweled liquor and said reflectively, "Not the town, just the mines. The damn thieves made off with two payrolls last month. If I find out who they are, they will swing as that idiot bank robber did."

"Bank robbers, too?" She knew she had to ask the question, although pain swelled through her. The sight of her friend Jimmy hanging from the quickly constructed gallows was something she did not want to remember. "I would have thought Sheriff Bancroft was too competent to allow such in this area."

He swirled the brandy in his glass and watched its hypnotic motion. "He is new, and the only thing he has stopped is one drunkard. The train robbers still live. When we capture them, they will not hang until we have gotten our satisfaction from their executions." Looking at her, he mistook the strained expression on her face for a fear totally different than she was feeling. "Don't worry, Katie. They are not interested in a young gal like you. They want the gold riding in the mail car."

When the door from the kitchen opened to

reveal Taylor bringing the soup, she was glad she did not have to answer. Lyndon's words made her more determined than ever to have this deception completed quickly so she could get Ethan and leave Montana.

Deciding a change of subject might ease the terror in her enough so she could eat, she asked calmly, "What is it that you do in Copper Peak, Lyndon?"

She heard Taylor's startled gasp as his hand holding the ladle paused over her dish. More swiftly than his employer, he recovered enough to continue serving. Lyndon stared at her as if she suddenly had sprouted horns.

"What do you mean?"

Lifting her spoon, she tasted the soup before answering. "I did not realize it was such an odd question. I simply wondered what you did in Copper Peak."

"I own Copper Peak," he boasted. He folded his arms on the table and leaned forward to hold her eyes with his gaze. "This is all mine. The copper mines, the town, everything and everyone you can see from your window belongs to me."

"There's enough money in prospecting to live like this?" She smiled inwardly when she saw how he had to control his temper not to bristle at her insult, which appeared unintentional.

He snapped, "Copper may be the most important mineral in this country's future. Electricity is popping up everywhere, and people will need copper for the wires. Easterners are swearing by those new telephones, and copper will be necessary to connect the telephones to a central switching station."

Katie was pleased she had introduced a topic that required her to do little more than nod and smile between infrequent questions. Throughout the meal, Lyndon ranted on about the future of the copper-mining industry, the horrible prices that allowed him less profit than he thought was his due, and the idiocy of his employees and competitors. She relaxed and ate while he shoved his food about his plate as he questioned the sanity of anyone who had sold their worked-out silver mines to the Anaconda syndicate, which discovered enough copper to make its members millionaires.

When her dessert plate was empty of the last bite of the chocolate cake, a treat she could not remember having before, but would ask to be served again soon, she waited until he took a breath amid his monologue.

"If you will excuse me, Lyndon, I must retire. I did not sleep well during my journey." She smiled as she rose, forcing him to do the same. "This is all so interesting, but I truly cannot keep my eyes from closing." Turning her head away, she faked a delicate yawn covered by a discreet hand.

"Of course, Katie, you must go to sleep. I'm sure you will find your room very comfortable."

The light response she was ready to make dried up in her suddenly arid mouth. She could not mistake the expression in his eyes. When she had been standing before the mirror in the drawing room earlier, she saw the same lust burning on his face. Lyndon Flynn's reputation as a lecher was whispered throughout Copper Peak. Even she, an outsider, had been aware of it. He took whatever woman he wanted, but she had staked her trust on Sheriff Bancroft's assertion that she would be safe as Lyndon's daughter. As she stared at his gaze moving with serpentine coldness along her form accented by the lines of the gown, she feared she had gambled foolishly.

"Good night," she managed to say without stuttering.

He intercepted her path to the door. Capturing her by the arm, he halted her from leaving. Katie tensed as he turned her to face him. When his mouth lowered toward her, she took a deep breath to scream, although she knew that no one in the house would gainsay Lyndon's wishes.

The slightest pressure of a kiss against her icy cheek was accompanied by a rumbling "Good night." She stared wide-eyed at him as he stepped away from her until the stench of brandy did not make her stomach roil.

"Good night," she repeated as she forced herself to make a dignified exit.

Hurrying to her room and readying herself for bed, Katie tried not to think of how Lyndon would treat her if he discovered she was not his daughter. She doubted if he would send her directly to the gallows. First he would see that she suffered as Eugenie St. Pierre had. Although she tried to force those images from her head, they returned to taunt her. She reclined on the mattress finer than any she could recall. Rolling on her side, she looked out the window at the moon sweeping through the clouds above the mountains. In this busy house, she experienced a loneliness unlike any she had ever known. While she lived here in sumptuous luxury, her brother languished in a Butte jail.

A moan escaped her lips as she wondered if Sheriff Bancroft was being honest with her. She had no reason to believe he would tell her the truth. He had promised that when this hoax was done, whenever that was, he would arrange for Ethan to be released, but he had lied to her before. If they were successful, he might renege on his vow to help the Forresters.

She sat up, unable to lie still. Burying her face in her hands, she asked herself how she had come to this. There had been a certain prestige and status in being a train robber. She had peers and understood the rules intimately. This was so different. Even before a day had passed, she knew this was a mistake.

How long could K.T. Forrester convince everyone she was Katie St. Pierre? She shivered as she thought again of what Lyndon would do to her if he discovered the game she played. Already he made it clear he wanted to atone to her supposed mother by giving his daughter everything. He spoke of new clothes and a maid and luxuries she had not imagined.

Almost as much as this charade, the resurgence of forgotten memories frightened her. She could not remember sitting at a fine table or living in a house like this, but scenes blurred by a young child's misconceptions gave her clues of how to manage in this environment. From the time Ethan was old enough to ask questions, she had avoided answering them. Not because she did not want him to know the truth, but because she could recall so little of what had been. Only the sparse recollections of loving arms and the scents of jasmine perfume as sweet as the soap in the bathroom. More came back to her in this house than in the many years since they had left . . . Home.

Questions exploded in her head. Eli had been born nearly ten years before her and had been almost nineteen when he took his young sister and baby brother from their home. He had brought them West. He soon found that the best way to provide for the children was crime. As soon as K.T. was strong enough to hold a pistol and control its recoil, he trained her as his assistant. She remembered all that, but wanted to discover what had been before.

She dropped back on the pillows to stare at the emptiness of the night sky. What had happened to her in the past had become as important as the present. When she assumed Katie's life, she found things she had not known she lost. If they were necessary for her survival, she must regain them immediately.

CHAPTER EIGHT

Katie learned how different her life had become when she rose the next morning. Lyndon met her in the front hall as she was returning from breakfast. It took all her strength to respond calmly to his smile and accept his wet kiss against her cheek.

"Would you like a tour of your new home?" he asked in a jovial tone that matched the one he had used last night after his fourth brandy.

"Mrs. Grodin showed me around earlier."

"Not the house." The impatience she guessed was characteristic had returned to his voice. "I meant Copper Peak."

Her laugh sounded fake in her ears, but he simply grinned as she answered, "La, Lyndon, I must be an idiot! How wonderful to see your little town! I need to arrange my things better in my rooms, but I should have plenty of time after your tour. There can't be that much to see."

His face reddened with suppressed rage as he waited while she took her bonnet from the hatrack and tied it under her chin. Then he led her outside, where a buggy far fancier than Sheriff Bancroft's was waiting to take them into the village nestled in the valley below.

Broad hands around her waist lifted her easily to the running board. As she sat on the velvet cushions, he walked around to the driver's side. He pulled himself up to sit next to her.

"You are a skinny little thing. Mrs. Grodin will be determined to put some more flesh on your bones." He patted her shoulder, but drew his fingers back when she gasped with what was clearly pain. "Katie, did you hurt yourself?"

"I'm so embarrassed," she murmured as she forced her mind to work through the morass of anguish. "I bumped my shoulder on the sharp edge of a dresser last night. It's still tender this morning."

"You must be more careful."

She smiled weakly. "I can assure you I have no plans to hurt it again."

Although he gave her a bewildered glance, he said nothing more. He picked up the reins and slapped them sharply on the back of the horse. She saw that the animal was accustomed to such abuse, for it compliantly started toward the gate.

Katie did not speak as she noticed things about the estate that she had not seen when she arrived with Sheriff Bancroft the previous day. Buildings clustered beyond the main house, but whether they served as servants' quarters or stabling for the animals, she could not guess. The low roofs gave no clues to their use and contrasted with the expansiveness of Lyndon's home.

The leaves had become a variety of shades to add color to the green darkness of the distant hillsides. Few of the trees in the compound appeared very old. Like everything in Lyndon's path, the old trees hardy enough to survive the fumes from the smelter had been cleared to make way for the new and far more pretentious trappings that proclaimed his wealth.

She gripped tightly to the wrought-iron ornament on the side of the buggy as he drove through the gates and toward the town. The steepness of the road did not frighten her, but the trail was rough with the recent rains and jarred her aching shoulder until she had to bite her lip to keep her moans within her.

Copper Peak existed in the shadow of the mine situated on a hillside on the opposite side of the valley from Lyndon's house. The stench from the smelter hovered over the countryside, settling into everyone's senses and turning freshly washed laundry into a sickly green. All the buildings carried the scars of the dirt that had seeped into the wood.

The main street was less busy than the last times she had come into town. She averted her eyes as they drove past the gallows that waited for its next victim. The act forced her to look into the sheriff's office, where she could see a man she did not know gesticulating wildly. He paused as he noted the buggy driving by and turned to look out the window. She returned his stare without emotion, for she refused to be intimidated by the residents of Copper Peak. If she acted as if she had nothing to hide, they might not be tempted to ask dangerous questions.

Lyndon halted the buggy in front of the store where she shopped whenever she came into town. Knowing that the storekeeper must be a member of the sheriff's marauders kept her from fearing he would denounce her before her companion. She watched as Flynn came around to her side of the buggy. He held up his hands to assist her down.

As she had with Sheriff Bancroft, she simply put her hand against his palm. She stepped down with aplomb worthy of a queen and gazed about as if she had never had a chance to explore Copper Peak.

"What a quaint place!" she said as she opened the parasol she had not needed while riding in the covered buggy. "I daresay it looks like something out of photographs of the wild West."

"Montana Territory is sparsely settled, my dear, but someday it will be as fine a state as any of those east of the Mississippi." He pointed to the mine whose shadow blanketed the town. "Wealth awaits us beneath the earth, as well as a fortune in lumber on the hills. Soon Montana will be a state."

"Isn't that wonderful?" She brushed dirt off her sleeve in a derogatory motion that negated her compliment. Keeping her eyes lowered, she was able to prevent him from seeing how she enjoyed disparaging everything he considered important. She refused to let him know that she shared his pride in the glories of the territory.

"Shall we go?"

"Where?"

He pointed overhead to the sign moving with the breeze. "This is Copper Peak's finest and only emporium. I thought you might want to look around in here. Most women enjoy shopping. Are you the exception?"

"I'm afraid not," she said, laughing.

"My dear?" He held out his arm and waited for her to respond in the proper manner.

Katie hesitated, but knew she had no choice. She put her fingers on his sleeve and wished she could race away from this man she did not understand. If she had the money Lyndon did, she would be enjoying a good life in a fine city instead of crouching on a hill overlooking Copper Peak and playing the part of a vengeful, greedy god.

He opened the door of the crowded room, which had not changed in the weeks since she had been in the store. The few customers stopped talking immediately as they saw who came into the shop. Furtive stares were fired at Katie, but she guessed it was not *her* presence that silenced the shoppers.

Giving her no chance to look at anything, Lyndon led her to the counter. He slapped on it to gain the store manager's attention. Haggerty came rushing over while his assistant cowered in the shadows, not wanting to be seen.

The storekeeper halted in mid-step, but whether

his surprise at seeing Katie was real or feigned she could not tell. He brushed his dark hair back from his high forehead and straightened his apron. As he settled his gold-rimmed glasses more tightly on his nose, he boomed, "Good morning, Mr. Flynn. It's a pleasure, as always, sir, to see you."

Lyndon ignored his fawning and said coolly, "Haggerty, this is my daughter Miss St. Pierre." Turning to the woman by his side, he added in the gentle tone he used each time he spoke to her, "My dear, Haggerty helps the employees of Flynn's Copper Mining Company and their families select items to make their lives more comfortable."

"Hello, Mr. Haggerty." Katie smiled as boldly as the shopkeeper. This meeting had been inevitable, but she wanted to show the men in Sheriff Bancroft's gang that she had gained an importance in this plot that they could not have foreseen. They had given her this role, but she alone would decide how to play it. Glancing about at the filled shelves, she pulled off her gloves. "Are we obligated to shop here as well, Lyndon?"

The disgust in her soft voice brought forth open-mouthed wonder in Haggerty. During a seemingly impromptu meeting of several of the village residents at the saloon last night, the sheriff had explained how well K.T. Forrester was playing her part as Flynn's daughter. All of them assumed that Jonah was exaggerating in the hopes that this ploy would be more successful than past ones. Haggerty saw how accurate the sheriff's estimation had been and how assured she had become of her own power in such a short time. This did not bode well for any of them.

"Haggerty can order anything you need, Katie," Lyndon told her.

She ran her fingers over the bolts of material on the shelves. The fabric was finer than any she had worn before the past two days, but she dismissed it as inferior quality. "I hope so, for I cannot appear at any functions dressed in this." She spun and smiled coyly. "You do have social functions in this place, don't you, Lyndon?"

Out of the corner of her eye, she noted the reactions of the witnesses to this exchange. Haggerty was scowling when he thought that neither of them was looking at him. The women in a small group at the end of the counter tried to hide their loathing for Lyndon Flynn and, to a lesser degree, his demanding daughter.

"I'm sure we can find some social functions to please you in Butte, my dear."

"Butte?" As soon as she said it, she wished she could take back the too-enthusiastic reaction. Haggerty would report to Sheriff Bancroft quickly that she was eager to go to the city where her brother was imprisoned. Somehow she must lessen his suspicions. Regaining her bored voice, she murmured, "I have heard about that cow town. Can it offer much more than this outpost?"

A rumble of outrage at her insults raced through the room, but she pretended to be indifferent to anyone's opinions but her own. Acting as if everything were too inferior for her to bother with, she asked Haggerty to take down a box of ribbons from a higher shelf.

He blew dust off the top before placing it on the counter. None of his regular customers could afford the luxury of velvet hairbands, but he did not doubt that this and many other luxuries would now be disappearing from his shelves. When he saw K.T.—no, Miss St. Pierre, he reminded himself—glance at him, he could not believe that she winked at him. An involuntary grin settled on his lips. Although he had been against using her, she might prove a good conspirator after all. She had been in Copper Peak for less than a day and already was depriving Flynn of some of his wealth.

"I like this one," she said, pointing to a royal blue riband. "And that one." She giggled with childlike charm as she held up a length of velvet. "Oh, Lyndon, isn't this one lovely? I swear it is as white as Grandmère's hair!"

"Take as many as you wish, my dear. Haggerty, just wrap them and send them up to the house." He walked away, obviously tired of looking at anything as trivial as hair decorations.

Katie chose a half-dozen more, but when the storekeeper put them in a pile with the others, she set them aside. "Give these to whoever deserves them most," she whispered. "I think Lyndon Flynn has a few debts to the people of Copper Peak."

"Of course, Miss St. Pierre," he answered aloud, but he could not conceal his surprise. That K. T.

159

Forrester would be generous with her newfound wealth was the last thing he had expected.

"I shall be back again to do more shopping." She patted the gift ribands and winked at him to show that she intended to repair a few wounds in the town in the only way she could.

"Why are you doing this?" he whispered.

Glancing at Lyndon standing impatiently by the window, she whispered "He stole my friend's boots before he hanged him. Your sheriff is not the only one who wants revenge." In a normal voice, she said, "Thank you, Mr. Haggerty, for your kind service."

"My pleasure, Miss St. Pierre."

Katie smiled as he winked at her as brazenly as she had at him. Walking across the room, she did not glance at the other women. She put her hand on Lyndon's arm and said, "Whenever you are ready. I am finished."

"All right, my dear." He opened the door and escorted her out into the cool sunshine. "I trust you enjoyed your shopping spree?"

"You were right. Women love to buy pretty things." When he handed her into the buggy, she asked, "Where to next?"

He did not answer as he turned at the call of his name. Katie frowned when he walked away without explanation. His expression told her he was troubled, but she could not guess why, for she did not know the man hurrying along the boardwalk. She debated jumping down to eavesdrop on the conversation, but hesitated while devising an excuse for such an action.

"Good day, Miss St. Pierre," she heard before inspiration offered her an answer.

She smiled as Sheriff Bancroft tipped the broad brim of his hat toward her. She had never seen him in the saddle. He handled the spirited horse with the skill of a cavalryman.

"Good day, sheriff."

"Acquainting yourself with Copper Peak?"

Tilting her parasol, she gazed up at him from beneath the flimsy bits of silk dripping over its edges. Her eyes followed the strong breadth of his shoulders before rising to his smile. When she discovered he had been aware of her scrutiny, she felt the unfamiliar heat of a blush rising along her cheeks.

Jonah leaned forward to place his arm on the half-opened top of the buggy. He watched the color deepen in her face as he added, "This is an uncommon sight and a charming one."

"Lyndon brought me into town to show me where the stores and such are." She found it easier to disregard his comment, for she did not want the flush to divulge her true feelings further. Changing the subject away from her and the strange sensations Sheriff Bancroft created, she said, "That is a fine horse."

He patted the neck of the black horse. "He's a good steed. Steady and surefooted on these treacherous mountain roads."

"I'm sure." Lowering her eyes, she wondered if there was any topic they could discuss in public that would keep him from alluding to the recent past they had shared. She wondered why he did not find it as terrifying as she did to hint at the truth when Lyndon stood within earshot.

"Do you ride, Miss St. Pierre?"

"Yes, of course." She took a deep breath to steady her quivering hands as she saw Lyndon moving to join them. It was too late to learn what Flynn had been talking about with the man who was now racing away toward the road leading to the mines, but this gave her a chance to continue to flesh out the character she had assumed. "Mama always said a lady needs to learn to ride, so she arranged for me to take lessons as a child. That was good, for riding well was a necessity when I moved to Mr. McGwein's plantation."

"McGwein?" asked Jonah with open bafflement. When he noted the rage on Flynn's face, he guessed this must be part of the past she had created for Katharine St. Pierre. As soon as possible, he must learn what she had told Flynn, so he could play along with the charade.

Katie concentrated on continuing her story. She patted the neck of the horse Sheriff Bancroft was riding. If she managed this well, she might find a way to get out of the house to recapture the freedom of riding the open fields along the Divide. "I so love horses."

"Then you must choose one in the stables to call your own, my dear," gushed Lyndon.

"A stable?" She did not have to feign her surprise. "You have a stable of horses?"

"Not as many as your mother's in-laws, I am sure," he said with a tinge of bitterness, "but enough so you should find a mount suitable for a lady's gentle handling."

Jonah smiled as he imagined Katie on a quiet mare. She would be bored and push the poor beast beyond its capability. He recalled the glimpse he had had of the powerful horse she had ridden on the flight from the train.

"Thank you," she was answering when he returned his attention to the conversation. Her eyes glowed with anticipation at selecting the mount she wanted.

"We bid you good day, sheriff," said Flynn with the abruptness that everyone in town had become accustomed to experiencing.

"Trouble at the mine?" Jonah asked.

Flynn glared at the younger man as he climbed into the buggy. "How in hell—excuse me, Katie—how did you know?"

Jonah pointed toward the distant figure on the road leading to the gray buildings at the top of the grade. "The only time Bushee moves like that is when he has discovered some disaster he doesn't want to take the blame for. If you need my assistance, Mr. Flynn—"

With a curse, Lyndon slapped the reins. Katie grabbed at her seat as the buggy erupted up the street. Glancing back, she was not surprised to see a smile on the sheriff's face. Sheriff Bancroft would be pleased with anything that caused his enemy trouble. The sudden thought that he might have orchestrated this plagued her as they rode at a breakneck speed up the hill.

Lyndon stopped the buggy at the house only long enough for Katie to jump down before he applied the whip to the horse and sent the carriage careening along the road again. Watching the wild vehicle, she climbed the steps to the house.

When she reached the porch, Taylor was standing there watching the dust blown up by the buggy wheels. "Trouble again?" he asked.

"Again?"

He did not hesitate before answering, a sign that his upset overrode his normal diplomacy. "Some of the miners are angry about the wages and living conditions Mr. Flynn offers his employees," he said.

From the distress on his face, she translated "some" to "many." From what she had seen, Lyndon gave as little to his employees as possible. That there were problems came as no surprise to her. It would seem that Sheriff Bancroft and K.T. Forrester were not the only ones eager to see Lyndon Flynn pay for his crimes.

The seriousness of the strike at the company became clear as Lyndon spent nearly every waking hour at the mine offices. Exactly what was happening no one in the house seemed to know or was willing to divulge. Katie asked each of the servants to explain it to her, but they all had ready excuses to avoid telling her anything. Even Taylor, after his first disclosure in a moment of stress, remained tight-lipped.

Lyndon refused emphatically to discuss it, telling her that she should not worry her pretty head with thoughts of business, which, after all, was men's work. Although she bristled at the comment and wanted to demand an answer, she knew that her alter ego of Katharine St. Pierre would accept such a response gracefully.

Day after day, she was confined to the grounds within the walls surrounding the house. Each morning, she rose and listened for the sound of the mine machinery to tell her the conflict was over. She went across the hall to a guest room to look for the fumes pouring from the smelter. Everything remained silent.

The town below seemed just as deserted until she began to wonder if the workers had decided simply to leave in disgust. No miners walked up the hill. No women hung laundry in the tiny, grassless yards. Even the children had disappeared from the playground not far from the railroad tracks. Only the steady schedule of the train continued the same, but its whistle had a mournful sound.

Cut off from the events around her and imprisoned in the house, Katie chafed at her invisible bonds. She chose a fine black gelding from the few spirited horses remaining in the stable, for Lyndon was as merciless to his beasts as he was with his employees. Learning the quirks of the horse called Sloe Night gave her something to fill her days, but she and the horse quickly grew bored with riding only in the exercise yard. As closely as the groom watched to be sure she did not hurt herself while in his domain, she had no chance to sneak past the gate for a ride among the trees.

One morning after her ride in the stableyard she asked the groom to adjust the stirrups on the sidesaddle she hated. After years of riding astride, she found the unwieldy saddle a ridiculous contrivance, but bowed to convention to protect her secret.

Katie spun at a sound rumbling from beyond the front gate of the house. Smoothing down the close-fitting jacket of her riding habit, she glanced at the groom's uneasy face, as colorless as his white mountain of hair.

"What is that?" she asked.

The groom murmured, "Miss Katie, I think you'd best go up to the house."

"But what or who is it?"

"Troublemakers from the mine have been whispering to anyone foolish enough to listen that they should confront Mr. Flynn. It sounds as if they convinced the most idiotic ones to come to the house."

She frowned as she asked, "How do you know all this?"

"I listen, Miss Katie. I hear what's being said, but that don't mean I agree or disagree."

Without replying, she hurried toward the house. Even from across the brown-grassed lawn, she could see the iron gate shiver as the men beyond refused to wait for it to be opened. She heard the groom shout to her to dash for the house. Over her shoulder, she saw him hurrying the horses into the stable so they would not become victims in the madness.

Katie lifted her skirts to run as the front gate surrendered to the clamoring beyond it. A flood of men the same color as the earth around her poured through the narrow opening. With instincts honed by years of eluding capture, she sought shelter, and learned how hopeless that search would be within the wall. The only trees were too narrow to hide her, and the sun announced her presence with a shadow that matched her every move.

A shout warned her she had been sighted. Gauging the comparative distance to the house or the stable, she chose to turn back to hide with the horses. The sound of pounding feet behind her added speed to her feet.

She grasped the door handle. In disbelief, she tugged a second time. The door refused to open. She pounded on it and screamed, "Open up! It's Katie! Let me in!"

Glancing over her shoulder, she saw several men advancing on her with expressions that told her they were eager for trouble. With her back to the rough boards of the barn, she tried to slide away from them. Their laughter sent her racing blindly back toward the house.

Hands grasped her. Shrieking her terror, she struck out at the man who held her. She broke away only to be captured by other greedy fingers.

Material ripped as she fought to escape the faces distorted by her fear. This was not the kind of battle she had learned to fight, for she had no way to protect herself against the men holding her. She screamed when her hat was pulled from her head. Cascades of dark hair dropped into the men's faces and startled them into loosening their grips momentarily.

That second was all Katie needed. She wrenched herself out of the voracious pack and fled toward the only haven she had. A pain burned in her side as she ran in the heavy gown. As her fingers touched the railing of the porch, she gave a sob of hysterical relief.

An arm around her waist dragged her back from the steps. Her throat burned with her screams of outrage as she was twisted to face a man who seemed as cadaverous as a corpse. Filthy hair matted with dirt clung to his head and dropped past his collar. Tugging her against his tattered overalls, he leered into her terrified face.

"Well, well, lookie here. If it isn't the grand Miss St. Pierre." His raspy voice blew his reeking breath into her face.

She shoved against his arms and spat, "Release me, sir! This instant!"

"This instant?" he taunted. The men behind him laughed when he added, "Pretty Kate, we ain't half done with you yet."

"Let her go. Your quarrel is not with her."

Silence dropped onto the men clustered on the lawn as if they suddenly had entered a church. Every eye settled on a man they considered the antithesis of the good that was preached in the small clapboard sanctuary in Copper Peak. Katie tried to escape while they faced the devil in the form of Lyndon Flynn.

The hollow-eyed man chortled and shoved her toward the steps. "Look at her, Flynn. Your bastard is dressed in velvet and satin while our families wear rags."

An arm steadied her, and she glared up, ready to shout abuse. Instead she locked eyes with

Lyndon, who had come down from his pedestal on the porch to rescue her from the rage. The leader of the miners growled an incoherent threat as he took a step forward to grip Katie's other arm.

"Take your filthy hands off me!" she spat. Shaking her arm, she tried to break his painful grasp.

"Release her, Reilly, if you want to work in Montana ever again."

"We must talk!" insisted the man, but his voice was more respectful as he was daunted by his boss. "You can't avoid us forever, Mr. Flynn."

"Let my daughter go. Then we can discuss this as men." His small eyes narrowed more. "That is what you want to be, isn't it? Or just the animals you are acting like?"

Uneasily Reilly glanced at his silent allies and saw that their thoughts matched his. Since they had followed the lure of jobs to Copper Peak, they had seen their womenfolk suffering Flynn's abuse. They all wanted revenge, but only the heat of excitement of breaking into this previously unviolated preserve had led them to try to hurt Flynn's daughter. That would not satisfy them. They wanted more than simple revenge of a wrong for a wrong. A share of Lyndon Flynn's wealth was what they desired.

The miner released Katie's arm slowly. She glared at him as she obeyed Flynn's terse order to go into the house. Feeling the multitude of stares pricking through her clothes, she hurried up the steps. Her boots sounded too loud in the preternatural quiet.

As she reached it, the front door opened only wide enough to allow her to enter. Taylor swept her into the foyer and the arms of the teary Mrs. Grodin.

"Look what those beasts have done to you!" the housekeeper exclaimed. "Let me take you upstairs so you can change."

Katie pulled herself out of the pillow-soft embrace. Spinning to confront the butler, she cried, "Don't lock that door!"

"Mr. Flynn ordered—"

"I don't care! Don't lock it!"

She raced into the drawing room. Flinging open the door to the gun cabinet, she disregarded the glass crashing against the wall. She grabbed a rifle, cracked it open to check the chamber, and hurried back into the foyer as she snapped it closed.

Lyndon's shouts for the miners to leave his property before they lost their jobs and ended up in jail for rioting only brought louder rumbles from the crowd as Katie edged the door open again. The whey-faced leader demanded that Flynn negotiate as he had promised, or . . .

The sound of the rifle firing in the clear morning air silenced the shouts, the echo ringing from the mountains back into their ears. Even before the noise had faded, Katie had cocked the Winchester and aimed it at the miners' spokesman.

"You heard my father! Get out of here. This is no shotgun loaded with salt. At this range, I can cut you in half."

A snicker broke the men's fascination with the

sight of the slender woman holding them captive with the rifle. Katie smiled coldly and lifted the barrel. Easily she squeezed the trigger. The twang of the bullet breaking off the metal tip of the weather vane on the barn warned them she was a worthy adversary.

"Gentlemen?" she asked quietly. She leaned the butt of the rifle against her thigh and cocked the gun again. A cold smile strained her tight lips. "I believe Mr. Flynn asked you to leave."

Almost as one, the defeated miners turned to flow back through the gates, their spirits broken by a petite woman who dared to fight more ferociously than they. Lyndon shouted orders to the servants to set up a guard to protect the house. Then he turned to his daughter.

"Where did you learn to shoot like that?"

She tossed the rifle to him. The uncomfortable smile remained on her face as she lied with the new ease she had acquired, "I learned all kinds of survival skills when I lived on Mr. McGwein's plantation, Lyndon. Times were not pleasant after the war with the freed slaves and the poor whites eager to gain control. A woman had to be willing to protect herself, if she wanted to go out. As I have never found a cloistered life to my fancy, I chose to be very, very good with a rifle."

If she expected gratitude, she was disappointed, for he snarled, "I never want to see you with a gun in your hand again. Do you understand? My daughter is no common trash to be acting like that."

"I understand." She spun on her heel and went into the house.

When the door slammed in his face, Lyndon looked from it to the rifle in his hand. As he had so often, he wondered how the child he had never known could be this chameleon. Sometimes Katie was the epitome of the perfect lady, but occasionally he saw signs of another woman, more resilient, stronger than a lady born to the lush life of New Orleans should be.

He pushed the disturbing thoughts from his mind as he hefted the gun and went into the house. It was time for an ultimatum of his own. Although he did not want to give her credit, he knew that Katie's bravery had aided his efforts to destroy the loose organization among the miners. He could not let the opportunity pass to crush it completely.

CHAPTER NINE

As suddenly as it had begun, the strike was over a week later. Lyndon came home late one night whistling a tune and ordered his brandy in the library. Telling Katie only that everything was fine, he sent her to bed. When she started to protest, he repeated the command. Even so, she would have refused, except that Mrs. Grodin drew her out of the room. Her whispered explanation of how Lyndon planned to celebrate breaking the attempts of the workers to organize brought a flush of embarrassment to Katie's cheeks. She hurried to her room, anxious not to meet the woman due to arrive from the bordello over the saloon.

Life returned to her usual routine. Each morning, Lyndon kissed her warmly on the cheek and went off to his office. Katie struggled to find something to do during the day, for she had no interest in domestic matters and left everything

in Mrs. Grodin's far more capable hands. The
hours passed with torturous slowness until she
could dress for dinner and the steadily less in-
tolerable company of the man she had come to
call her father in her mind.

Lyndon made every effort to charm her. He
brought her small gifts from town and sat with
her each evening instead of wandering through
Copper Peak in search of his newest female victim. Although his eagerness to touch her waned,
she was never unaware of the glitter in his eyes
as they appraised her.

Her life was easy, luxurious, and boring.

She was wandering about the huge house, wondering why there was absolutely nothing to do
when the butler called, "Miss Katie, do you wish
to see Sheriff Bancroft?"

Katie fought the temptation to say she had no
intention of wasting her time speaking with any
law officer. It would have been amusing to see
Sheriff Bancroft's rage as he was barred from
the house. She could have stood in the window
and watched as he drove away, furious at her.
That would have been perfect, if she was not so
bored in the big house. Arguing with the sheriff
would allow her to forget how much she hated
this role he forced her to play.

"Send him in, Taylor. I will speak with him."

She stood to look in the mirror opposite the
door. Absently she patted her hair into place.
Not that it had any chance to become disar-
rayed, for every minute of her day was spent in
this too-spotless house. Never again would she
wish for the easy life she had thought would be

exciting! She had learned how dull the life of a fine lady could be.

She turned slowly as he entered the room. Her breath caught in her throat, and she wondered how she could have forgotten the handsome strength of his coiled body. With his hat in his hands, the glow of his auburn hair came alive in the autumn sunshine bursting through the tall windows. Only the uneven securing of his string tie detracted from the perfection of his startlingly well pressed clothes.

For the first time, she was curious who cleaned his clothes and took care of the little house he lived in. The twinge of something she could not deny was jealousy astounded her. She should not care who tended to the needs of this man who used her without compassion.

"Hello, Miss St. Pierre," Jonah said with the perfect courtesy he had come to exhibit to her.

Extending her hand, she murmured, "What a surprise, sheriff!"

"This isn't a social call." He closed the door of the small parlor, not caring if he shocked Taylor and the rest of the household with his forward actions toward Flynn's daughter. "The payroll train was robbed last night."

"Robbed?" She glanced over her shoulder guiltily. Her raised voice might be heard beyond this room. "When?"

"About eight."

"At eight I was having dinner. If it was not you—" She gulped her words into silence. This life was making her too soft and allowing her to forget to think before she spoke.

He nodded fiercely. "None of my friends heard about this until early this morning when the train finally arrived in Copper Peak. I just got done checking the mail car with Flynn."

"And?" she asked.

"Same as before. Sliced across the throat." When she turned away, he demanded, "Who did it, Katie?"

She shook her head. "It can't be Ethan. You still have him up at Butte. Not that he would do such a thing anyhow." She smiled sadly. "My baby brother is much gentler than I was when the miners came here."

"I heard about that, Katie," he snapped, allowing her to distract him momentarily. "That was damn stupid of you, showing your hand that way."

"Lyndon listened to how I learned to shoot on my stepfather's plantation. All he said was I must not do that again."

Jonah hated having to agree with his enemy, although for a totally different reason. "He's right, but forget the miners. I'm interested in the robbery."

Knowing he was judging her by her reactions, she looked him squarely in the eye and said, "You know it was not me. You know it was not Ethan. That's all the Forresters."

"I can add. You and baby brother and Jimmy Schurman make three. There were four of you that first time."

"You must have seen shadows."

He twisted her into his arms. Although she was dressed in the fine togs Flynn had given

176

her, the stubborn set of her face brought to his mind the weeks she had been tied to his bed while her arm healed. "Lie to me, honey, and I can send another telegram right away to the marshall in Butte. Little Ethan wouldn't like the new treatment they could give him."

"Sheriff, you promised!"

"So did you!" he returned with equal heat.

She smiled as the echo of footfalls from the foyer forced him to release her. In a whisper, she spat, "I promised to be Katharine St. Pierre. Nothing else." With a sigh, she added, "It could not be one of mine."

"Then there's someone else who would steal the payroll at the cost of a man's life."

Shivering, she wrapped her arms around herself. That was a fact she could not ignore. Someone had stalked the payroll train and killed with cool precision. As successful as the murderer had been, he or she might become braver and strike out at other people he might consider rivals—such as she.

She glanced at the gun cabinet. Lyndon had said nothing about the broken glass in the aftermath of the confrontation on the porch, but it had been repaired. A lock prevented her from obtaining a weapon to protect her from the unknown threat.

"What can we do?"

"We can go for a buggy ride." When she stared at him as if he were mad, Jonah chuckled. "That is the second reason I came up here. I think you and I need to talk about what happened to you before you arrived here, *Katharine St. Pierre*. I thought we could do it while taking a buggy ride."

"A buggy ride?" Her eyes lit with eagerness at the thought of feeling the fresh breeze in her face again. To her, there seemed little difference in her captivity tied to the sheriff's bed or in this wondrous house where her every move was watched. "Should I?" she asked more quietly.

Jonah wanted to chuckle, but her eager face touched his heart, no matter how much he wanted to stay distant from this sprite who would disappear in an instant were it not for the threat he held over her head. In a gentle tone, he replied, "I wouldn't have asked you if it was inappropriate, K.T."

"Katie," she corrected. When he grimaced, she laughed lightly. Putting a flirtatious expression on her face, she sashayed away, flouncing her full skirts. She used her broadest drawl to add, "La, sheriff! I would have guessed you could remember my name."

"Does that mean you will forgive me and go for a ride with me?"

"Perhaps to the first," she said with a coy smile as she leaned over the banister in the foyer, "and definitely yes to the second. I must get my hat, if you will wait for me, sheriff."

With a wave of his hand, he motioned her up the stairs. "Hurry! This day is too lovely to waste."

Jonah drove the buggy past the edge of town in the opposite direction from the mines. When she asked where they were going, he smiled mysteriously.

"We'll be there soon. Why don't you use this time to tell me who McGwein is?"

Laughing lightly, she leaned back on the cushions and placed her feet against the dashboard. Her gown dropped back to reveal the top of her half-boots and a hint of black stockings. With the town of Copper Peak behind them, she did not have to sit straight like a perfect lady. It felt wonderful to relax.

"Sheriff, Mr. McGwein is a product of my imagination. The stepfather of one Katharine St. Pierre."

"Stepfather? And who else have you created in that fertile field in your head?" After she explained quickly, he laughed. "That's quite a tale, Katie, but you say your dear father swallowed it?"

She removed her parasol and placed it on the floor. It was a nuisance, and she enjoyed the warmth of the autumn sun on her. "Every bit. He feels so guilty for abandoning his daughter to a lascivious uncle that he cannot do enough for me."

"Is that so?"

Glancing at him, she saw that his mind was clearly on the next step of his plot. She sat upright and turned to him. "What do you have planned, sheriff? If you would only tell me what you had planned, I could do more to help you and get this finished as soon as possible."

"You are doing quite well now, Katie." He

179

smiled at her as his hand released the reins and settled on hers.

She stared into the blue depths of his eyes and wondered how she had never noticed the ebony speckles dotting the sapphire. The no-longer-strange sensation she experienced whenever he was near swept over her, weakening every bone in her to the fragility of dandelion fluff. When his hand rose from her fingers to reach for her cheek, she could not break the fascination of his eyes.

The buggy bounced roughly as the horse left the trail to avoid a fallen tree, pulling Sheriff Bancroft's attention back to his driving. He held the reins tightly as he eased the carriage back onto the path. Clutching the side of the carriage, she asked herself how she could act this way with a man who wanted only to use her.

Suddenly he tossed the reins to her and shouted, "Drive!"

"Where?" she cried in astonishment while she wound the straps around her wrists as Eli had taught her.

"Anywhere. Fast!" He whipped his pistols from their holster. Instantly he aimed at something she could see only by its shadow among the trees.

Katie was glad she had a good grip on the straps when he fired, for the horse bolted at the sharp noise. Making sure she did not lose the leather cutting into her palms, she let the horse take the buggy away from the trap set by the unseen assailants. She resisted the urge to look back as Bancroft shot again. If he had wanted her help, he would have given her one of his pistols.

Although the horse was at a full run, she shouted for it to go faster. Being unarmed in the midst of a gunfight unnerved her. She concentrated on keeping the carriage from tipping over on the uneven surface. Her arms ached, and she was sure her left shoulder would be pulled from its socket as she struggled to hold the reins.

Only when strong hands settled over hers did she pull back to bring the horse slowly to a walk. She did not dare to halt the carriage completely, for their ambushers could be following.

Bancroft drew her hands from the reins and turned them over to see where the leather had cut into her palms and the tender inside of her wrists. Bloody welts swelled in a crisscross pattern. She pulled her hands away from him and demanded, "Are they gone?"

"Yes," he answered without his usual sarcasm. "Katie, you need some attention to those hands. I did not think—"

"I am fine. I normally wore gloves when I rode, so my skin is not as tough as yours."

"I noticed."

She retorted to cover her own delight with his softly spoken compliment, "This isn't the time for flowery talk, sheriff. Did you get any of them?"

"I scared them."

"They will be back then."

"But not today." He turned the buggy to follow a lesser-used path leading eastward into the mountains. "I will send Peabody and some of

181

his underworked buddies out to clear the trail when we get back to Copper Peak." His gaze caught hers as he added, "Thanks, Katie, for your help."

A pain seared through her as she was about to shrug. Her half-spoken retort became a moan. When he halted the buggy, she batted away his hands reaching for the buttons at the neck of her high collar. "What in hell are you doing?"

"Looking at your shoulder."

"Keep your hands off me! My shoulder is fine, and I don't need you poking at me."

His mouth twisted with unuttered rage as he noted the paleness of her face that contradicted her snarled words. Knowing it was senseless to argue with her, he picked up the reins and set the horse moving along the faint trail again.

When Jonah turned the vehicle down into the river valley, Katie clutched the side. She recognized this elbow of the rushing river where it cut through the trees. It marked what had been her territory until a few weeks ago when the man by her side had stopped her larceny with a bullet.

Her back straightened until she was sure the muscles would never be relieved from their cramping spasms. Outwardly serene, within she was quivering with fear. If Ethan had found a way out of the Butte jail, he would be here. Bancroft had not mentioned anything about a jailbreak, but that was information he would not share with her.

Since she banished him from the Forrester gang, she had heard nothing of Les Proulx, but she doubted if he had left the area when there were victims to be found around Copper Peak. Without the Forrester gang in contention for the prizes, he might be able to garner some alone. Perhaps by changing his tactics and robbing travelers on a lonely road, like those who had just attacked them. She froze as she wondered if Les had been involved in that. He would have granted her no mercy if the ambush had been successful, for he had made it clear she would be sorry she had expelled him from the Forrester gang.

"Lovely country, isn't it?" mused Jonah as if to himself. "Unforgiving." He pointed to the snow-covered peaks majestic in the distance.

"Lovely."

At her terse response, he shot a quick glance and saw how tensely she sat on the leather seat. Like a cornered fox. Despite her outward change into Katharine St. Pierre, the hunted K.T. Forrester had now reappeared as they approached the location he had scouted just a few days before. Her reaction told him how accurately he had guessed.

With a smile, he leaned against the buggy seat and stretched one arm along its back. The tips of his fingers curved around her right shoulder until she shrugged them away. He did not accept her silent rebuff easily. To show her she was not in charge of the situation, he caught her upper arm in a strong grip.

"Sheriff, you should not—"

"No one is here to care if you are Katie St. Pierre or K.T. Forrester."

Flashing a furious glance at him, she demanded, "And what makes you think either of those women has any desire to be pawed by you? Just because I made my living by robbery, sir, doesn't mean I welcome your hands on me."

"Relax, Katie. After I tended to you for so long, do you think there are many secrets you have from me?"

A strangled moan came from her lips as she stared straight ahead. She did not want to think of that time when her life had depended on his care. Somehow she had been able to erase from her mind all the details of how he dealt with her daily needs.

When he spoke, her head popped up as she stared at him. His gentle words were the last ones she had expected to hear. "Forgive me, Katie. I shouldn't have said that." He withdrew his arm from around her shoulders. "It's just that I could not have imagined how you would look dressed up as a lady."

"How do I look?"

"Do you need the compliment so badly, honey?" He grinned at her. "You must have seen the expression in Flynn's eyes when you walked into his drawing room the first time."

"I saw it," she answered in a voice thick with disgust.

Jonah took his eyes from the uneven path to look at her. "Then you must know how lovely you look."

"Lyndon has a reputation for chasing anything in a skirt."

"Forget it!" He leaned forward so his elbows

rested on his knees. "I try to give you a compliment, and you throw it back in my face. What does it take to convince you that you are beautiful?"

She did not answer. During the years Eli trained her to replace him as leader of the Forrester gang, he never mentioned her appearance. Praise came for alertness and fast reactions. More than once, he had urged her to keep her curls in braids and wear looser clothes, but she had thought that was for ease of movement when they worked, not to keep the other men in the gang from noticing her femininity.

"Here we are," he said a few moments later and stopped the buggy.

"I know," she said and looked at the cabin, hoping it was empty.

"Home, sweet home."

Viciously she spat, "How perceptive of you, sheriff! So what exactly is the point of driving me out here if you know that already?"

Dropping the reins, he turned her stiff form to face him. The coolness of her features did not fool him. He knew how upset she must be to see her home. When she gasped, he watched the pain flee across her face before it vanished again behind her controlled mask.

He glanced away from her to note again what she was seeing for the first time. In the month since Katie had been shot, the cabin had been visited by someone intent on challenging the Forrester gang. The yard was littered with debris tossed through the shattered window. Even the bank of the creek had been desecrated by holes uprooting the vegetation.

"Is there anything you want to get while we are here?" he asked softly.

She forced her eyes from the broken door of the cabin to meet his sympathetic gaze. Without waiting for him to help her, she slid from the seat of the buggy. She said nothing as she walked up the steep path to the door and peered into what once had been her home. Tears weighed heavily in her eyes while she tried to swallow past the unfamiliar lump blocking her throat.

She pushed aside the plank that hung on a single hinge. It crashed to the ground behind her, but she did not look at it. Her gaze roved about her home in disbelief. The cabin had been ransacked. Even the bunkbeds had been upset and lay in broken strips of wood good only for kindling. Rage overwhelmed her sorrow. Whirling, she saw that the sheriff had followed her into the ruined cabin.

"Is this your work?" she demanded. "Why did you have to destroy it? When you release Ethan, we don't intend to stay here. You didn't—"

"I didn't!" He avoided her gaze as he looked again around the room he had discovered in this condition the previous day. Whoever had done this had wanted to create the maximum damage possible.

Katie forced her shock deep inside her. At first she had been sure that Sheriff Bancroft had ordered this destruction to remind her of her obligation to him, but she believed him when he denied it. Not because she expected him to be honest with her, but because he would be happy to gloat about such antics if he had been involved. Wanting to hide her pain, she turned to run her hand along the remains of what had been her changing screen. The small shack had not been a lovely house like the place where she lived with Lyndon, but this had been her home.

"What were they searching for, Katie?"

She did not look at him as she murmured, "There was nothing here of value other than our foodstuffs, which were in plain sight on that shelf . . ." With a soft moan, she pointed to the spot where only a bent nail marked the location of what had been her small pantry. She squared her shoulders as she went on more calmly, "Other than the weapons we carried, Ethan and I had nothing of much value."

"The money from the last robbery?" He pulled off his hat as it brushed a rafter, bringing down a shower of dust. Shaking his hat clean, he stated with irritation, "You must have some of that left. You couldn't have spent it all so quickly!"

"We did not keep our share of the money in the cabin. Anyone who was familiar with the Forrester gang would know that." She smiled with the icy control he had seen exhibited during her recovery. "Don't ask, sheriff. If Ethan did not take the money before he left, it's safe where it is. As I don't need it now, I won't satisfy your curiosity by showing you where we hid the packet."

"That money should have been mine." The false serenity of his tone warned her of the strong emotions he hid. She had learned in the past weeks that she had met her match in masking the truth.

With a laugh, she retorted, "What a shame, Sheriff Bancroft! I admit to being smarter than you. Is that a crime in Montana?"

"If it was, it should be punishable by the spanking you needed years ago to halt your sass." His eyes twinkled as he backed her steadily into the corner clogged with broken furniture.

"Don't touch me," she warned. "You'll be sorry, sheriff. I fight dirty."

He chuckled as he paused. "I bet you do, honey, and if I'm going to roll around on the floor with you, I would prefer it to be in a much more friendly manner."

Katie hated the heat that brightened her cheeks. No one else made her blush like this, and she wanted to rip the arrogant smile from his face. Pushing past him, she stormed out of the cabin. She did not know which was worse—his easy assumption that his handsome strength appealed to her or the fact he was right.

Putting her hand on the side of the buggy, she decided this must be the final irony in the ridiculous situation. Of all the men who had shared her life since Eli brought them West, none of them had ever urged her wordlessly to relinquish her strong self-control and let them discover the K.T. Forrester she wanted no one to know. None until she met Jonah Bancroft.

"Do you want help up?" came a voice behind her.

"Yes, thank you."

She held out her hand, but he put his hands

on her waist and lifted her to the seat. He did not release her and leaned across the side to keep her close to him. His fingers stroked her lower back gently, but he made no effort to pressure her again with unspoken suggestions she wanted to ignore.

"Thank you," she repeated, hoping he would accept her words as an order to take his hands off her.

"Can I ask you a personal question?"

Unsure what to reply, she searched his face and saw none of the normal arrogance displayed there. The honesty of his expression frightened her. She did not want him to be sincere with her, for that would be another step toward something other than enmity. Although she wanted to shout that she had no desire to reveal anything intimate to him, she heard herself answering "Yes" as she lost herself once more in the cobalt of his eyes.

"Has someone threatened you lately?"

"That's personal?" She chuckled with relief. Shaking her head, she asked, "You mean has anyone threatened me other than you?"

"Katie, this isn't a joke! Look at your house. Whoever did that was coldly methodical. Can you imagine what would have happened to you and baby brother if you had been there when the ransacker and his friends arrived?"

Peeling his fingers off her, she tightened the ribbons of her bonnet. "*They* would have been the ones in trouble. I am as competent with my Winchester as I am with the handgun."

He rounded the front of the horse and leapt

into the carriage. "Dammit, woman! You could be in tremendous danger, and you don't even act as if you care."

"I have always lived with peril, sheriff. I'm no longer afraid of things that pop from the bushes."

His hands brought her to face him. Once again, his gaze worked its odd magic on her, stealing her will and the desire to spit curses at him. With her fingers entwined in her lap, she regarded him as if mesmerized, resisting the temptation to raise a finger and brush the lock of hair back behind his ear. When he spoke, she watched his mouth and the movement of his mustache to escape the power of those compelling eyes.

"Katie, what are you afraid of?"

"You know."

He tilted her chin up so she could not avoid his eyes. "I don't, honey, but I know that only fools are not afraid. No one has ever intimated that you are a fool. What scares you?"

"Captivity. Knowing my life isn't my own to control."

"Like now?"

She did not look away as she said tersely, "Like now."

Relinquishing his hold on her eyes, he picked up the reins and spoke a soft command to the horse. The rig moved slowly in a circle before turning toward Copper Peak. Water splashed over the front of the dash as they crossed the creek and climbed the gentle slope on the other side.

Katie listened to the distant cry of a hawk

and envied the freedom of that fierce hunter.
Once she had been able to roam as she wished
across these hills in search of prey or simply to
enjoy the fingers of the wind combing back her
hair as she set her mount to its best speed. She
had dreamed of climbing one of the higher peaks
and sleeping in the damp mist of a low cloud,
but that might never happen if she was forced
to continue in this game that had no rules and
no foreseeable ending.

The buggy moved easier as it gained the top
of the ridge and the slight indentation of the
seldom traveled trail. Bancroft kept the horse to
a walk as they drove under the canopy of trees.

She did not let her wonder become visible
when he steered the carriage toward the creek
again. This was not the way to Copper Peak. A
cramping in her stomach accompanied her fear
of what he planned on this side trip. Although
she ached with sorrow from seeing her house
vandalized, she could imagine many worse sights
in the desolation of these mountains.

When he stopped in a clearing among the
trees, she peered about in trepidation. Bancroft
leapt from the seat, tied the horse to a nearby
tree, and walked back toward her. Silently she
looked from his face to his outstretched hands
offering to help her from the carriage. She wanted
to ask what he wanted to show her, but the
trembling in her stomach would betray her as
soon as she opened her mouth.

Putting her hands on his shoulders, she was
not surprised to find they were as hard as the
tree trunks around them. He lifted her with no

effort and released her the second her feet touched the floor. Without speaking, he walked away from the carriage. For a moment, she considered staying where she was, but she had learned how futile it was to go against Sheriff Bancroft's silent edicts.

Holding up her skirt, she wished for the ease of her denim trousers as she followed him toward the creekbed. The thick clumps of vegetation caught at her, threatening to topple her into the water. When she reached the auburn-haired man gazing at the opposite bank, she left an arm's length between them.

He turned to face her, and she felt all the color drain from her features. In his hand was one of the pistols he had fired at the men who had tried to ambush them. At his order, she gazed at him in astonishment.

"Here."

Katie raised her hand to close around the weapon. Like a traveler who has crossed a desert without water, she welcomed the delight of the butt of the gun against her palm. Except for the last month, she could not remember a time when she had not worn one or more pistols in a holster at her hip or slung over her shoulder. Almost reverently she stroked the cool steel and the highly polished wood set into the handle.

With a sigh, she offered it to him. He used a single finger to reaim it toward the ground. His finger moved along the barrel until it reached her hand. While he stroked the surprising softness of her skin still mottled with the marks of the reins, he admonished, "Katie, you of all people should be aware of the dangers of pointing a loaded gun at someone."

"Loaded?" She gasped the question, although she could think of nothing but his touch that created such odd feelings within her. The first time she had experienced this melting in her center was when he helped her into the wagon the day she had come into town with her brother. Since then, it had grown stronger. She wanted him to stop because she feared being unable to control her errant emotions, but was even more afraid he would not continue.

As softly as if speaking of something more personal than a pistol, he said, "I know you must be miserable in Flynn's house. You weren't made to be a hothouse flower kept simply to be admired by those about you. I thought a little sport might interest you. Go ahead and fire the rounds." He laughed with a sudden return of his usual acidic wit. "Fire them as long as it is not into me."

"You have many restrictions, sheriff."

His hand on her wrist kept her from eagerly lifting the gun to sight it on a tree stump on the far side of the sparkling river. At the same time, he tilted her face up to meet his uncompromising gaze. "Katie, I think it would be better if you called me by my given name."

"I'm not sure I should." She pulled away from him and walked a few paces through the scrub toward the riverbank.

"Why?" he called after her. "Because Lyndon Flynn's newly found daughter is too high-class to be keeping company with the village sheriff?"

Whirling, she caught her skirt on the prickly plants. She jerked it away as she stated, "No, not because of that. Because I don't think I want to be your friend, Sheriff Bancroft. How long until you have succeeded and obtained your revenge? Then you can do whatever you want while Ethan and I will return to our lives of waylaying trains. I can't imagine having a friend who is eager to hang me."

She did not wait for his reply. She spun to sight on the target she had chosen. With easy efficiency, she fired off the six bullets in the gun. As she lowered it, she waved away the malodorous black smoke filling the clearing and wondered if anyone would ever devise gunpowder that did not choke a sharpshooter. She did not rub her shoulder, and was pleased that the wound had caused such little difficulty when she held a gun again.

"Perfect. Six hits!" came the enthusiastic appraisal from behind her.

Katie walked back to the man and pressed the warm gun in his hand. "I told you I don't miss what I aim at."

"So why didn't you shoot me on the train?" he asked as he reholstered the weapon. With his other gun's cylinders filled, he did not think he would need to worry about reloading immediately. He kept her from walking past him by catching her arm and forcing her to look at him. No taunts sounded in his voice when he said, "I didn't think you were squeamish, Katie."

"I'm not. I just don't consider it justifiable to

murder someone who has proven his idiocy by drawing his weapon and not shooting."

He bristled. "I don't make it a habit to shoot people in the back."

"You shot me in the back!" She slowly eased her arm out of his grasp.

"That was different. I thought you had killed Meyer."

She shook her head. "You lost me for a while in the trees. How did you know I was the same one you had met on the train? I could have been anyone out for a ride."

Leaning against a tree, he regarded her with cold rage. "You never give up, do you, honey? I followed you closely. I knew you were the little fool who robbed the train. If it had been simply the money, I would have been angry, but not enough to shoot you." His lips strained in a grin. "I'm honest enough to admit I wanted the pleasure of seeing the one who beat me twice hang on my command."

"But unfortunately you have been denied that pleasure."

"Not so unfortunately." He stepped forward until his shadow draped her in purple light.

Katie stared up at his face and wondered why he had to be so tall. His imposing stature gave him an immediate power to daunt her, but she fought it. When he took her hand, she wondered what he had planned. With her finger, he traced the uneven surface of the tin star on the left side of his weskit.

"This gives me the right to put a rope around

your slender throat, Katie, and order you to die."

When he led her finger to move along the circumference of her neck, she did not know how to answer him. All during this ride, it had been as if she were with a stranger, a man who was Jonah Bancroft and yet was someone totally different. He terrified her and lured her closer to solve the mystery.

"I can't stop you," she answered quietly. "By virtue of your size, you are stronger than me. If you want me to hang, I will."

"What is wrong with you?" he demanded in the same tender voice. "Why do you urge me to do what I have no desire to do?"

"Nothing is wrong with me. Those are the facts, aren't they?"

"Yes, those are the facts, but there is no reason why you have to die if you want to live."

She pulled out of his arms. Flinging out hers, she embraced the mountains and wished she could pull them around her to comfort her. She longed for the ability to ride where she wished and do what made her happy. All of that had vanished with the concussion of a bullet cutting through her to leave her powerless. As she glanced to the man standing by the carriage, she knew that the healing of her shoulder had not regained her any of the power she had possessed when she led the Forrester gang. Everything she was, as well as her life, depended on this man's whims.

"Will you take me home, sheriff?"

"Of course."

She walked back to the carriage and held out her hand so he could help her. Silently he assisted her to the high seat. She watched his lithe movements as he took his own place next to her. When he reached for the reins, his leg brushed her skirt, sending a yearning for his touch lurching through her.

"Thank you, Jonah." She smiled as his name floated from her lips. Only as she spoke it for the first time did she realize that she had been calling him that in her mind for weeks.

"My pleasure, Katie. I trust we can go riding again sometime soon."

"I hope so." She laughed with honest happiness when he took her hand and placed it securely on the crook of his elbow. "I have enjoyed today."

"Despite the arguments?"

"Half the fun is arguing with you."

He chuckled as he regarded her dark eyes crinkled with amusement. "I agree, honey."

CHAPTER TEN

"I shall be a bit late for dinner this evening, my dear," Lyndon murmured around the crumbs of his breakfast biscuit. "I must arrange for hiring a service to guard the payroll shipments. This last robbery proved that I must do more to keep my money secure than I have in the past. With all my other work at the office, I am sure I won't be finished to eat by seven."

"May I go with you?"

Lyndon lowered his bone china cup to the saucer with a loud click that filled the room. The servants found that tasks needed their immediate attention in the kitchen, but lingered close enough to the door to hear the explosion sure to come. Miss Katie's emergence as something other than the pretty ornament her father yearned for her to be needled Mr. Flynn. Since the confrontation with the miners on the front yard, she had been reluctant to reassume her role as lady of the manor to match his self-image as the baronial ruler of Copper Peak.

Not that the staff had any reason to complain about Miss Katie. With the growth of her assurance came a friendliness and compassion they had never guessed any child of Mr. Flynn could feel. Certain that she would want to run the house, he had turned over the management to Miss Katie, who promptly told Mrs. Grodin to arrange the work as she saw fit. Unlike ever before, the servants found they enjoyed working in the house.

Heavy brows underlined the furrows in Lyndon's forehead as he tried to affix Katie to her chair with a malevolent glare. When she did not cower before him, he was secretly pleased. He did not want his only child to be a limp dishrag, tossed about by others, although he wished she was more susceptible to his fierce stare.

His voice remained deceptively calm as he asked, "Why do you want to go to that filthy place?"

"You speak of the mines all the time," she replied reasonably. "The servants speak of them, as do the people in town. Even the sheriff when he calls here discusses this and that about them." She tapped her napkin against her lips in a ladylike motion that concealed any errant expression the mention of Jonah Bancroft might create. Raising her eyes to meet his stern regard, she added coolly, "I'm stuck in this horrible place. Therefore, it behooves me as even a reluctant resident of Copper Peak to be conversant on this most important topic. If you do not have time to teach me, I'm sure the Mr. Bushee you talk about would take an hour or two from his labors to help."

"Bushee?" He snorted. "That fool? He knows less about copper mining than you do. I'll take you into the office. Isler can show you about. He can earn his pay for a change. All right. Meet me on the porch in ten minutes if you wish to go." A paternal smile of pride creased his face as he added, "My dear, you should wear something less charming than that frock. Even the office can be filthy. You wouldn't want to ruin your pretty dress."

Katie rose, pleased with this chance to leave the house again. "I will be downstairs again in ten minutes. Thank you, Lyndon."

He caught her hand as she moved past him toward the door. When he tilted his face toward her in an obvious order for her to kiss his cheek, she felt her stomach churn with distaste. She commanded her breakfast to stay put as she compliantly bent. A quick peck against his skin she hoped fulfilled her obligation, but she discovered how wrong she was when he put his hand on the nape of his neck.

Horror strangled the words beating in her heart as he kept her lips poised directly over his. Off-balance, if he pushed on her head, she could not prevent him from kissing her. She had no place to put out her hands to push herself upright, for she did not want to touch him.

When he spoke, his seemingly innocuous words further fueled her fear. "Until I saw you, Katie, I was sure my memory had fooled me into believing Eugenie was as lovely as I remembered her. You prove to me I was right. Such a pretty child you are, my dear. So pretty."

"Lyndon," she forced herself to say, afraid of what would happen if she remained silent, "if you don't want me to delay your leaving for the office, I must go now so I can change."

"Don't change, my dear."

Deliberately misunderstanding him, she gasped, "But, Lyndon, you just said—"

He shook his head until his jowls vibrated. Releasing her, he stood so abruptly that she had to step back to keep her nose from hitting his shoulder. Without looking at her, he snapped, "Ten minutes, girl! And don't be late, or I will leave without you."

Hurrying from the room, Katie wondered how much longer she would be able to escape these terrifying incidents that happened so often. Her father wanted to seduce her, and the only thing halting him was his belief in their familial relationship. So far, she had been able to convince him she did not understand the meaning behind his blatant caresses, but she did not know how long that would continue. Nowhere in the house did she feel safe. Even her dreams had been invaded, for she suffered the sensation of being stalked through the darkness.

It was something she must deal with alone. Jonah would chuckle at what he would see as an overreaction. If she suggested he help her parry Lyndon's flirtations, he would laugh louder. In this one thing, she knew he would be right. She must deal with this alone and use Lyndon's lust for his daughter to effect the revenge which would gain her twenty-five thousand dollars and her brother's life.

Wearing a dark skirt and a simple blouse trimmed with the bare minimum of lace, she tied on her narrow-brimmed straw hat. It had no flowers to be ruined by dirt brought into the mine office. When she rushed down the staircase curving like a dark rainbow in the morning sun, the bonnet bounced off her head. Laughing, she caught it before the velvet ribbons struck the floor.

This chance to get out of the house she intended to enjoy. Most of her disquiet had vanished by the time she climbed into the carriage. Enough of her characteristic distrust remained to please her that she had arrived before Lyndon so she did not have to suffer his touch while he assisted her into the buggy.

He came out onto the porch several minutes after the appointed time and grumbled something at her. It was the only thing he said to her as they drove through the gate and down into Copper Peak. She did not attempt to break the silence, for it was more comfortable than the continual round of lies. Slowly she was becoming accustomed to Lyndon's widely fluctuating moods and understood most of them. From the tight set of his jaw, she guessed he was upset because he had allowed his longing for her to overcome his few moral constraints.

When they stopped before a storefront in the middle of town, she was surprised. She had noticed the plain building before, but never guessed this was the heart of Flynn's Copper Mining Company. Nothing on the door or the narrow window announced its identity. For a moment, she was curious about the anonymity of the building, then she realized it was not modesty but the opposite that kept a sign from the office.

Everyone in Copper Peak and beyond knew where Lyndon Flynn managed his massive holdings. There was no need to waste money for a sign, which would be redundant. A king did not label his castle. Katie stored that insight with the other details she was learning about him.

Lyndon opened the door to allow her to precede him into the plain room. A wrought-iron railing divided the outer office into two unequal parts. The narrow front section contained an uncomfortable settee next to a small pot-bellied coal stove. Dusty flowers had been jumbled haphazardly into a china urn. She was not sure if they were dried or simply dead.

She noticed how industrious all the workers became as Lyndon opened the swinging door in the half-wall. As she walked with him between the two rows of tables, she felt secret glances following them. The silence was unnerving, and she guessed the office was very different when Lyndon was elsewhere.

"Isler?" bellowed the thick man by her side.

A man popped out from behind another worker. Of a slight build, he wore a green shade over his eyes, so she could not see his expression other than the vapid smile that always greeted Lyndon. His few strands of thin hair had been combed in an odd pattern across his almost bald pate. Pushing up the elastic garters holding his sleeves in place, he answered, "Yes, Mr. Flynn?"

"I have a busy morning, so I want you to give Miss St. Pierre a tour of the offices. Have her back to me in exactly one hour."

Katie felt fury burning impotently within her at Lyndon's portrayal of a feudal lord ruling absolutely over all he could see. She respected those having power, and using it for profit was something she understood, but this obvious belittling of an employee enraged her. She had been the leader of the Forrester gang long enough to know that power meant nothing without the loyalty of her followers.

As Lyndon walked away, he added over his shoulder, "One hour *exactly*, Isler!"

Silence followed in the man's wake until he went into his private office and slammed the door. A low mumble of discord sounded in the corner most distant from Katie, but those closer did not dare disparage Flynn when his daughter might carry tales to him.

"Miss St. Pierre, if you will follow me?" Isler gestured toward where he had been working. When she started to follow, he asked, "And how are you enjoying your sudden good fortune here in Copper Peak?"

Stopping in the middle of the room, Katie stared at the man's pleasant smile. She suspected it concealed a darkness she was too well acquainted with and wondered if this was the mysterious final member of Jonah's gang. Weeks ago, she had decided it must be someone working at the mine. It was the one part of the town unrepresented by the gang members she knew.

Until she was sure, she must continue her charade. She glanced about the room and sniffed. "Mr. Isler, I truly think you should remember that Mr. Flynn asked you merely to give me a tour of the office, not to ask about my personal life."

"I beg your pardon," he murmured, but she caught a hint of amusement in his eyes. Even if he was not Jonah's ally, he certainly was not Lyndon's obedient servant. "If Mr. Flynn didn't mention it to you, I'm his office manager and act as a liaison between the various aspects of the company."

"I thought Mr. Bushee was his assistant."

Isler chuckled, and his dark eyes crinkled with lines left by too many days in the hot sun. "How shall I put this politely?"

"He is my father's lackey?"

"Exactly." He changed the subject as he pointed to the papers littering the cluttered table. "If you will look here, Miss St. Pierre, you will see one of the most important tools of our work. These are maps of the region. The known location of minerals is marked on here. Gold, silver, sapphires, and, of course, copper are all to be found in these mountain storehouses."

Katie's finger traced the rivers along the map to orientate herself. She was not surprised to see that the shack she had lived in had been built by a miner who gave up the useless attempt to find gold alone the river. Other shacks were marked as well, and she noted their locations for future reference.

Taking her hand, he moved it toward a brilliantly colored blob in the middle of the map. "This is the main mine of Flynn's Copper Mining Company."

"It goes from here to here?" she asked, amazed at the size of the vein.

Isler hushed the amusement of the men working at the table. "It goes from here to who knows where. No one has found exactly where the lode ends. While it remains pure, the company will continue to dig out each ounce. We—" He was interrupted by his name being called from across the room.

A young man came forward with some pages in his hands. He smiled, and Katie recognized him instantly as the charming man she had encountered on the train. Without his Eastern-style clothes, she had not noted him in the room.

"Why, hello, Mr. Brown."

"Miss St. Pierre, this is a pleasure." He could not keep his infectious smile from his face, for he had never expected the daughter of the exalted Lyndon Flynn to remember a man who had overstepped himself when he met her.

Aware of the interest in their impromptu conversation, Katie kept her role firmly in mind as she asked, "And how do you find Copper Peak, sir? As interesting as you had hoped?"

"Yes, miss." Enthusiasm widened his grin. "Far better than the offices I worked in back in Atlanta."

"I'm glad." She turned her back on him, clearly indicating the interview was completed. She hated the necessity to be like this, but Katharine St. Pierre would not allow too much familiarity from her father's employees. "Mr. Isler, you were saying . . . ?"

He said quietly, "If you will excuse me for a moment, miss, I shall deal with this matter before we continue our tour."

"Of course. I shall wait over there." She pointed to the window at the front of the office.

Allowing her skirts to sway with the gentle rhythm of a ladylike stroll, she went to gaze out at the splendor of the Continental Divide. This was not the outing she had wanted. Her curiosity about the actual mining had been whetted, but this view of geological maps and account books did nothing to satisfy it.

She watched the people passing on the streets. Miners with their dirt-encrusted bodies bent by hard labor, and their equally overworked wives trudged along the boardwalk without raising their heads to look at the main office of Flynn's Copper Mining Company. They were a broken people, whose dreams of wealth had been doomed by the realities of the mean existence in Copper Peak. Wondering how her father could live his fine life on the hill while his employees suffered, she fought the bitter bile of hate rising in her.

Never could she let Lyndon guess her real emotions. Nor could she allow Jonah to discover that she did not consider Lyndon the horrible beast he had described to her. Lyndon Flynn was a lecher and a man interested only in his own profits, but that made him no different from many other men she had known.

"Miss St. Pierre?"

"Yes?" she asked as she looked at the plump man who had addressed her.

"Mr. Flynn wants you in his office immediately."

"Thank you."

She was not the only one curious about this sudden command, she realized as she crossed the room. Each eye followed her until she opened the door and entered the private office. Instantly she was in a startlingly different world. Carpets covered the floor, and the walls had been decorated with wallpaper and pictures of the mine instead of the plain whitewash of the outer office. Her eyes went to the imposing desk in its center.

"You wanted me, Lyndon?" she queried when he did not seem aware of her presence.

He looked up from the pages spread across his desk. Standing, he beckoned to her. When she stood next to him, he ordered, "Look at this!" He waved a page under her nose.

She grasped it to halt its flapping long enough so she could make out the words. Quickly she scanned the letter and saw the name that would be known throughout Montana and the mining community. "Marcus Daly"! She looked at Lyndon to find him grinning like a child with an unexpected sweet.

When she did not say anything instantly, he added with impatience, "Daly is coming to Copper Peak to talk to me, Katie. He wants to buy the company." Rubbing his hands together, he chuckled. "Oh, yes, he wants my company, for it has been a thorn in his side for too long."

"Will you sell it?"

"How would you like to see San Francisco or New York or Paris, my dear? All that and more

208

we could do with Daly's money." His eyes sparkled with greed. "He has heard that Clark wants the company as well."

"William Clark of the Colusa copper mine?"

"Who else?" he demanded. Dropping into his chair, he did not offer her the same courtesy. She noted there was no other chair in the room. His employees would have to remain standing when they came to petition him for a favor or to report on the various aspects of the mine. His grin widened as he pointed the page at her to emphasize his point. "They both want the company. Or more specifically, they both want to keep the other from getting it. This could be very, very profitable."

Katie became more confused by his words. In the past weeks, she had seen that Lyndon thrived on the power and prestige of owning his mine and Copper Peak. She could not imagine him relinquishing that for mere money. Tightly she asked, "So whoever makes the best total offer gets the company?"

He had been rereading the letter. As if he had forgotten she was in the room, he looked up, startled. A greasy smile oozed across his face. "Best total offer? It is too bad you were not a man, Katie. I wouldn't consider selling the company if I had a son with your intelligence to give it to when I retire. Yes, I am waiting to see what they offer. Money, political favors, stocks, whatever. Then I will make my decision."

"And?"

"I will let you know when I, and I alone, decide." He waved his fingers at her. "Why don't

209

you run back to the house, my dear? I'm sure you have many little projects to keep you busy."

Katie refused to be dismissed by Lyndon as coldly as she had dismissed Mr. Brown. "Lyndon, I want to see the mine."

"The mine? You mean the shafts?" He guffawed. "That is very amusing, Katie."

"Why can't I?"

"Women don't belong in a mine. Go home, my dear."

Determined not to follow his order, she begged, "Please, Lyndon. Mr. Isler can take me and will be sure I don't go anywhere dangerous." In her most wheedling tone, she repeated, "Please, Lyndon."

He glanced from her pleading face to the letter he wanted to savor. If he did not agree, he would not be able to deal with more important matters. With a snarl, he snapped, "Go ahead! Just don't come crying to me if you ruin your dress."

Knowing exactly what she must do, she bent and performed the distasteful act of kissing his cheek. She hurried out of the room to inform Mr. Isler that he would be escorting her farther afield than the mining office.

The office manager did not seem surprised that she had convinced Lyndon to allow her to visit the main mine. Merely nodding, he reached for his coat hanging on a peg behind the door. He handed her into Flynn's buggy and leapt into it. With a quick order to the horse, he drove along the middle of the street and turned up the hill toward the mine buildings.

So suddenly did Mr. Isler pull back on the reins that Katie nearly rocked off the seat. He did not attempt to apologize as he waited for the lone rider on the road to meet them.

It did not surprise Katie that the man on the horse was Jonah Bancroft. He had a propensity for being about whenever she left the house. She wondered if he did not trust his allies to watch her movements or if, as she hoped, he simply wanted to see her. Angrily she banked that thought. She did not want to deal with the sheriff any more than necessary, but she was beginning to believe he did not feel the same.

"Good morning, Katie, Isler."

The office manager started at Jonah's familiarity with Flynn's daughter, but said nothing. He did not like the smile on his friend's face. It confirmed what Haggerty had whispered in his ear before they parted after their last meeting at the saloon. Jonah was becoming too interested in the woman beyond the parameters of his desired revenge. None of the men wanted to be the one to confront their leader with this accusation, but as Isler watched the sheriff talk to Miss St. Pierre, he knew something must be done soon.

"So you convinced him to let you go down in the mines?" Jonah laughed as he winked at the man driving the buggy. "And you are accompanying her, Isler?"

Katie answered when the office manager hesitated, "Lyndon is agog by the letter he got from Marcus Daly. He would have agreed to anything to get me out of his office so he could delight in his good luck."

"What letter?"

She saw the glance exchanged between the two men and knew she had been correct when she guessed that mousey Isler was the fifth man in Jonah's gang. It no longer angered her that they were able to keep a spy close to her all the time, for she had become accustomed to the inevitable. If she complained, no one would heed her, and she admitted she would have been as suspicious of Jonah if the situation were reversed.

Quietly she explained about the letter that had arrived from Butte this morning. "And Clark is interested as well."

"That I knew," said Jonah, "but I never suspected that Flynn would consider these offers seriously. What has he said, Isler?"

The clerk shrugged. It stung that the letter had gotten past him without his seeing it. Since he had started working for Flynn four months ago, nothing had reached his employer's desk without his examination first. When this important note arrived, he had missed it because he had been busy giving this woman a tour.

"He's been mum on this, Jonah. I think he will listen to them this time."

"Dammit!" Jonah pounded his hand on the dash of the buggy. "He can't pack up and leave now." Blue fire scorched Katie as he looked at her. "You have to talk him out of it."

"Me?" she gasped.

"He idolizes you. Surely you can use your feminine wiles to urge him to turn down what Daly and Clark offer."

She leaned forward and patted him on the

shoulder. "My dear Sheriff Bancroft, if you are suggesting what I believe you are suggesting, you can take your ideas directly to hell."

Isler's laugh wiped the astonishment from Jonah's face. Fighting back his rage, the sheriff glared at the smiling woman. Katie had become too sure of herself, but she was pivotal for the success of their plot.

"I wasn't suggesting you seduce him, but that is your prerogative, my dear Miss St. Pierre," he said coldly. "Just remember, if he leaves before we are finished, it may bode poorly for dear baby brother's future health." When she did not answer, he continued, "I think I would like to have a tour of the mine as well. It's been a long time since I've been down in the shafts."

Katie wanted to tell him his company was not welcome, but she decided not to waste her breath. Her first exhilaration at seeing him had become the familiar rage and frustration. Once again, he reminded her with a few words how helpless she was in protesting his edicts. She settled back in the buggy and fumed as Isler snapped a command to the horse.

It seemed odd to build the entrance into the earth at the top of a hill, but Katie did not mention that. She was too uneasy with Jonah's accompanying them on this tour to think of anything else. As the buggy climbed the steep slope, it appeared as if each building were built atop the one behind it. Smoke rose from the many smokestacks of the smelter to darken the sky to a sickly gray.

The inside of the building they entered was a

darker shade of gray. She made no attempt to step around the dirt, for her skirt had become stained with the filth within two steps. Everything smelled soiled and musty. Dank odors from the open earth poured from the shafts at the far end of the room filled with machinery she did not recognize.

Involuntarily she flinched when the rumble increased, and the floor quivered with the power of the compressor. A rattling was heard from the shafts. Slowly a hoist rose to reveal the cage in which they would ride to the first level below ground.

"You don't have to go," Jonah whispered.

She glared at him. "Why? So you can taunt me for being a coward?"

"It isn't cowardly to stay above ground."

"I want to see what it is like."

He smiled, and she was startled at the flutter in her stomach as she saw the warmth in his eyes. "That doesn't surprise me, Katie. Shall we go?"

Despite her words to him, she almost changed her mind as she stepped into the metal-bound box that served as an elevator. Her body tensed painfully as the ground-level floor slowly rose over their heads while they dropped down into the intermittently lit shaft. The lanterns were hung at odd intervals. From blackness, they would enter eye-burning light before leaving it for the ebony again.

A steady glow announced their arrival at the first drift, as the miners called the horizontal levels of the mining shafts. She noted Jonah had to duck so his head did not strike the timbers supporting the tunnel. A parade of scantily dressed men caught her attention. Although Lyndon had mentioned the heat in the tunnels, she had not thought about it until she entered this stygian world. With the poor ventilation, heat had nowhere to escape but up the narrow vertical shafts. Most of the heat stayed to plague the miners, who considered themselves lucky if they could spend a few minutes each shift in a room where ice was brought to help them cool off before returning to their tomblike work areas.

Isler warned her to watch her footing as he led the way down the steep incline leading to the next level underground. From there, they must follow the path of the giraffe, the ore-carrying cart designed to travel at an angle. Every step brought new danger.

Katie dampened her lips before she forced her feet forward to follow. Suddenly she regretted her insistence that she visit the mine. This was not adventure. This was braving the gates of hell to taunt the power of Satan. The horrible image of being smothered by a cave-in froze her to the earth. On the infrequent occasions when she wondered how she would die, she had imagined it would be on horseback or in a bungled robbery, not in the bowels of blackness, suffocating from tons of rock over her head.

"You don't have to go."

She could not read the expression on Jonah's face in the spare light, but his words again dared her to show her fears. That she would not do. "I am going," she stated before walking slowly toward the lantern bobbing in Isler's hand in tempo with his steps.

They walked for what seemed like miles along twisting tunnels before the mining manager stopped. When the tunnels opened into the darkness, guardrails had been put into place to keep the unwary from wandering off to their deaths in one of the unmarked chasms. The timbers were spaced more evenly than the lanterns, for even Flynn knew the foolishness of scrimping on such safety. A mine disaster would cost him employees and valuable time digging out the shaft again. Echoes of distorted voices rang along the tunnel below the strident sounds of the equipment battling the rock to steal its treasure.

"There. See that gleam?" Isler paused and raised the lantern toward where his finger pointed. "That's chalcocite. Solid copper. That is what makes Flynn's Copper Mining Company profitable. The miners drill into it and blow it out of the wall. All the debris is gathered up and sent up in buckets to the main drift. Then it's on its way to the smelter where the copper is reduced to its usable form."

She touched the rock, which was sharp from the samples cut from it to be tested above ground. Stories of the purity of the copper brought from the Montana mines had not been rumors. Even her uneducated eye could detect the large amount of the metal bright in the glow of the lantern.

"This is a new find," he continued. "Somehow it got bypassed before. There are many other places where the men are working now, but they are deep down, and I wasn't sure how long you wanted to stay in here."

"This is fine, thank you." She had seen enough. All she wanted now was to escape from this prison which was worse than any she had suffered. She did not know how the miners could come down in this hole day after day, month after month, for the paltry salaries Lyndon paid.

"Let's go," seconded Jonah, as he saw the paleness of her face in the light.

Isler smiled at their reactions. He had felt the same until he had forced himself to become accustomed to this nether world. Motioning to them to follow, he led them back toward the hoisting shaft.

Katie carefully skirted the bare-chested men sweating in the shaft. Her own clothes clung damply to her, impeding every step, and she thought longingly of the bath she would take when she returned to the house on the hill. It would be luscious to soak away all the perspiration rolling in thick droplets along her back and plastering her hair in tight curls to her face.

Lost in her thoughts, she failed to remember Isler's primary injunction of watching where she placed her feet on every step. The heel of her right boot slipped into a crevice. When she did not notice and tried to step forward, it popped off and knocked her from the narrow path.

She screamed as she tried to twist away from the wooden fencing along the walkway. A strong arm around her waist kept her from hitting the thin slats and tumbling into the dark pit beyond the railing. Shouts of warning were distorted grotesquely along the stone passage, but she did not hear them as she clung to her savior. Through

217

her mind careened the images of falling down
... down ... ever downward into that black
incision in the earth.

Gentle, comforting fingers stroked her back,
offering her unspoken solace. She did not lift
her face from the nest of flannel that moved
with his breathing. That common motion eased
her trembling more than anything else, for it
represented the life she might so easily have
lost.

Slowly her eyes rose along the front of the
shirt loosened at the neck to reveal the expanse
of muscular chest, past the rock-hard chin and
unsmiling lips, up the russet splash of mustache.
Unable to speak, she felt her knees weaken with
the concern cascading from his compassionate
eyes. He continued to caress her knotted shoulder blades. Slowly she relaxed but did not step
away from him. A happiness she did not recognize suffused her, urging her to stay close to
him.

As never in the past, she noticed how his mustache accented the shape of his lips before flowing out across his cheeks. Her fingers moved
across his firm skin to clasp behind his neck to
keep him from releasing her. Staring into his
eyes, she wanted to drown herself in the blue
oceans hiding many mysteries in their depths.

His arm tightened around her nearly impercep-
tively to press her closer to his body as soaked
with perspiration as hers. At the same time, his
breath cooled her overheated face. A desperate
hunger to feel that mouth against hers unnerved
her, but she took no time to think of why she

would feel this way about a man who wanted her as a tool to exact his revenge. Such hatred could not enter her mind when she stood in his eager embrace.

Isler's voice broke the fascination she had with the shadows dancing on Jonah's face in the tempo of the flame in the lantern. "Is she hurt, Jonah? If Flynn—"

"She is fine," Jonah interrupted before the mine manager might slip in his distress to reveal what must stay hidden. Even in a near catastrophe like this, none of them could forget the specter of the hangman's noose.

At his words, Katie stepped away without looking at either man. Silently Jonah cursed Isler for speaking when he had. In Katie's eyes he had seen her longing for what she had refused emphatically at her old hideout. He would have been quite happy to oblige her by kissing her soft lips.

He took her hand and said, "Let me help you, Katie."

Taking a step up the tunnel, she wobbled. Only now did she discover why she had almost fallen. She looked back to see Isler plucking her broken heel from the crevice. When he tossed it into the air, she reached over his hand to catch it before he could. He chuckled at the wry expression on her face.

The man holding her hand did not seem so amused. "You can't walk out with a broken shoe."

"I will be fine, Jonah," she assured him. To prove it, she started past him. She gasped when he halted her and swept her up into his arms.

Automatically her arm went around his shoulders so he did not drop her, but as she looked up into his shadowed face so near hers, she knew she need never worry about that. There was a throaty gentleness in her voice she did not recognize as she asserted, "I can walk. The tunnel is steep."

"If it becomes too much for me, I will put you down," he answered with a chuckle that crawled into her blood and set her pulse to dancing to a wild tempo. He repositioned her so her head leaned against his shoulder. Her damp hair flowed along his warm-smelling skin as her face pressed against the curve of his neck.

The invitation he offered was one she could not resist. She relaxed against him and found a comfort she had never suspected existed. All her life she had fought for what she wanted. For these brief moments of incredible bliss, she let him care for her as if she were something too precious to risk.

She closed her eyes and listened to his heartbeat muted by his damp clothes. Beneath her, his muscles rippled with the effort he expended to carry her along the slope. She became aware of his fingers along her ribs and supporting her legs. Where they touched her through her layers of clothes, her skin was vividly alive.

Although she had thought he would put her down when they reached the hoist, he insisted on carrying her to the buggy. He placed her carefully on the seat with obvious reluctance. Touching the boot heel in her hand, he said, "Maybe you should wear these more often, Katie. That was fun."

"Sometimes I think you must be mad," she admonished playfully. Her light words combated the too-strong emotions flying through her and tempting her to put her arms around him again.

"Just sometimes?" he retorted with a laugh. "What do you think about me the rest of the time?"

She picked up the reins to drive herself back to the house. "I don't know," she answered with sudden honesty. "Don't ask me that, Jonah." With a quick order to the horse, she sent the rig down the road toward the village.

Katie did not look back to see him become gray with the dust rising in her wake and sticking to his damp clothes. If she risked a glance toward him, she might turn the buggy around and demand he take her in his arms again. That would be more dangerous than the most daring robbery she ever had attempted, for she might lose her heart to a man she no longer was able to despise.

CHAPTER ELEVEN

Although Mrs. Grodin and Taylor were capable of dealing with all the preparations for Mr. Daly's visit to the Flynn home without Katie's interference, she double-checked every detail. She was sure the housekeeper and the butler tired of explaining to her what had or had not been done, but she wanted to be sure this business meeting went as Jonah wanted. Only by making it appear that Lyndon was on a par socially with the Dalys and the Clarks could she help him bargain to get the best price for his company.

Jonah had told her exactly what she must do. If Lyndon's already inflated sense of worth was increased, he would demand more than either Daly or Clark was willing to pay for the company. Any negotiations would then fail, and Lyndon would have to remain in Copper Peak until Jonah's still-undefined revenge was completed.

Katie assured herself for the fifth time that the guest room was ready. Then she braced herself for what she had to tell Lyndon and came down the stairs.

She knocked on the door of the library, which served as Lyndon's office when he wanted to work at the house. A grumble ordered her to come into the pleasant room lined with books he had bought for appearance, not to read. Fringed lamps gave a soft glow to the room now darkened by clouds as rain fell heavily on the house. The light brightened the dull colors of the rug and glittered off the gold embossing on the frames of pictures purchased for their investment value.

"Ah, Katie, how are things going for Daly's visit?"

A smile felt stiff on her face as she dropped to sit on the crimson horsehair settee. She spread her velvet skirts to complete her pose of the perfect lady. It was the one that worked best when she wanted to get something from this surprisingly simple man.

"It should be wonderful this evening." She lowered her eyes as if ashamed of what she had to tell him. "Lyndon, don't be angry with me, but I forgot to tell you that I invited Jonah Bancroft to the dinner party this evening."

He glanced up from his paperwork to snarl, "You did what?"

"I invited—"

"I heard!" Rising, he surged around the edge of his desk to stand over her. As he saw the glitter of tears in her eyes, his bluster vanished.

223

She had learned how effective her softer emotions were at cracking through his anger. Each time it happened, he told himself that next time her feminine tactics would not work, but he could not refuse his only child anything.

Katie rose to put her fingers on the well-starched sleeves of his shirt. When she felt his arm around her shoulders, she placed her head against the scratchy wool of his vest.

"Lyndon," she whispered, "I thought you and Mr. Daly would enjoy playing cards as you told me you do in Butte and at the Montana Hotel in Anaconda. With a third to join you, I thought . . . I'm sorry if you are angry with me."

Stroking her incredibly fragile arm, he murmured, "Of course I'm not angry with you, my dear. You only did what you thought was best. Daly is a common man, and I doubt if he will be offended to sit down to the table with the town sheriff."

He tipped her face up so he could place a kiss on her cheek. For a moment, the familiar longing to taste her rose lips instead of the coolness of her cheek swirled through him. If only she were not his child . . . He swallowed harshly as he fought the craving he had suffered since she arrived. There was no alternative but to find another woman to help him forget the erotic fantasies he relived each night as he dreamed of bedding Katie.

"Go and get yourself ready, my dear. I know that ladies have many things they must do before they dazzle us men with their beauty. Did you get your new gown?"

"Yes, Mrs. Kane delivered it this afternoon. She did not want me driving to her shop in the rain."

He gave her a gentle shove toward the door. "Then go and bathe, my dear. I will see you after I meet Daly at the train."

Katie was pleased to escape so easily. Racing up the stairs, she decided to do as he ordered. It might be the last chance she had to enjoy this soft life, for certain hints that Jonah had given her suggested he was readying the noose to tighten around Lyndon's neck. He continued to refuse to tell her anything specific, but a smile had betrayed him when she asked him when he would institute his revenge.

In her room, she sent Betsey away until she was ready for her. Despite Lyndon's promise to find her a maid, he had been unable to obtain anyone who would work for the miserly pay he offered. Katie had accepted Mrs. Grodin's suggestion and her help to train Betsey to assist her. The young maid proved grateful not to work in the kitchen and tried conscientiously to serve Katie. That the youngster was inept Katie did not mention to anyone, for it suited her fine that Betsey simply followed orders without question and left her alone when Katie wanted to be by herself.

She started the water running in her tub and went into the bedroom to undress. Pulling on her dressing gown, she padded about the room in her bare feet. The wool rug scratched her feet as she listened to the hushed swish of the water. She dropped into a chair and stretched her legs out in front of her.

What tonight might bring was something she did not want to think about, but it was better than the other thoughts crowding her mind. In the days since she had visited the mine, she had found herself imagining her next meeting with Jonah too often. Although she warned herself over and over that this attraction was worse than crazy, she was no more able to halt it than she could halt a train with her bare hands.

Shedding her wrapper, she climbed into the tub and sank deep in the water. Its warmth soaked into her to loosen the tightness of her body. Reaching for the delicately scented soap, she rubbed it between her hands until she had worked it into a lather that felt like satin. Her eyes closed as she recalled the time when Jonah's skin had been separated from hers by only a few layers of cotton and silk.

"Forget about him!" she ordered herself aloud.

With a sigh, she realized that such commands were impossible to follow. Her recalcitrant heart refused to listen to anything but its own soaring sound of happiness each time she saw Jonah.

She scrubbed her hair with a vengeance as she worked off her frustration with her own ambivalence. It was idiotic to think so much about him, and she intended to stop as soon as she could. Even if it took forever!

Leaving the tub gurgling its strange song, she left damp footprints behind her on the rug as she hurried to her bedroom. She sat at her dressing table and combed the tangles from the dripping strands. As she had too often, she listened to the chime of the clock in the hall below.

So much had happened since she had come here nearly two months before and listened to those bells tolling away the quarter-hours. She sought within herself for the woman she had been. If she allowed K.T. to vanish, she would not be able to resume her life she had loved so dearly. As she rang for Betsey, she vowed to remind herself every day of her precarious situation in this house and what would happen if she allowed this luxurious life to seduce her into believing it would last forever.

Katie was not surprised the train was delayed. The morning rain had become freezing sleet, clinging to the iron rails and slowing the train to a crawl. Nor was she surprised when Taylor announced, exactly on time, that the sheriff had arrived.

"Good evening, Jonah," she said as he entered the drawing room. Her calm voice gave no clue to the state of her stomach, jumbled with delight in seeing him dressed formally. For the first time, she could imagine him in a fine home in New Orleans. His black frock coat was cut away to reveal a vest of the same color. A high collar was closed with a maroon ascot that matched his trousers. The only other hint of color on his elegant clothes was the badge peeking from beneath his coat. Although she could not see it, she guessed at least one pistol hid there as well.

"And to you, Katie." He smiled, his waxed mustache as stiff as the hair lacquered to his head in the prescribed style. "You certainly make it a good evening when I see you looking so lovely."

"La, Sheriff Bancroft," she said in her most "Katie" voice, "you will turn a girl's head with such compliments."

He did not respond to her teasing. In a more serious tone, he answered, "I wasn't fooling, honey. You look fabulous in that gown."

Smoothing the pale pink crepe de chine of the full skirt, she delighted in the silk ribbons of the same shade accenting the flounces along the front. She adored the ruffles along the deeply rounded neckline and the train that trailed several feet behind her when she came down the stairs.

"Mrs. Kane did a wonderful job with it, didn't she?"

"A gift from 'Daddy,' I assume?"

Her smile vanished. Why did he have to be so vindicative tonight when she felt like a fairy tale princess attending her first ball? This was supposed to be a magic night when a train robber could sit down at the table with two of the most powerful men in Montana. His words wrenched the illusion away from her.

When she did not answer, Jonah moved past her to look at the rain flooding the window. "Did you have any trouble convincing him to invite me? When I did not hear otherwise, I assumed I was welcome tonight."

"I told him I invited you."

"That was it?"

She raised her chin arrogantly as she wanted to laugh at his astonishment.

228

"That was it." She sat on the settee and watched as he prowled the room. "Why are you working yourself into a tizzy? The train is simply late."

"I know. I just want to be sure everything goes well this evening."

"It will."

He whirled to face her. "You are damn sure of yourself, Katie. Don't forget this isn't a game."

"I never do." When he began to pace the room again, she asked, "Why don't you sit down?"

Jonah paused by a table where Taylor had arranged the tray he would take into the men after dinner. In addition to the requisite bottles of brandy and whiskey, there were several packs of playing cards. He picked up one and shuffled the cards.

"Why the cards?" he asked.

"Lyndon says he often plays cards with Mr. Daly." She watched as he handled the cards with easy competence. Suddenly he was not the New Orleans gentleman she had envisioned, but a Mississippi riverboat cardsharper. "I convinced Lyndon they would enjoy having a third tonight to make the odds more exciting."

He chuckled without humor. "I wonder if you'll break Flynn or me first, honey. He can afford to dress you like that, but did you consider I may not be able to afford to play poker with high rollers like those two? I take it you will not be joining us. I'm surprised you don't like cards, Katie."

"I never had the opportunity to learn." She glared at him as she said in a tight voice, "I was too busy honing other skills."

229

He tossed the cards back on the tray. Crossing the room, he said, "With Elijah Forrester's aptitude at the card table, I would have guessed he'd taught you how to cheat at poker as well as he did."

"Eli said ladies do not play cards for money."

A volley of laughter exploded from him as he regarded her stiff, perfectly correct pose. "But they can ransack trains?" he taunted.

"Jonah!" she gasped, glancing over her shoulder to be sure his words were not overheard.

"No one's there. Don't be so jumpy, honey. It's not like you."

"Not like me? What do you know about the real me?" Her voice escalated sharply with rage.

His smile infuriated her more as he went to the bar. Uncorking the decanter that held Lyndon's finest brandy, he poured himself a hearty serving. He leisurely walked to where she sat in a sunrise cloud of the pink gown.

"I know plenty about the real you."

She started to rise as he sat, but his broad hand on her wrist kept her next to him. Trying to pull away, she learned instantly how futile it was to fight his greater strength. She subsided to snap, "I'm tired of your threats!"

"If you took that statement as a threat, you misunderstood me." Calmly he took a sip of the brandy. With a grin, he offered the glass to her. "You don't play cards. Do you drink?"

"Not that."

Jonah chuckled, sure his amusement would raise her ire further. Each time he was with Katie, he learned of another of the contradictions in her character. A train robber with the keenest eye he had ever seen for target shooting, she could use language that would cause most women to swoon. Despite that, she considered herself too ladylike to play poker or drink hard spirits.

"Honey, let's not fight this evening. We are going to be too busy making sure things go well."

Her reply was halted by the sound of wheels on the driveway. Leaping to her feet, she looked at the man still sitting. He took her hand and rose to stand between her and the door.

"They're here," she said needlessly.

"It will be fine, honey." His finger under her chin brought her face up to look at him. "You will do perfectly tonight."

She wanted to speak of the fear in her center and the importance of this evening to everything they had worked for, but she was lost in the caress of his eyes. When she felt his hand at her waist, pulling her closer, she put up her fingers to his face. Lightly she touched his recently shaven face and recalled the first time she had seen him shave. Then they had laughed together and conspired together, never imagining they would be other than reluctant allies.

"Jonah, I—"

He placed his finger against her softly parted lips. Silently he cursed the men he could hear talking on the porch, for it was not his finger he wanted on her mouth. "Hush for now. Your guest is here, Miss St. Pierre."

Taking her elbow, he steered her to the door just as the two men blew into the foyer on the wind-driven rain. They shed their soaked mackintoshes into Taylor's quickly wet arms. Turning, Lyndon stopped in mid-word as he beheld the beautiful woman he could claim as his daughter. Quickly he stepped between her and Bancroft to draw her forward to meet one of the men known far from affectionately as Copper Kings.

"Katie, this is Marcus Daly. Daly, my darling daughter Katharine."

Flashing a quick glance at Jonah, she saw he had noted as well how Lyndon did not mention that her last name was different from his. She forced her attention back to the decidedly Irish gentleman in front of her. Despite the excellent cut and fabric of his clothes, his ruddy cheeks and stocky build bespoke his background of the same low class that had spawned Lyndon Flynn. The tint of his native country colored his words, although he had left Ireland more than thirty years before.

"Katie, is it?" he crooned. "Such a fine name for a fair colleen. Where has your jealous father been keeping you, lass?" He turned to Lyndon and smiled past his drooping mustache. "Surely you will be bringing her into Butte for the Copper Kings' ball next month. We need everyone to attend so we can raise money for the Democratic party."

"To defeat Mr. Clark?"

Daly's ever-present smile dimmed momentarily as he glanced at the man standing next to Flynn's daughter. The description his informers had given him of the upper-level employees at

Flynn's Copper Mining Company did not match this tall man dressed as dapper as their host.

"Oh," said Lyndon to break the strained silence, "Marcus, this is my sheriff, Jonah Bancroft." Later he would explain how his daughter had offered the spontaneous invitation to the sheriff. Remembering his role, he added, "Brandy?"

"Sounds excellent." Daly held out his arm in Katie's direction. "Allow me the honor, Miss Flynn."

"Please, Mr. Daly, call me Katie," she said hastily before explanations became necessary. "I am afraid I find formality uncomfortable among friends."

"Aye, and friends is what we all shall be. Now tell me how a lovely lady like you has missed the attentions of all the young bucks in Butte."

Katie kept him busy with the lies she spun so easily. Tonight was one night when Lyndon would not listen too closely to what she said, for he wanted her to say anything to charm his guest. She noted that her father was beaming at her quick conquest of the Copper King.

Hours later in the drawing room, Katie sighed as she accepted the cup of coffee from the tray Taylor held out to her. After thanking him, she added, "Will you close the door on your way out?"

"Of course, Miss Katie. If you want anything, just ring the bellpull behind you."

"Thank you," she murmured. As soon as the door closed behind him, she kicked off her slip-

233

pers and put her feet inelegantly on the stool in front of her. She pressed her hand against her side and condemned her corset with every curse known to Lucifer. There had been distinct advantages to her free life, such as not having to wear such constricting garments all evening long.

Her finger traced the rim of the cup as she decided the night had been a rousing success. Throughout the formal meal with its many delectable courses, she had exerted all her wiles, as Jonah was fond of calling them, on the spry Irishman. Effectively she had prevented the men from discussing business while, at the same time, boosting Lyndon's already overblown sense of self worth. He was sure to turn down any offer Daly made.

When the door opened with the breathless whisper of well-oiled hinges, she could not hide her surprise that someone was invading her haven. Her scowl altered abruptly to a smile as she saw Jonah hold his finger to his lips. Like a naughty child sneaking into the parlor on Christmas morning, he closed the door as quietly behind him. Only when it was latched and he turned the bolt did he relax.

"You were so convincing at the table tonight, I was unsure if that yawn after dessert was real or simply another act," he said as he crossed the room to sit beside her.

"I'm too tired and tense to sleep." She leaned back against the cushions so she could admire his handsome profile. When he slipped his arm along the top of the sofa, she closed her eyes to delight in the tingles coursing through her.

"How is your shoulder, Katie?" When she looked at him, surprised at the sudden question, he smiled gently. "I know weeks have gone by, but I should have asked you before this."

She whispered, too afraid of the strong longings within her to speak louder, "It is fine, as long as I don't strain it too much."

"Is it up for some dancing?"

"Dancing?"

Laughing again, he stood smoothly and held out his hands to her. He pulled her into his arms. "You are shorter than usual," he announced.

She lifted her dress enough to show him her stockinged feet. "I am afraid some old habits are hard to break."

"Then I shall be especially careful of your toes."

Before she could respond to his outrageous statement, he began to hum a waltz. With the same ease as when he rode, he whirled her slowly around the room. She kept pace with his fluid steps, recalling the times she had danced with Eli as he taught her what he thought she must know so she could enter society when they made their big strike.

Placing her head against the satin trim of his lapel, she forgot the past, the future, and all of the present except the luscious sensation of moving together. The magic disappeared when he stopped singing and said, "Damn!"

"What is wrong?"

"I can't remember the rest of the song."

She whispered, "That's fine. Just start over. We will dance to the beginning and never have to worry about the end."

"Or we could dance to a real orchestra. With all the talk tonight of the Copper Kings' ball, I thought it would be a pity if the prettiest lady was accompanied solely by her father." He did not loosen his arms around her as he asked, "Would you allow me to escort you, Katie?"

"To Butte? You want to take me to the ball?"

"You don't need to sound so shocked." He framed her face with his hands. "What astounds you more, Katie—that I can attend or that I want to take you?"

"Both," she replied with sudden honesty. When he touched her like this, she doubted if she could lie to him.

He smiled at the confusion on her face. A single finger ironed out the creases of puzzlement on her forehead. "Honey, I must get back to the poker game. The excuse I gave them garnered me a few minutes with you, but they will be suspicious if I'm gone much longer. What is your answer?"

Katie reached up to touch his face as he had done to her. It took all her strength not to pull away from the searing power that burned from his skin through hers. That she could initiate this rapture came as a wondrous surprise. Her eyes settled on his lips as they had done too often lately, and she mused again about how sweet they would feel on hers.

"Katie?"

She blinked as she tried to recall what he had asked her. So precious were the fantasies she could create of Jonah that she could become totally immersed in her dream world.

"Yes." She repeated in a more normal voice, "Yes, Jonah, I would be delighted to have you as my escort to the Copper Kings' ball."

When he took her hand and lifted it to his lips, her gaze followed his motion as if she were in a trance. At the fervent touch of his mouth on it, she was sure that nothing had ever felt so grand. Holding her hands, he brought them to his shoulders. He released them slowly. Once he was sure she would not move them, he slipped his arms around her waist and invited her into his embrace. One hand stroked upward along her back to cradle her head at exactly the right angle for his lips.

"We shall have a grand time showing these snobs how to have a good time, Katie," he whispered as his mouth descended toward hers.

Her eyes widened when she pulled away from him. This was insanity. She should not be feeling sensuous yearnings for Jonah Bancroft, for he was the one man she could never be totally honest with. If he kissed her, he might discover how he stripped her of all sense with nothing more than the chance passing of his hand over hers.

"No, Jonah." She hid her hands in the fullness of her skirt. "I think you should return to the poker game."

"You think I should—?" He lowered his startled voice when he saw her wince as she had when he checked the wound he had inflicted on her. This time the flayed edges of her agony were invisible. "If that is what you want, Katie."

"It isn't seemly for you to—to do that."

"A kiss never hurt anyone, not even Lyndon Flynn's perfect daughter!"

Katie cried, "That isn't fair! You made me—I mean, you—Oh, just leave me alone!" She whirled away from him.

"All right, be alone, if that's what you want."

She bit her lip to keep the tears from cascading down her cheeks as she listened to his footsteps beating the carpet. A muttered curse accompanied the opening of the door. When it closed, her shoulders sagged, and she asked herself why she had been so foolish. A single kiss would not have changed anything so irrevocably that she could not have things as she wished when this farce was over.

Bending, she picked up the cup and saucer and placed them on the tray. Taylor would be sure to clear them when he turned out the lights. With a sigh, she walked toward the door. It opened nearly in her face to reveal Jonah. His stone-hard face broke into a mischievous smile which she recognized as the one that meant disaster for her. Involuntarily she backed away enough to allow him into the room.

He closed the door without speaking. His broad hands were iron strong but gentle as he grasped her arms and brought her close to him. The fierce glow in his eyes emphasized his words as he stated in a husky whisper, "Dammit, Katie, kiss me before I go mad from longing to feel your soft lips."

She was given no chance to protest before his mouth captured hers. With a tenderness she did not expect, he wooed her lips by teaching them

238

the texture of his. As lovingly as he had taken care of her during her recovery, he caressed her with questing kisses. Her fingers stroked his arms, feeling his muscles hard beneath the coarse material of his coat.

When he raised his head to look down into her eyes glazed with emotion, he smiled to lessen the fierce acidic hunger in his middle. He tilted her head back so she could not glance away from him.

"When we go to Butte, I may be dancing with some of the other women at the Copper Kings' ball while you fulfill your social obligations, but my mind will be filled with the sweet fantasies of holding you, Katie."

Again she broke his embrace as all color fled from her face. "No," she whispered, "don't talk like that."

"Why not?" His face became the uncompromising one she was too familiar with. "Don't you like how you feel when I kiss you?"

Katie considered lying, but knew it was useless. The way she had melted against him when he held her must have told him the truth. "I like it when you kiss me, but we cannot have any future. You are the town sheriff, and I am . . . what I am. A relationship of any kind other than enemies is impossible for us, Jonah." Gathering her skirts in her hand, she opened the door. "Good night."

She was gone, racing up the stairs as rapidly as her unshod feet could carry her. Without looking back, she could feel Jonah's piercing eyes cutting through her to seek the strength of her attraction to him. She vowed never to allow this to happen again, although the thought sent a pain from her heart outward to ache in every pore of her body.

Out of view at the top of the stairs, she paused and tried to slow her rapid breath enough so she could hear Jonah returning to the card game in the small room at the back of the house. She had been wrong when she thought she could control this relationship enough so a single kiss would change nothing.

It had changed everything by revealing the state of her rebellious heart. She wanted Jonah to kiss her again and again and again until she was swallowed by the strange enchantment of this emotion she did not dare call love.

CHAPTER TWELVE

Katie untied her apron as she walked down the front stairs. If she did not hurry, she would be late meeting Jonah who had promised to take her into town to visit Mrs. Kane, the seamstress. This morning she had been so busy she barely had time to consider taking an hour for a fitting.

In spite of her disinterest in the subject, Mrs. Grodin's continual insistence in having Katie accompany her on her daily rounds was forcing her to learn something about managing a house. The housekeeper never mentioned how elementary the questions were that Katie asked.

Draping the organdy over her arm, she ran her fingers along the banister and smiled as she checked to see there was no dust. She could not believe how much she had been changed by living in this house. Even a few weeks ago, she would not have cared if a layer of dust dimmed the wood or been gratified when Mr. Daly told her, just before leaving Copper Peak yesterday, how efficiently her house was run and how he looked forward to seeing her again in Butte.

She paused as she heard voices in the hall below. In some ways, she remained the hunted K.T. Before she entered any new situation, she made sure she was aware of who waited beyond her sight. As she listened to the two familiar voices, her hand clenched on the railing.

"Thank you," said Jonah as he took the roll of greenbacks Lyndon offered and put them in his pocket. "It is kind of you to pay up so quickly, Mr. Flynn."

"Don't think I am doing this because I am pleased that a no account sheriff is taking my daughter to the Copper Kings' ball, but a wager is a wager." Lyndon grumbled, "I never expected she would agree to let you escort her."

The younger man's smile was evident in his satisfied tone. "Never bet on women, Mr. Flynn. they will do the opposite every time."

"*You* bet on her!"

"I bet on *me*. I was sure I could convince her to let me take her to the dance, although I didn't realize such an invitation obligated me to escorting her to the seamstress for her fittings."

Katie seethed on the stairs. A bet! That was all she was to these men. A wager, a chance for sport . . . a joke! Just when she had dared to let her heart care for Jonah, he proved what she should have known all along. The only thing of importance to him was his damnable revenge against Lyndon.

She shoved her apron into the top of the umbrella holder in the hall, not caring that the ties hung over the outside. Grabbing her cape, she vowed that Jonah Bancroft would pay for this insult. When a bright idea struck her as to exactly how, she struggled to contain her laughter. Simple revenge might be the best.

Her smile was firmly in place when she entered the drawing room. She waited until the two men standing by the fireplace turned to see her. Nearly identical expressions of pleasure crossed their faces as they noted how closely her new dress clung to her body. As she walked toward them, the fullness at the back swished along the rug.

"Hello, Jonah. How kind of you to arrive so promptly. I did not want to be late for my appointment."

"Shall we go then?" He placed his hat on his head and reached for the cloak she had folded over her arm. When he felt her shoulders quivering beneath his fingers, he risked a glance at her face. Her expression was bland while she told Flynn the approximate time they would be returning.

Something was bothering her, and Jonah intended to find out what it was. Although she had said nothing to him of Flynn's reaction to her, it was clear her so-called father wanted a far more intimate relationship with pretty Katie. The swell of rage bursting through him was startling. He assured himself quickly that it was not jealousy he felt, but a protective reaction because he had forced her into this.

More than once he tried to introduce the subject as they drove the short distance to the seamstress's shop. She ignored him as she prattled on about the material for her dress and the many fittings, and wouldn't they have a grand time in Butte, and had he heard the latest news about the trouble at the mines. He fought the temptation to tell her to be silent. It was most unlike Katie to chatter aimlessly and added to his concern about what was really upsetting her.

When he stopped the buggy in front of the nondescript house that matched all the other plank buildings in Copper Peak, except for Flynn's fabulous house, she waited with uncharacteristic patience for him to help her from the carriage.

"Oh, thank you, Jonah," she purred as she pulled her hand out of his. "La, I daresay I could not manage it by myself in this dress."

"Katie, why don't you tell me what is wrong?" When she turned away without answering, he grabbed her arm and twisted her back to face him. "Dammit! Tell me!"

"Sir, what is wrong is that you are treating me with your normally boorish manners." She eased her arm from his grip. Brushing the wrinkles from her velvet sleeves, she made it clear he had bruised her genteel sensibilities. "If you persist, I must ask you to leave."

Jonah watched in disbelief as she entered the dress shop. It was as if his dearest dream was transforming into a nightmare. How could she have become Katharine St. Pierre? That woman did not exist! Yet an urchin who once delighted in larceny had breathed life into something that should have been only a creature of his imagination.

For a moment, he considered leaving her and letting her find her own way back up the hill. Then he realized that only would widen the inexplicable gap between them. Two nights ago she had been warm and sweet in his arms as he explored her lips. Something had caused her to change into this too-polite stranger. He was determined to find out what it was.

He went into the modiste's shop, which he immediately decided had been designed to make men uncomfortable so they would agree quickly to any purchase to escape from its lush interior. Hats, parasols, and dress models were covered with lace and swatches of fabric in every conceivable color.

Mrs. Kane burst out of the back room, her bun of silver hair bouncing, to answer the bell tinkling over the door. "Why, sheriff! Is something wrong?" She laughed and pressed her hand to her full bosom. "Of course! You brought Miss St. Pierre in, didn't you? You sure know how to charm her, don't you?" She winked at him broadly before ducking back into the other room. Her happy chatter drifted throughout the shop.

Jonah stretched out his legs as he sat in the too-short chair. He felt as if he had entered a child's dollhouse. Listening to the lyrical sound of female voices, he glanced at the magazines spread on a small table. *Godey's Lady's Book*, *Leslie's Illustrated*, *Child's Home Companion*, nothing of interest to him, even if the most recent issue was not three months old.

He leaned back in the uncomfortable chair and closed his eyes. It had been far into the morning hours before he got to sleep last night. The meeting with his "gang" at the saloon had gone well, although he was tired of defending Katie to them. If they had not seen how Flynn doted on his "daughter" with their own eyes, he refused to explain yet again what they disregarded. Finally he had convinced them that she would not betray them and that she should not be dealt with harshly.

A hint of a smile tipped his lips as he recalled the accusations they had shot at him of being unable to think clearly because he was developing an attraction for Katie. On that, he had to agree with them. From the moment he saw the slight woman in her poke bonnet and plain calico dress, she had haunted his dreams. That no one in town could tell him exactly who she was and where she was from, other than hints of a sheep farm in the higher altitudes, added to his curiosity. Closing his eyes, he reveled in the fantasies that had been filling his mind too often lately and wondered if Katie imagined the same delights.

In the fitting room Katie's thoughts were about him, but hardly the sweet passions he was envisioning. She was so irate that she could barely force herself to be pleasant to the seamstress. Mrs. Kane did not comment on her terse responses, but kept her normal gossip to a minimum, which pleased Katie. She was going to have to show Jonah exactly what she thought of being the object of a wager between him and Lyndon.

"All done, Miss St. Pierre," announced the modiste. When the young woman continued to stare at the mirrors ringing the room, Mrs. Kane repeated slightly louder, "All done, Miss St. Pierre. Miss St. Pierre, are you ill?"

Abruptly Katie broke her fascination with her thoughts of retribution to realize the woman was talking to her. "I'm fine, Mrs. Kane. When do you need me again?"

"Tuesday will be fine."

"Afternoon again?"

"Any time is fine, Miss St. Pierre."

Katie simply nodded. As Lyndon Flynn's daughter, she rated the best service Mrs. Kane could offer. If someone else had an appointment when Miss St. Pierre arrived, that other customer would have to wait for the shop's premier client. Everyone understood and outwardly accepted that.

Pulling on her dress, Katie stood with ill-concealed impatience as Mrs. Kane's assistant helped her hook up the back. When the slow task was completed, she thanked the girl perfunctorily and left the room with a crisp farewell to the seamstress.

"Finished," she told Jonah in the same tone she had used when she came down the stairs in the white house.

Jonah stood and stretched. When she felt his admiring eyes roving along her again, she tied her cloak around her shoulders and tightened it to hide her form from his view. She smiled tightly when he offered his arm. This was not the place to let him know exactly how she felt about his little game with Lyndon.

247

The few people passing on the street avoided speaking to them as they crossed the boardwalk to the buggy. She suspected that the townspeople considered their sheriff a traitor for taking up with Flynn's daughter. If only they knew the truth . . .

When they were seated side by side in the narrow buggy, Katie asked with nonchalance, "Must we go directly home? Are you busy this afternoon?"

He looked at her with bewilderment that wiped the hard edges from his face. The boyish expression urged her to forgive him, but then she remembered what she had overheard him say in the drawing room.

"Do you want to go somewhere, Katie?"

Fighting to keep her voice light, she said, "For a ride. It has been a while since we have had any length of time alone, and I thought we had the perfect excuse today."

"And I know the exact place." He picked up the reins and gave a sharp command to the horse.

She sat next to him and listened while he spoke of matters from the town. She wanted to shout that she did not care about what had happened in Copper Peak or at Flynn's Copper Mining Company, but she stewed silently and watched the road in front of the carriage. He was driving east from town, so she guessed he was going to take her to the deserted upland meadows where they could have the privacy to do whatever they wanted. She eagerly anticipated the chance to show him exactly how wrong he was about how she felt.

Even the sound of the compressors was silenced by distance as Jonah slowed the buggy when they approached a stand of trees. She took a deep breath and discovered the freshness she had forgotten in the valley below.

"Do you miss this?"

She looked up at him, and then away. This was the wrong time to believe he truly cared about her. He reached for the brake to keep the buggy from rolling. As he leaned forward, she reached down and pulled the pistol from his holster. Before he could react, she pressed it against his ribs. He froze.

With a laugh, she ordered, "Hand me your other one, Jonah."

Shock registered in his voice as he gasped, "Katie, the gun is loaded! Get it away from me before something happens. This isn't something to joke about."

"No?" She chuckled again as she saw the rage on his face. "I think this is incredibly amusing. The other one, Jonah." She jabbed the barrel into the tender spot between the smallest bones of his side. "Now!"

Slowly he lifted the other gun from the holster on his opposite hip. Not for a moment did he think about contesting her for it. He might be stronger, but she had proven already she could shoot quicker. He could not have drawn before she fired, even if he wanted to risk hurting her again. Turning the pistol over in his hand, he offered the grip to her.

With a smile, she took it. "Out!" she snapped, waving the gun to second her order.

"Katie—"

"I said 'Out,' Sheriff Bancroft!"

He did not remove his gaze from her smiling face as he slid off the buggy's bench and onto the ground. When he tensed to leap to one side, he heard the click of the hammer. He halted instantly.

Katie leaned over the side of the buggy so her eyes were on a level with his. The pistol rested easily in her hand, never wavering from the middle of his chest. "You are too trusting."

"Fun's over. Give me back my pistols."

"Odd. I thought the fun was just beginning." She laughed at the fury on his face as she settled the gun more comfortably in her hand. "This is a fine weapon. You favor a Colt, I see."

He fought his impulse to reach for the gun and pull it from her hand. With the sharp sound edging her laugh, he was not sure she would refrain from pulling the trigger. "Why don't you tell me what you want?" he suggested, deciding he could not force the issue physically.

"What I want? You should know by now. One small miscalculation, sheriff, and your whole plot crumbles. I have a weapon. I can go to Butte and take my chances at freeing Ethan."

"A telegraph message can reach Butte before you." He continued to be calm. Although he had come to enjoy Katie St. Pierre's company, he realized how little he truly knew about K.T. Forrester. She might have been lying about murdering the guard on the train. If she had done that, she would have no concerns about adding another to her list of victims. He added hastily,

"I will have the marshall waiting for you, Katie. Can you guess what would happen to you in that prison?"

She refused to be intimidated by his threats. "He will be alerted only if you can sound the alarm. How long before you are missed, sheriff? Do you and your cronies meet regularly? Or will it take until Lyndon comes searching for his absent daughter and discovers both of us have disappeared?"

"Katie—"

"Yes?" She grinned at him. "Go ahead and beg, sheriff. Never let it be said that I didn't give you an opportunity to beg for your life. I like that word. Go ahead, sheriff. Beg."

He shook his head and crossed his arms on his chest. "You won't shoot me."

With a chuckle, she lifted the gun and squeezed the trigger. The bullet hit a rock to the left of his ear. She waved aside the black smoke as the twang of the shot faded into the distance. "Want to wager on that?" Her eyes grew hard as she added, "Just as you wagered with Lyndon that you could coerce me into accepting your invitation to the Copper Kings' ball in Butte."

"Is that what is bothering you?" He laughed as he relaxed slightly. "I made that bet with Flynn the day you arrived. It was the best way to be sure I got to see you regularly."

"So you could be sure I didn't betray you?"

As he nodded, he noticed the tears glittering in her eyes. "Of course," he answered slowly.

Katie asked herself what other answer she had expected. Jonah had made it clear from the beginning that she was nothing but his method of gaining his revenge. When she felt her finger clench on the trigger reaimed at his chest, she wondered why she did not shoot him. She was tired of being used.

Her gaze moved along his handsome face, and she knew the truth. She could not shoot this man. When his only crime was breaking her heart coldly, she was unable to act as his executioner. Slowly she lowered the gun and placed it next to her on the seat. Picking up the reins, she slapped them on the horse's back.

She gasped in pain as her wrist was pinched by strong fingers. Looking up, she saw Jonah stretching over the step of the buggy to hold her. "That hurts!" she cried.

"Good!" He scooped up his guns and put them back in their holsters with his right hand as he held her with his left. Then he leapt onto the buggy seat beside her.

"Is there something besides the bet that's bothering you, Katie?" he asked with outrageous serenity as she struggled to pull away from him. He laughed as his arm around her waist kept her close.

"Let me go! I don't want to discuss my personal business with you, Sheriff Bancroft!"

"Jonah!" he corrected.

She spat back, "Sheriff Bancroft is your name, isn't it, sir?"

As if she had not spoken, he continued, "Yes, there is something wrong with you today." He put a single finger under her chin and tilted her face toward his. "But it is nothing that cannot be taken care of like this."

252

His hands held her motionless as his lips captured hers. At first gentle, they became as demanding as everything else about him. She stiffened at the caress of his mouth, but he dared her to prove to him that he was wrong. Hesitantly, her hands moved along the iron strength of his arms. When she touched the breadth of his back, he pressed her against the back of the seat.

She gasped as the warm tickle of his mustache moved along her face as he pelted her skin with rapid-fire kisses. Instantly he retook her mouth, devouring her senses as he lured her into the spiraling vortex of his desire. His tongue teased hers when her lips parted to welcome his exploration. As it moved along the slippery sweetness of her mouth, he discovered secrets hidden even from her, leading her on a swirling, wild pattern of passion.

Her fingers entangled in his hair brushing the back of his collar. She did not want him to stop kissing her as she became aware of every inch of herself against him. When he pushed her straw bonnet back, his lips followed the line of the silk ribbons. She tightened her hands on him as she relished the stroke of his rough face against her soft skin.

When his tongue found the lobe of her ear, she gave a surprised cry of delight. His gentle laugh puffed into her ear, making her tingle to the tips of her toes. As her fingers clenched along his back, she fought the currents of rapture to bring his mouth boldly back to hers. She wanted to feel its adoration of her lips.

He raised his head slightly, and his words were accented by his mustache brushing against her. "Holding you like this is something I have wanted to do for a very, very long time, Katie."

"A long time?" she whispered.

"Ever since I saw you in town with Ethan." He cursed his own stupidity as she stiffened in his arms. By speaking of that day when he had ordered her friend to die and, more importantly now, had seen her brother well enough to identify him as Ethan Forrester reminded Katie of their enmity. When he put his fingers against her cheek, she tried to bat them away.

She ordered, "Release me, Jonah!"

"Stop it!" he snapped with the full force of his frustration. "When are you going to stop acting like a child? You are a woman. Don't you think you should start acting like one?"

Katie seethed, sure she had never been as angry as she was now as she glared up at his infuriated face. "And how does a woman act?" A coquettish smile did not match the fire in her dark eyes. "Do you prefer me as simpering, snotty Katharine St. Pierre? Is that how I should be? Do you want me to say, 'La, Sheriff Bancroft, I daresay you could sweep a girl clear off her feet with such antics. My head is spinning.' Is that what you want? I don't! I want to be myself! Simply because I can ride and shoot better than you doesn't mean I am not a woman."

His arms slid from around her. Sadness filled his eyes as he shook his head. "That isn't what I mean at all. I admire your ability with a gun, but you have to grow up and learn that life is not simply an adventure."

"I know that!" She laughed with sharp pain. "Oh, I learned that early. When everything I loved disappeared suddenly to leave me and my brothers with the choice of learning to prey on those foolish enough to leave themselves vulnerable or of starving, I discovered life is no adventure. Adventures are what regular folks have when they go for a lark in the mountains. When this is your life every day of the year and your life depends on your prowess, it is nothing but hard work. And, if you think pretending to be Lyndon's daughter is fun, then you are more off-target than I thought."

"Katie, I never said this would be fun."

She did not look at him as she whispered, "Just take me home, please." Tears burned in her eyes as she wished he would take her back to her home in the cabin on the ridge where she could be herself again. She did not want this fine life. She did not want these obligations and burdens.

She did not want to fear she was falling in love with Jonah Bancroft.

Silently he drove back toward town. During the long drive through the windswept mountains and along the dusty street, neither of them spoke. Katie remained silent because she was afraid of the words that might spring from her lips if she let any sound past them. She tried not to think about whether Jonah felt the same, for such thoughts brought only more misery.

Leaves blew across the driveway of the house as they passed the gate. The buggy halted in front of the porch. Jonah did not jump out as he normally did. Instead he turned to take Katie's hands between his. "Honey, can I hope you will go to the ball with me? No, don't say it. The main reason I want to take you is that I need to be there to see that Flynn does as he should, but," he added quickly as a flash of pain raced across her face, "Katie, any chance I have to be with you is a special occasion." He stroked her cheek and kissed her in the spot warmed by his touch. "Katie?"

"I will let you escort me to the ball," she answered as she scurried down from the carriage. "No, don't walk me to the door. I don't want to talk to you any more today."

Taylor waited, as always, to open the door for her and welcome her into the warm comfort of the house. He did not say anything when the sheriff did not follow her. With a simple greeting, he accepted her cloak and watched as she ran into the drawing room and closed the door.

She drew back the curtains to watch the carriage leave through the front gate. At least Jonah was being honest with her when he said her company was the *second* most important reason he had for wanting to go to the Copper Kings' ball. Maybe that truthfulness was a start.

But of what? Even when she heard the answer in her heart, she did not want to acknowledge it. Never had she been scared of danger, but she was terrified now.

She was terrified of loving Jonah Bancroft and knew she could do nothing to change the future when that love might bring them to ruin.

*   *   *

Through the sleepless night, Katie remonstrated with herself over the foolishness of fearing the one man she should trust. When, at dawn, she knew it was useless to stay in bed when she could not sleep, she dressed in her riding clothes to go for an early run on her horse.

She yawned as she pulled on her well-tailored blazer. As she buttoned it, she rounded the top of the stairs to see a group of servants clustered below her. The sibilant sound of their gossiping was clear in the morning silence. All the whispers halted when the maids noticed her on the stairs behind them. She descended the few steps to stand with them on the landing.

Her voice cracked as she gasped, "Did I hear you say the sheriff has been shot?"

The maids glanced at each other and the floor, but no one answered Katie. When she implored them to tell her the news, the distress on her face urged the tallest to speak up, "Miss Katie, I jes heared from Joey in the stables that Sheriff Bancroft done got hisself shot."

"Are you sure?" When the girl nodded, Katie asked the question she did not want to know the answer to. "Is he dead?"

"Don't know. All I heared was he done got hisself shot."

Katie whirled and raced down the stairs. Taylor came into the foyer as he heard her rapid steps. When he saw her reaching for her cloak, he said quietly, "I just heard the news, Miss Katie. I trust you will forgive me for ordering your buggy for you."

257

"Thank you, Taylor," she murmured as she threw her arms around him. She needed his friendship desperately while she fought the fear trying to strangle her. "Tell Lyndon where I am. I will be back with the truth about Jonah as soon as possible."

"Send one of the lads if you need anything, Miss Katie."

She nodded, unable to say more. Whether he opened the door or she did, she only knew she was running for the buggy. She grabbed the reins from the stableworker holding them. More times than she could count she had wished this masquerade was over, but she had not imagined it would come to an end this way.

Jonah could not be dead!

CHAPTER THIRTEEN

Duncan, Jonah's ally from the telegraph office, opened the sheriff's door at her frantic knock. Although he did not seem surprised to see her, he said only, "I think it would be better if you came back at another time, Miss St. Pierre."

She regarded him coolly, although she felt anything but calm. "I suggest, Mr. Duncan, that you step aside and let me in. If I have to come back to see Sheriff Bancroft, I will find it necessary to bring my father's rifle with me." Giving him a second to digest her threat, she added, "I want to see him, Mr. Duncan."

"All right." He opened the door and motioned for her to enter. Quickly he closed it as she ran through the quiet room.

"Where is he?' she asked when she peered into the bedroom to discover it empty.

"Not here."

"I can see that!" Her voice rose as she ordered, "Tell me where he is!"

Duncan calmly sat on the sofa where she had been drilled on her lessons of New Orleans night after night. Stretching his arms along the top, he said, "I can't."

"If you don't tell me where Jonah is, I will—I will—"

"What will you do? Run and tell the town that Sheriff Bancroft isn't in bed recovering as he is supposed to be?"

Katie did not like to admit defeat, but she knew she would garner no information from Duncan like this. What these men had planned she did not care about, for all she wanted to discover was if Jonah lived. Slowly she sat in one of the chairs grouped around the table. The strength that had propelled her at top speed down the hill deserted her as she whispered, "Mr. Duncan, at least tell me if he is alive.'

"Why? So you can learn if you must find another escort to the Copper Kings' ball?"

Lustrous tears filled her eyes as she gasped, "That isn't fair!"

"What is?" He relented as he sat forward and lost his faked pose of nonchalance. "He is alive, Miss St. Pierre, and we intend to keep him that way."

"But I can't see him?" When he did not answer, she asked in resignation, "Will you at least tell him I came to see how he was?"

Duncan grunted something she was sure meant Jonah would never hear of her visit, but she could not win this argument by continuing it.

260

Jonah could be almost anywhere in the mountains surrounding Copper Peak. Even if she knew where these men had their hideout, she was sure the wounded man was hidden so well that she never would find him.

Rising, she turned to the door. She did not tell the telegraph operator farewell, and he said nothing to her. Her eyes closed in anguish as she saw the gleaming letters on the sheriff's office window. Jonah's world where he had been so alive and vital. She hurried to the buggy and clambered into it, afraid of the weakness of the tears flowing along her cheeks.

When she returned home so quickly, the servants did not know whether to ask for news or offer consolation or both. Mrs. Grodin met her at the door to envelop her in a motherly warmth that brought back distant memories of gentle kisses easing the pains of scraped knees.

"I don't know!" she answered to the whispered questions. "They won't let me see him. Dr. Havering wants him isolated for a few days so he will rest." Her lies gave her no comfort, but might keep the curious from endangering Jonah.

Throughout the day, she wandered through the house like a wraith. Each window she passed, she looked out wondering if the mountain framed by the glass was the one where Jonah hid. Tears, so rare for her, kept bubbling from her eyes, but she wiped them away quickly. The skin under her eyes grew red and raw to announce the sorrow she could not conceal. She searched in her heart for the acceptance that he might die and she would never see him again. Nothing but rage and fear could be found.

When had Jonah become so important to her? From the second they first met as enemies, she had been intrigued by his inherent power. At the sight of his handsome features, she had felt the stirrings of what she now realized meant she wanted to sample the stroke of his lips on hers. She hated him. She admired him. She feared him. And she loved him.

No one bothered her as she struggled with her grief and fear. She skipped both breakfast and lunch. Only as the night darkened the house did Mrs. Grodin interrupt her solitude.

Katie looked up at the knock. When the door opened, she greeted Mrs. Grodin in a barely audible voice. The housekeeper closed the door and brushed the loosened strands of her silver hair back from her face.

"Miss Katie, Mr. Flynn will want you to come to dinner tonight. He has sent the message that he will be bringing company to dinner."

"Company?" She bit back her curse. Lyndon must have heard the news, which would have flown through the village. When he learned of Jonah's injury, he should have known how upset she would be.

Mrs. Grodin hurried through the sitting room to disappear into the bedroom. When Katie could not understand her mumbled answer, she went into the chamber to discover the housekeeper instructing Betsey to lay out one of her finest gowns. Her heart ached with the resignation she had experienced when Duncan would not share any details of Jonah's wound with her. If Mrs. Grodin had been instructed to have the maid make such elaborate preparations, this must be a most important visitor. Perhaps Lyndon had arranged a meeting that was impossible to cancel at the last minute.

"Shall I help you, Miss Katie?" whispered Betsey.

She scowled as she looked from the flustered maid to the strangely silent housekeeper. There was more amiss here than the disturbing tidings from Copper Peak.

"Mrs. Grodin, if you tell me the truth now, it might make it easier as the evening passes."

The white-haired woman sat without asking permission, another sign of her intense distress. Katie said nothing of it as she chose another chair. Her maid waited without speaking and crumpled the material of the gown Katie would wear to dinner.

Dampening her colorless lips, the housekeeper said, "Mr. Flynn has spent the day in town. At the saloon, from what I hear, celebrating his good fortune in dealing with Mr. Daly from Anaconda. He—he is bringing a—a—"

"A dancehall girl?" Katie wanted to laugh at the housekeeper's squeamishness, but a sudden rage stripped her of any amusement. While his daughter waited anxiously for word on the condition of one of his most valuable employees, Lyndon had been arranging an assignation.

Taking the dress from Betsey, she tossed it on the bed. "You can put this away. I won't be wearing it this evening."

"Miss Katie, Mr. Flynn was very explicit that you·would join them this evening." The flustered Mrs. Grodin flitted about the room like an overweight black bird, her dark dress flapping behind her.

"I don't feel well. You may tell Mr. Flynn that I have retired early."

"You must eat!"

She smiled at the reappearance of the kind, competent woman she admired. "A tray would be pleasant, but not much, for I have little appetite."

The housekeeper nodded, but went from the room slowly. Until this evening, Miss Katie had been willing to follow her father's edicts. This rebellion would garner the suffering woman only more trouble. The servants had been respectful of her worry about her friend Sheriff Bancroft, but Mr. Flynn thought first and only of himself.

Mrs. Grodin's fears materialized as soon as the master of the house returned home. Smelling of cheap whiskey and with a decidely under-dressed woman on his arm, he swept into the foyer and tossed his hat to Taylor. He murmured endearments as he grabbed his black-haired harlot and pawed her while removing her cloak. The butler kept his face sternly immobile, but wished he did not have to be a witness to this depravity.

With a voice slurred with liquor, Flynn demanded, "Where is my Katie? She was to be here to meet me and Veronica."

"Miss Katie sends her regrets, sir," answered the butler with cold composure. He ignored the whore's shrill laughter at his imperturbable posture. "She plans to sup in her room, Mr. Flynn."

"Does she?" Drunken rage reddened his face. Taking Veronica's blue-veined hand in his, he surged up the stairs.

Taylor stared after them in horror. He hurried into the dining room to find Mrs. Grodin and try to devise a way to help Miss Katie.

When the door crashed open, Katie leapt to her feet. She tightened the neckline of her dressing gown as she saw the glitter of Lyndon's eyes. Wrapping her other arm around her waist, she faced him squarely.

"Good evening, Lyndon." Her voice was as perfectly correct as Taylor's.

"Why in hell aren't you dressed for dinner?" he bellowed. Since he did not release Veronica, she came into the room with him.

The whore's eyes widened as she saw the beautiful room granted to Mr. Flynn's daughter. If she was careful in her planning, she might be able to devise a way to stay in this wonderful house as his permanent woman. She had been warned when she came to Copper Peak a month ago how the owner of Flynn's Copper Mining Company treated his women in bed, but she could tolerate some physical abuse and degradation if she could live in a place like this.

"Some classy joint!" she murmured.

Katie took her eyes from the woman dressed in wisps of red and black silk that barely covered her to meet the rage on Lyndon's face. "I told Mrs. Grodin to inform you that I am feeling poorly tonight."

"You look fine."

"After the news of the sheriff being shot today, you should understand I am understandably upset about my friend being hurt."

With a roar of laughter, he said mockingly, "If that is the only problem, my dear, I can find you another man eager to escort you to the Copper Kings' ball."

No one was more surprised than Katie when her hand struck his face with a resounding smack. He pressed his palm to his reddened right cheek. Rage altered his face into a horrendous mask as he raised his hand. When she did not cower away from him, he turned his back on her ashen features. Grasping his companion's hand, he dragged her from the room and slammed the door.

Katie collapsed into a chair. As she stared at the door, she wondered what her impulsive action would bring. Her outward defiance might have been forgiven, but she was unsure if Lyndon would pardon her after the scene acted out before his harlot.

She buried her face in her hands and sobbed as she had not been able to do all day. Her tears fell for everything wrong in her life. For Ethan, for the plot that might come to an end tonight because of her ungoverned temper, but mostly for Jonah and the love he could die without knowing she wanted to give him.

A second night without sleep had left its signs on Katie's face when she came down to the dining room the following morning. From habit, she went to the sideboard and served herself from the dishes kept warm there. The scent of eggs and fried meat sickened her, so she took only a single biscuit before pouring herself a cup of fragrant coffee.

Sitting at the table, she placed the cup between her elbows and leaned over to let the steam billow into her face. Maybe it would loosen the tight skin around her eyes, for no amount of washing had cleansed the area of the salt left by her many tears. Her muscles ached with each breath she took, but she forced herself to move.

Already she had decided she would ride back into town this morning to confront Duncan and demand to see Jonah. If she did not get permission to visit the injured man, she would threaten the very thing the men did not want. A hue and a cry to help find the missing sheriff might cause Duncan to cooperate quickly.

At the sound of heavy footsteps, she glanced up from her coffee. No emotion crossed her tired features as she saw Lyndon enter the room. His own lack of slumber slowed his movements, but he was smiling.

"Good morning, Katie."

She rose as she said, "Good morning."

"Stay. She won't be having breakfast with us."

Fatigue gave her the courage to be reckless. "It is not your whore I don't want to sit with. It is you! How could you bring her here last night?"

"Just because Bancroft was foolish enough to get himself winged by a bullet when he tried to stop another robbery of the payroll train doesn't mean the whole town should go into mourning!" he snapped. The plop of scrambled eggs on his plate caused him to wince, and he rubbed his aching head. Irritably, he ordered, "Sit down, young lady. You and I have much to discuss."

She refused to be browbeaten by a man suffering from too much of the saloon's rotgut whiskey. With the quiet dignity that no longer seemed odd on her lips, she said, "I agree, Lyndon, but there is no sense discussing it when we are both short on sleep and you are barely able to function. Good day!"

He shouted after her, but she refused to acknowledge him and went without pausing to the coat rack. Pulling down her heaviest cloak, she closed it around her. As she was putting on her bonnet, Taylor came rushing out to ask if she wanted the buggy. He sent a lad scurrying to the stable to have it brought around for her.

"Will you be home for lunch?" he asked with gentle concern.

"I'm not sure. It may be a while before I return, because I intend to see Sheriff Bancroft this afternoon." She smiled as she drew on her suede gloves. "I will see him, even if I have to drag Dr. Havering from his office to issue the order."

Taylor chuckled after the door had closed. His good humor faded as he heard Mr. Flynn bellow for Miss Katie again. Deciding a hasty retreat was his best chance of missing his employer's rage, he hurried to the kitchen to warn Mrs. Grodin and the rest of the staff about the horrendous day ahead of them.

In the buggy driving at a sedate speed down into the village, Katie tried to arrange her demand in the best possible way. She wanted Duncan to know she would not be rebuffed today, but if she angered him too much, he would never cooperate with her. Drawing back on the reins, she halted the carriage in front of Jonah's small house.

Before she could climb down, the door opened. Her first, irrational hope was that it would be Jonah coming to reassure her personally. She banked that dream as she saw the telegraph operator walk to the vehicle. He was not smiling as he jumped onto the seat next to her.

"Drive!" he snapped.

"Where?"

"Just drive. Out of town. East."

Although a flurry of questions beat against her lips, she clamped them closed and obeyed. When she turned the horse onto the road paralleling the railroad tracks, her companion said nothing. She did not know if he was angry that she had guessed this was the trail they needed to follow to get to Jonah.

The cold, damp air threatened precipitation, but nothing fell to make their silent trip more uncomfortable. Katie knew that Duncan despised her more than any of the other men in Jonah's gang. She refused to cater to his patronizing attitude by begging for more information. Watching the road in front of them, she steered the rig competently along the uneven path.

When they were more than five miles from the village, he ordered her to stop. "Here?" she gasped. There was nothing in sight that could offer shelter to a wounded man. Rugged banks of stone challenged the trees clinging precariously to them. She was familiar with this stretch along the tracks and knew that no prospectors' cabins stood nearby.

"Here. Turn around." When she did not do as he ordered quickly enough, he shoved her forward. Her protests became a shout of outrage when he placed a bandana over her eyes and tied it behind her head. "Shut up! If you keep squawking, I will gag you, too."

Katie gasped as he pressed her back against the cushions. The smell of residual gunpowder was pungent close to her face. She did not need eyes to know he was pointing his pistol in her face. In a whisper, she said, "I understand, Mr. Duncan. I will be quiet."

"I thought you would."

She lurched against the side of the carriage as he gave a low command to the horse. Clutching the supports for the canvas of the buggy's roof, she tried to keep from sliding off the seat or against the man. When the wheels bounced off the road, she wanted to shout out a question, but she remained silent. If this was the only way she could get to see Jonah, then she must accept their idiotic precautions.

Duncan hissed a warning to her not to move when they stopped. The buggy bounced as he jumped down. She listened to his feet moving through some sort of dried vegetation as he came to her side. His broad hands lifted her from the seat and placed her roughly on the ground. When she swayed, he gripped her arm and spun her in a different direction.

He told her nothing about the small obstacles on the ground in front of them, so she tripped more than once before she heard him open a door. Her toe stubbed painfully into the door sill before she could obey his order to step into some sort of shelter. The door closed behind her, and she heard a bolt slide into a lock.

When she did not feel him take her arm again, she used her other senses to decide whether she was alone. Musty dampness reeked in her nose, but it was not the aroma of burnt powder. That made her believe that Duncan had locked her in this place and gone out.

Fear burst through her. She did not doubt that the others in Jonah's gang wanted her dead. If their leader had been killed, this might be their method of dealing with their unwanted ally. Her fingers shook as they reached for the knot behind her crushed bonnet.

She lifted the blindfold from her eyes. Glancing around, she frowned. The room contained a table and chairs, but mostly piles of debris. Gaps in the unchinked wall allowed in bits of gray sunlight. Walking to the filthy window, she used her cloak to wipe off a spot large enough so she could see through the handblown glass. The wavy image of the shadow stretching over the train tracks identified her location immediately as the small building by the water tower eastward along the spur off the main Northern Pacific rail line.

"Recognize this place?"

With a gasp at the voice she had feared she would never hear again, she whirled to see Jonah standing in the shadows at the back of the shed. She started to raise her arms so she could throw

271

them around him, but paused as she regarded him with bewilderment. There was no sign of a wound or bandage anywhere on his clothes filthy with dust.

"You aren't shot!"

He chuckled as he closed the distance between them. "You don't need to sound so disappointed."

Irrationally, she felt fury explode within her. "Do you have any idea how worried I have been? I have not slept in two days! I—I . . ." Her voice faded away as she began to laugh, softly at first, then with a soul-healing catharsis that filled her eyes with hysterical tears.

Jonah welcomed her into his arms. When her laughter turned into sobs, he continued to stroke her back and whisper in her hair. What he said mattered little, but he wanted her to know he had not intended this to hurt her. Only the impossibility of sending her a message had kept him from telling her the truth immediately.

As the storm within her lessened, he brought her face away from him so he could see her cheeks. He ran his finger along their dampness and realized that, through all the trials she had suffered with him in the past months, this was the first time he had seen her cry. This outburst of emotion showed him what he had suspected lately, although her actions often denied it. Katie cared for him far more than she wished to.

A gentle smile matched his words as he murmured, "Honey, I'm sorry you have been worried about me. It was necessary."

"Necessary to let me think you were dying?" She touched him tentatively, afraid this was simply a hallucination. When his fingers covered hers to hold them against his chest, she dared to give him a watery smile. "I didn't want you to die, Jonah."

"Neither did I!" His voice softened again as his mouth descended toward hers. "When Duncan told me how upset you were, I told him to bring you out here as soon as he could."

His lips touched hers, and she dissolved into his arms, surrounding herself with his strength, which she longed to have around her forever. When his mouth rose from hers, she saw the fatigue that dimmed his eyes.

"What happened?" she whispered. "Why this charade, Jonah?"

"The train was robbed."

"I know." She drew away from him as she explained, "I heard yesterday. Was it you? I thought you and your gang had decided to choose a safer method for amateurs."

"These bandits were like none I have seen before, honey. They swept down on that train as if they wanted to destroy her." His voice grew hard as he added, "And they did. Less than a minute after they rode away, the mail car blew sky high. The shock of seeing that stunned us long enough to give those bastards a chance to take a shot at us. Haggerty was hit."

"Haggerty? Not you?" As an afterthought, she added, "How is he?"

"He died this morning."

"Oh," she breathed. She recalled the many times she had met that member of Jonah's gang. With his job in the store, he seldom could leave Copper Peak and had served primarily as a gatherer of information for them. "I'm sorry, Jonah."

He smiled sadly. "Me too, honey. We devised the story that I had been the one hurt because less questions are asked if a sheriff is shot than if a shopkeeper is found bleeding by a train where he should not be. Later he will be a hero in town for taking the bullet meant for me when . . ." He paused as pain crossed his face. Shrugging his shoulders, he sighed. "I don't know exactly what lies we will devise, but it won't help Haggerty or his wife. I had hoped we could save him. Like when you were shot, I convinced Doc Havering to help, but this time the help came too late."

Katie felt tears refilling her eyes. She did not cry for the near-stranger who had died, but for the man who held out his arms to her. The members of Jonah's gang were held together by a loyalty she respected. How and why they had joined him in his determination to ruin Flynn she had never asked, for it was not important.

Her fingers against his cheek tilted his mouth over hers. She wanted the touch of his lips again to soothe the never-ending pain of death. As her hands encircled the nape of his neck, she gave herself to the passion building so swiftly through their anguish-wracked bodies.

"Katie, Katie, my love," he whispered as he pulled her so tight against him that his gun belt could be felt through her many layers of petticoats. "Honey, I want—"

A derisive chuckle drowned his words, instantly separating them. Katie glared at Duncan and the other members of Jonah's gang. The mine manager, Isler and the train conductor named

274

Lenny stood behind the red-haired Duncan. When she would have stepped away, Jonah caught her hand and held her next to him.

His voice was as calm as his stone face. "Has everything been taken care of in town?"

Isler nodded. "The minister took charge of the body and said the ceremony will be tomorrow morning. A message has been sent to Flynn." He glared at the woman standing too close to their leader and wished she had been the one killed. None of them trusted her or her seductive claws, which appeared to be firmly entrenched in the sheriff. Only Jonah's insistence in continuing with their original plan kept Isler from pulling his gun and getting rid of her right now.

"Good." Jonah pulled out a chair from the table and motioned for Katie to sit in it. He doubted that she had missed the hatred for her in the eyes of his men, but noted that she remained serene. Tempered by the fire of her rough life, she would not be daunted by voiceless threats. "Everyone sit. There are some things we need to discuss now."

Lenny hesitated. "With her here?"

"Now."

For a moment, Katie thought the men would balk at the order, but, grumbling, they took their seats.

"So now what?" asked Isler.

"We continue, of course." He looked at his other friends for confirmation. "This was a fluke. If I had not been eager to keep Flynn off my back by catching these robbers, we wouldn't

275

have been watching the payroll train. We should keep our goals firmly in front of us and forget everything else."

Katie shook her head. Her fist striking the table startled the men. When they turned to look at her, they saw that the ladylike Katie St. Pierre had vanished to be replaced by the wily K.T. Forrester. Her dark brows bowed over the scowl on her face. In the silence, she did not have to speak loudly to make her point.

"Once is a fluke. Twice cannot be discounted."

"Twice?" demanded Duncan. "What is she talking about, Jonah?"

The tall man met her eyes steadily. Jonah said, "Katie, I know you are talking about the day we drove out to your old hideout, but that was just chance."

"And this wasn't?" When no one answered, she continued, "You can dismiss the facts if you wish, but someone is after one of you. It may be Haggerty or you, Jonah, or any of you. If you ignore this, whoever it is will continue until he is successful, if he hasn't been already."

Jonah hesitated before answering. That her mind accustomed to dealing with larceny had seen this connection while he missed it irritated him, but he could not allow his bruised pride to keep him from accepting her theory. He had forgotten about the attack on them. He should have been suspicious when there were no future ambushes on travelers in that area, for his deputy was incapable of dealing with criminals that competently.

"You can't be taking this hogwash seriously, can you?" demanded the conductor when Jonah stared reflectively at the opposite wall. "How do you know that Miss *St. Pierre* isn't just doing this to destroy our effectiveness?"

"Don't listen to me!" she snapped. "That satisfies me perfectly. I would be glad to be done associating with fools who insist on disregarding the facts." She stood and reached for the blindfold she had tossed on the table. "Mr. Duncan, I would like to be taken back to town now."

The telegraph operator growled, "You don't give orders here, girlie. If—"

"Take her back to town," said Jonah quietly.

"Jonah, you may kowtow to this whore you can't wait to sleep with, but—"

Katie shrieked as she was shoved aside. The table was up-ended to crash against the wall, but no one noticed. Every eye watched as the sheriff's fist struck Duncan's nose. The redhead went down, but he bounced back to his feet. He swung wildly, and Jonah blocked his arm without difficulty. With the same ease, he knocked the shorter man off his feet again.

Duncan started to rise, but swayed. Reaching down to help him up, Jonah was caught off guard by the fist that struck him in the mouth. He spit blood, but smiled as his arm swung a final time. This time when the telegraph operator hit the floor, he did not move.

"Pick him up," Jonah ordered, wiping the stream of blood from his mouth. "When he wakes up, tell him I want to see him at my office tomorrow first thing. C'mon, Katie," he added to the silent woman. "I will take you back to town myself. It's about time I let people see I have recovered from my malady."

She said nothing to the men who watched her with open rancor. That Jonah would defend her like this from his own friends left her speechless.

When she handed him the bandana, he stuffed it in his pocket. He could have told Duncan it was futile to try such games with Katie. There was not a stone on these hills she would fail to recognize. He grimaced as a piercing pain set his head to aching when he wiped his mouth on his sleeve. If he was lucky, he would not have to repeat that lesson in respect.

Easily he lifted her into the buggy and jumped up to take the reins. As they began along the deserted road, he noted how straight she sat. He expected her to be upset. Beneath the brash exterior, she was a gentle spirit.

"You are wondering why I hit Duncan," he said to break the silence.

"Yes."

He took his eyes from the road for a moment as he heard her terse answer. He explained, "You were the leader of the Forrester gang. Sometimes you have to show that you mean your orders to be followed without question, right?"

"Yes." A tightness in her chest kept her from saying anything else. She wondered how she could have been so foolish as to believe he had been defending her questionable honor. Someday she must learn that fairy tales did not happen to women like her. Men as handsome and charming as Jonah Bancroft had little interest in a woman who survived by robbery and deception.

"You must have had to deal with someone trying to undermine your authority."

"I threw Les Proulx out of our gang when he tried to steal my share of the money one night."

He gazed into the darkening sky that had begun to spill snow. "How did a little thing like you deal with him?"

"I pinned his arm to the wall with my knife." When he chuckled, she added, "Then I told him I didn't want to see his ugly face again."

"Leaders have to be tough, right?"

She looked at him and noticed the snowflakes that spotted his mustache in a strange pattern. "Yes."

Pulling back on the reins, he halted the carriage. His arm around her swept her close to him. "That's all true, but that's not why I hit Duncan."

"It isn't?" Her eyes searched his face to see the truth her heart desired. She tipped his hat back so the brim did not strike her in the forehead.

"You know why I hit him."

"Because he insulted me?"

He shook his head as his finger traced the slim line of her nose. "No, honey. I hit him because he spoke the truth in part."

"He called me—"

"Not that part, but the part about wanting to have you next to me through the hours of the night you could make so sweet."

Hungrily he pressed his lips to hers. The slight pain of his cracked skin he ignored. As if they had been separated a lifetime, they savored the luscious kiss. Her fingers knocked his hat to the floor of the buggy as she put her arms around him to feel the strength of his body overwhelming her. The howl of the wind vanished as he leaned her back against the narrow seat.

She raised her fingers to halt him as he reached for the ties of her cloak, but they settled on his shoulders when his hand moving along her found the curve of her breast. A fervent sigh of longing drifted from her lips as his fingers gently sought along its upsweep to find the buttons of her shirtwaist. Knowing she should halt him, she did not want to do anything to cause him to take his hand from her. Deep inside her, she felt an emptiness she longed for him to fill with his warmth.

His mouth seemed determined not to miss a single inch of her skin. Each time she started to protest when he undid another button, he silenced her with a heated kiss that burned to her very center, releasing a sweetness that flowed outward to urge her closer to him.

When he pulled apart her gaping blouse, she did not feel any cold, for he bent to taste the flavors of the skin she had allowed no other man to touch. Her fingers twisted in his hair to keep him close to her when the stroke of his tongue sought beneath the lace of her chemise to tease her sensitive skin.

"Katie," he whispered, "I have missed you so deeply the past two days. Come home with me tonight."

His words reached through the webs of enchantment to bring the icy clutches of reality. When she put her hands up, she did not touch him, afraid of being lured back into his spell once more. Instead she rebuttoned her shirt. His fingers halted her before she could close it completely.

"I can't!" she answered. Glistening tears distorted her vision while she wished she could agree with him as her heart wanted. That was impossible. "If ever I had considered entangling my life with a man, it might have been you, Jonah, but nothing can change the fact we are what we are."

"I know. A sheriff and a train robber!" Bitterly he asked, "Can't you forget that for once?"

"Never, and it's more than that. You are from a fine family in New Orleans. I know that without you telling me. Where I am from is a mystery I will never have answered." She sighed as he opened his mouth, but motioned him to silence. "You are going to say that doesn't matter, for you are making me no promises beyond tonight."

He watched as she finished buttoning her shirt. When she looked up at him, he wondered if she had ever been more beautiful than at this moment when she opened herself to him as she never had before. He ran the tip of his finger along her silken cheek and asked, "And for you there must be more than one night?"

"K.T. Forrester and Katie St. Pierre are not so different about that, Jonah. I'm sorry."

"So am I, honey." Putting his arm around her, he kept her in the shelter of his body so the frozen wind did not burn her with its fierce touch. He knew he would have a difficult time releasing her when they arrived in Copper Peak.

CHAPTER FOURTEEN

The bell over the door rang without its usual brightness as Katie entered the store. A cluster of women standing near the cast-iron stove's sparse warmth glanced in her direction and hastily away.

Ignoring the baleful glances, she went to the counter where Haggerty's assistant Barlow awaited her uneasily. The playful flirting she had endured when he believed she was a female sheep rancher had disappeared into fearful stammering as he judged every word before he spoke to Mr. Flynn's daughter. More than once, she had wanted to tell him to open his eyes and see the truth.

"Is Mrs. Haggerty in?" she asked in a carefully lowered voice.

"Umm . . ." He colored as he fought to speak without saying the wrong thing. "Miss St. Pierre, I don't know if you have heard about Mr. Haggerty's accident, but—"

"I heard. That is why I am here. May I see Mrs. Haggerty?"

He hesitated, then decided he could not make this decision himself. Asking her to wait, he went into the back room. The curtain in the doorway dividing the store from the living quarters fell heavily back into place.

Katie made no effort to speak to the other women. She knew that if she went to them, they would drift away on lame excuses, not wanting to be infected by the sickness they were sure she had inherited from Lyndon. Her tales of how kind he was to her would bring only more rage, for their daughters suffered at his hands while she was coddled.

Quicker than she expected, Barlow called, "Miss St. Pierre, Mrs. Haggerty asks if you want to come upstairs. She prefers not to come downstairs now."

"I understand."

As she stepped through the small swinging door to the back of the store, she felt the cold stares of the women cutting into her back. It was useless to attempt an apology, for only the truth would satisfy them. Then they would despise her more for being K.T. Forrester, who had deprived them of their income by stealing the payroll.

A door waited at the top of the stairs behind the curtains. Barlow knocked once before opening it. Ushering Katie in, he closed it behind her. She stared around the simple room, which brought to mind her own home now ruined on the mountainside.

Bright gingham curtains hung at the trio of windows that allowed the sunshine to enter the small chamber. It brightened the embroidered cloth covering the round table and the braided cushions of the three chairs. The well-worn carpet had been scuffed by many feet. She walked only as far as the first chair so she could look beyond the patched settee to see a woman kneeling on the floor.

A gaunt woman, Mrs. Haggerty had made no effort to repair the damage left by her grief. Puffs beneath her nearly colorless blue eyes showed her hours of suffering since learning her husband had been killed. Only when she stood and moved toward Katie could the younger woman see what she had been tending.

"A baby!" gasped Katie involuntarily as her eyes riveted on the cradle. In it a child not more than three months old played with its toes, blissfully ignorant of the death of its father. Inanely she said, "I didn't know, Mrs. Haggerty."

"He was his father's greatest joy." Tears cascaded without shame along her face.

"I'm sorry." She added, when she saw the hatred on the woman's face, "I truly am sorry, Mrs. Haggerty. Your husband will be missed by those who care about what happens to Copper Peak."

Mrs. Haggerty stated with icy pride, as she brushed her disheveled brown hair back from her face, "If you are here to tell me Mr. Flynn expects us out, you can tell him—"

"No!" Katie interrupted her. "I don't know what Lyndon has planned for the store, but I didn't come here to tell you that. He wouldn't ask me to do such an errand for him, even if I had been willing."

The woman's eyes narrowed suspiciously. From the midst of her sorrow came the memory of who this well-dressed lady truly was. Except for the new clothes her father had Mrs. Kane make for her, everything this brunette wore had been selected by Mrs. Haggerty under Sheriff Bancroft's critical eye. If this whorish train robber threatened her, she could repay her in kind. Her thoughts glowed in her red-ringed eyes as she demanded, "Then exactly why are you here, Miss St. Pierre?"

Katie wished she could ease the other woman's agony, but no simple words would convey the grief she understood all too well. Again she fell back on the trite. "To tell you how sorry I am your husband was killed."

"Well, you have done your duty, Miss St. Pierre. If you will excuse me, you must realize how distressing a day it has been. I have just come from the cemetery and the funeral."

Katie nodded. "I wanted to come, but was told it would be best if I didn't attend, although I admired Mr. Haggerty. Your husband was an honest man who always treated me fairly when I did business with him."

"Thank you for the belated eulogy, Miss St. Pierre," she said bitterly. "Now why don't you leave?"

Katie refused to be dismissed. "Are you staying? I know Jonah needs—"

"I don't care what Sheriff Bancroft needs, Miss

St. Pierre." The power of her mourning filled her voice as it elevated on every word. "My husband is dead! Don't you understand? Maybe you have never suffered so to comprehend how it hurts to lose one you love."

"I know!" Katie's polite facade disappeared as she spat, "I know all too well! My older brother was hanged earlier this year, and my other brother waits the same fate in a Butte jail. If he dies, I will have lost all of my family."

Mrs. Haggerty stared at her as if she had never seen her before. After a long minute of silence, she motioned for Katie to sit on the couch. Katie accepted and spread her fine velvet skirts on the tattered brocade. Her dark eyes followed the woman as she went to the kettle on the stove and poured water into two cups. When Mrs. Haggerty brought them back to the sitting area, she spoke soft words of gratitude for the cup of tea the older woman held out to her.

"You are welcome, Miss St. Pierre." A weak smile shone amid her tears. "I never thought I would say this to any of Flynn's family, but I'm sorry I acted as I did."

"I'm the one who should apologize." Her voice was as muted as the widow's hushed tones. "I barged in here when you are still in the grip of your grief. May I ask if you plan to stay in Copper Peak?"

"That won't be my decision. Flynn owns everything. In the past, he has made it clear he has no obligation to the widows and orphans left behind after a mine accident. As soon as the bodies were laid in the ground, the survivors were asked to leave so the employees replacing their loved ones could have a place to live."

Not wanting to defend Lyndon, but unable to agree outwardly with Mrs. Haggerty, Katie found it easier to ask another question. "Do you want to stay?"

"I know what you want to ask, Miss St. Pierre—"

"Please call me Katie. The other name is too long, and you know it is not mine."

Another wisp of a smile crossed the tragic mask of what had been an attractive face. "Katie, I was mistaken, wasn't I? You aren't here on behalf of Lyndon Flynn. You are here to seek help for Jonah Bancroft."

"He does need an ally here in the center of town to gather information for him." She placed her cup on the table and folded her hands on her knees. "Jonah does not know I am here today. He doesn't want me to become involved in—in that facet of his business."

"I will think about it. My friends are here in Copper Peak, and I don't want to leave before I see my husband's work finished." She paused as the baby began crying. "Excuse me a moment."

Katie watched as she picked up the fussy child. Like her, this youngster would have no firm recollections of its father. She hoped it would have more than the ghostly images of a mother to comfort it as the years passed. So many things she thought she remembered, but when she had tried to speak of them to Eli, he laughed them away and told her she must have been dreaming to imagine such a fine home as the one that existed in what she thought were her memories.

When Mrs. Haggerty noticed her odd expression, she offered, "Would you like to hold him?"

"Me?" Katie suddenly felt inept in a manner she had never experienced. The last time she had held a baby would have been Ethan. In the rough world where she had been raised, she shared no feminine experiences with other women. The few women she had met were prostitutes whom Eli refused to let her speak to. She could never understand his strange standards, for he taught her to be an accomplished gunfighter and robber, but insisted she learn the graces of a lady.

"If you don't like babies—"

"No, no!" A wry grin stole the last vestiges of snobbish Katie St. Pierre from her face. Gentle awe at the small size of the kicking baby in Mrs. Haggerty's arms softened her features. "It is simply that I am not accustomed to such little ones."

"Then you should be. Someday you may have youngsters of your own." She instructed Katie on how to hold the child and placed the baby in her lap.

Katie touched his dough-soft cheek and ran her finger along the downy texture of his chubby arm dimpled at the elbow. Although winter was readying its power beyond these walls, Mrs. Haggerty had dressed him lightly so he could kick and wave his hands to entertain himself. Some past warning urged her to be very careful as she stroked the fine golden silk along his head.

"What a beautiful baby!" She did not dare to take her eyes off the child as she asked, "What is his name?"

"Bourne Haggerty, Jr."

Surprising herself with her own bravery, Katie lifted him so she could look directly into his curious blue eyes. She laughed as he reached out to pat her nose with pudgy fingers. At the sound, he pulled them back and stuck his thumb in his mouth.

A knock sounded at the door. "No, no," said Mrs. Haggerty with a laugh. "Please hold him while I answer that. It's most likely just Barlow. He's afraid to make any decision without consulting me."

Katie smiled as she balanced the baby on her lap again. With one hand behind him, she dangled her other hand in front of his eyes. The bangle on her wrist sparkled before him and, with a delighted gurgle, he grabbed for it. She laughed as his fingers closed awkwardly around the thin gold.

"Good afternoon, Mrs. Haggerty. I trust I am not interrupting."

Katie whirled at the voice she would notice no matter what else was happening. At the door stood Lyndon Flynn, filling the narrow portal. The baby gurgled, and Flynn looked past Mrs. Haggerty to see Katie sitting on the sofa. His cold smile vanished into his most intimidating scowl.

"What are you doing here?" he asked as he pushed past the widow.

"I came to offer Mrs. Haggerty my condolences on the tragic death of her husband." She grinned involuntarily as the baby put her bracelet into its toothless mouth to test its flavor. "Be careful," she warned him gently as she pulled it away and offered her finger to replace the bangle. Glancing back at Lyndon's ferocious frown, she added, "Mrs. Haggerty was kind enough to invite me in for a cup of tea."

Without taking his eyes from his daughter who was becoming more independent every day, he snapped, "Take your bawling brat, Mrs. Haggerty."

"Lyndon—"

"Katie," he interrupted fiercely, taking her arm in the seconds after Mrs. Haggerty retrieved her baby, "you and I will talk on our way back to the house. Ma'am," he said to the ashen-faced woman standing in the middle of the room, "you have until tomorrow at sundown to have your personal items cleared from this establishment."

Rage erased all of Katie's common sense. Ripping her arm away from him, she said, "Nonsense! Why are you sending her away? She has done nothing wrong and knows more about running this store than any new shopkeeper you will be able to find."

"Stay out of this."

With a glance at Mrs. Haggerty to warn the woman not to betray her, she asked, "Why did you think I came here, Lyndon? Because you are so busy with the dealings with Mr. Daly, I wanted to handle this detail for you. I have been quizzing Mrs. Haggerty about the management of the store. She has been handling much of the ordering for the past year, and the other employees come to her for guidance. You would be mad to dismiss her."

Lyndon did not ask the other woman to verify what Katie was saying. It would be unseemly to accuse his headstrong daughter of lying in front of this storekeeper's wife. But then he wondered why he should believe her. Katie had a gentle heart, and this might be her way of showing compassion for the Widow Haggerty. He did not want to tell her that much of his anger had come from seeing her with a child on her lap and knowing the time would come when he would lose her to another man who could love her as he was denied.

Quietly he answered, "You are right, Katie. Mrs. Haggerty, come to the mining office tomorrow, and we will discuss arrangements for your continued work in Copper Peak."

"Yes," she managed to say through her shock, "yes, Mr. Flynn." She looked at the astonishment on Katie's face and wondered if the sheriff knew how much power his creation could wield over the owner of the copper company.

"Come along, my dear." He took Katie's arm, but much more kindly.

Unsure exactly what had happened or why, Katie scooped up her cloak and called a rushed farewell over her shoulder as Lyndon hurried her down the stairs. They went through the silent store without stopping to speak to anyone. Only when they were seated in the fancy carriage did he speak.

"I don't expect I shall have to tell you this again, Katie," he said in a low tone which did not lessen its threat. "You are not to become involved in my work. It's no place for a woman.

You tend to the house and your duties there. My daughter will not clutter her pretty head with business matters. Do you understand?"

"Yes," she answered, although she seethed at his words. She wanted to tell him that she had managed the Forrester gang more efficiently than he did his company.

"And you will obey?"

"Yes."

She smiled in the shadow of her bonnet as he grunted with satisfaction. If he believed her false vow, he was as naive as he had accused her of being. Choosing a subject she was sure he would think more appropriate for her station and gender, she began to prattle about the dress Mrs. Kane was making for her. By the time they reached the house on the hill, she had convinced him again that she was his devoted Katie who would listen to his edicts and pretend she did not see the lust in his eyes.

Taylor peeked into the dining room where Katie was discussing next week's meals with Mrs. Grodin. So hastily did he talk that his words tumbled over one another. "Miss Katie, there is a gentleman from Butte here to speak to Mr. Flynn. When I told him Mr. Flynn was unavailable, he insisted on seeing you."

"Where is he?" she asked as she rose and pulled off her apron. A caller of such importance to make Taylor lose his normal composure could not be met with a dusty apron over her dress.

"I asked him to wait in the drawing room, Miss Katie."

"Very well. Please send a boy down to the office. Mr. Flynn will want to be informed immediately."

Peering into the mirror, she ascertained that she looked presentable enough to meet a visitor. She smiled at the housekeeper and went across the foyer to the drawing room. Her surprise at finding the double doors closed was masked by the time she opened one and stepped into the room.

A well-dressed man was examining the paintings on the wall, but turned at the sound of her footsteps. She regarded him without emotion. "I am Katharine St. Pierre. And you are?"

He held out a pudgy hand that felt soft and sweaty as he shook her hand. His dark eyes did not miss an inch of her in the time it took to lift her fingers to his lips. "I am Upton McSherry, representing Mr. William Clark of the Colusa Copper Company."

"Mr. William Clark?" she squeaked. Instantly she swallowed her shock and motioned to the sofa. "Please forgive my surprise, sir, but this is quite unexpected."

"It shouldn't be, Miss St. Pierre. After Mr. Daly's recent visit to Copper Peak, you must have realized Mr. Clark would be interested in assuring Mr. Flynn that he received a fair price for Flynn's Copper Mining Company."

Her smile tightened. Beneath his slick words, this man was as unscrupulous as his employer who fought Daly for control of the political future of Montana. She wanted to throw his words back in his face. Neither Clark nor Daly was interested in anything other than outdoing the other in their continual war of wits and dollars.

"How kind of Mr. Clark," she murmured. When she felt his eyes settling on her bosom, she said, "I noticed you enjoying the paintings. Are you fond of art, Mr. McSherry?"

"I find landscapes pleasant, but I must admit a preference for the human form." He smiled with oily obsequiousness. "May I say you are indeed lovely, Miss St. Pierre? The tales of your charms have reached Butte, but I must admit you are far lovelier than mere words can convey."

"Thank you." Her short answer deflated him. If he had expected embarrassment or fury at his forward words, she would not oblige him.

Deciding that the tactics which had succeeded so wonderfully with Lyndon would be equally effective with this fool, she began to talk about the upcoming social events in Butte. She saw his eyes grow glazed with faked interest as she spoke on and on about the imaginary functions she had attended in New Orleans. Laughter built in a bubble within her, but she did not let it explode to let him suspect she was playing with him.

Relief crossed his face when the door opened and she knew, without looking, it was Lyndon arriving. She surged to her feet and ran to him as if she always greeted him enthusiastically.

"Lyndon, see who is here! Mr. McSherry has come all the way from Butte and Mr. Clark, who wants to be sure Mr. Daly does nothing to cheat you. Isn't it kind of Mr. Clark to care so much about us?" When she saw Lyndon's eyes narrow at the implicit insult in Clark's patronizing attitude, she knew she had prejudiced him against McSherry before they met.

"McSherry," he said shortly, "I don't do business in my home."

The lawyer tried to keep from glaring at the pretty woman whose naive comments might destroy all he had intended to do. "Excuse me, Mr. Flynn. I thought you might not want my visit to be common knowledge ... under the circumstances."

"My people think and say only what I allow them to!"

McSherry wanted to fix the damage his own words were creating. Picking up his case, he said, "Mr. Flynn, if you would look at these papers from Mr. Clark, you might—"

"I told you I do not do business in my home."

Katie decided the situation had deteriorated enough not to need her assistance any longer. Putting her hand on Lyndon's sleeve dusty with dirt from the mine, she hid her curiosity about why he would be in the shafts, where he seldom went. "Lyndon, if you will excuse me, I will let you gentlemen tend to matters that would only clutter my feminine head."

"Go ahead, my dear," he urged, missing her sarcasm. He was too intent on subduing this whippersnapper that Clark had inflicted on him.

Just outside the room, she paused and heard Lyndon say, "And don't think I won't take this up with Clark when I go to Butte next week. Tell him I will see him on Tuesday afternoon. Do you understand?"

Instead of returning to her housewifely tasks as Lyndon expected, Katie seized her cloak, whipped it over her shoulders, and ran from the house to the stable. A quick order had the buggy readied for her. Within minutes, she was driving through the spitting snow down the hill toward the village.

She reined in the horse in front of the sheriff's office. Easily she leapt from the vehicle and tied the reins to a bar in front of the boardwalk. Her smile blossomed forth as she went into the dusty, nearly empty room.

Jonah turned from the board where he was hanging a new "Wanted" poster. His grin wider than her happy expression twisted her heart into a fierce rhythm. Her gaze traced his lips as she yearned to feel them on hers, in the unfettered passion she had discovered in his arms.

"Is something important happening or is this purely a social visit?" He leaned on the desk as he leered at her until she laughed. "Can I say I hope it is the latter?"

"Then you will be disappointed, I'm afraid." As fast as she could speak the words, she told the exciting news of the visitor at the house on the hill.

Jonah's lackadaisical attitude disappeared instantly. "Clark this time?"

"Yes, and, Jonah, Lyndon is much more willing to listen. He made an appointment to meet with Mr. Clark when we go to Butte next week."

He came around his desk to regard her with an expression she could not decipher. "You didn't mention that you were going to Butte, Katie."

"With all that has been happening, it must have slipped my mind." She shrugged as she untied the ribbons of her hat. "It isn't that important. Lyndon wants to buy me some clothes unavailable in Copper Peak."

"What a nice father you have!" he said with an abruptly cruel snicker. "No wonder you don't want to risk his displeasure by admitting you might care for his lowly sheriff. Then 'Daddy' might not buy you these expensive gifts."

Her face displayed her confusion. Watching him as he paced like a trapped mountain lion across the room, she asked, "Jonah, what is wrong with you? I thought you would want to hear about McSherry right away."

"I did."

"Then why are you angry with me?" she asked reasonably. This sudden transformation from the charming man who had teased her when she entered his office was too strange. So many times they had exchanged nasty retorts, but this astounding bitterness she could not understand. "I have not said anything to anyone about our relationship. From the beginning you told me to act like Lyndon's daughter. I am, but that doesn't satisfy you. What do you want of me?"

"Nothing! Go home to 'Daddy,' honey. I am sure you will have no trouble convincing him to give you anything you want."

Shock did not silence her. It vented the frustration she had stored within her since the beginning of this fiasco. "I think I finally understand you. You hate the fact that Lyndon isn't the beast you envisioned him to be, don't you? You set me up in his house, hoping he would abuse

297

me, so you could feel justified to do whatever you have planned." She settled her bonnet back on her head and hastily retied the ribbons. "Well, I'm sorry to inform you, Sheriff Bancroft, that Lyndon had been nothing but kindness to me, treating me only as a father should treat his daughter. If that sticks in your craw, don't come cawing like a broken-winged crow to me!"

He halted her before she could open the door. "Where in hell do you think you are going?"

"Home! Like you told me. Aren't I always a good little girl and do exactly as you tell me?"

With a snort, he pushed her back into the room. "Honey, you have never listened to an order in your life. If you think I'm going to let you go back to Flynn and betray all we have worked for, you are as crazy as you are acting."

Pointing to the cell, she said quietly, "Open it then, and put me in, for that's what you want, isn't it? The fact I have been used well infuriates you. So why don't you treat me horrendously as you usually do?"

"Horrendous? You call this horrendous?" He halted her gasp by seizing her mouth with his. With the enticing pressure of his lips, he sought to seduce her into submission. When she turned her head away from him, he heard her whisper, "Don't, Jonah."

"Don't? You don't want me to kiss you?"

Pain creased her forehead as she gazed up at him and the rage she could not comprehend. "Just don't use something incredibly sweet as a weapon against me. If you were not so bull-headed, you would know I have no intentions of betraying you. I want my brother to live." Her eyes widened when he showed his surprise at her words. "Have you forgotten about Ethan? Jonah, he hasn't been—?"

He shook his head, wondering how he could betray himself more readily than he accused her of doing. Releasing her, he went to his desk and stared at the posters hanging on the wall. "No, baby brother has not been hanged. When are you leaving for Butte?"

"The beginning of next week."

"I will see you when you get back so we can make our plans for the trip in for the Copper Kings' ball."

Katie hesitated at the door, wanting to say something, but unsure what. Inside she knew what she wanted. She had come here eager to enjoy the enticing delights of his lips, but all they had offered her was heated words of anger. Now she felt bereft, but she would not beg him to kiss her.

"All right. I will send you a message when we return."

"Do that."

The closing of the heavy door behind her clanged like a prison door in her heart. She was the one imprisoned in a love she could not offer to a man she could not understand. Just when she began to think he might want more than just her body next to him in his bed, he showed her the truth.

She must forget about loving Jonah Bancroft. She just wished she knew how to accomplish such a hopeless task.

CHAPTER FIFTEEN

The train pulled out of the station, heading east toward Butte. Its whistle screeched a farewell to Copper Peak and cut into Katie's heart as she sat in a seat near the window. She listened to Lyndon's grumbling about the inadequacies of a company that could not run its trains on time, but her eyes remained on the false fronts of the town.

She had not guessed how long the days could be when she was unable to see Jonah. During the days when she had feared he was dying somewhere, that fear helped her cope with the slow passage of time. It was so different when she knew he was working in his spartan office in town while she waited alone on the hill.

When she had told him she did not understand what he wanted, that was the truth. Over and over she reviewed the conversation in her mind, but she never discovered exactly what she had said to trigger his rage. Slowly she had to admit the change had come before then. It had come the day he returned to Copper Peak after Haggerty died, after she refused to become his lover.

She answered Lyndon absently as she wondered why she had passed up her chance for a brief happiness. The rapture she savored in Jonah's arms had no comparison, for it released her soul to soar into his as they melded their hearts together in joy. He had chosen to woo her sweetly, for he could have forced her to be his any of the nights she slept alone in his bed.

The steady clack-clack of the wheels on the rails and the rhythm of the train offered her no comfort. Clutching her bag, she wondered if she should ask Lyndon to get her cloak for her. The flimsy silk of her fancy gown could not keep out the cold that had settled on the valley in the past week. As she rubbed her bare forearms, the gold lace draped over her fingers.

"Nice to have you aboard today, Mr. Flynn, Miss St. Pierre."

Katie stared at Lenny as he handed Lyndon back their tickets. He winked at her while Lyndon was putting the stubs back in his wallet. It continued to amaze her how these men delighted in their game. If they were found out, they would die as horribly as Eli had, as quickly as Jimmy had before her eyes. Their revenge seemed more important to them than their lives. She could not understand that obsession.

As the train climbed slowly along the mountain trails before dipping into the cuts blasted through the rock, she leaned back in her seat and closed her eyes. When she felt a hand on her shoulder, she looked up to see Lyndon regarding her with the concern that gradually was overshadowing his baser emotions.

"My dear, are you feeling poorly?"

"I'm fine," she said with a weak smile. "I did not sleep well last night." *Or the night before that*, she added silently. Since she had feared Jonah was dead, she could not remember sleeping a full night. Instead she rose to pace the floor or stare sightlessly out the windows.

"Don't be too excited about Butte." He kissed her cheek lightly. "It will seem very primitive compared to New Orleans, but I think you will enjoy your time there while I tend to business."

She let him describe the business district of Butte to her and pretended she had never been there. Occasionally, Eli had taken them into the big city to enjoy a stage show or to look at the goods in the shop windows. Then, she could not have imagined that she would someday go to those same stores to choose whatever she wanted.

Swallowing a sob, she looked at the passing scenery spotted by the snowflakes that had been falling since before dawn and wished she had never met Jonah Bancroft. Then she would not have to suffer this unfamiliar insecurity. Until he had forced her to live the life of a stranger, she had always known what to do. That was no longer true.

Sorrow and fatigue lulled her to the lullaby of the train. Her eyelids became heavy, and she had to struggle harder each time to open them.

Seduced by sweet dreams, she let sleep take her far from the pain of reality.

She had no idea how long she had been asleep when a sound jolted her awake. A second blast of the whistle shrieked from the engine through the train. Katie tensed instantly as she tried to see why the conductor was racing toward a woman who sat with her children. This was not the sound the steam engine had made when they pulled into a station.

Lenny shouted, "Hold on, everyone! Emergency stop!" The words were barely out of his mouth when the train jolted to a halt.

Only Lyndon's arms around her kept Katie from striking the seat in front of her. She banged her head against the window hard enough to create stars in her eyes. Pressing her hand on her forehead, she leaned against his shoulder. His awkward patting made her head spin faster, but she said nothing.

Looking at her with concern, Lyndon ignored the complaints of the other passengers as he signaled to the conductor, who somehow had managed to stay on his feet and keep the youngsters from panicking. "What in hell is going on?"

"My guess is something's on the track," Lenny answered as all the passengers waited fearfully for his verdict. They did not want to be stranded along a lonesome stretch of track in the increasing storm. He smiled coldly as he saw Miss St. Pierre regard him with wide-eyed shock and knew she understood the situation better than any of the other passengers. "What, I won't know until I check."

"Then check, man!"

Katie blinked as she watched the conductor scurry away. Something on the track. So often the Forrester gang had used that technique to halt a train. She had never considered the possibility of hurting people aboard, for they always built a bonfire to alert the engineer to the danger in time to halt the train without derailing it.

Outside the car, the treetops rocked with the power of the storm, which had become a blizzard. She could not see much farther than the gravel along the tracks. This deserted region was the perfect location for a robbery. Wrapping her arms around herself, she shivered at the thought of meeting the gang that had dynamited the mail car to steal the previous payroll sent into Copper Peak. Perhaps one of the passengers had brought a fortune along to take East after a big strike. Such information always reached ears eager for it.

Shadows amid the trees told her what she feared was happening. It was ludicrous for her to be sitting on a train being robbed. Her fingers itched for a gun to protect herself and the other passengers, but she knew if she reached for the rifle over the door, she would betray herself to Lyndon sitting beside her.

When she saw Lenny reaching for the weapon, she relaxed somewhat. He must be skilled with a rifle if Jonah had chosen him to be a member of his gang. On the small chance the bandits came into this passenger car, he would halt them immediately.

"Sit quietly," the conductor urged. "I'm going

to check the next car forward to be sure everyone there is safe." When a large man demanded
that he not leave them defenseless, he smiled
tightly. "I will be back in a few minutes. They
aren't interested in you, mister, unless you have
gold lining your long underwear."

A ripple of nervous laughter spread through
the car, but halted as the door closed behind
him. Katie had not listened to the exchange.
Her eyes remained on the horses intermittently
visible between surges of the snow. If the gun-
men did not leave soon, it might mean trouble
for the passengers. Normally it took no more
than a few minutes to take the money sack from
the mail car and ride into the concealing trees.

"Don't be frightened, Katie," Lyndon urged,
reading her quiet appraisal as fear.

She turned on the seat and smiled at him.
"I'm not afraid. Like the conductor said, they
aren't interested in anything except whatever
gold the train might be carrying. I—"

Her words halted as a scream sounded from
the rear seats. She half rose in shock as the door
at the back of the car burst open. Two men with
bandanas concealing their faces strode in to stare
at the terrified passengers one by one. Lyndon's
hand on her arm reminded her of the ridicu-
lousness of the situation. She was on the wrong
side of the gun.

"Sit," he ordered silently. "Don't draw attention to yourself."

"Which one of you overstuffed pigs is Lyndon
Flynn?" called the taller man.

"Oh!" she gasped at the shout. She put her

hand over her mouth to hide her grin, but Lyndon was intent on glaring at the robbers. The voice had told her what she had thought was too absurd to be possible. The man hiding his features behind the navy bandana was Jonah Bancroft.

He did not look at her, and she was not surprised. In this uneasy situation, he could not be thinking about his single ally. Jonah dared much to confront his nemesis this way. After his months as the lawman in Copper Peak, it was very likely that Lyndon had come to recognize his sheriff's voice, which ordered again, "Lyndon Flynn, I know you are here! Stand up so I can see your ugly face!"

"I am Lyndon Flynn." He rose with the courage that had enabled him to fight his way from a poor laborer to the owner of much of this section of Montana. "Why don't you show you have some intelligence and get out of here before the conductor comes back?"

"We have business to discuss." The handkerchief fluttered with every word.

Katie could not help being fascinated by the resurrection of Jonah as a thief. When she had met him in this persona before, they had been competitors, and she had not been able to appreciate his calm control of the circumstances. If he had been prone to panic, they both might have died the first time they tried to rob the same train.

His gaze settled on her. Her temptation to smile faded as she met his eyes as cold as the gun in his hand. The weapon pointed unerringly at her. She feared he actually might pull the trigger. He had shot her once.

Her throat grew tight as she tried to breathe. In her pampered life as Lyndon Flynn's daughter, she had forgotten the compulsions that drove desperate people to robbery and murder. After her argument with Jonah, he might have decided she no longer was valuable to abet him in his revenge. Her heart halted for a painful second as she recalled him accusing her of betraying him. She wondered if this was the way he planned to rid himself of Flynn and her in one masterful stroke.

"Who is she?" he demanded with convincing ignorance of her identity. "Your mistress?"

"Sir, you insult my daughter with your tasteless allegations." Lyndon's broad hand nearly covered her shoulders shaking with astonishing fear.

"Your daughter? Well, this is a charming turn of events." Katie could not see if he was smiling or simply enjoying sarcasm as he grasped her arm and jerked her to her feet. When Lyndon started to step forward to help his daughter, the pistol in Jonah's hand pressed to the brim of Katie's bonnet. The bulbous man halted in midstep. As if this were nothing more than a Sunday call, Jonah asked pleasantly, "How are you, Miss Flynn?"

"Miss St. Pierre," she corrected tightly. She wished he would give her some clue as to what he intended with this prank. When she spoke again, she heard the passengers frozen to their seats gasp at her audacity. "Will you release me, sir, before someone does something stupid?"

The frosty laugh she recalled from the beginning of their relationship augmented her terror. This was not the tender Jonah who had come to visit her and take her for rides in his buggy. She wondered if she knew the real Jonah Bancroft. Of one thing she was sure. If she betrayed his identity to Lyndon, she would die before she could finish speaking.

She breathed a sigh of relief when he lowered the gun from her temple. His cohort, whom she guessed was Duncan, moved forward as Jonah placed his weapon in his holster. The telegraph operator pressed one of his guns painfully into her breastbone while keeping the other pointed directly at Lyndon.

"Anyone moves, and this lady dies." No one murmured a sound, but everyone guessed he would do as he threatened.

Katie glanced at Jonah when he released her. She was backed up against the side of a seat. Duncan's sparkling eyes dared her to move and give him the chance he wished for to kill her. She watched as Jonah pulled a second bandana from his pocket.

"Cooperate, Miss St. Pierre, and I will let you live a while longer."

"What—?" Her voice escalated into a surprised scream of outrage as he tied the bandana around her head as a gag. With the same ease, he wrenched her wrists behind her and bound her hands. Each time Lyndon opened his mouth to protest, the second criminal pulled back on the hammer of his pistol held against the woman.

Katie's fear became rage that Jonah would

treat her so. If he wanted to hurt Lyndon, he did not need to be this cruel to her as well. When he dragged her back against him, she tried to twist out of his grasp, but his arm became a clamp around her middle. Fury sparked in her dark eyes when he turned to her supposed father again.

"Mr. Flynn, this train is too crowded to discuss the delicate business we have to deal with. I think we shall adjourn this meeting to another time and place. To insure your presence and cooperation, we will return Miss St. Pierre to you then." Even his mask could not hide the sun-darkened skin crinkling around his eyes as he grinned. "We will return her to you when you have met the requirements you'll be informed about shortly."

"No!" cried the distraught man as the thief made it clear he was taking Katie with him. Visions of the abuse his beautiful daughter would suffer raced through his head. Involuntarily he remembered her mother's screams the first night he forced her into his bed. As never before, he had sympathy for Eugenie whom he had taught through harsh lessons to be obedient. He did not want his precious child to be used in the same way. "Don't take Katie! I'll do as you wish if you leave her here."

"But don't you see?" taunted Jonah. "You'll do as I wish because I have her." He picked her up easily and, with a flurry of petticoats, tossed her over his shoulder. His arms clamped her thrashing legs to his chest. "You will do as I wish, and so, Mr. Flynn, will she."

Lyndon grasped the back of a seat. His ruddy

face became devoid of all color. Helplessly he watched as his daughter's bold abductor walked past his cohort, who still pointed two guns at him. He called his daughter's name in a broken voice, but no one heeded him as she was borne out of the car.

Struggling to escape, Katie gasped as the full strength of the storm struck her face and sliced its snowy fingers through her gown. When she felt Jonah catch his balance on the slippery gravel of the roadbed, she halted her efforts to convince him to release her. If he fell on this ice, she would be hurt. At the moment, she cared little if he was injured.

She gasped as the air in her lungs was knocked out when he flung her face down across the saddle. The leather beneath her creaked as he put his foot in the stirrup to swing up behind her. He lifted her like a sack of flour across his knees and shouted an order to his horse.

The crack of a rifle shot sounded behind him, but the bullet did not come near them. She closed her eyes as she wondered if it was Lenny signaling them to flee. No other shots resounded as they crashed through the thick underbrush leading up the mountainside. She winced as a shrub nearly hit her nose.

Jonah jerked her upright so she sat on his knees. His eyes above the kerchief broadcast his amusement with the degradation he had inflicted on her. Holding her close so his cloak blew over her to protect her from some of the wind, he steered his horse carefully through the increasing snow.

"This is far enough!" he called to his friends.

They drew their horses closer so they would not have to shout over the screech of the banshees riding the storm wind. As they pulled their masks down over their chins, she saw all of them grinning with triumph.

"We did it!" shouted Isler. His meek self had been left behind with his accounting books at the mine office. Glitters of vicious satisfaction glowed in his eyes. "That bastard will do whatever you want now, Jonah."

"I told you she could help us bring him to his knees!"

Another round of laughter sent a renewed explosion of panic through her. Her gaze went from one face to the next, but each one told her what she had guessed on the train. The purpose she was to serve for Jonah and his friends had come to an end, and she was no longer necessary to them.

Jonah glanced down at her, and his smile broadened, but she felt no solace. She wanted to demand that he tell her what he planned, but nothing came from her lips except an angry mumble which elicited more guffaws from the men.

"You know what you must do," Jonah said to his allies.

"And her?"

"I'll take care of her. Do you want to watch?"

Wide brown eyes could not hide her terror when he smiled at her. His fingers brushed her side as he reached for something at his hip. She hated him for making her cower away from him as he lifted his gun from the holster.

311

Laughter lightened his threat as he said calmly, "I don't intend to shoot you, honey. Not yet, anyhow."

Katie could not believe her eyes as Jonah raised his pistol by the barrel high in the air. She still did not think he would hurt her even as he brought it down on her skull. Her final thought as she lost consciousness was of betrayal.

A moan cut through her agony. Katie did not realize it was her own voice that ached so fiercely in her skull. Her eyes burst open. Jonah had kidnapped her from the train. Comprehension came quickly. His plot had worked exactly as he wished. He had wanted her to insinuate herself into Lyndon Flynn's life, which she had done with more success than she believed possible. Then to repay the man for past crimes, he stole the one thing Flynn valued more than his copper mines.

The only question remaining was what Jonah intended to do with her now. She had served her purpose. He had made it clear he did not keep useless things around to bog him down on his path to vengeance.

Escape was her only option. When she tried to sit, she was not surprised to find her wrists tied to the bed posts. The ropes had been rigged so she could move slightly, but could not reach the knots to release herself.

She struggled upright and stared at her prison. Nothing distinguished the one-room cabin from any of the dozens dotting the countryside. Log walls were broken only by a door, for the luxury of a window was not important to men more interested in looking at sparkles of gold or silver than at the towering mountains surrounding them.

A fireplace offered a warmth that made the blankets over her stifling. She started to kick them off, then realized how high her skirts had risen along her legs. Modesty seemed more important to her than comfort, especially under these circumstances when she had no idea if she would live long enough to worry about the perspiration dampening the silk of her gown.

Other than the bed where she had been left, a single bench pushed under a shelf was the only furniture in the room. A rag rug was a surprising splash of color on the wood slab floor. She jerked her eyes from its brilliant reds and blues to look inward for the strength she would need for her coming ordeal. If she had some clue as to what Jonah intended to do with her, she would feel more competent to deal with it.

She moaned again as she moved her head too rapidly. Even without touching the tender spot, she guessed that a large lump marked the spot where Jonah's pistol had struck her. Even in retrospect, she could not believe he would hurt her so heartlessly. Just days ago, he had held her in his arms and let her sample the delight he could create with his mouth sliding along her bare skin.

The stamping of boots beyond the walls broke into the seductive thoughts that lured her into forgiving him for his abuse. She tensed on the bed, although she knew how hopeless her dreams of fleeing were when she was tied so securely to the headboard.

When the door opened, Katie saw it was still snowing. She had expected to watch this storm from the luxury of a Butte hotel.

She said nothing as she watched Jonah walk in with an armful of wood. He placed it on the floor close to the stove so the snow would melt off it. Casually he slipped his coat off and hung it on the back of a door latch. He sat on the bench to pull off his ice-frosted boots. Only when that was done did he look at her.

"So you are awake, K.T.?"

Her sharp answer died unspoken when he used the name she had not heard in so long.

"It's not very comfortable to be tied up like this, sheriff." She made no reaction to his surprise at what she called him. If he had not intended to return to the enmity between them at the beginning of their uneven relationship, he would have continued to call her "Katie." Her voice remained serene as she asked, "Where are your friends?"

"Back in Copper Peak." He folded his hands on his knees and leaned forward. Snow melted from his hair and dripped in large drops from his mustache and eyebrows. "They did not want to be marooned up here in the snow. Wives and children might be made to suffer if my friends were inexcusably absent in the aftermath of this afternoon's activities."

"And you?"

He smiled. "Didn't you hear, honey? I'm on my way to Billings to contact the U.S. Marshall about the trouble at the mine."

"And me?"

"What about you?"

The tip of her tongue dampened her arid lips. He was the cold man she had first met. In no way would he help her. She would be forced to belittle herself before him to gain the information she needed. Despite her efforts, her voice trembled when she spoke. "What are you going to do with me, sheriff?"

"Call me by my name, and I might tell you."

"Jonah, no games," she begged. Her fear emerged from her plea.

He rose to sit on the edge of the bed. Gently he untied the knotted ribbons of her ruined bonnet and tossed it on the floor. Her thick hair cascaded around his hand as he tilted her head. Slowly, so slowly she wondered if he wanted to continue to torment her, his lips lowered to hers. Their light caress urged her to lift her hands to clasp behind his neck. She groaned against his mouth when she tried to move them, and pain throbbed from her shoulders throughout her whole body.

Reaching for the knife he wore on his gunbelt, he said with obvious regret, "You do look incredibly desirable bound to the bed like this, Karleen Tamara Forrester. Like something out of an adventure story."

"You wouldn't think that if your hands hurt as mine do!"

As he sliced through the ropes, she could not be unaware of his form so close to hers. The odor of cold pine had accompanied him into the cabin, but it was overpowered by the virile musk

315

of his body brushing hers as he worked to cut her bonds. She rubbed her scorched wrists to relieve the pain of the rope burn.

"Thank you!" she snapped when he placed his knife back on his belt. Her eyes remained on his face, but she was aware of him undoing the heavy leather band. When he leaned forward to place it on the floor, she noted exactly where he placed it.

"Such gratitude!" He chuckled as he moved closer to her. "When a beautiful maiden is rescued from danger, she is supposed to reward her champion with a kiss."

"But you are the villain as well as the hero." She let him recline her back into the pillows as she brazenly taunted him. He would expect nothing else from her, and she must not make him suspicious enough to guess the thoughts in her head.

He smiled. "Then I should let you slap my face before you kiss me. Would that satisfy you?"

"Maybe."

With another laugh, he pressed her into the mattress. Light, teasing kisses along her face urged Katie to forget what she had planned, but she refused to let him continue to use her until he must kill her. As his lips roved along her neck, daring her to melt into the flame of desire, she put one arm around his shoulders. The other reached toward the floor.

Carefully, so slowly she feared he would guess why she tensed beneath him, she withdrew the pistol from his holster. Turning it in her hand so she held the barrel, she used the butt to push the belt under the bed where it could not be grabbed quickly.

"Oh, Jonah," she murmured to keep his attention on her lips and not on the hand steadily lifting the gun from the floor. "That feels so wonderful."

He chuckled, the victorious sound returning to his voice. Smoothing her damp hair back from her forehead, he gazed down into her glistening eyes. "You are the one who is—" His smile faded as he felt the sharp tip of his gun barrel against the back of his ear.

"Up!" she ordered. "Let me up!"

"Katie, we have been through this too many times. That gun is loaded." Even as he was protesting, he obeyed her commands. He could see the anger she had hidden blossom forth to show him how he had broken her heart by stealing her from the train.

"So was the one you pressed to my head earlier."

He shook his head as she slid off the bed to stand in her stocking feet on the cold floor. Both of them ignored her dress slippers sitting near the footboard. "Honey, I would not have risked killing you."

"And Duncan?"

"I think . . ."

She scowled. "Oh, he was hoping I would give him a reason to pull that trigger. I could see that in his eyes." She used both hands to hold the gun steady as she backed away from him. Wisely he did not move. He simply watched as she circled toward the door. "I know why you

317

did this. You wanted to give something to Lyndon that he could care about, so you could steal it from him. You—"

He interrupted sharply. "That is not why I took you off the train."

"Just shut up!" she cried. "I don't want to hear your lies. I am not going to waste my time while the snow piles up on the mountainsides. Good-bye, Sheriff Bancroft."

"You aren't leaving, K.T."

"I am! D-dammit!" She stuttered on the word she had not said in so long. More vigorously she repeated it with a satisfied smile. "Dammit, Jonah Bancroft, you aren't going to tell me what to do any longer. You have had your revenge. I'm leaving."

Rising, he took a step toward her. He shook his head. "No, honey, you aren't leaving. You are staying with me since you want to as much as I do."

"How in hell do you know what I want? You never cared how I felt during this whole mess! Stay back!" The gun wobbled in her hands as she raised it to point at his chest. "You can't stop me. I can shoot you before you can get your other gun."

He lifted his hands in the air. "I have no intentions of drawing against you. I know you are the better shot." As he continued to close the distance between them, he added, "I know also that you are staying here."

"I will shoot you," she reiterated, but her voice quavered.

"Will you? Go ahead, if you wish. I cannot

halt you if you want to pull that trigger." He smiled with the coldness she wished was on her own face. "But before you kill me, you will hear why I took you off that train, K.T. It had nothing to do with Flynn. When I devised this plan, I figured it was easier to let you and my allies think exactly that. The truth is I brought you here so I could have you to myself." Pausing directly in front of her, he did not look at the gun pressed against the buttons in his shirt.

Katie looked up into his eyes and saw the truth in their azure depths. What else she discovered there frightened her more than anything in her life. She backed away from him, as she had vowed never to do before any man. When she bumped the uneven logs of the wall, she gasped harshly.

Her gaze followed his right hand as he held it up before her. Trembling fingers could barely lift the pistol as she placed it in his empty palm. She sagged against the wall when he took it and walked across the room to put it in his holster.

A gentle finger beneath her chin brought her jeweled gaze back to him. Through her tears, the lamplight gave his face a gleaming glow. She closed her eyes when he bent to place his lips against her damp skin.

"My dear . . . ?" He laughed lightly. "What do you prefer to be called tonight? K.T., Karleen, or Katie?" He framed her face with his hands and whispered, "Open your eyes."

She did as he ordered to discover his face mere inches from hers. As if it had a mind of its own, her hand rose to stroke the wind-scoured roughness of his cheek. He stepped closer to her until her body was sandwiched between the hard strength of his and the wall behind her.

"Jonah?"

He smiled. "So easy it is for you to choose what you wish to call me. I think I shall make it as easy on myself and call you 'my love.' " All humor left his face as his fingers entwined in her hair. "I love you, my love."

Her gasp was swallowed by his mouth over hers. He was not gentle as he explored the softness of her lips with his own. Insistent, demanding as much pleasure as he gave her, he enticed her into the sweet madness. When her hands slid along his neck to the breadth of his shoulders, his arms swept behind her to press her more tightly to him.

All thoughts of escape vanished as she surrendered herself to this sweet captivity which offered her more freedom than she had ever known. Seeking deep in her mouth, his tongue contained the heat of velvet left on a sunlit stone. It caressed hers and released the lightning-fast electricity coursing along her.

Stepping away from her, he whispered, "Will you stay with me tonight, my love?"

"Yes." She did not add that she was his for as long as he wanted her. No more would she think of the differences that had brought them together to enjoy this love. Nothing mattered but the glow in his eyes, urging her to forget everything except the promise of rapture.

With her hand in his, he led her the few steps from the door to the rumpled bed. He paused next to it and reached for the hooks along the back of her dress. As he bent to undo them, he kissed her on the forehead. She closed her eyes to delight in the touch of his lips on her cheeks and along the slant of her nose. A soft smile parted her lips as he kissed both corners.

So bemused was she by his playful antics that she gasped as he pushed her loosened dress from her shoulders. A blush brightened her cheeks when he released the silk to let it whoosh softly to the floor. With a flourish and an exultant laugh worthy of the rogue he portrayed so well, he untied the petticoats thickening her slender waist. The cotton skirts dropped into the drift of her dress.

He groaned with unsated desire and tugged her close to the hard line of his body. Kisses seared her skin with their fierce heat and melded their mouths together as she twisted her fingers into the pelt of his auburn hair. The hunter had trapped his prey in a snare of sensuous, sinuous love.

When she moaned against his mouth as she squirmed against him, he held her so tight she had to strain to breathe. "No!" she gasped as she wrenched her lips away.

"Katie?"

With a laugh, she pulled away and rubbed her skin marked in pink. At his confused expression, she laughed with a gentleness that sank through his skin to stoke the escalating craving to touch her, to kiss her, to feel the silken texture of her body all around him.

"I don't think it's meant you should wear that

when you hold a woman dressed only in her chemise, sheriff." She pointed at his tin star.

Easily he slipped his weskit off and let it fall unnoticed to lie atop her discarded clothes. When he felt her unbuttoning his shirt, he forced himself to let her finish before he held her as he wanted. Her slim fingers slid along his bared chest, touching him as lightly and as fleetingly as a butterfly. A groan he could not restrain escaped from his lips.

When he stroked her hair tumbling in wild abandon along her shoulders, she slid her arms beneath the opened shirt to touch the sleekness of the skin covering the smooth muscles along his back. As he brought her close to him again, she gasped at the warmth of his chest against her. The pulse of his heart ruled her as his lips tasted hers once more. She did not let his mouth leave hers as he bent to put his arm under her knees. Easily he lifted her into his arms. He placed her in the midst of the crumpled blankets.

When he felt her shiver, he teased, "Cold?"

"No."

"Scared?"

"Should I be?" she retorted with typical outspokenness.

Shaking his head, he loosened the laces on the front of her chemise. His voice was hushed as he pulled aside the silk to reveal what his eyes had yearned to see. "No, honey, you have no reason to be scared unless you are afraid to know the happiness only you and I can share."

He leaned over her to taste the succulent skin bared before his eyes. She wondered how she could survive the strength of the desire building to a detonation within her as she felt his body pressing her deeper into the embrace of the mattress. When the tip of his tongue moistened the downy surface of her breast in a circular path, she breathed his name with a craving she could not deny.

"Not yet," he murmured against her as his mouth created a spiral across the flat plane of her abdomen.

"What?" she whispered. Lost in the ecstasy of his touch while he drew off the last of her underclothes to leave her open to his heated gaze, she could not be aware of such mundane things as words. The sound of her accelerated heartbeat careened through her ears, urging her to move to its tempo.

"Want me as you have wanted nothing else in your life, my love. Want me as I want you."

She opened her eyes to look about herself in puzzlement when he moved away from her. The smile returned to her eyes as she discovered him standing by the side of the bed. He pulled off his boots before unbuttoning his denims. Rising to her knees, she put her hands on the belt loops and drew the trousers down the lithe line of his legs. Her skin rubbed against his as she slid along him in an unhurried, luxurious caress. He kicked the denims aside and, with a growl, pushed her back into the pillows.

Laughing, she caught at his arms to pull him down over her. The amusement in her eyes transformed abruptly to a more potent emotion as she felt the naked warmth of his body over hers.

Her dark eyes closed when his mouth took hers to lead her on the enchanting path to ecstasy.

She faded into a happiness so intense it became an agony of its own. Wanting the flicks of his tongue against her never to stop, she feared she would go insane with the sensations ravishing her. The soft cry of his name matched the melting within her as he sampled the source of the pulse pounding through her. Her body swayed with a tempo she could not control.

Her fingers brought his mouth back to hers. She gasped deep into it when he found a welcome far in the warmth of her body. The intoxicating bliss she had felt was overwhelmed by the surges of savage sweetness roiling in her body moving in perfect rhythm with his.

When he whispered her name against her ear, she succumbed to the undeniable might of her love for him. In that idyllic moment, she gave up her oneness to be a part of him for all of eternity. She released her soul to gain a freedom, an exhilaration, an unnamed need to find satiation for this thirst. She drowned in a mountain lake of pleasure, sinking deep to float in the arms of the man she loved before the eruption of rapture lifted them together far beyond the silvery peaks to paradise where their love detonated into ecstasy.

The screech of the wind brought Katie back from her soaring journey among the clouds. She became aware of the lumpy mattress beneath her. Moments before, it had been as soft as the finest eiderdown blowing on the breeze.

Opening her eyes, she met Jonah's gaze regarding her with a warmth she viewed so seldom in his eyes. She brushed the recalcitrant curl from the middle of his forehead. Softly she said, "I didn't tell you that I love you, too."

"Yes, you did, my love." His finger traced her lips. "You told me here." Picking up her hand, he pressed the palm to his mouth. "You told me with these." His irreverent grin returned to his lips as he stroked the curves of her side. "You told me with all parts of your lovely body. Yet I must admit I enjoy the sound of those words on your lips."

"I want you to call me Katie."

"What?" he asked, puzzled at the sudden change of subject.

She smiled a she rested her face on the furred texture of his chest. "I want you to call me Katie. I have enjoyed being a lady again, and you have taught me how wonderful it is to be a woman in your arms."

Stroking the silken strands of her hair stretching past her waist, he mused, "Who would have thought a bungled robbery would bring you to me, Katie?" He tipped her chin up so he could see her bright eyes as he continued, "And to think I was angry because I thought I had lost out on a fortune that night. Little did I know that my good fortune was just beginning."

"Obviously!" The tartness had returned to her voice. "You won when you wagered with Lyndon about taking me to the Copper Kings' ball."

He laughed as he rolled her onto her back, so he could lean over her. "Tonight I will collect my prize."

"You didn't wager—"

His fingertip traced the lines of shock creasing her forehead. "Of course not, my love. I would not risk losing the one thing I want for my own more than anything else in the world." A wicked twinkle came into his eyes as his mustache tipped in a smile that warned her of the mighty emotions boiling within him, demanding satisfaction. "And what I want is you, Katie, my love."

Instead of teasing him in return, she whispered softly, "I'm yours, Jonah." Nothing more did she have a chance to say as he stripped all sense from her with his fiery kisses.

CHAPTER SIXTEEN

Katie nestled into the warmth of the bed. Happiness created a gentle glow around her. She did not question the source of this quiet joy of release from the shackles of fear and falsehoods. Lying in the easy caress of the blankets, she closed her eyes and willed the dream never to end.

"I know you are awake," came a husky voice not far from her ear.

At the rumble of laughter, she convinced one eye to open and peer over the mound of blankets. A smile brightened her face as she saw Jonah sitting on the edge of her nest. She settled more comfortably into the bed so she could watch for his next move, but inherent distrust ruled her no longer. Instead of tensing fearfully as she prepared for his latest prank, she felt a surge of the newfound love that had welcomed her so sweetly to paradise during the night.

"Good morning, Jonah," she whispered, not daring to speak louder. If this rapture vanished, she was not sure she could find such perfection again.

"Good morning to you, my love." He stroked the tangle of dark curls flowing across the pillows and recalled the luscious sensation of her hair teasing his bare skin. Bending forward, he tasted the welcome of her lips still soft from his rapid massage of kisses during the love-filled hours before the sun rose.

"What smells so good?"

"Breakfast. Are you hungry?"

"Ravenous!" she announced. She started to sit, then recalled she wore nothing beneath the blankets.

His finger reached over the edge of the covers she held close to her and drew them away. In the throaty tone of the passion which had returned more insistent each time they sated it during the night, he whispered, "Me too, but I want you, my love."

"Jonah!"

Lifting her hands to the buttons of his shirt cold from his trip out into the snow for wood, he let his fingers run along her warm skin. She raised her arms to enfold him once more in the love she craved as much as he did. She wanted the kisses, the touching, the ecstasy, and the sweet embers of love burning in the afterglow of their love.

Even hours later, it was not easy to leave the cocoon beneath the covers. Jonah laughed when he turned from the fireplace. He shoved a log

328

into the red heat of the fire before coming to her, rocking from one bare foot to the other as she fought the cold with the blanket around her.

"Is something wrong, Katie?" he teased.

"Where did you put my clothes? You can't expect me to stay like this all the time."

He smoothed her hair back from her face and tilted her mouth under his. The still-rapid pulse of her heart could be felt through the thin quilt. The fiery emotions seldom lying quiescent within her had exploded to bathe him in glorious rapture when he held her in his arms and learned the most intimate secrets of her slender body.

"My love," he murmured as he raised his lips, "I would love to keep you like this all the time. Ready and eager for my love." When she breathed a soft agreement to his invitation, he thought of how he would love her again and again before the night draped them in the velvet darkness of starglow.

"I'm cold, Jonah." She laughed when she stepped away from him. "Where are my clothes? I don't see them anywhere."

He shrugged and sat on the bed. "No clothes? That's amazing, honey. Maybe you should get back in bed and warm up."

"Jonah!" Exasperation raised her voice as she regarded him with frustration.

Chuckling, he rose and went to his saddlebags. He withdrew some clothes and tossed them to her. She lifted the shirt to find it was long enough to drop to her thighs. Holding up a wool sock, she wrinkled her nose in disgust. Even when she had worn an outfit much like this one, she had chosen cotton stockings to cover her legs. She hated the scratchy heat of wool.

She looked across the room at him and saw his challenging expression. Although he must know exactly where her dress was, he had no intention of returning it to her. Suddenly she did not care. She was not Lyndon Flynn's pampered daughter this morning. Instead she had become the woman she once had been, carefree, free-spirited, and eager for adventure.

Within minutes she had the long shirt covering her and sat to pull the socks over her feet. They rose nearly to her knees, leaving little skin visible between them and the tail of the cream-colored shirt. She twirled about the room on her toes. The socks caught the splinters in the rough floor and threatened to topple her, but she simply laughed.

Jonah held out a cup of coffee to her. "You look simply wonderful, Katie."

"Don't I, though?" she retorted in the same, light tone. The truth was she felt like dancing.

The coffee steamed in her face, and she drank it greedily. Until she tasted its rich sweetness, she had not guessed how thirsty she was after all his kisses stole the breath from her throughout the night. She thanked him for the bread and eggs he fried quickly over the fire. While he dished out his own meal from the cast-iron pan, she sat on the bench and ate.

"Good?" he asked when he joined her.

"Umm," she mumbled through a mouthful of food. When he laughed with the easy amusement she had heard in his voice since he lured her into his arms last night, she looked up at his smile. "I am very, very hungry."

"You should be."

Despite her effort to keep her face as jesting as his, she blushed to a deep rose. His terse response concerned feelings too precious to be spoken of, even to the man who shared them. She kept her eyes on her plate as she said, "If you will recall, Jonah, I have had nothing to eat since yesterday at breakfast."

"I didn't mean to embarrass you."

"No?"

He could not halt his delight over her unswerving attempts to remain in control of every situation. "If you must know the truth, the answer is yes. I did mean to tease you. Eat up, and we will go out to see how much snow got dumped on us last night."

"We aren't going back to Copper Peak?" she blurted before she could halt the words.

"Do you want to go back?"

Katie regarded his guarded face and wondered how long it would be before they could trust each other totally. The weeks of suspicion could not be erased even by the sweet caresses that brought them a love they never expected. Even as she sat next to him, dressed in the too-large clothes, with her body longing for his touch, he could not believe she truly loved him.

"I never want to go back," she said with the honesty she so seldom displayed. Putting her dish on the bench next to her, she slid her hands along his arms. "I love you, Jonah Bancroft, and I don't want to shorten by one second the time we have here."

"I love you, too, honey." He kissed the tip of her upturned nose and winked broadly. "If you are done with your breakfast, why don't you finish dressing? You can't go out in that." He pointed a fork toward the door. "You can wear my other boots."

"You certainly were well prepared. Food, clothes, and this hidden bower."

He wrapped a long arm around her waist and pulled her against him. There was no humor in his voice as he said intensely, "When you want something as much and as long as I have wanted you, Katie, you make damn sure everything is perfect when your dream is within your grasp."

Overwhelmed by the emotion glowing in his eyes, she drew away from him and hurried to dress. So little she knew about Jonah Bancroft, but she loved him.

As she latched the boots around her ankles, she glanced at him slipping on his heavy coat. Jonah Bancroft, sheriff of Copper Peak, might love her, but she knew what the future would bring. There could be no permanent love for them, which made these stolen moments more precious.

No sign of her troubled feelings showed on her face when she placed her hand in the one he offered. She forced the dreary thoughts to the back of her head as she felt the cold rip her breath from her. Blinking in the brightness of the sunlight dripping through the sieve of the clouds, she gazed at the miniature mountains of snow obscuring the landscape.

With a laugh, he pulled her out into the drifts.

Katie pushed through the waist-high snow piled by the wind against the cabin wall. She squealed as the snow sprinkled over the top of her boots. Even with the too-long pants bunched into them, both of her feet could have fit into one boot. Taking his hand, she let him assist her across the open snowfield. When he paused, she looked at the magnificent scenery.

The sharp profiles of the mountains rose to their fluffy crowns of clouds. Above the treeline, only shadows on the snow defined the cliffs. Eye-smarting sunshine reflected off the white ground. Lower, the ponderosa pine carried their burden of heavy snow with dignity gained through the many winters they had struggled in this harsh climate. It was an awe-inspiring sight, but the beauty could not hide the dangers inherent in such a wild landscape.

"Right here," he said in answer to a question he had spoken only in his thoughts. He grinned as he looked down at her face barely visible between his old hat tied on with a bandana and a scarf pulled up to protect her from the cold. "Someday I'm going to build a house right here."

"I thought you might go back to New Orleans. You speak so fondly of the city."

He lifted her easily onto the frigidly unforgiving surface of a boulder left by the retreat of the last great glacier, whose descendants still haunted the Divide to the north. Leaping up to sit next to her, he pointed at the distant vistas. "Look at that view. Mountains climbing directly to heaven beyond a sky so blue and enormous you'd think it was an ocean. Why would I want to go back to overheated, crowded New Orleans when this can be mine?"

"You'd give up train robbery for this quiet life?" she teased.

"I don't love that life of crime as you do, honey." He turned her to look at him. With a calmness that could not hide the entreaty in his eyes, he asked, "How about you, Katie? Could you give up your criminal life to live such a quiet, uneventful life?"

She slid down from the rock and began to walk back to the cabin. After a few steps, she felt his hands on her shoulder. She shrugged them off and spun awkwardly in the enormous boots. Somehow she regained her balance before falling in the snow.

"Don't ask me that, Jonah. I love you, but loving you has not changed what will happen when we leave this aerie. You may have taken down the 'Wanted' poster for the Forrester gang from your office wall, but my description is available to every other lawman in the territory. I made my decision years ago as to what I would be. I cannot change now."

He clasped his hands behind her. "If you want those posters to vanish, I can arrange that by having Duncan send a telegram stating I have hanged one train robber known as the leader of the Forrester gang. K.T. Forrester vanishes for good."

"I don't know if I want K.T. to vanish forever." Pain flashed through her as she saw the shock on his face. "Jonah, it may be that I can change what I am, but I don't know if I want to.

I miss the excitement of my life and the companionship I had with my brothers and the men who rode with us."

"And the love we have means less than that?"

"Don't ask me that. I don't want to choose."

Leaning her against him, he said, "There's no need to think of that when we have all this loveliness around us. Forget about the future. Think only of now."

"I'm trying."

"That you are," he agreed with a laugh. He released her as she grimaced at him. When he turned to look at the magnificent scenery frosted with the fresh snow, he missed the glitter of mischief in her eyes.

Scooping up a handful of the wet snow, she formed it into a ball. Her laughter sounded the only warning before the snowball struck Jonah above his collar. At the impact and the cold particles dropping heavily down his back, he whirled to see her fleeing toward the door of the cabin. Easily he cut off her path of escape.

"No you don't!" he crowed as he caught her. "This time you are going to pay for your crimes, honey."

She shrieked as he picked up a handful of the wet flakes and let them fall in a white cascade over her head. Exerting all her strength, she shoved him away. Her eyes watched in horror as his feet came up from under him and he fell back into the snow to lie motionless next to the patch of ice where he had been standing.

"Jonah?" she cried, unsure if he was jesting with her again. When he did not move or answer, she dropped to her knees next to him. She put her hand on his shoulder and shook him gently. "Jonah, this isn't funny. Jonah? *Jonah?*"

Her voice rose on each repetition until she wanted to scream out her horror. Never had she thought their joking would lead to tragedy. Pulling off her glove, she put her hand close to his lips and was pleased that his breath warmed her palm. She stared at his long form in the snow. It would be impossible for her to get him into the cabin alone, but to leave him there would risk frostbite.

She brushed particles of snow off his face and glanced up in fright. The silver clouds were turning dark. From experience, she knew that the soft flakes could turn swiftly into a deadly blizzard. Leaning over him to prevent the snow from covering his face, she prayed that inspiration would offer her a way to get him inside.

Arms caught her and spun her into the snowbank. Shock allowed no other emotion in her mind as she looked up at Jonah's smile. When she realized he had tricked her, she spat, "You two-faced bushwacker! Let me up! Do you know how horrible it made me feel to see you lying there?"

"You feel mighty fine right now, honey." He kissed her fiercely, holding her between his arm and the hunger on his lips.

Katie turned her head away from him so she could whisper, "Take me home, Jonah."

"Home? Back to Flynn?"

Katie laughed as she looked at him. If ever the day came that they could not chuckle at one another, she was sure the greatest joy would have disappeared from her life. Wrapping her arms around his shoulders made bulky by his heavy clothes, she gave him a sly glance from under her eyelashes white with snow.

"Take me home to our house, Jonah. I know exactly what I want *now*!"

"The same as I, my love."

The coffee steamed comfortingly in her face as Katie leaned against Jonah's legs. With the fresh air early in the day and the body-sapping hours of love, she found she had no energy to raise the cup to her lips. There was no need to talk in the darkness. The silent communion of kindred spirits spoke what words could not say. With his hand stroking her back in an aimless pattern and her arm draped over his knee, they savored the music of the fire crackling on the hearth and breathed in the pungent scent of burning pine.

She thought back to other winters and other fireplaces. There she had found friendship and love, but nothing like what Jonah offered her. Although he treated her as a delicate lady, he was not afraid to challenge her to do what most men would shirk. He forced her to be someone she was not, but allowed her to be herself more than anyone else ever had.

Who was she? Was she K.T. Forrester, anxious to return to her life of larceny and high jinks? Or had she become Katharine St. Pierre, a woman eager to have a life of fine things and be pampered by those around her? She was beginning to consider herself both and neither.

337

When she looked into blue eyes as fathomless as the deep lakes clinging to the mountains, she knew that it did not matter who or what she was. All that was important she found in the arms of the man she loved.

In the bright sunshine of the next morning, Jonah came into the cabin just as Katie finished washing her face in the water she had heated over the fire. The pail had a layer of ice on it that she could not break with her fist.

"Good morning, darling," she called.

"I'm glad you're up," he answered quietly. "We have a long trip ahead of us. We are riding down into Copper Peak. It's time to go home, Katie."

"What?" she gasped, sure she had misunderstood him. She had not thought about the time when this sweet interlude must come to an end. All her thoughts had been of the distant future when she must decide what her life would be and what part Jonah would play in it.

He did not look at her as he tossed her the silk dress and petticoats she had been wearing when he carried her off the train. Without explaining where he had hidden them, he said, "I'm taking you to Flynn. The Copper Kings' ball is coming soon. If we are going to attend—"

Rising, she came around the bench to stand before him. He pulled her onto his lap and brought her head to rest against his shoulder. She whispered, "I don't want to leave, Jonah. When we go back, it will be as it was."

"Not quite." He kissed her forehead and added,

"We cannot be the same after what happened here."

"And this is the end of that?"

He laughed. "My love, don't be foolish! Of course not. We will find chances to meet in Copper Peak. I am not going to give up what we have found." Framing her face with his broad hands, he added more seriously, "Katie, what I must do down there isn't finished. Until it is, I'm not free to offer you anything but stolen moments. When what I came to Montana for is completed, then we will have the discussion we must. This will give you time to decide what life you want. I don't want to be away from you for a single second, but there is no choice."

Although Katie wanted to argue that there were many choices, she knew it would be a waste of time. When Jonah spoke in this somber tone, he could not be swayed by any tactics. Wanting to cry, afraid that she would awaken to find this all had been a dream, she went to the bed and spread her clothes on it. Silently she unbuttoned the shirt and reached for her chemise.

The stroke of lips against her shoulders sent a sweet shudder through her. With a sob, she whirled to fling her arms around his neck. His hands lowered the cotton shirt down her body as he murmured, "I must hold you one more time, Katie. Let me love you before we return to the hatred again."

"Love me, Jonah." She gazed up into his eyes coming closer as his lips descended toward hers. "Love me forever."

* * *

With Katie before him in the saddle, Jonah urged his horse along the deserted street. The last warmth of the sunset barely penetrated his coat. Although Katie had not complained once during the slow journey from their mountain hideaway, he knew she must be suffering the bite of winter.

The cold wind swirled along the street, creating small twisters of dried snow. He drew his horse even with the lights bright in the sheriff's office and let out a shout. Instantly his deputy emerged from the warm glow within. He nearly laughed when he saw Peabody's shock.

"Sheriff? Is that you? Go up to Flynn's! He's as mad as a wet hornet! Someone abducted—Oh!" The last word came out in a gasp as he noted who sat in front of the sheriff.

"Ride ahead," ordered Jonah calmly. "Let them know we are coming. Tell them to ready Miss St. Pierre's room. She's very chilled."

Peabody nodded so hard that it appeared his head would bounce off and roll up the deserted street. When he leapt onto his horse waiting patiently in front of the office, he struck its rump with his hat. This one time he did not dread confronting Flynn. The terrifying man who owned Copper Peak would be exultant to hear the good news.

Jonah chuckled as the incompetent deputy raced up the road leading to the brightly lit house on the hill. Wrapping his cloak tighter around Katie, he asked, "How are you doing?"

She looked up at him. "Cold. The next time you plan something like this, please warn me ahead of time. I will wear something other than a light traveling gown."

"But you look so pretty in it." He tightened his arms around her and savored the caress of her body against his.

"That's what you said when I was wearing your clothes."

Picking up the reins, he felt her nestle closer to him and wondered why he had bothered to come back to Copper Peak. He could have taken Katie and kept going to someplace where no one would have recognized him or guessed her to be Flynn's missing daughter. Only his determination not to let Flynn escape from his revenge had brought him to this small blot on the mountainside again. He bowed his head into the wind and urged the horse toward the next chapter in his plan to destroy Lyndon Flynn.

Katie struggled with her ambivalent feelings as they rode through the gate of Lyndon's estate. She could not wait for the chance to be warm, but she did not want to think of giving up what she and Jonah had savored on the mountaintop.

When the horse stopped in front of the house, Jonah slid from the saddle and lifted her to the ground. He kept his arm around her as they walked toward the porch. Taylor had the door open before they reached the steps. His shout of "Here she is!" reached out to welcome them into the warm glow beyond the portal.

"Let me help you," whispered Jonah in her ear as they crossed the wide verandah. "Remember, you have been an unwilling captive for the past two days."

"Jonah, I don't—"

"Honey, you have to. This is far from over. We must see it through, or Ethan will suffer . . ."

She stiffened in his arms as she saw the hardness return to his face. Suddenly she wondered if the lovemaking on the mountain had been only a charade. Why should Jonah remind her so coldly of how her brother's life continued to depend on her ability to convince everyone she was Lyndon's daughter?

"I understand, sheriff."

"Sheriff?" he repeated, incredulous. "No, Katie, that is not—"

Flynn surged forward to pull his daughter from Jonah's arms before he could say more. "Katie! Oh, my poor child!" He held her close as he felt her tears dampen his shirt. In his wildest imagination, he could not guess why she was crying.

"Lyndon," she sobbed, "just let me go to my room. I want—I want . . ." She did not know what she wanted other than to escape from the man she had dared to believe loved her.

When he nodded and released her, he asked, "Of course, my dear. We can talk later, but first, don't you want to thank the sheriff for rescuing you?"

Jonah understood her confusion enough to realize she was struggling to see the truth. He stepped toward her to take her hands. His smile hid how he tightened his fingers over hers when she tried to pull away. This ludicrous misunderstanding must be cleared up before she worked herself into a frenzy.

"Katie, I'm glad I was able to bring you home

safely. I promise you I will do everything I can to see that any man who hurt you pays for that heinous crime. You are too special to be injured in any way, even by hastily spoken phrases which could not have meant what you thought."

She stared up at him and tried to decipher his words to be the apology she yearned to hear. On his strangely candid face, she saw the truth she could not deny. He hated forcing her to continue this game and would prefer to have her living with him in the small house opposite his office. The words she had heard as a threat meant something else totally. He did not want to see Ethan die. Only her sorrow at returning to Lyndon's house and her lonely bed had tricked her into blaming him for her sorrow.

"Thank you, Jonah. I will never forget what you have done for me." She smiled involuntarily as she saw the leap of passion lighting his eyes.

"I trust I may call on you tomorrow to see how you are."

"Lyndon?" she asked like a dutiful daughter.

The man with a cheek-cracking smile on his broad face gushed, "Of course, my dear. Whatever you want. You know the sheriff will never be turned away from our door after his gallant rescue of you."

As if the subject was painful, she put her hand to her forehead. She swayed to the sound of warning shouts from the many servants filling the foyer. When she was scooped up into strong arms, she leaned her head against the chest that had been her pillow for the past two nights.

"Katie? Katie, child, are you ill?" called Lyndon.

With a performance worthy of the star of any traveling troupe of actors, she murmured, "La! I didn't realize how weak I was. Thank you again, Jonah."

"My pleasure. I would be glad to take you upstairs if you think you are unable to manage the stairs."

She battled her urge to smile as she glanced surreptitiously at the crowd of people. No one seemed to suspect they were lying. When she saw the haggard faces of Taylor and Mrs. Grodin, a twinge of guilt tormented her. During the days of ecstasy, she had not once considered what those who cared for her in Flynn's house would feel.

Realizing that everyone waited for her answer, she smiled with a martyr's resolution. "You must be so tired after all the excitement today. I still cannot believe how quickly you bested those three criminals all by yourself. I am sure I can—"

"Nonsense!" He felt the unaccustomed heat of embarrassment beneath his collar. With a few oblique words, she had made a hero of him. It was a notoriety he did not want and certainly did not deserve, but, as he saw the smiles on the faces of Flynn's staff, he knew he would be lauded by everyone in town except those who knew the truth. He turned to his employer and asked, "Mr. Flynn?"

"Go ahead, sheriff. No one would deny you the honor of taking Katie upstairs to be sure she is safely home."

As they led the parade going up the long staircase, Jonah growled in her ear, "No more cock-and-bull tales of my so-called heroics."

"La!" she said in a low tone, but with a hint of laughter. "I didn't guess you to be a modest man."

"I'm not, but I don't want your dear 'Daddy' to become my best friend because I saved his daughter."

She did not reply as she rested her head against him and felt the movement of his muscles as he carried her with little effort up the long, curving staircase. Mrs. Grodin hurried ahead of them to open the door to Katie's rooms.

He placed her on the bed and left as he saw Mrs. Grodin pulling clean clothes from Katie's armoire. Flynn was waiting in the sitting room. Jonah closed the door and nodded as his employer pointed to a chair. Gratefully he sat, allowing muscles tight from the long ride in the cold to relax slightly.

Flynn cleared his throat before saying, "Bancroft, I can never reward you appropriately for what you have done to save Katie."

He shrugged. "It was mostly dumb luck, Mr. Flynn. I got blown off course by the storm and happened to stumble on horse tracks where there should have been none. I followed them and found Katie with her kidnappers."

Flynn ran his hand across his face, making the wide jowls longer. More than once he started to speak, but the words did not come easily to him. Events of more than twenty-five years ago had played through his mind the last few days, except that Katie had taken her mother's place as he struggled as futilely as Eugenie's champion had to protect her. Then . . .

"Was she raped?" he asked bluntly.

"I didn't wait to question her captors. By myself and needing to protect her, I could not risk letting them awaken while we were there." Jonah added, "She hasn't said a word about what happened."

The curse Flynn breathed seemed hardly adequate to lessen his shock. Jonah watched him closely as the hard man crumbled before his eyes. Hiding his exultation, Jonah soaked up all the details to share with his allies. The first part of their plot had been successful, for Flynn understood well what those who cared about the fate of Eugenie St. Pierre had suffered when he forced her to be his private whore.

"Mr. Flynn? Sheriff?" They turned to see Mrs. Grodin in the doorway to the bedroom. She smiled with fatigued happiness. "Miss Katie would like to speak to both of you."

Jonah hesitated as Flynn rushed into the room. Although his employer clearly would refuse him little tonight, he did not know if that generosity included allowing him again in the sanctum of his daughter's room.

When Flynn shouted to him impatiently, Jonah winked at the housekeeper. He listened politely when Mrs. Grodin said she would be back with hot drinks, but was thinking only of the woman in the far room. Pausing in the doorway, he relished the scene of Katie looking so soft and feminine in the lacy bed jacket. She was propped against a mountain of pillows, and her hair flowed loose once more, urging his fingers to touch it.

Katie looked past Lyndon as the man she dared to trust with her heart entered the room. Holding up her hand to him, she said, "I trust you do not think ill of me, Jonah, for acting so boldly as to ask you to come in here. I fear that improprieties have been the least of my concerns for the past two days."

At the strangled sound from Lyndon, she wondered what lies Jonah had told him. The ashen features of her father told her what he feared. Jonah's ploy had succeeded at the very thing she had accused him of attempting. Lyndon would be thinking she had been subjected to all sorts of physical abuse. She did not have to look at Jonah to know he wanted his enemy to continue thinking that.

"You should rest," Jonah urged. "I'm sure you have slept little since your abduction."

She almost laughed. He knew exactly how few hours she had spent sleeping in the bed they shared. "I think that is a wonderful idea."

"Tomorrow," interjected Lyndon, "Doc Havering will check you to determine—if you are well." When he saw her face flush, he knew she guessed exactly what he meant.

Closing her eyes, she begged, "Lyndon, must I have the doctor inflicted on me after what I've been through? Can't it wait a few days?" She refused to submit to the horror of having a doctor touch her so intimately, for Lyndon would want to be sure his daughter remained a maiden he could marry off advantageously. With several days' grace, she might devise a way to put off the damning examination completely.

"Of course, my dear, of course. I didn't mean to upset you more. Look. Here comes Mrs. Grodin with something to help you sleep. The sheriff and I will leave you to your pleasant dreams, and I shall see you on the morrow." He bent his round form to kiss her cheek. Patting her hair, he murmured, "It's so good to have you home, Katie."

"It's so good to be home," she lied as she looked at Jonah and wondered when they would be together again. In a breathless voice, she added, "Thank you for everything, Jonah."

"My pleasure." His eyes twinkled as he picked up her fingers and pressed them to his lips. "Until tomorrow."

"Tomorrow."

Katie watched as the two men went out of her room to leave her with the navy shadows clinging to the corners. Dropping back into the pillows, she stared at the canopy over her head. Tonight she would dream of being in Jonah's arms again. It was a dream she would savor every night until she could make it come true.

CHAPTER SEVENTEEN

In front of the strange mirror in the strange hotel room, Katie brushed her hair and stared at the strange person in the reflection. Slowly she turned to look at the room where she had just finished unpacking her things for the visit to Butte. Oak moldings glowed with new varnish and dimmed the dusty colors of the wild prints of the garish wallpapers.

A knock kept her from sighing with dejection. She put the silver-handled brush on the marble top of the dressing table and went to the door. When it opened before she reached it, she forced a smile on her face.

Since her "rescue" from the unspecified criminals, Lyndon seldom allowed her out of his sight. If she sought some privacy, it soon was interrupted by Lyndon with a ridiculous excuse. She wanted to be grateful that he cared so deeply for her, but she could not. Each intrusion reminded her of her captivity as this man's daughter. Even when Jonah called, Lyndon found excuses to intrude on them.

Joviality not normal for Lyndon Flynn boomed as he asked, "How do you like your room?"

"It is fine." She clasped her hands in front of her so she could hide her frustration.

"I'm directly next door. With the many folks coming in for the ball, we were fortunate to be given such fine rooms next to each other on such short notice. I had canceled our reservations when . . ." His voice trailed off as a horrified expression crossed his face.

Katie had seen it often during the past week. That she had told him nothing of what had happened to her during her supposed abduction continued to haunt him. Only Jonah's whispered injunction that she not relieve Lyndon's perverted fears of what she had suffered kept her from having sympathy for him.

Turning away from him, she toyed with the perfume bottles on the dressing table. "And where is Jonah staying?"

"Sheriff Bancroft also found a room on this floor." He put his hands on her shoulders and added, "Katie, we must talk."

"I have told you I don't want to talk about that. I cannot face it yet. Give me time." She repeated the words she had said so often. Until she knew what lies Jonah wanted her to tell, she must maintain her silence.

His broad hands brought her to face him. Leaning forward so his thick face was close to hers, he said forcefully, "My dear child, I don't want talk of that, for I know how it upsets you. I want to speak of Sheriff Bancroft."

"Jonah? Is there some problem with him?" Her nonchalance vanished as she quivered beneath his grip.

"Sheriff Bancroft," he corrected, struggling to restrain his fury with her reaction. Again he told himself that it was to be expected that Katie would form some attachment to a man who had rescued her from the depravity of her captors. Her words made him more determined to say what he must before this idiocy went further. Holding her expressive eyes with his, he stated, "After the Copper Kings' ball tonight, I do not want you to see him socially again."

Katie gasped, "Not see him again?" Her mouth straightened with a stubborn streak she had kept hidden during her portrayal of Lyndon's daughter. "You know that's impossible. Copper Peak is a small town and—"

"I said socially, Katie." He smiled coldly. "He isn't of your class. When you marry, you must choose an appropriate husband."

"One that you select?"

His scowl deepened. Grabbing her arms, he pulled her close to him and shook her until the hair held demurely at the back of her neck loosened to fall down her back. It cascaded over his hands in a rain of dark silk and shadowed her body so revealingly outlined in her dressing gown. The perfume she was wearing drifted over him like a magic potion. Entwining the fingers of one hand in the hair at the back of her head, he did not hear her cry of pain.

351

Katie tried to pull away from him, but his bulbous body retained the strength of his youth. Her hands against his chest had no effect on him as he drew her tightly to him. When she cried out for him to stop, a smile twisted his lips in the seconds before they covered hers. The painful pressure drove her head back against his arm.

When she felt his tongue against the fortress of her mouth, she turned her head away and cried, "Lyndon, are you mad? I'm your daughter!"

As if she had become as hot as the flame of desire within him, he released her. She rocked back on her feet and grasped the uprights of the bed. With her fingers against her mouth she wanted to wash clean of his invasion, she regarded him with white-faced horror.

"Katie, I—I—"

"Go away," she whispered as she flinched away from his outstretched hand begging her forgiveness.

She heard the door close but did not look across the room. Running to the washstand, she poured warm water from the pitcher into the bowl. Over and over she scrubbed her face, longing to eradicate any memory of his touch. She now knew that she had to escape from Flynn's house as soon as possible.

It took her only a few minutes to redo her hair and dress to seek help. She pulled on her dark green traveling suit and buttoned up the jacket with its red piping. Her black button-topped shoes made little sound on the crimson rug as she hurried along the hallway toward the stairs.

352

In the lobby she went directly to the mahogany desk. The clerk smiled ingratiatingly at her. Ignoring his well-practiced expression, she asked, "Will you please give me the number of Sheriff Bancroft's room?" She knew how outlandish her request was, but she offered no lie to explain why she wanted such information.

"It's 17, Miss St. Pierre, but if you are looking for Sheriff Bancroft, I can tell you he just left."

"Thank you." She hesitated and reached for a piece of paper next to the ink well. Hastily she scribbled a note which said nothing but her urgent need to see him. Folding it, she offered it to the clerk. "Will you see that he gets this as soon as he returns?"

"Yes, Miss St. Pierre." His smile broadened when he felt the coin she had placed beneath the paper to insure his cooperation.

Katie did not hesitate as she walked toward the door. Although she longed to speak to Jonah about what had happened in her room, this gave her the opportunity she had prayed for when she first heard they were going to Butte. With their trip shortened by Lyndon's insistence that they come only for the ball and leave immediately afterward, she must take this chance she had feared she would not have.

As she walked along the street, she noticed how much more permanent Butte appeared to be than Copper Peak. The shadow of the mines on the "richest hill on earth" hung over the city, but there was a jovial, devil-may-care feeling on the streets. Although few here shared the wealth of the Copper Kings, they did not suffer from the despair known so well by the citizens of Copper Peak.

The fine residences were set apart from the frame houses of the employees of the mines, but the streets were safe during the daylight for any woman. Not that Katie did not have many men look her way and more than one whistle at her. She simply was too involved in her own anticipation to notice the admiration.

She nearly walked past the building she wanted. None of the gilt on the window of its counterpart in Copper Peak had been painted here. Taking a deep breath, she opened the door and went into the office that resembled Jonah's. The "Wanted" posters were clumped together on one wall, and the floor was thick with dust ingrained in the boards. At the single desk, a man bent over a pile of papers. He did not look up at the tinkle of the bell over the door.

"Good afternoon," mumbled the deputy in a bored voice. When she answered, his head popped up like a marionette hooked to a string. He bounced to his feet, sending his chair careening against a wall and crashing to the floor.

Straightening his rumpled vest holding the star that proclaimed him a deputy marshall, he came around the desk. He reached to tip his hat, but with an embarrassed grin realized that his hat hung on a peg behind him.

"I am looking for a deputy to help me." She was pleased she had disconcerted him. It might make it easier to get in to see Ethan, who must be imprisoned beyond the door with the bars in the window.

"Yes, ma'am. I mean, that's me, ma'am." He nearly slobbered like a big-footed puppy eager to please her. Thinking there must be an important reason why a lady dressed in forest green velvet and lace would call at the jail, he asked, "I'm Deputy O'Malley. Can I help you?"

She smiled coyly and watched the result. The deputy could not keep his eyes on her face as she spoke. The form-fitting suit had been the right choice. "Deputy, do not think this request odd—"

"Of course not, ma'am," he gushed, so anxious to please that he did not wait for her to finish. His ears reddened beneath his blond hair when he realized how foolish he sounded.

"I would like to see one of your prisoners."

He nodded. He would be glad to offer her a tour of the whole jail if that was what she wanted. "Which one?"

"Ethan Forrester."

"Forrester?" He broke his fascination with her curves to state, "Don't have anyone here by that name since they hanged Elijah Forrester almost a year ago. Is that who you mean?"

Katie nearly lost her composure. Something must be wrong. Before she betrayed herself, she remembered her role. She smiled and put her gloved fingers on his arm. "Deputy, I did not mean that one. I'm talking about Ethan Forrester. He would be much younger than the one you hanged."

"Nope, ma'am. We don't have anyone with that name here."

"Are you sure?" she blurted. When she saw

355

his eyes narrow in the beginnings of suspicion, she forced herself to laugh lightly. Pressing her hand to the fall of lace at her throat, she brought his attention back to her feminine form he so clearly admired. "I shall have to admonish my friend. She told me you had that bandit here. After he stole my purse in a holdup, I wanted to see him behind bars. Oh, well. I guess it doesn't matter." She let her voice drop into the husky whisper that always worked best with witless men. "Thank you so very, very much, Deputy O'Malley."

"Yes, ma'am. You're welcome, ma'am." He paused before adding, "If I can do anything, anything at all, to help you, don't hesitate to come back."

"I will. You may be sure of that."

It took all her strength not to slam the door behind her. Someone had lied, and she feared she knew exactly who it was. Tears burned in her eyes as she fought to swallow past the lump closing her throat. She had trusted Jonah with her heart, and he continued to be false with her.

A rush of hope filled her as she wondered if it was possible he had not been the one to make the mistake. He had shown her a telegram he told her came from the marshall here in Butte. If she checked the telegraph office, she might discover . . . she choked back a sob as she knew how futile this hope was, but she had to be sure before she accused Jonah.

Crossing the street as she headed for the telegraph office, she cared little about the risk of not looking to be sure no cart was racing toward her. At that painful moment of enlightenment, she thought only of how she had been betrayed and prayed it would all be untrue.

The door to the telegraph office creaked as she opened it. She ignored the crash of the loose glass in the door as it slammed behind her. A clerk raced to the counter to remonstrate with the careless customer, but swallowed his words as he saw the pretty woman crossing the narrow space to him.

Katie straightened her shoulders aching with her burden of truth. Her smile stretched her lips painfully, but she tried to make her expression realistic. The lie came easily to her lips. "I'm sorry to bother you, sir, but would it be possible that you keep a record of all your wires?"

"Of course." He folded his arms on the counter and said with a sly, conspiratorial wink, "That's how the company makes sure we give them the money they have coming to them."

"Thank goodness. Could you do me a favor? My name is Katharine St. Pierre. My father is Lyndon Flynn. I asked for a wire to be sent from Copper Peak to Butte about ten weeks ago. I was wondering if it had arrived properly." She lowered her eyes modestly. "It was for a Christmas present for Father, but the tailor tells me he never received the order. Could you check?"

He grinned and pulled a bound book from beneath the counter. Opening it, he ran his finger along the page. "To Semmes' Tailoring Shop? No, Miss St. Pierre. Nothing logged in from ten weeks ago."

"It might not have been exactly that date. Would you check the week on either side?"

"No need. Nothing logged from Copper Peak around that time."

"Are you sure?" She saw his scowl and realized she was pushing too hard, but she must discover the truth she did not want to face.

He whirled the book so she could read the spidery handwriting. "Look for yourself."

Katie saw that he was not trying to hide anything from her. The half-formed hope that official wires were kept separately died when she saw several entries of messages sent to and from the marshall's office, none of them about Ethan.

She could not ignore the facts any longer. Jonah had lied to her. In retrospect, she wondered how she could have been so stupid. She had known they were sending a false telegram to Lyndon. It had been a simple step in the plot to do the same to her.

"Thank you," she managed to say. Her eyes blinked rapidly to dam the tears pressing against her lashes.

She spun and walked out of the office before he could reply. Wandering along the boardwalk, she knew she must go back to the hotel and confront both men who wanted to rule her. Instead she strolled in the opposite direction. Somewhere in this city she should be able to find a quiet spot and sob out her agony that the man she loved had used that love only to twist her more closely to him.

No smile complemented the silken confection Mrs. Kane had made for Katie. She stood in front of her dressing table and pinned flowers in her hair. A box sat to one side. It had been waiting when she arrived back from her walk, but she had not opened it. With a dejected sigh, she lifted the top to see the wrist corsage of hothouse flowers.

Opening the card, she read the short message. "For one more beautiful than these fragile flowers. All my love, Jonah." She crumpled it in her hand and threw it across the room. More lies. That was all she got from him.

Despite her rage, she placed the lovely flowers on her right wrist. She wanted to keep her left hand free in case she needed to deal with him or with an amorous Lyndon. As she took a step toward the door, she paused. Lifting her full skirts of the palest coral, she repositioned the sheath of the knife she had bought in a pawn shop on one of the less elegant streets. She did not intend to be defenseless again.

Her skirts whispered against the carpet as she walked down the stairs to meet her escorts to the ball. When she saw Lyndon sitting on one of the chairs against the wall, she noted the paleness of his features. His hand was pressed to his chest, and as she came closer, she could see he was struggling to breathe.

Instantly Katie forgot what he had done that afternoon. In comparison with Jonah's duplicity, a heated kiss was a misdemeanor she could forgive. She put her hand on Lyndon's arm. "Are you feeling ill?" she asked gently as he struggled to his feet.

"Leave off, child. I don't want to be nagged by you tonight. The business I have with Clark and

Daly is too important. A bit of indigestion from
that rich lunch we had is all. It will pass."
When he saw the distress in her luminous eyes,
he relented. How he had suffered when he imagined her in the hands of his enemies! If it had
not been for Bancroft . . .

As so many times in the days since she was
returned to Copper Peak, he found himself wondering what she had endured. His hardly subtle
questioning gained him nothing, for Katie deftly
deflected each query by saying she did not want
to think of that time.

Footsteps approaching on the parquet floor
interrupted his musings. That must be Bancroft.
He could understand his daughter being grateful to the sheriff for his rescue of her from her
captors, but he did not plan to let that relationship exist after tonight. His daughter must have
a suitor of higher class than a drifter who managed to win himself a tin star.

Before Bancroft could interrupt, he must apologize to Katie for his foolishness earlier that
day. All afternoon, he had fought the pain in his
chest and the guilt of lusting for his darling
daughter.

"Katie?" When she looked up at him, he
cupped her chin in his hand. "My dear child,
forgive me. I was angry this afternoon and have
suffered since thinking how I might have hurt
you. I promise it will never happen again."

Tiredly, she nodded. "I know, Lyndon. I know
you made a mistake, and it's forgotten." She
wanted to add she had made a much greater
one when she gave Jonah her love. Her smile

tightened as she heard the voice which only this morning had made her heart leap with longing. Now it only reminded her of how stupid she had been.

Katie held up her cheek for Jonah's perfectly casual kiss. Inside she battled the memories of his lips moving along her, urging her to release her tightly restrained emotions until she fell into the passionate orbit he created. Anguish surged through her as she gazed up into his sparkling eyes, made a deeper blue in the reflection of the royal tie closing his collar.

It took all her strength to keep from taking his arms and shaking him and demanding that he tell her what else he had lied to her about since they began this masquerade. A pang centered over her heart. He had been false about Ethan. She feared he had been as dishonest about the love he offered her.

None of that showed on her face as he smiled at her. His loving expression fired her rage to a fever pitch. She wanted to whirl away from him and spit out the truth. Only the dimmed song of love in her heart halted her.

"You look lovely tonight, Katie."

"Thank you."

He blinked at her short response, but did not ask any questions. Instead he greeted Flynn and apologized for being delayed. His excuse was waved aside as Lyndon took his daughter's arm and walked across the lobby to leave him looking after them.

What was bothering Katie enough to leave him a note with the desk clerk he had not discovered. Curiosity teased him about her obvious distress, but he could not ask her in front of Flynn. He smoothed his frock coat and knew he could question her when she twirled in his arms on the dance floor.

The fine carriage carried them quickly to the house where the ball was being held. Jonah was pleased the distance was short, for neither of the two sitting across from him said anything during the ride. He had seen immediately that Flynn was not feeling well, but it was Katie's unusual silence that was disquieting. He had expected she would be bubbling with excitement at this peek into the life she yearned to have for her own.

A liveried footman helped Katie from the carriage and held the door for the men. His quiet instructions sent the vehicle to wait with the others while he escorted the guests to the house. They were ushered into a foyer of immense luxury. A carved balustrade led the eyes upward to a Palladian window through which the moonlight poured to caress the stairs. Heavily gilded lincrusta formed the ceiling over their heads. Its pattern was accentuated by the shadows cast by the electric lamps, glaring bright to eyes accustomed to gaslights.

Past the gaudy furniture lining the walls, Katie could hear the delicate sound of a waltz played by the orchestra brought from Chicago especially for this event. She handed the butler her cloak and wondered at the choice of music. Waltzes seemed too tame for men who were so hard and mercenary and, she added silently when she met Jonah's eyes, interested only in themselves.

She ignored the arm he offered to her and turned to Lyndon. When he finished grumbling about the ineptness of the maid who had dropped his silk top hat, he compliantly let his daughter take his arm. He continued to complain as they walked along the long hallway to the room set up for this evening as a lavish ballroom. It hid his need to lean on her as the pain grew sharper through him.

At the entrance to the ballroom, he mumbled something about a whiskey and left his daughter to her companion. Katie watched him lurch across the crowded room and wondered what was ailing him. His breath had not been tainted with liquor, so he was not the drunkard he appeared. She decided she had enough problems of her own without worrying about him. Once he found Daly or Clark and could talk business, he would be fine.

"Shall we, Katie?"

She looked at Jonah. Knowing she could not clutter up the doorway all evening, she put her fingers lightly on his sleeve. He walked her toward the side of the room where ceiling high windows were topped by stained glass. They had to push their way past the many other guests making the huge room stifling. The clink of glasses and the snippets of conversation created a countertempo to the violins. He paused away from the bright lights of the crystal chandeliers.

"They look lovely on you." His fingers went from the elastic holding the flowers to the soft texture of her skin visible beneath her lacy gloves. "My love, why don't we dance, and we can talk undisturbed?"

"I don't want to dance," she said tightly. "I think I would prefer to watch."

"Watch?" He smiled. "Katie, you must show everyone how beautifully you dance. I have been waiting for the chance to dance with you as we did the night you accepted my invitation to the Copper Kings' ball."

She did not meet his gaze as she looked at her gloves. The flowers on her wrist were wilting in the hot room. Their early demise seemed the final insult she could take when the last of her newly acquired illusions had been ripped from her. Choosing a seat behind her, she lowered herself into it gracefully.

"I don't want to dance with you, Jonah."

When he dropped to sit next to her, she flinched as he slid his arm behind her on the upholstered back of the small sofa. She did not have to look at his face to sense his rage, for it billowed over her like a noxious vapor from the Copper Peak smelter. His fingers beneath her chin forced her to turn toward him. If she had resisted, he would have insisted, and she was not sure that she could halt him.

"What is wrong with you tonight, Katie?" he asked, more confusion than fury on his face.

Disregarding the temptation to smooth the ruts from his forehead, she answered only, "Nothing is wrong."

"Nothing?" He lowered his voice which had exploded over her and caused others to turn and regard them curiously.

"Excuse me, Sheriff Bancroft. I see my father looking for me." She rose and smiled at his confusion with the coldness she felt burning in her. "Thank you for escorting me here, sir. I trust you will find your own entertainment for the rest of the evening."

She did not look back at Jonah as she crossed the room to where Lyndon was involved in an argument with a bald-headed man she did not recognize. She hoped that Jonah would feel some of the betrayal swallowing her in its dark maw. Revenge was something he should understand. It was the only thing important to him, certainly more valuable than Katie St. Pierre.

Quickly she corrected herself. She was still and always would remain K.T. Forrester. That she was becoming caught up in this charade showed her the time had come to bring it to an end. If Jonah had not gotten what he wanted, that was his problem, because she was going to leave as soon as they went home to Copper Peak. There were a few items she wanted to collect before she went to find out where Ethan truly was.

A male voice halted her. "Miss St. Pierre?"

"Why, Mr. Daly!" She gave him her warmest smile, not caring if it helped or hindered Lyndon's business dealings with the owner of the Anaconda. Her part in those games was over. From this point forward, she would do what she wanted to do. Despite his cutthroat reputation, she liked this charming Irishman. "What a pleasure to meet you here tonight."

"Would you forgive an old man for interfering?"

"You, sir?"

He motioned to a man standing behind him. "This is Fraser Spalding who works in my office. He is a shy fellow, but cannot hide that he would enjoy dancing with you."

Shy was the last word Katie would have used to describe the handsome man lifting her hand to his lips as he bowed in her direction. His silk evening suit glistened in the light nearly as brightly as his raven hair. When he stood, she looked up into eyes darker than hers. They moved along her in candid admiration. A tremor ran along her back when his deep voice filled her ears.

"Miss St. Pierre, I trust you will forgive Mr. Daly for his introduction."

With a smile toward the spry man who smiled through his brush of white whiskers, she answered, "Mr. Daly knows I would forgive him almost anything."

Winking at them, Daly walked away to look for other conquests in his battle to see Clark lose his power in Montana. He smiled, sure that Miss St. Pierre would remember this incident and convince her father to listen more closely to the offers that Marcus Daly had for him.

"Would you care to dance, Miss St. Pierre?" asked the man still holding her hand.

"Yes, thank you." She let him lead her through the crowd toward the dance floor. Without looking anywhere but directly in front of her, she knew that Jonah watched every move she made. That made her more determined to prove she could have a wonderful time with another man.

Mr. Spalding put his arm around her waist as he lifted the flowing skirts of her dress. Easily he maneuvered her into the pattern of the dance. She stared at the onyx studs closing his shirt as he twirled her competently around the floor.

"You dance beautifully, Miss St. Pierre."

She lifted her gaze to his face and forced a smile she did not feel. "How kind of you, sir! I was afraid a country girl like me would be out of place here."

"I daresay you are not a bumpkin. Your accent tells me you are from the part of our country where ladies recall their place as a joy to be admired. Too many of the ones out here seem to think they are the same as men. I suppose you have heard of the efforts to give women the franchise."

Her smile tightened slightly. "You don't believe women should have a part in the political decisions of Montana when it becomes a state?"

"Why would you want to fill your pretty heads with such tiresome matters?" He drew her closer to him and let his fingers slip around to her back.

"Why indeed?" When she tried to step away, he kept his arm too tight to her. "Mr. Spalding, I think you are forgetting yourself," she whispered in the calm tone that Jonah would have known was a sign of danger. She cursed inwardly at the stray thought of him that had entered her mind to distract her from this so-called gentleman.

He did not loosen his grip. Instead his hand stroked her back through the fine silk of her gown. When she hissed a second warning, he chuckled. Putting his mouth close to her ear, he whispered, "Why don't we go to a quiet place, Miss St. Pierre, and you can tell me about the adventures you have been having?"

"Adventures?"

"Come, my dear. Surely you know the whole of Butte is abuzz with the story of your capture by brigands who kept you to themselves for nearly two days." He leered down into her shocked eyes. "What you enjoyed must have been very exciting."

She tried to stop in mid-step, but he kept her twirling to the dance. "Sir, when I tell my father of the type of men Mr. Daly hires, you will learn you have done your employer a great disservice."

His expression of glee told her what she should have guessed as soon as he passed the boundaries of polite behavior. He might be collecting pay from Daly, but she guessed he also was being compensated by Mr. Clark for certain services of undermining his enemy's efforts to buy Flynn's Copper Mining Company.

Suddenly they halted. Katie's nose nearly hit the blinking eyes of Mr. Spalding's shirt closures. When she stepped away, Jonah was standing behind the obnoxious man.

No sign of rancor sounded in his voice as Jonah said, "May I cut in?"

"No!" snapped Spalding.

"Of course," answered Katie at exactly the same time. As much as she hated how Jonah had used her, he had been a gentleman about it most of the time. He never would have taunted her for something that should have been a taboo subject. "Good evening, Mr. Spalding." As she stepped into Jonah's arms, she called over her shoulder, "Give my best to Mr. Clark."

"Clark?" asked Jonah. "I saw Daly introduce you."

"Did you?" She fought the ease of being in his arms. Although her mind shouted her anger with his falsehoods, her body recalled the joy of being so close to him. When he whirled her about the floor until they reached a distant corner, she struggled between happiness and hatred.

She did not protest when he took her hand and led her from the dance floor to an alcove where they could speak without being overheard. From the clenched line of his jaw, she knew that he intended to have this discussion. As she wanted the same, there was no sense in taking perverse pleasure in denying him this chance to talk.

No sooner had he seated her on the plush window bench than he demanded, "Tell me what is wrong."

"You lied to me," she replied simply.

"About?" he asked coolly. He never took his eyes from her ravaged face.

"About Ethan." When he opened his mouth to respond, she halted him. "Don't lie to me again, Jonah. I have been to the marshall's office and to the telegraph office. I know the truth."

He lounged against a wooden column and watched the dancers whirl about the floor. "So what now, Katie?"

"You aren't going to deny it?"

"Why should I? It's the truth. I have no idea where Ethan Forrester is. If I did, I would not do anything to keep him from hanging. It would generate questions we can't afford to have asked."

Tears burned in her eyes, but her voice was strong with hatred. She rose and stared at him without fear. "Then this must be good-bye, Jonah. I don't want anything more to do with you."

He grasped her shoulders as she tried to step past him. Easily he twisted her into his arms. "Really? You want none of this?" His voice was thick with husky longing. A smile crossed his lips in the second before they touched hers.

Her hand struck his face forcefully. When he pulled back in shock, she gathered her skirts to rush back to the ballroom. Again he caught her arm. He smiled coldly when she glared at him.

"Go ahead and scream if you want, Katie. I thought you would want to understand why I did what I did."

"You wanted to control me by threatening the one person I love in this world."

A wave of pain crossed his face. "The only one?"

She spat, "You know I love you too, now, but I am doing my damnedest to convince myself how stupid it is to love a man who treats me as you do."

"Listen, honey. Really, listen." He bent down so his eyes were level with hers. "Then if you want to slap me again, I will stand still for it. Katie, I love you. That was something I couldn't foresee when this began, so I couldn't guess the time would come when I would regret the lie that Duncan and I devised."

Tears filled her eyes, but she fought the softening in her. He had spun his lies with the skill of a storyteller so often that she did not want to trust him again. "That was months ago. You could have told me the truth."

"When?" He stopped her as she started to reply by placing his finger on her lips. "When, honey? When you showed me that you would be a good ally without that threat over your head? You would have vanished within seconds, and I didn't want to lose the woman who fascinated me. Should I have told you during those two days we had on the mountains? More than once, I thought I should, but I could not bring myself to risk the love we found there. Honey, don't you understand? I could not be honest because I wanted you to stay in Copper Peak."

She moved away from him and sat on the windowseat. He might be honest with her, but she could not be the same with him. More than ever, she knew what she must do. Pasting a smile on her face, she listened to herself speak of how she forgave him for being unable to find the proper time to confide in her. It was the truth, but she did not speak of her intention to leave Lyndon's house as soon as possible.

As he took her hand and brought her to her feet and into his arms, he whispered, "Katie, I love you."

"I love you, Jonah," she answered. Holding up her lips for his kiss, she added, "And I always will."

CHAPTER EIGHTEEN

The main street of Copper Peak was busy as Katie drove along it, but everyone made a wide path for her buggy. The hate and fear the villagers felt for the man they called her father had clearly washed over onto her.

She was careful not to slow the buggy as she passed the sheriff's office. Since the discussion that Jonah considered a reconciliation, she had pretended to accept the life she led in Copper Peak. Lyndon had made no effort to keep the sheriff from his home. To the contrary, he seemed more comfortable when a third person was in the room. It unnerved Katie to realize that he could not trust himself even after promising her not to try to kiss her again. His odd actions added to her determination to be done with this deception of hers.

Craning her neck, she could see that Jonah sat at his desk in his office. Several men were speaking with him, and she hoped they would keep him busy while she did what she must. It was too dangerous to pause to see if they were his cronies or simply some of the miners he considered his friends.

Without looking toward either side of the street, she drove through the village. She ordered her fingers to stop trembling as she drove to the end of the street and turned the vehicle back to approach Jonah's house from the rear. Gossip might betray her. If she failed this time, she knew he would never allow her another chance. Exactly what Jonah might do she did not want to speculate.

She stopped the buggy and climbed out cautiously. It did not surprise her to find the rear door unlocked. Since she had arrived in Copper Peak, she had heard of no incidents of burglary in any of the small houses. No one possessed anything of value for anyone to risk their lives to steal.

When she stepped inside, it seemed strange that she had lived in this small cabin nearly a month. That time had become like a dream, but she knew she must recapture that sense of Jonah as an enemy, which he soon would be again. Within the week, she planned to be dressed in denims and riding the hills to seek her brother. If she was going to do that, she must have her weapons. That was why she was invading Jonah's home.

She kept her back to the wall as she moved into the kitchen end of the main room. When she had been Jonah's captive, she had discovered where he hid her guns. If he had not moved them, she would find her way out of this insanity within seconds.

She reached up to the shelf over the stove and found her quarry. With a racing heart she brought down the holster whose leather girth had worn to fit her hips exactly. Withdrawing her treasured gun, she smiled as she checked to find the cylinders loaded and extra bullets in the slots along the holster.

She ran her fingers along the smooth barrel and the grip inset with mother-of-pearl. Although Eli had sworn by the accuracy of his Colt Peacemaker, she preferred this lighter-weight Smith & Wesson pistol.

She hurriedly strapped the holster on beneath her long coat, then closed the door behind her and scurried into the buggy. A quick order to the horse brought the vehicle around and onto the street again. Just as she was about to relax with a silent celebration of victory, she saw Jonah standing in front of his office. He motioned for her to come to talk with him.

Pulling on the reins, she smiled with the ease she had learned since she became Katharine St. Pierre. "Hello, Jonah. It looks like snow again, doesn't it?"

"The train was attacked again last night."

She allowed her shock to show as she asked, "And?"

"They didn't get the money. Flynn's extra guards helped fight them off. One of the bandits was killed. They brought him here."

"Not Ethan?" she gasped, afraid to hear the truth.

He leaned forward and patted her hand. "Honey, I wouldn't tell you news like that here on the street. No, this was a two-bit hustler named Red Carlington."

"Red?"

"You know him?"

"*Of* him. He rode with the Armstrong brothers for a while in Wyoming. I didn't know he was still alive."

Grimly he said, "He isn't. I just wanted to let you know before you heard of the robbery attempt that baby brother has not been gunned down on the job."

"I must get home," she said. "Lyndon has been feeling poorly."

"Still?"

Seeing the concern on Jonah's face, she knew it was not over Flynn's health. He simply did not want Lyndon to die before he had the gratification of seeing his revenge completed. She could not understand why he had not finished it after kidnapping her. There was something he was waiting for, but she could not guess what it was.

"He hasn't recovered from the indigestion he had in Butte. It keeps recurring, but he refuses to change his ways or see Dr. Havering."

Jonah nodded and shrugged. "If you can't convince him, no one can. Go ahead. I'll let you know what else I hear about this robbery attempt."

"Thank you." She raised the reins and let the horse take her home.

When she arrived, she was told that Lyndon was resting in his room and did not want to be disturbed. She left a message with Pemberton, his valet, to call her as soon as he was ready for supper. In the days since they returned from the ball, she had become accustomed to eating alone in the huge dining room.

The house was too quiet in the long hours of the evening. Mrs. Grodin tried to interest her in feminine pursuits, but Katie had no inclination or aptitude for embroidery. As the time dragged on, she took the wretched piece from the bag by her chair. Grimacing, she looked at the uneven stitches puckering the material and wondered how she could be expected to master in a few weeks what most women had a full childhood to learn.

Satisfaction ran through her as she recalled the pistols hidden at the back of her armoire. She promised herself that she would ride out in the morning for some practice shooting. Everyone in the house would be shocked to discover the real direction in which her talents had blossomed.

"Miss Katie?"

She glanced toward the door to see Taylor peeking in. "Yes?" she called.

"Sheriff Bancroft would like to speak with you."

"Send him in."

When Jonah came to the door, she lowered her needlework to her lap as a false smile settled on her lips. Any excuse to be done with these tangled threads was welcome, even Jonah Bancroft. Warning her idiotic heart to calm its happy beat, she watched him walk across the room.

"Why, Jonah, what a pleasant surprise! I thought you would be busy investigating the train robbery."

He did not respond to her smile or her words. In a strangely cold voice, he demanded, "Where are they, Katie?"

Quickly she had to decide between outrage and puzzlement. She chose the former because it was what he would expect from her. "I might be able to answer your question, if you told me what 'they' are. Just once I wish you would start a conversation at the beginning instead of in the middle."

"No, no," he said as he shook his head. A wry smile appeared uncomfortable on his lips. He lifted his hat to point at her to emphasize the fury in his words. "You aren't going to fool me this time! You are the only one who knew where they were."

"Who are 'they'?"

"A pair of matched Smith & Wesson .44 caliber pistols."

In feigned horror, she rose to stare at him, sending her embroidery hoop bouncing on the carpet. Her voice cracked as she spoke, but she did not want him to know it was the threat of laughter that made it rise. "My guns are gone? Oh, no! What will I do when—?" She covered her mouth with her hand and widened her eyes before glancing fearfully at the hall.

Jonah grasped her shoulders. Too many times he had seen her portray innocence when her devilish mind was bent on causing mischief. She tried to wrench herself out of his grip, but he simply laughed as he refused to release her.

"Not this time, honey," he warned. "I know you took the guns. This afternoon, right? Then you calmly talked to me on the street as if you were returning from a pleasant ride in the country. If you are thinking of skipping out on our deal, I—"

"What will you do?" she interrupted sharply. She did not attempt to deny his accurate guesses, for to do so would give them credibility. "What can you do to me, Sheriff Bancroft? Not pay me the twenty-five thousand dollars you promised?" She laughed. "You never intended to give me that tremendous sum. It was only a bribe to buy my help. Will you send me to hang?" Raising her hand, she ran her fingers part way around his throat before he jerked his head from her. "Shall we die together, my love?"

With a curse, he pushed her away. He did not know whether he was more sickened by her threats or how she degraded the love she seemed eager to toss aside in order to return to her life of robbery. Abruptly he wondered if she had been lying, just as he had lied about her brother, from the beginning. He thought of her willingness to allow him to seduce her after she put up a token resistance. Her enticing allure might have been just another act by the consummate actress K.T. Forrester.

"Damn you!" he snarled. "Have it your way!"

"I certainly intend to!"

He continued as if she had not spoken, "I will deal with the rest of my plan without you, honey. Stay or leave as you like. I imagine you plan to stay with your wonderful Daddy who gives you the luxury I never could."

"You give me anything?" She snorted in a most unladylike fashion. When she put her fisted hands on her hips, in spite of the dress she appeared the fiery robber she had been when he shot her. "All you have given me is trouble and heartbreak, Jonah Bancroft! Why should I long for more of that?"

He pressed his hat onto his head so hard the brim became misshapen. As he raged toward the door to the hall, he called over his shoulder, "That's fine with me. Call off the wedding!"

"What wedding?" she asked, startled.

"Ours!"

"What?"

His smile was colder than any she had ever taunted him with. He put a hand on the door frame as he assumed a pose of nonchalance she was sure he did not feel. "I thought we might get married when this was all over, but . . ."

Shock weakened Katie's knees. Her hand on the back of the chair guided her onto its cushion. She wanted to speak . . . to retort with anger that she did not want to bind her life permanently to his . . . to announce she had no idea how to respond to his outrageous proposal . . . to whisper how she loved him. Inhibited by the conflicting thoughts spilling helter-skelter through her head, she said nothing.

When she felt a hand smoothing the hair loosened from the bun at the back of her neck, she closed her eyes. She did not want to love Jonah.

"Is this what you wanted?"

With a graceful flourish he dropped to one knee in front of her. His hand scooped hers to bring it to his lips for a kiss.

"Do you want a proposal on bended knee, honey? Katie, I love you. Why not marry me? Then we can fight for all of eternity." His smile vanished as he became somber. "Katie, marry me. Forget how and why we met. Just remember how much we love each other."

"Jonah, this is so unexpected," she murmured with lame triteness. Then her face hardened suddenly as she snapped, "If you are doing this to tease answers about—" She hesitated before adding, "—about things from me, I can tell you—"

"Tell me yes, honey." His other hand stroked her colorless cheek as he exulted at being able finally to disconcert her into speechlessness. "I mean this honestly. After the love we have shared, did you think I would let you disappear from my life?"

Pushing his hands away, she leaned back in the chair to put space between them. She could not think clearly when he touched her. Then she believed all his cleverly spun lies, which surrounded her in a caress nearly as sweet as his fingers upon her skin.

"I don't know what to think any longer," she lamented.

"Do you love me?"

She answered quickly, knowing how senseless it was to lie at this point. "Yes, dammit, I love you!"

His hand moved along her arm resting on the chair. Amusement tinted his voice as he answered, "You don't have to make it sound like it's a dreadful curse to love me."

"Isn't it?" Again she shoved him away. Rising, she crossed the room to escape from his overpowering masculinity. When she was so close to him, when she could smell the heady, musky scent of his body, she could not imagine denying him the love she yearned for with all her heart.

Just when she thought she had her life in her own control again, he had come to tease her errant heart into insanity one more time.

"I want to be K.T.," she whispered.

Across the room, Jonah heard her desperate plea for her freedom. He knew he could not offer her that wild life, but wondered if she was only running away from the first thing in her life that had frightened her. Pushing her to see the situation logically would send her fleeing from him more swiftly. When he discovered the pistols missing this evening, he had rushed to Flynn's house, afraid he already was too late to keep her in his life.

Quietly he suggested, "Let's go for a ride. We need to talk, honey, where we don't need to worry about being overheard."

"Jonah, it is dark. Lyndon doesn't want me to go out with you alone."

"Afraid?"

At last, she met his gaze steadily. Strength filled her as she wondered why his apparently jesting words reached deep into her and found the truth she tried to mask even from herself. She closed the distance between them until she stood bare inches from the tin star shining dully in the lamplight.

"Yes," she whispered. "I'm afraid of you and this love that strips me of all reasonable thought."

"That is the curse of love, Katie." He put his hands on her slender shoulders as she moved into his embrace. With his mouth close to her ear, he murmured, "Yet, conversely, it brings us a joy we can find with no one else."

"I don't like being out of control of myself or anything else."

He chuckled before teasing her ear with the tip of his tongue. When he heard her eager gasp of delight, he knew he must have her for at least a short time.

"I know," he answered. "Katie Bancroft will be a martinet in her household."

Stepping back, she regarded him with a wry smile. "Damn sure of yourself, aren't you, sheriff? Why do you think I would marry a man who has shot me and accused me of all kinds of skulduggery? I should hate you."

"But you don't."

"No, I don't."

Laughing at the regret in her voice, he held out his hand to her. She put hers in it and walked with him to the front door. He did not listen to the lie she told Taylor as he took her cloak from the peg. Draping it over her shoulders, he smiled at the butler.

"Tell Mr. Flynn we will be back as soon as possible."

"Yes, sheriff." Taylor did not allow his thoughts to show. Although Miss Katie had always been honest with him, he doubted if she was honest tonight when she spoke of helping the sheriff at his office. He had noted the sparks of unsated love in the eyes of the two walking across the snow-frosted porch hand in hand.

If Miss Katie had decided to take a lover as her father did, Taylor would not betray her to Mr. Flynn. The love affair would not be allowed to last for long, for he had overheard Mr. Flynn dictating a letter to Mr. Daly about references for a Mr. Fraser Spalding who worked for the head of the Anaconda syndicate and wanted to court Miss Katie.

Jonah stopped the buggy in front of his house. With the streets empty of pedestrians, he knew that no one was likely to see him take Katie into his house. Not that he cared. As things were going, the culmination of twenty years' waiting should come soon. Then he would have everything he had yearned for, and pretty Katie as well.

Watching while he lit the lamp on the table, Katie moved stiffly when he motioned for her to sit on the sofa. She felt uneasy as she did as he silently requested. Although she had been here just hours ago, the house seemed different. She had been a prisoner here and a thief. For the first time, she felt shy in Jonah's home.

Beyond the windows, she could see the gentle snowfall covering the ugliness of the town. The icing that accented each blade of grass and every indentation in the wood buildings made Copr Peak pretty for the first time.

She flinched when Jonah touched her. "Is something bothering you, honey?"

With a laugh, she put her fingers over his on her arm. Her eyes twinkled as brightly as the lights on the fresh fall of snow. "Maybe I have become too respectable. I feel very uncomfortable sneaking away to be with you."

"I can take you home."

"No!" She looked unswervingly at him. Seeing his smile, she relaxed and let him settle her against him on the settee. "I want to be with you, Jonah, but . . ."

He stroked her shoulder as he sympathized in a tenderly ironic voice. "I understand. You have your image as the daughter of Lyndon Flynn to live up to."

"Don't speak of him now!"

At her vehemence, all his good humor vanished. "Honey, what has he done?"

"Nothing since that one time in Butte, but I wonder what it will be like when he is feeling like himself again." She put her hands on his shoulders as she looked with supplication into his face. "I don't know how to deal with a man who . . . He believes he is my father, but does—does that!"

Rising, he brought her to her feet. "Let me help you forget everything but our love, Katie."

"Yes," she said almost desperately.

She leaned her head against him as they walked together into the bedroom. When he closed the door, she felt a twinge of regret that she must remember all the days he had locked her into this room. She did not want to think of those days when she despised him. All she needed was his love.

Her gloomy thoughts disappeared as he twirled her into his arms and tasted the delights waiting for him on her lips. He smothered her depressing memories when he chuckled and slipped his arm beneath her knees. Lifting her, he dropped her on the bed as he had the day she tried to escape. He leaned over her and smiled.

"I know what you are thinking, honey. Once I imprisoned you here."

"Yes, and I hated it and you."

"I don't hate you, even if you keep me as a captive of your heart. I want to love you."

She gripped his flannel shirt and pulled him closer. "Then stop talking and love me."

"Yes, ma'am, Miss St. Pierre," he returned with a laugh.

As soon as his mouth touched hers, the jesting vanished. She raised her arms to his shoulders and surrendered to the power of their love. A yearning stronger than any she ever experienced made her its thrall. It urged her fingers to hurry as she unbuttoned his shirt and pulled the light material aside.

Feverishly, she helped him undo the many hooks along her blouse and skirt. At the touch of his naked chest against her skin, she moaned with unbridled longing. Her fingers swept along his smooth muscles and felt his reaction deep in her mouth as he pressed her to the bed.

She entwined her legs in the longer length of his sinewy limbs. When he twisted so she could look down into his hooded eyes, she sampled the flavors of his skin. The banquet she had enjoyed for such a short time whetted her appetite for more of the ecstasy. From the sandy surface of his bewhiskered face to the uneven satin of his chest, she let her lips explore every angle of his hard body. As he abandoned his senses to the passion sweeping through both of them as if they shared one mind, she delighted in the broad stroke of his hands urging her to yield up her heart to him.

When his hands gripped her arms and tugged her mouth back to his, she gasped. His eyes sparkled with the fire within him as he leaned over her. He gripped her wrists and pressed them to the mattress as his mouth silenced her shock. Probing deep with his tongue, he did not allow her to move beneath him. A need so strong it became almost anguish surged through her.

Holding her arms together over her head, he let his mouth and fingers explore her with the intimacy she had ached to know again. She fought against his gentle enslavement as she writhed in mind-dissolving desire. A sharp cry escaped from her lips as his tongue moved along her curves.

"Let me go!" she gasped as she tried to escape his hands holding her to the bed.

"Never!"

Her blurred gaze was caught by his fierce eyes. As he was welcomed by the velvet softness of her body, she felt his fingers release her arms. She raised them to his shoulders as she tugged his mouth to hers. At the touch of his fiery lips, she lost herself to the need to satisfy this craving that stripped her of every other emotion. The driving, pulsing, powerful voracity consumed her in its flames. She melted to be one with the man who had driven her to this passion, and who she loved with all her heart.

A gentle kiss urged Katie to open her eyes. Weak fingers rose to touch his face displaying his amazement at the strength of the love they had found. That expression brought joyous tears to glisten like dark jewels in her eyes, for knowing he was as overwhelmed by their passion as she was made what was magnificent even more perfect.

"I didn't believe it truly would be as wondrous to be in your arms as I recalled on the nights when I couldn't sleep," she whispered as she rested her head on his shoulder. "But it is!"

"You couldn't sleep?"

Her fingers traced the firm planes of his face. "Jonah, I would lie awake and think of how much I wanted to be with you here." She rolled onto her stomach so she could look up at him. "I nearly drove down uninvited to see if you felt the same."

"I did." His hand stroked her dark hair. "Someday soon, this will be ours any time we want. I hate to ask you to wait a while longer, my love, but—"

"Your work isn't finished." Bitterness crept back into her voice. "Jonah, maybe you have done enough. I don't want to risk our love for your hatred."

"Nothing will keep me from loving you," he

vowed. Leaning her back in the pillows, he kissed her to seal the promise he had no intention of ever breaking. When she smiled, he was sure nothing could prevent him from fulfilling his dreams centering around this woman ... not even the final destruction of the man who considered her his daughter.

CHAPTER NINETEEN

Lyndon was in a jubilant mood when Katie came into the dining room to greet him at midday. As had been his habit before he took her in his arms in Butte, he bent his tall frame to kiss her cheek. "Good afternoon, my dear. You look like the first daffodil of spring."

Glancing at her soft yellow frock, she grinned impishly. "I thought you would like me better dressed like this than as I was an hour ago. This morning after my ride, I cleaned the horse's stall. I smelled like the lowest stableboy."

He frowned. "You shouldn't be doing chores out there. I have a full crew to handle the custodial tasks."

"I like working in the stables. Time has been heavy on my hands with all the wonderful people here taking such good care of me."

"Here." He handed her a glass of lemonade. "This will refresh you."

Putting her fingers lightly on his arm, she looked up into his face. "Lyndon, we must talk about something. I had a discussion with Jonah last night." When he did not reply with the anger she expected, she turned to look at him. Her brow furrowed as she saw the queer expression on his face. "What's the matter, Lyndon? Are you ill?"

His hand pressed to his chest as his face turned an inhuman shade of gray. Like a rag doll, he sagged to the floor. A low groan escaped his blue-tinged lips as his features contorted with a pain he could not tolerate.

Katie dropped to his side. She screamed in terror, "Mrs. Grodin!"

The housekeeper ran into the room followed closely by the butler. One look at the prostrate man and the panic-stricken Katie warned her of the seriousness of the situation. Miss Katie did not become hysterical over nothing. She urged, "Miss Katie, stay calm. Just talk gently to him. Keep him awake. Taylor, send for Dr. Havering. I will get some of the boys to carry him upstairs."

"What is it?" Katie cried.

Over her shoulder as she rushed away, Mrs. Grodin answered, "His heart."

His heart!

Katie tried to still her trembling fingers as she held them up to keep the sun glaring through the window from his eyes. When he had told her over and over it was simply indigestion, she wanted to believe him. Not knowing what she said, she prattled while her other hand remained n his on his chest. As the spasm passed, the painful grip on her fingers eased.

Though his face did not regain its normal color, Lyndon whispered, "I don't want to die now, my darling Katie."

"Don't say that. You aren't going to die! You are going to get well." She kept her fear out of her falsely cheerful voice.

"I should die happy having met you. When I think of what you and Eugenie suffered—"

Gently she leaned over him to kiss his cheek. "Hush. I don't want to hear you speak of dying again."

"Stay with me, Katie," he murmured. "Please."

She could not ignore the pleading in his eyes. "Of course, Lyndon. As long as you need me, I will be here."

Katie felt her terror lessen slightly when Mrs. Grodin returned. The burly men with her picked up the stricken man carefully. Before the housekeeper followed them upstairs, she turned to the young woman rising to her feet. Miss Katie's face was nearly as pale as her father's.

"Are you all right, Miss Katie?"

Katie ignored the question as she watched the slow procession through the dining room. "May I come up also?"

Mrs. Grodin hesitated. A young lady should not be attending a man by his bedside, even her father. Then she nodded and placed her arm around Miss Katie's quivering form. "Come along, dear. It will hurry his recovery to see your pretty face by him. He has become so fond of you."

"Will he live?" She voiced her greatest fear with trepidation.

"This isn't his first attack. We can only wait and see what Dr. Havering says."

"Not his first one?" She turned to look at the housekeeper as they climbed the stairs side by side. "Why didn't someone tell me?"

Mrs. Grodin did not answer as she rushed to tend the ailing man. Pausing by the door, Katie wondered who else knew of Lyndon's failing heart. She closed her eyes and leaned on the wall. She was sure that Jonah had learned of or guessed his enemy's condition. This explained why he was waiting patiently for something to happen, but what this heart palpitation would mean to Jonah and his plans, she could not begin to understand.

As soon as he arrived, Dr. Havering ordered everyone to leave the room so he could examine his patient. In the hallway, the women waited uneasily for a word from the doctor. As Katie paced, she tried to envision what would change when Lyndon recovered. When the door opened, she twirled in a mixture of fear and hope.

"Are you Katie?" asked the doctor in his rumbling voice.

"Yes, sir."

"Come in. He insists that you receive the instructions for his care instead of his valet." His disparaging glance seemed to dismiss the young woman as being inadequate to handle any chore. "Come along, girl." Without further explanation, he closed the door in Mrs. Grodin's anxious face.

He led Katie through the suite she had never entered. It was larger than hers and far more elaborately decorated, as befitted the master of the house. Over the marble fireplace in the sitting room hung a portrait of a woman and a man who resembled Lyndon slightly. Katie wondered who they were. Lyndon had never spoken of another family.

Dr. Havering explained his prescriptions and their dosages, adding, "If he doesn't make sense, Miss St. Pierre, it's because I have dosed him for the pain."

"I understand." He opened the door to admit her to the bedroom before bidding her a good day. She was startled. She had thought he would come in with her to see Lyndon.

"Dr. Havering?"

"Yes, Miss St. Pierre?" he demanded shortly.

She hesitated. His officious manner made it impossible for her to tell him that she had never been in this bedroom before. Fearing that her face glowed as rosily as the heat pouring from her cheeks, she could not tell the doctor that the man everyone thought of as her father wanted her to share his bed. She lowered her eyes and said merely, "Thank you, doctor."

"Hmph!" he snorted. "I don't know why Lyndon wants a child like you around him. You women are all alike! Soft and pampered. How's this country going to maintain its supreme spot on the globe if its females cannot cope with a small crisis?"

His words stung her into forgetting her manners. "Dr. Havering," she replied with cold dignity, "I'm quite capable of coping with a crisis." She did not tell him how she had dealt with every medical emergency afflicting the Forresters and their partners.

He repeated his derisive "Hmph!" before adding, "Good day, Miss St. Pierre. You are keeping your father waiting."

It took all her strength not to slam the door after him as he strode away. Then she wondered if Dr. Havering, like everyone else in the valley, hated Lyndon. She forced her irritation aside as she went into the bedroom. The patient did not need to see her agitation when he was ill.

In the large oak bed, she saw Lyndon propped up beneath the silver coverlet. With a smile to hide her qualms and her hands clasped in front of her, she crossed the room like a young child approaching a stranger.

"How do you feel?" she asked in a near whisper.

"Better, my dear." He smiled at her. The expression was so normal that relief came to her instantly. "Just having you here is the best medicine I can have."

"The doctor has told me what we need to do to get you well. If you are good, you will be up soon."

Lyndon slid his hand across the cover to take her hand. His fingers stroked her soft skin as he stared up into the worry-darkened eyes of the vision before him. He was determined to best this affliction. He did not want his time with his dear Katie cut short.

"Sit down. Pull up a chair and sit beside me."

"Shall I sit with you until the medicine takes effect?"

He smiled. "Stay as long as you like. I never tire of your sweetness." His pale eyes scanned her face. "How are you doing, Katie?"

At first his question startled her. Then she laughed. "Just like you, I too am doing better. We are going to get you better so you don't terrify me again!"

"If anyone can help me, it is you, Katharine Tamara."

"Katharine Tamara?" she repeated, puzzled. "Why do you call me that?"

Picking up her hand, he put both of his around it. "You told me your name is Katharine Tamara St. Pierre, as it shall be until some wonderfully lucky man changes it. Humor me, my dear. I like the lyrical sound of your name." He yawned. "I think the powders are working. By tomorrow evening, I shall be up again. Havering said this was just a mild tremor."

Not wanting to disagree with him, she smiled and nodded. She sat beside him until he was asleep. Gently she eased her fingers out from under his hand. She kissed his forehead lightly as she whispered a soft farewell. She informed Lyndon's valet, a taciturn man in his middle years, to call Mrs. Grodin if there was anything amiss.

Wearily Katie went down the wide stairs. Taylor met her in the hall and asked her to come with him. He led her to the dining room where Mrs. Grodin waited. She sat down at the table as they requested. When she stared unseeing at the plate before her, a glass was put in her hand, and she was told to drink.

She choked on the strong taste of the brandy, but gratefully took another, smaller sip. She needed its calming effect. "Thank you."

"Will you be all right, Miss Katie?"

"I'm fine, Mrs. Grodin." Raising her eyes to the two, she motioned for them to sit. When Taylor hesitated, she added, "Please join me. I need to talk to someone." She swallowed past the blockage of fear in her throat. "I was wondering if I should leave. I don't want to add stress to Lyndon's heart."

Taylor exchanged a glance with the housekeeper before he answered, "Don't talk of leaving, Miss Katie. Mr. Flynn has no other family, and it is harder to be ill when one is alone. All he has is his valet Pemberton, and he is such a disgusting creature, I am not sure if he helps or hinders Mr. Flynn's health."

"Taylor!" Mrs. Grodin admonished.

He did not attempt to apologize. " 'Tis the truth, Mrs. Grodin. Miss Katie, must you go? I was under the impression this was your only home. Do you have another place to live?"

"No," she answered swiftly, not wanting to reveal Jonah's proposal of marriage until she could tell Lyndon of it, "but I fear that this attack is partly my fault. My sudden appearance may have been too much for Lyndon."

Mrs. Grodin patted her hand. "Child, Mr. Flynn is happy with you here. If anything, your visit has delayed this attack. But if it makes you uneasy to be near illness, then we do not want to keep you here."

"That is no problem. I have never been squeamish." She took another sip of the brandy that relieved the tightness of her tense body. The tales she could tell them to prove her assertion they would find unbelievable.

Mrs. Grodin looked at her with a critical eye. "If you aren't going to eat, you should lie down. You look peaked, Miss Katie. Don't forget to think of yourself. The stress will affect you as well as Mr. Flynn."

Katie nodded, struggling with her sudden fatigue. When she rose, she felt her knees turn to rubber. Sitting down abruptly, she put her hands over her face and began to cry as the belated reaction struck her. She did not admire Lyndon, and since his kiss in the Butte hotel, she found his company loathsome. Despite that, it bothered her to think of him dying.

"I'm fine," she gasped through her sobs as they tried to comfort her. "I am really. It's just—just—"

"We know," Taylor murmured. He aided her to her feet and put his arm around her waist.

Carefully he guided her to the front stairs, where he gave her into the care of the housekeeper. He had longstanding orders from his employer on what to do in a situation like this. If he did not put them into motion, he would find himself being reprimanded severely by Mr. Flynn. In the past, he had hesitated to obey, but this time was different. As he watched the women slowly climb the stairs, he called for one of the houseboys to run into town to the telegraph office.

Mrs. Grodin assisted Katie into her room. She closed the drapes to darken the bedroom to a firelit twilight. Urging her charge to lie down, she promised to call if Mr. Flynn's situation changed.

"You rest now, Miss Katie."

"I will," she promised.

She listened for the hallway door to close before burying her head in the pillows. Desperately she sought sleep to escape her fears. Hours passed before she could erase from her mind the scene of Lyndon collapsing.

Katie walked cautiously across the floor with her eyes fastened on the cup in the center of the tray she carried. The coffee sloshed nearly over the rim. As a nurse, she was a failure, but her patient was doing well despite her lack of skills.

Entering the bedroom, she called, "Good morning, Lyndon."

"Ah, breakfast." He grumbled to himself as he pushed himself up to a sitting position. The continued bedrest ordered by the doctor irritated him, but he did not want to risk another heart palpitation so soon after the other. "Has Offerdahl arrived yet?"

She smiled as she placed the tray on his knees. "A telegram arrived. He will be here this evening. Now, will you stop worrying about the company? Mr. Isler has everything under control. He asked me to sign some forms he had to send out this morning. I hope you don't mind."

Although his grimace said the opposite, he mumbled, "Of course not. The company must be tended to, even if I'm confined to this damn bed."

"Eat!" she urged. She did not want to tell him when he was in this grumpy mood that it had been more than a few papers Isler had brought to her. The mine manager had urged her to assume leadership until her father was well. When she balked, he told her she had no choice. He could make the decisions necessary to keep the company running, but he must have her signature to validate any orders.

Lifting a spoonful of scrambled eggs to his mouth, Lyndon paused. He said in a weak voice, "If something happens to me, Katie—"

She put her hand on his. "Lyndon, don't speak like this."

"I must. If I survive this attack, there will come a time when I won't. You must be taken care of." He looked down at the food on the tray for a long minute before he said, "You have a cousin."

"A cousin?" For the first time in weeks, she suddenly felt uneasy as Katharine St. Pierre. Slowly she asked, "Do you mean those cousins back on Mr. McGwein's plantation upriver?"

He smiled, and his thick jowls moved at an odd angle. Taking her hand, he pulled her closer so he could kiss her cheek. As he had too often, he wondered why this beautiful woman was his daughter.

A twinge cut across his chest. As if from a distance, he heard her soothing voice urging him to rest. He would, but he had to tell her the truth he had hidden from her since her arrival. "You must hear this."

"All right, but, Lyndon, please do not excite yourself."

"My brother was with me in New Orleans. He found a woman eager for the company of a Union soldier, unlike your mother . . ." He cleared his throat and looked away from her. When he continued, he stared at a distant wall as if he could see the past. "She fell in love with Theodore. When he was to be sent to fight, she went to his commanding officer to beg for a change in his orders. It was to no avail. I saw her only once after that when she came to inform me she was to have his child. Theodore was killed in battle, and I never heard from her again."

"So you do not know if it was a boy or a girl?"

He shook his head. "All I can tell you is that Theodore's mistress's name was Rayna Dubois. Find her when you are alone, Katie. You shouldn't be by yourself again."

"Lyndon, this is unnecessary." She tried to smile, but the muscles in her face refused to cooperate. "The doctor said you should be fine."

With a snarl, he ordered, "Be silent! I know how serious this attack was. I want you to be taken care of. Don't forget her name."

"I won't." She did not want to argue when his face was such a strange color.

He shook off her soothing hand. "What is her name?"

"Rayna Dubois," Katie answered quietly.

"Don't forget it."

When she promised to remember it always, she had no idea what that vow would bring her. At the time, she wanted only for him to rest. Taking the tray he was not interested in finishing, she left him to Pemberton after reassuring him that she would be back later to entertain him.

Taylor met her at the foot of the stairs. Before he could speak, she translated his happy expression enough to ask, "Sheriff Bancroft?"

"Yes, Miss Katie." He could not hide his delight in having the sheriff come to strengthen her. "I asked him to wait in the library."

Tiredly, she nodded. "Thank you."

When she entered the room, Jonah turned and asked, "How is he?"

"Much the same," she answered with a sigh as she closed the thick door so they could speak without the fear of eavesdroppers. "He hates being kept in bed, so he's doing too much too soon." Sitting in a chair, she folded her hands in her lap. Her shoulders ached with the stress of the last two days. "I have never seen a man so miserable."

"You feel sympathy for that bastard?"

Exerting all her strength, she forced herself to look up at him. "He is ill. I would have sympathy for a sick dog."

"He's worse than a dog!"

"Why?" Holding out her hand to him, she begged, "Jonah, will you tell me why you hate him so strongly after two decades?"

His face contorted as he wrenched her to her

401

feet. He took her by the shoulders and shook her harshly before shoving her away, clearly deciding that she could not see sense. As he walked toward the fireplace, his silhouette was as unyielding as the massive mountains hovering over Copper Peak.

When he said nothing, she repeated her question. Sharply he stated, "Because that bastard you are so worried about killed my father."

Katie stared at him, unable to form a coherent thought. In the weeks she had been forced to be Katharine St. Pierre, she had created a history for her alter ego and the others in this fateful triangle. She had assumed that Eugenie St. Pierre was related to Jonah and that she was the one he longed to avenge.

She crossed the room. Jonah turned at the rustle of satin, his emotions bare on his surprisingly vulnerable face. Gently she took his hands in hers. She gazed up into his sorrowful eyes as he wrapped his arms around her while she stepped closer to him.

"Will you tell me?" she whispered.

"You don't want to know, Katie." Leaving one arm around her waist, he raised the other so he could touch the softness of her cheek.

A rueful smile dimmed the compassion in her eyes. Somewhere along the way to Jonah's goal, they had forgotten their beginnings. Perhaps that was not so bad, for they had found a love that neither of them had expected would be theirs. One final wall separated her from the man she loved. If she could knock it down in the aftermath of Lyndon's collapse, she might begin to believe they could be successful at this game and survive it.

"I'm not squeamish, Jonah. I think I should know."

"That's right. You aren't squeamish, are you?" He grinned suddenly. "Since you have become Katie St. Pierre, it is not easy to remember . . . what was before. All right. If you want to know the truth, I'll tell you, honey."

He steered her to the sofa and seated her. Although he hesitated, he sat next to her. Silence filled the room with grim anticipation. Taking his hand, she held it between hers. She wanted to let him know she ached for him.

A fleeting smile showed his appreciation before he began his tale. His eyes grew dim with the memory he wanted to erase with his revenge. "I was not yet ten years old when the Confederacy lost their finest jewel. New Orleans controlled the Mississippi, and, without its lifeblood, the Confederate States of America were doomed. The Union Army under General Benjamin Butler was given the task of punishing those who were foolish enough to defy the laws of the United States."

"I remember," she murmured. At his startled expression, she said, "You told me before . . ."

"Before," he acknowledged. Never could they forget how easily a thoughtless word might betray them. Putting his arm around her shoulders, he gazed past Katie as he continued with his painful recollections.

He had had little sense of impending doom when he and his father left their home for a trip to the wharves where the senior Bancroft had his business. Traveling by coach through the streets of New Orleans, they saw few signs of the occupation by the Union Army. Young men in uniform clustered on corners, but the streets were always busy anyway.

Then they had heard the scream of a terrified woman. Ordering the carriage halted, Randolph Bancroft leapt from it to leave his young son peering from the open door. He walked to the sidewalk and confronted a trio of men surrounding a woman nearly hysterical with fear.

"Why don't you gentlemen leave this lady alone?" Jonah heard his father ask with his usual courteous tone, although Randolph Bancroft must have been enraged.

"She is belittling the Union," a thick man retorted. "General Butler has ordered that any woman insulting the Union or its representatives should be treated as the harlot she is. I was just explaining it to this one. Why don't you get the hell out of here?"

"No, sir, don't leave me with them," cried the woman. "I was simply on my way to market. They—"

"Shut up, whore!"

Randolph moved to halt the man's hand as he lifted it to strike the cowering woman. "Will you desist, sir?"

The answer was one never expected by a youngster raised in a loving home amid the genteel life New Orleans was famous for worldwide. The man who was obviously the leader turned to face Jonah's father. He had lifted his pistol and fired point-blank into the man who had tried to keep him from taking the woman he wanted.

Katie turned away to hide her overflowing eyes as Jonah continued to speak without emotion of watching his father's face vanish into a bloody mass of pulp. He had seen little more as the coach driver shouted an order to the horses. As the carriage sped away, a horrified child vowed to repay the man who shot his father.

"I learned later that the woman was Eugenie St. Pierre, the daughter of a well-to-do family. She had been betrothed to a man serving with the Confederate Army. The man who accosted her was named Lyndon Flynn. When he left New Orleans, she discovered she was pregnant. Fortunately, the child died at birth. Although her fiancé returned alive at the end of the war, she would not allow him to sully his name by marrying a fallen woman. She spent the rest of her life in a convent in the center of the city." His voice faded as the scenes of the past disappeared to be replaced by the quivering shoulders of the woman sitting next to him.

Silently he pulled her into his arms. He was amazed that comforting her gave him the greatest solace he had ever known. Within him grew the yearning to be sure that Katie never suffered as he had. Or never again, for his hand had been the one to order the death of her friend at the gallows.

Tipping back her head, he gazed into her eyes glistening with tears. "My love," he whispered.

"I'm sorry, Jonah. I'm so very sorry."

"I have become accustomed to those memories after twenty years." He stood. "I have work to do. I will be back this evening to see how you are doing."

Rising, she urged, "Come to dinner, Jonah. It's awful to sit there alone night after night. I need you with me."

When he held out his arms to her, she went willingly into them. She was sure she would never question her love for him again. The revelation of the pain that drove him to destroy the man who had murdered his father allowed her to strengthen her alliance with him.

CHAPTER TWENTY

onah leaned on the mantel of the fireplace in
he drawing room. His after-dinner glass of
randy caught the light of the fire on the hearth.
So how is he, Katie?"

"After this horrid week, the doctor is hopeful
f a complete recovery."

"You don't seem upset by that news."

Her eyes widened. "Upset? Why should I be
pset to hear he is going to live?"

Taking a deep drink of the brandy, he re-
arded her with the derision she had not seen
n his face since the onset of this charade. "Some-
mes you act so stupid, Katie. I know you are
ntelligent. Certainly you know your esteemed
ather called in his lawyers again for a consulta-
on last night."

"Yes, I greeted them myself. Mr. Offerdahl
rought his partners. They were busy with
yndon until nearly nine o'clock. You would

have thought they could have waited until h
was feeling better to come here with all thei
papers to be signed."

"And?"

"And what? Why are you talking in riddles
Jonah?"

He chuckled. Crossing the room to where sh
stood, he put his arms around her waist an
pulled her into his embrace. "Duncan has bee
keeping me very well informed about the tele
graphic dialogue between Flynn and his attor
neys. The reason for this sudden deluge of lawyer
is that Lyndon Flynn rewrote his will yesterday
Once he has a few details ironed out, Flynn'
Copper Mining Company will be the sole prop
erty of one Katharine Tamara St. Pierre Ban
croft when he dies." He smiled, his exultatio
glowing in his eyes. "Don't you understand
Katie?"

"I understand all too well." She pushed agains
him, but he refused to release her. "You hav
received your revenge and more than you eve
expected. You don't care if a man must die fo
you to get your satisfaction."

"Don't be silly, honey. I didn't try to convinc
Flynn to leave his holdings to the daughter h
cannot trust himself not to seduce. You did that.
He grinned as he ran his hand along her slende
form. "Soon you will be richer than even you
devious, greedy mind could have wished."

Pain seared through her. "Is this why yo
asked me to marry you, Jonah? So you coul
gain possession of the one thing Lyndon prized?
Her betrayed heart gave her the strength to brea

408

his hold on her. She stepped back from him, too hurt to care if she bumped into the furniture. Later she might feel those bruises, but, as she saw the truth in his eyes, she suffered from the greater agony within her.

"Katie, I—"

"No! I won't listen to any more of your lies." She clutched the back of a settee and smiled icily. Even though she was dressed in fine satins, he recognized the wily K.T. Forrester he had seen so seldom since he convinced her to be his ally. "To think I felt sorry for you when you told me why you came to Copper Peak. Such a grand plot it was, Sheriff Bancroft! Based on ideals of love and justice, but you perverted them as much as Lyndon ever did. The only difference is that the one you used is me! No more! Get out!"

He put the empty glass on a table. When he reached for her, she shied away from him. Rage ripped his compassion from him. "You cannot throw me out, honey. This isn't your house!"

"With your help, it may soon be." Folding her arms over her chest to maintain her dignity, she raised her chin high. "Sir, I have asked you once to leave. I trust I will not have to call Taylor to have you escorted from the premises."

Knowing she would do as she threatened, he whirled toward the door. She flinched at the sound of it slamming hard enough to rattle the pictures on the walls. Tears seared her eyes as she bent to weep out her grief at learning too late that the man she loved had had an ulterior motive for everything he did. Even his love had been given with the expectation of a grand reward in return.

Katie smiled absently at Taylor as he came down the steps. In her hands were the papers Lyndon had requested that morning when she finished explaining to him what had happened at the mine the previous day. She sorted through the papers to be sure they were in order. Bushee had delivered them to her in a confused melange, but she suspected he only wanted to prove her incompetence. She brightened as she recalled that Lyndon had spoken of how he must get rid of his assistant. Perhaps then more of the profits would go to the people who deserved them, instead of filling Bushee's bottomless pockets.

She went over the news Lyndon had asked her to obtain for him. Although he was no longer bedridden, he depended on her to run many of his errands. She was pleased to keep busy. Having her mind full of other matters kept her from thinking of Jonah and his cruel twisting of her heart.

The offers from both Daly and Clark to purchase the company were waiting for him in the office in Copper Peak, but the letter he'd been waiting for from his lawyers in Butte about some information he was eager to have had not arrived. A telegram yesterday had told him that the thing he needed should be on the evening train along with the payroll from the bank in Butte, but he had hoped the papers he wanted might come earlier.

"Miss Katie?"

Pausing, she looked up from the work to say, "Yes, Taylor?"

"Mrs. Grodin asked me to remind you that this is the afternoon you were going to assist her with the plans for the Christmas party."

"Of course. Let me take these to Lyndon first. I will meet her in about fifteen minutes." She grimaced as she added, "I can't pretend I'm sorry to be done with hearing all the gripes from the mines."

Taylor chuckled at her usual humor, which had been sadly missing in the house since he had overheard heated words between her and Sheriff Bancroft. Although he had been unable to distinguish the actual words, there had been no mistaking the anger between them.

Katie's slippers made little noise on the plush carpet. She kept her mind purposely blank so as not to dwell on the sorrow that was her constant companion. Working with Isler in signing the papers necessary to keep the company running had occupied her for a while, but she now had to face the emptiness of her life in this big house without the anticipation of seeing Jonah.

Hushed voices intruded on her grim thoughts as she approached the library. Katie edged closer to the doorway, not daring to believe what her ears told her.

"Those are high terms, Proulx," warned Lyndon's deep voice.

"The information is worth it." A familiar laugh halted her heart in mid-beat. "It's less than what will be stolen from you tonight when the payroll comes in on the late train."

411

"How—?"

"Your moves are no secret, Flynn." The insinuating voice must be accompanied by a crooked smile if the speaker had not changed in the months since she had seen him last. Katie could not stay to listen to the rest of the conversation.

Les Proulx! If her onetime partner was in the house, she was not safe. She had to ride into town and warn Jonah. If Les saw her, their plot would be exposed. If they did not flee, they would suffer the power of Lyndon's fury.

She placed the suddenly unimportant papers on a table in the hall. Keeping her eyes on the open door of the library, she backed away until she had put enough distance between her and it so the men would not hear her furtive footsteps. Then she turned to hurry toward her cloak hung on the coat rack.

Buttoning the dark wool under her chin, she scooped up her bag. The few dollars within might be the only thing they could salvage to start anew. She wondered what Jonah would say when she told him her ex-partner was dealing with Lyndon. Jonah might laugh in her face and accuse her of trying to fool him again, but she knew she must alert him to the danger in the white house on the hill.

As she moved stealthily toward the door, she heard an unmistakable click. She whirled to confront the gun held in Les's hand. Her eyes in her colorless face rose from it to his broken-tooth smile. Behind him, with his hand on the bottom newel post of the stairs, stood Lyndon, a shocked expression overcoming his rage with whatever Les had told him.

After letting the suspense build for nearly a full minute while none of them moved, Les said jovially, "Howdy, K.T.! You sure do look different all decked out like a fine lady."

"Proulx," ordered the other man coldly, "lower that gun. Get out! I don't care what information you have. I won't have you threaten my daughter."

"Daughter?" Les hooted with laughter as he risked taking his eyes from Katie to see the fury on Flynn's face. When she moved minutely, he affixed her again with his heartless stare. She could see he was anticipating obtaining the revenge he had vowed when she banished him from the gang. "Is that what K.T. convinced you? That she is your daughter? So you don't know who she really is, do you?"

"Les . . ." Katie halted herself. She would not beg him to spare her, but was ready for him to expose her. The servants must be watching, and the word would swiftly reach town of what had happened here. Jonah might hear before he left to prepare for the robbery. The fast-moving truth might save his life, for she feared hers already had reached its end.

He rested his thumb confidently on the hammer. "Do you want me to tell him, K.T.? I never thought I would live long enough to see you frightened!" When she did not answer his taunt, he glanced over his shoulder. "Mr. Flynn, I don't know why she is pretending to be your daughter, but that there is K.T. Forrester, leader of

413

the Forrester gang who has been robbing you
blind."

"K.T.? Katie?" Flynn's facile mind comprehended the plot instantly. He shoved the slighter
man aside and advanced on the woman.

Katie backed slowly toward the door. She put
a hand behind her to reach for it. If she could
open it, she might be able to race down the hill
to safety. Duncan or Isler might give her sanctuary. If they were there . . .

Waiting for the well-remembered agony of a
bullet cutting through her, she spun to grip the
door knob. She had to reach Copper Peak and
stop Jonah. She must. She did not want both of
them to die.

All her plans were foiled as she felt strong
hands gripping her upper arms. She was slammed
against the wall. Fearfully she met the fury twisting Lyndon's face, but she made sure he would
not guess how terrified she was. Her own face
remained serene.

"Lyndon, you are hurting me," she said, hoping she could convince him to throw Les out of
the house long enough so she could flee.

"Is he speaking the truth?"

Les interjected, "She will continue lying to
you, Flynn. You don't expect K.T. Forrester to
admit to this deception, do you?"

"Shut up!" he snarled. "Katie?"

"I don't know why you would believe that
two-bit train robber instead of me," she said.
When she saw sorrow in the second before rage
was emblazoned on his face, she knew she had
betrayed herself in some way.

414

"Train robber?" the huge man asked. He gripped her chin in his broad palm and repeated, "Train robber? How did you know that?"

"She worked with me. She masterminded—"

"Shut up, Proulx!" Lyndon glared at the man and warned him silently to lower the gun pointing at the two by the door. "Katie? Are you Katharine St. Pierre?"

Katie considered lying, then knew it was useless. Lyndon would not be treating her so harshly if he was willing to accept her falsehoods once more. She regarded him with the bravado which was all she had remaining to fight these two men who wanted to destroy her.

"I am not Katharine St. Pierre, Mr. Flynn," she said with the icy regality she had used so well during her time in this house. "I don't even know if there is such a person."

"You are K.T. Forrester?"

As much as she could with him holding her painfully to the wall, she nodded. She let pride lift into her voice as she answered, "I am K.T. Forrester, formerly the leader of the Forrester gang."

Footsteps approaching from the back of the house halted whatever abuse he planned to shout at her. He twisted her from the wall and pushed her rapidly ahead of him as he walked toward his office. When he passed Les, he motioned with his head for the man to follow.

She lifted the hem of her skirt, but before she could race away, fingers bit painfully into her arm. The odor of unwashed hair told her it was Les. If she looked at him, he would flaunt his victory before her. She did not intend to give him that pleasure.

Shutting the door behind them, Lyndon ordered, "Over there, Miss Forrester."

The name on his lips sounded so strange that Katie started. She felt an urge to beg Lyndon to reconsider, to let her live, to let her flee to the safety of his sheriff's arms. Even though she and Jonah had parted in anger, she was sure he would protect her, if for no other reason than to safeguard himself.

She had no chance to speak as Les shoved her roughly into the desk chair. From a drawer Flynn found a ball of twine. He tossed it to the man standing behind her. Knowing it was worthless to fight at this point, she compliantly followed Les's orders to put her hands behind her as Flynn went out into the hall. His statement he would be right back to deal with her sent shiver of fear through her.

Despite her cooperation, her traitorous partner whispered as he bent forward to bind her wrists with the twine, "Don't move, K.T. Mr. Flynn would not like it if I slit your throat."

"You wouldn't dare, you sniveling idiot!" she spat.

"No?" Fury distorted his life-scarred face. He pushed the flat of his knife against her throat so she could not breathe. When terror blossomed in her eyes, he drew it away to continue tightening her bonds painfully. "Be stupid, K.T., and you will get what they did."

She tried to speak, but only moaned as she could think of nothing but the fierce pain sear

416

ing her wrists as he tied them to the chair. "They" must be the train guards who had been killed mercilessly.

When he came around to regard his handiwork, he boasted, "So this is the end of the Forrester gang, K.T.? It would have been different if you had let me take over when Eli was hanged, but you Forresters are all alike. You are damned hard to get rid of."

"Rid of?" she gasped.

He patted her cheek in a patronizing motion. "For a woman, you are damn smart, but you are too trusting. You never suspected I hobbled your horse, knowing Eli would give you his. I thought I could take over the gang when he hanged, but you had Schurman mesmerized. Old Jimmy paid the price for selling me out to you when I finished him off by convincing him to do drunk what he never would have done sober. You have been a problem. You and that damnable gang who tried to stop us when we blew the Northern Pacific that night. Tonight all of you will be finished, and Les Proulx will own this valley."

Katie could not believe she had been so obtuse as not to see the snake in their midst. Of all he said, the one thing she riveted on was his plan to destroy Jonah and his cronies tonight. If she did not escape to warn him, Jonah would lead his men blithely into a trap.

The opening of a door caught her attention. She was not surprised to see a gun in Flynn's hand as he entered. Her arms strained against the sharp bite of the twine when she cried, "Lyndon, you must listen to me. This man—"

"I will listen to you," he growled. Holding the gun in front of her face, he said, "If you say anything to try to confuse the issue, Miss Forrester, you won't receive a second warning."

"Please, you must—" She halted as she saw his thumb reach for the hammer. Without glancing at Les, she knew he was smiling triumphantly, for Flynn would abet him in gaining a monopoly on the prizes rolling through Copper Peak.

"Why?" Flynn demanded, as he wiped sweat from his gray face. His shock at discovering she had lied to him had obviously strained him.

"After you hanged my friend Jimmy Schurman, I decided I would make you pay for his death." She congratulated herself on her inspiration. If Les were not standing directly behind her, she could have lied more easily. With him in the room, she had to be sure she said nothing he could disprove. "This seemed the simplest way. I had heard about your past alliances in New Orleans, so it seemed this would be the way to . . ." Her voice faded away, as she realized she did not know what she would have planned if her story had been true.

When she saw the fury contorting Flynn's face, she knew that explanations mattered little. He had consigned her to suffer already and was interested only in discovering her allies. That fear was confirmed when he shouted, "No simpleminded female train robber could have managed this alone. Who else is involved with you in this?"

"I don't know what you are talking about,"

she said with quiet conviction. By exerting the greatest effort, she could keep her eyes steady on his and appear to be telling the truth. Pain burned through her at the thought of what this cold man would do if he discovered the cabal led by his sheriff. She had not thought days ago that Jonah would be proved right in his warning that Lyndon Flynn was a beast who would turn on her. Nor had she guessed she would pay for that foolish naïveté with her life, but she would not let Flynn learn of the plot from her. In the same unwavering tone, she added, "I told you I decided to do this on my own."

Flynn raised his hand as if to hit her, but halted. Although he knew she was not his daughter, he had come to care deeply for her in the past weeks.

Not his daughter.

The thought turned around and around in his mind. If she was not his daughter, there was no reason not to treat her as he had always wanted.

Horror raced through Katie as she saw the glitter in his eyes. She could not mistake what it meant, for she had seen it often when he brought yet another strange woman into the house for a single night. If her hands had not been tied to the chair, she would have crossed her arms in front of her to block his gaze that disrobed her.

Licking his lips in eager anticipation, Flynn mused, "It's getting late. We have to get going if we want to spring that trap for those other criminals. If they're your allies, Miss Forrester, you can be sure that you will betray them before I'm finished with you."

Les stepped forward and raised his gun to her temple. "Let me take care of K.T., then we can leave."

"Fool!" shouted Flynn. He knocked the pistol away. The shorter man lowered his eyes before Flynn's glare. "If you kill her now, I never will get what I want from her."

At his new leader's orders, Les loosened the ropes that bound her arms to the chair. He tried to leer victoriously at Katie, but she ignored him as if he were of as little importance as the rug beneath her feet. Although his fingers itched for the grip of his pistol and the chance to repay her for humiliating him last time they met, he knew he must obey Flynn's orders. They had not talked money yet, but he was sure to garner a big reward from the copper king for betraying her.

"Get that," Flynn commanded, pointing to a paisley cape he had brought into the room.

Les complied quickly and draped it over the woman. Stepping back, he watched as Flynn put his arm around Katie's waist after tightening the shawl over her shoulders. The silk fringe concealed her bound hands and the pistol pressed mercilessly to her ribs. Each breath was a torture as the steel bit into her tender skin.

"I don't think I need to warn you to be sensible, Miss Forrester."

She kept her gaze on the closed door so he could not see the terror in her eyes. What he planned would be horrible. The urge to dissolve into panic increased as she felt his fat fingers stroking her side.

Retaining her dignity, perhaps her only tool to defeat him, she said icily, "Don't waste your breath, Mr. Flynn."

"You can forget the fake accent!"

A smile fled across her lips. With a short laugh, she retorted, "I have found that, for me, this is not false. My former life taught me to speak in this manner."

"A train robber?" He snorted. "Honey, train robbers don't talk like ladies." Pushing her ahead of him toward the door, he added over his shoulder, "Meet me in the stableyard, Proulx. I will be there as soon as I secure Miss Forrester."

"Yes, sir." With a laugh, he crowed, "Goodbye, K.T.! I hope you get everything you deserve!"

She resisted the urge to curse at him. Doing that would only increase his arrogant pleasure at her downfall. Walking with Flynn, she said nothing. His fingers tightened on her arms when they came into the foyer, but Taylor only looked up to nod a greeting before resuming his reprimand to the parlor maid for forgetting to dust the mantel.

Slowly they climbed the stairs. Next to her, she could hear the rasping breath of her captor. She knew he was pushing his heart to its limits with these antics, but he would not listen to her suggestion to relent. Any sympathy he would see as an attempt to elude her punishment for her deception, and she had to admit he was partially correct.

When they paused at the top of the stairs, he shoved her brutally toward his room. She groaned when her shoulder hit the heavy door, but she managed to stay on her feet. Throwing open the door, he pushed her into the sitting room.

"No, no," he said with a sadistic chuckle as she started to sit in one of the chairs. "That's not where I want you, my dear."

He locked the door to the hallway and gripped her arm. When the shawl slid to the floor, he paid it no attention. In his lair, there was no one to halt him from doing exactly as he wished with this beautiful woman who admitted she was not his child.

Katie stumbled into the inner chamber and against the massive bed. Falling to her knees, she banged her head on the siderails. Her eyes gave her a distorted view of the room as she struggled to her feet, determined she would not kneel to Flynn for any reason.

He motioned with his gun. "On the bed, woman."

"No, I—"

As she tried to flee, he shoved her back across the room. When her shin struck the small stepstool used to climb into the high bed, he laughed. She whirled to face him. Tears dribbled from her eyes, but she disregarded them and the pain searing along her leg. He snapped another order at her. She refused to move.

"I don't want to kill you yet, honey," he growled, "but if you insist, I will have little difficulty putting a bullet in the center of your pretty face."

Katie saw he was serious. That he was leaving for the train would grant her some time. If she used it wisely, she might escape from the fate he planned for her.

In spite of her efforts to appear unhurt, she limped as she turned to the bed. He waited until she sat on it. Grasping her wrists still bound by the scratchy twine, he raised them over her head and tied them securely to the headboard. Within seconds, her arms ached to the bone. She squirmed to find a more comfortable position, but froze when she felt his lascivious gaze.

She screamed when he ran his hands along her body. She could not have halted the involuntary reaction when she felt him touch her as only Jonah had done. What had been sweet in the arms of the man she loved made her skin crawl with terror at Flynn's fondling. Sliding his heavy hand along the plain front of her bodice, he began to chuckle with eager delight.

"No!" she screamed when he reached into the collar of the dark dress and pulled sharply. The heavy material ripped only a short distance, but gave him a view of the creamy skin hidden beneath her demure clothes.

With a vicious laugh, he walked to the bottom of the bed, grasped her left ankle, and pulled her body toward him. A shriek of pain burst from her as her arms were stretched agonizingly. She kicked at the hands holding her foot.

He batted her away easily and bound her slim ankle to the spindles of the footboard. She felt the seductive fingers of panic urging her to give in to terror. She closed her eyes as he caught her other leg and lashed it to the bed in the same degrading manner. Again he tightened the ropes much more than necessary and left her gasping from his torture.

A savage slap on the face brought her eyes open to reveal her tears. He smiled at her misery. "I'm glad you aren't Eugenie's daughter, honey. Or I should say, I'm glad you aren't my daughter. After I take care of those thieves, I will be back to deal with you."

"Mr. Flynn, I'm no different from the Katie I was this morning."

"But I no longer have to feel guilt for lusting after my own child." He watched her eyes widen in horror as he asked, "Do you know how many times I came into your room to stand by you as you slept and wanted to bring you back here to my bed? Now I have no reason to keep from doing exactly as I wish."

"Mr. Flynn, you must listen to me about Les Proulx. He—"

With a chuckle, Lyndon withdrew a handkerchief from his pocket. She was still urging him to listen to her as he gagged her. Her mumbles became a muffled screech as he ran a finger along the skin revealed by her ripped dress.

Eagerness filled his voice as he mused, "You look so luscious like this, I don't think I will untie you right away." He ran his fingers along her legs beneath her gown. Regretfully he sighed, "Later, honey."

Katie turned her head to follow his steps from the room. One tug on the ropes told her what she needed to know. He had secured her so well that she would never be able to break these bonds. When she heard him close the door, she knew that instructions would be left with the staff not to enter his room until he returned. She could expect no help from anyone in the house.

By the time Flynn returned, she would be so weak she could not fight his rape. She wondered if this was the same sadism that Eugenie St. Pierre had suffered, and prayed for that wronged lady's forgiveness for all the many times Katie had wished Miss St. Pierre had never existed.

Katie sagged into a semiconscious realm of pain. As each hour passed, she lost more of her will to escape.

A creak from the direction of the window brought her eyes open in new terror. She tried to cower as she saw a man approaching the bed. She knew it could not be Flynn because of the figure's smaller size, but she feared anyone who might be here.

When he bent over her, his face was revealed in the dim light. "Ethan!" she gasped when he pulled the cloth from her mouth. Instantly she forgot her agony. When he put his fingers to his lips, she added more quietly, "Where have you been?"

"Around." He grinned. "Living with far less excitement than you, it would appear."

He leaned across the wide bed and slit the ropes carefully at her hands and feet.

"Do you have horses?" she asked as she rubbed her aching shoulders.

"Two. Out behind the stable. You don't think Flynn will miss one, do you?"

"How did you get into the house?"

He laughed low so the sound would not carry past the heavy door. "That's a question I should be asking you, K.T. I couldn't believe what my eyes were telling me when I saw you riding with that old bastard through town. All gotten up like a four-bit whore." A scowl creased his forehead. "That's not what you are doing, is it?"

"Did it look like I was waiting here willingly for him?" she snapped. She leapt from the bed and winced as abused muscles screamed their refusal to obey commands. "Wait here. I have to get my pistols from my room down the hall. Then we can get the hell out of here."

"You won't get too far in that get-up. I came in the window from the porch roof. If you try it in all that lace, you are sure to fall."

Instead of arguing, she bent over to grasp the hem of her skirt and raise it above her waist. She ignored her brother's shocked expression as she turned her back to him. "Go ahead," she ordered. "Untie the petticoats. You'll have to learn to do it when you are with a woman."

When he chuckled self-consciously as he loosened the layers of cotton, she glanced over her shoulder to watch a warm flush oozing up his cheeks. She bit back the comment she was about to make. Ethan was not her baby brother any longer, and she could not fault him for looking for love as she had.

Kicking her loosened petticoats aside, she exulted in her sudden freedom of movement.

"K.T., what are you doing in this house?"

Motioning him to silence, Katie ordered urgently, "The story is too long, and we don't have the time. We have to ride to the train. We have to stop Jonah and his gang from walking into Flynn's trap."

"Jonah who?" He saw the truth on her face. Taking her by the shoulders, he shook her. "Geez, K.T., you cannot mean Bancroft! Why in hell do you want to help him?"

"I love him."

"Love? A lawman?" He grimaced as if she had told him she had been involved in the most perverted affair he could imagine. "You love Bancroft? Are you mad, K.T.?"

She whispered, meeting his dark eyes filled with disbelief. "Yes, I must be mad, but I cannot let him die."

CHAPTER TWENTY-ONE

Katie adjusted herself in the saddle. It felt wonderful to be riding astride again. Her skirt bunched up beneath her, revealing a long length of leg in dark stockings. She was glad she had been wearing this navy dress. It would blend with the night.

Even as she had skulked along the hallway and strapped on her holster, she had wondered how she could explain to her brother the thoughts flitting in the confusion of her brain. She felt she owed Jonah this rescue, for he had saved her life once. In her mind, she could hear Ethan saying it was Jonah's fault that she needed saving in the first place.

There was no time for such thoughts if she wanted to save Jonah.

She looked at Ethan, and he nodded. Waving her hand in the air in the signal she had used so many times in the past, she told him to start what might be the final robbery by the Forrester gang. She urged her horse to hurry down the hill toward the stopped train.

Flames from the engine end of the iron creature gave her enough light to be sure her horse could choose the safest path. She did not have the faith in this mount that she had in the one she had trained specifically for this work. Slowing the horse at the edge of the gravel roadbed, she slid off his back. She glanced in both directions, but saw no one. Not that she had expected to see Ethan, for he had too many years experience at making himself invisible in the shadows. What worried her was not meeting Jonah or any of his men. If they were not here, she did not want to spring the trap needlessly and find herself Flynn's captive again.

The velvet gown threatened to trip her on every step. If she had been dressed in her denims instead of the dark dress, Katie would have wondered if the past months had been more than a terribly realistic dream. Sneaking up on the train like this seemed so natural that she could hardly believe she had been away. The memories of being Katharine St. Pierre and hints of another life in the smothering warmth of New Orleans disappeared as she concentrated on her task.

Grasping the metal banister at the back of the car, she swung up to the steps quietly. She tried to hear what was being said past the open door. She heard Jonah's voice ordering the guard to give him the bag in the safe. Her heart began to pound with added adrenalin. She was too late. This would not be easy now.

She drew her pistol from the holster. Settling it comfortably in her palm, she surged up the steps. Her foot kicking the door open froze the men in the room. She did not look at the guard transfixed with shock at seeing a woman with a gun in her hand.

"Drop it!" she cried. When Jonah glanced over his shoulder in surprise, she repeated, "Drop it! Forget the damn money. Flynn is on to you. He's on his way here."

She spun at the sound of a victorious laugh behind her. Carefully she kept her gun pointing at the floor as she met the rage in the narrowed eyes of the man who wanted to kill them all. She tried not to show her fear as Lyndon Flynn's pistol was placed in the center of her chest.

"I'm afraid you are wrong, Miss Forrester. I am here." Flynn motioned with his head to the suddenly smiling guard. "Get out of here. Don't let anyone in this car until I call you. Under any circumstances! Do you understand?"

"Yes, sir, Mr. Flynn." He raced away like a rat seeking its hole.

Closing the door behind the man, Flynn never moved his pistol away from Katie. He used it to shove her closer to the bandit with his bandana still concealing his face. Although he longed to learn how she had escaped from his bed, he knew he could discover that later when he got his satisfaction from her. He noted with pleasure that neither of his captives made any sudden moves which would necessitate killing them.

f he had to slay them quickly, it would lessen he fun he intended to derive from them.

"Put them on the floor," he commanded. "All he guns."

Katie leaned forward to place her weapon care-ully on the filthy boards. If it discharged by nistake, it might bring death to them immedi-itely. She felt Jonah's hand settle on her shoul-ler as she stood. This was not the way she had magined they would apologize to each other for vords too hastily spoken. She ached for his arms iround her once more before she died. Tears seared the back of her throat when she realized hat farewell was the last thing Flynn would illow.

"Back away from them," order Flynn with inother triumphant guffaw.

She bumped into the hardness of Jonah's body is she tried not to step on his toes. His fingers in her arm stroked her gently in an effort to comfort her, although there was no use pretend-ng they could best Flynn when he held a gun to Katie's chest.

They stepped backward in unison until Flynn ordered them to stop. His boots touched the tips of the guns they had dropped, so he could pre-rent them from trying to grab one.

"Slowly, very slowly, take off that handker-chief. I want to see your face when you die." Flynn chortled with glee as her face became paler. His fierce gaze centered on the man be-ind her. He would deal with pretty K.T. Forrester ifter he killed the man who dared to infringe on is kingdom.

Jonah followed his enemy's orders explicitly but his thoughts were on Katie. She had risked her life by riding out here to warn him that this too easily stopped train had been a trap. Flynn called her "Miss Forrester," so someone had tipped him off to the plot. Instead of fleeing Katie had come to try to save him and had thrown away her only chance to survive.

The knot at the back of the bandana untied easily. He felt Katie tense as the glitter in Flynn's eyes told her he was about to meet another enemy face-to-face. Pulling away the concealing material, Jonah tossed it carelessly behind the stove.

"Surprised, Flynn?" he taunted when the man stared at him in thunderstruck silence.

Flynn did not want to admit exactly that, but he had never suspected that his trusted sheriff was the one trying to bankrupt him by stealing payroll after payroll. His eyes slitted as he looked at the unspeaking woman and wondered why he had not suspected Bancroft before. Bancroft had brought her to his house and had called on her often. Their attraction had been more than coincidence.

"Did you really think you could get away with this?" he snarled.

Jonah chuckled. "We nearly did, didn't we?"

The older man's face creased with fury. He grasped Katie's arm and wrenched her away from her lover. His smile deepened as he saw the sheriff take a step toward him before pausing with a sickly pallor beneath his tanned skin. Holding the gun to Katie's skull, Flynn watched

Bancroft's face grow long with fear. He knew he could force the man to grovel in any way he chose.

"Why?" he demanded.

Forcing his eyes from Katie's terrified stare, Jonah answered with the truth. "You killed my father."

"Father? Who the hell is your father, Bancroft?"

"You never knew him, but you killed him when he tried to prevent you from raping Eugenie St. Pierre."

As he wrapped his arm around Katie's slender waist, Flynn said, "So you carried on his quixotic quest to stop me? Was it your inspiration to send this train robber into my house pretending to be Eugenie's daughter? You should have known you could not succeed. You will hang, Bancroft, as a warning to anyone else foolish enough to try to steal what is mine."

"And Katie?"

"I would not think of giving my darling daughter over to the hangman." He used the sharp tip of the gun to push back her loosened hair. "It's a shame you shall die as futilely as your father, Bancroft. Neither of you could keep me from doing as I wish. While you swing in the wind, my darling daughter and I will retire to our home for some very private moments of grief at the treason of our sheriff. Very, very private, right, K.T.?"

She stared straight ahead, her back as stiff as the line of Jonah's lips. If she gave in to her terror, she would become a hysterical blob. Her fingernails bit into her palms. She could feel her pistol next to her boots. With it in her hand, she would show Flynn exactly how she wanted to treat him.

If only ... gazing at Jonah's face, she feared there was no "if only" for them. They had risked the whims of fate too many times and lost.

Flynn ordered, "All right, Bancroft. Slowly toward the door. If you try to skip out on me on the way back to Copper Peak, I will let your lover here take your place at the gallows."

"I understand," he replied grimly. He stepped toward the back of the car when the door crashed open.

"Flynn?"

The man holding Katie started at the tremulous voice behind him. Risking a look at the pale face of the man standing in the doorway, he growled, "Proulx, what in hell—?"

A rifle shot sounded. When Flynn flinched at the sound, Katie whirled out of his grip. She brought her fisted hands down on his right wrist. He did not drop the gun, but yelped in pain. Before he could decide who to take aim at, she dropped to the floor. She grasped her pistol and raised it.

Two gunshots sounded at once. Black smoke swirled through the car. Jonah surged across the room to find a weapon. He fell to the floor as a bullet whirled past his ear. In the room filled with burnt gunpowder, he could not be sure if anyone could see who was friend and who was foe. When his fingers found a pistol, he rose to his knees to take aim.

Instantly he realized he was too late. Only a

few feet from where he crouched, he could see two shadowed forms facing each other across steel barrels. Even as he aligned his gun to shoot at Flynn, he watched the man drop his weapon and clutch at his midsection. Katie propelled herself away from him as he toppled forward to lie in his own blood.

She did not lower her guard. The still-belching gun pointed at the man on the floor. Only when she was sure Flynn would not move again did she relax slightly. She turned to see Jonah stepping over the motionless forms of Flynn and the man who had called to him. He held out his hand to her, but she did not release the gun with its trail of eye-smarting smoke.

"Thank God you never lost those reflexes." He put his arms around her.

She pulled away to gasp, "How could you be so stupid? You had your revenge against that beast. What were you doing robbing this train?"

"Beast?" His eyes noted the ragged condition of her dress. "Katie, what did he do to you?"

She waved aside his concern. She was too angry to be bothered by useless sympathy. Lyndon Flynn was dead, but she still did not understand why Jonah had decided suddenly to resume his criminal act. "How could you pull a stupid, ill-conceived, adolescent prank like this? How could—?"

With a growl, he turned to pick up the bag he had been holding when she entered the car. When he heard footsteps near the door, he whirled to take aim at whoever approached without the signal he and his friends had devised to keep from shooting at each other. When a shadow appeared in the doorway, he prepared to fire.

"No!" Katie cried, and put her hand on his arm. "That's Ethan."

The young man he recognized from the faint memory of months past regarded him with the same wariness that Katie had when he nursed her back to health. Jonah did not lower his pistol totally as he regarded the rifle in Forrester's hand. If Ethan Forrester shot as well as his sister, he could kill Jonah without winging Katie.

"Bancroft, you've gotten what you wanted," Forrester said grimly. Not taking his eyes off his enemy, he added, "C'mon, K.T. You saved his worthless life. Let's get the hell out of here."

"Wait—" Jonah halted as he heard the click of the hammer of the rifle.

Katie stepped between the two men and knocked the barrel of the rifle toward the floor. "Don't point that at anyone you don't intend to kill, Ethan. I know Jonah is a lawman, but I love him." When she felt Jonah's hand stroking her shoulder, she added more coldly, "I love him even though he is an idiot."

The sound of a gunshot interrupted Jonah's retort. He smiled as the two Forresters tensed and raised their weapons in a motion that had been practiced enough to be instinctive. Before they could fire, he warned, "Someone is on their way here. That was one of my men letting us know. We have to get out of here."

"Where?"

"Flynn's house, for now. It would be best if it wasn't known that you and I were here, Katie."

"The guard—"

Ethan stated grimly, "He won't talk. I saw Les take care of him when he emerged from the car. One slice of a knife, and the man was dead."

Katie shivered as she leaned against Jonah. When she felt his arm around her, she let him usher her out of the car. All the many random actions of their lives had come to a culmination tonight along this isolated stretch of track. If Jonah's father had not chosen that route to take to the river . . . If she had not thrown Les out of the gang . . . She wondered what other strange actions would be explained tonight, but knew she intended to discover exactly why Jonah had come to this train when his revenge nearly had been in his hands.

CHAPTER TWENTY-TWO

Taylor met them at the door of the fancy house. Greeting them with his usual courtesy, he did not notice that Miss Katie did not remove her cloak as she excused herself to go up the stairs. She called behind her, "Taylor, will you escort Sheriff Bancroft and his friend to the drawing room? I will be with them in a moment."

"Yes, Miss Katie." He said nothing of his confusion at her odd action, but gestured for the men to precede him into the elegant room. After making sure there was plenty of brandy in the decanter, he drew the pocket doors closed to leave them to their privacy.

Ethan could not hide his awe with his surroundings, or his unease with Bancroft. His hands stayed near his hips where he could grab his pistols at the slightest provocation by the other man. Dark eyes were the only part of him that moved as his gaze followed Bancroft crossing the room.

Lifting the decanter of golden brandy, Jonah asked in a conversational tone, "A glass, Forrester?"

"No."

"You might as well drink it. It belonged to Flynn, and he has no use for it any longer." He smiled as he poured two servings and offered one to the other man. "She's a damn good shot."

"She never misses what she aims at," he unbent enough to say as he accepted the goblet. He took a sample sip and smiled at the smoothness unknown in the disgusting saloons he had been frequenting since K.T. disappeared.

Jonah chuckled. "Katie has told me that on more than one occasion. After seeing her proficiency with that pistol, I'm inclined to agree with you."

Silence settled uncomfortably on them as Ethan kept his eyes on the brandy in his glass. Neither man was sure what to say. With his revenge completed, Jonah had again become the lawman who would be obligated to hang the other man in the room.

Finally Ethan said, "Give us a day's head start, sheriff. We will stay out of your territory in return."

"Head start?" Jonah leaned on the back of the settee as he faced the hard features so like Katie's. In the months since "baby" brother had been hiding, Ethan Forrester had lost his softness to become as strong as his sister. "What makes you think I'll let her go?"

"You're going to hang her after all she has done for you?" Ethan placed his glass on a table, paying no attention to the liquid splashing on the valuable wood. "You bastard, I—"

Seeing Forrester's fingers reaching for the pistol, Jonah raised his hands slowly away from the guns he wore. "Whoa, Forrester, listen to sense. Don't be bullheaded like your sister. . . have no plans to hang her. I want to marry her."

"Still?"

Both men glanced toward the door, which stood slightly ajar. Framed by the dark oak, Katie looked from one tense face to the other. She did not need to know the course of the conversation that had urged her brother to draw his pistol on Jonah. Closing the door, she walked toward them with the rustle of pink satin. She ignored the wide eyes of her brother as he saw her for the first time in her complete incarnation of Katharine St. Pierre. All of her attention was on the man who held her heart.

"Jonah," she asked softly, for she did not dare to speak the precious wish aloud and have it be untrue, "do you still want to marry me?"

"Of course." He went to her and put his hands on her shoulders encased in lace. His fingers played with the uneven texture as he urged her deeper into his embrace. "My love, I have never changed my mind on that, despite your stubborn attempts to convince me that I am an idiot to love you."

Her hands clasped around his neck as his mouth warmed hers with the eagerness she had longed for during the days since he had left in rage. The familiar lure of his passion tangled her in its sweet web. When his face brushed her cheek, she moaned.

"Katie?" He tipped her chin so he could see the bruise left by Flynn's cruel treatment. "I'm sorry, honey. If I had not been in such a hurry to get to the train, I would have come to warn you that Isler had heard reports that Proulx was sighted near town yesterday."

Angrily she pulled out of his arms. "You knew that, and you felt it more important to steal the payroll than save my life?"

"I had to get into that mail car to save you, honey." When he saw her expression of disbelief, he picked up the bag from the settee.

Only now did Katie realize it was not the payroll, but a private mail bag. He took a handful of envelopes from it, and she watched silently as he sorted through them. When he ripped open one and shoved it into her hand, she looked from the crumbled page to his tight face. "What is this?"

"Read it," he ordered as he led her closer to the fireplace and its warm glow.

"I did. I don't understand. This is a birth certificate for Katrina—" She held it nearer her face. "—for Katrina Theodora Dubois."

"Katrina Theodora Dubois. Karleen Tamara Forrester. Same first and second initials. Same birthday."

"You mean this person is K.T.?" asked Ethan, voicing his sister's confusion.

Jonah said grimly, "Flynn's detective in New Orleans wired that this would be on the mail train tonight. Duncan informed me before sending the message to Flynn. If he had gotten it—"

She shivered as she interrupted, "He would have known they could find no one named Katharine St. Pierre. But I don't understand why you think this other person is me. It must be a coincidence that we have the same birthday and initials. I don't even know if I came from New Orleans."

"You did, honey. No, don't ask how I know. Read this, and you will understand." Jonah handed her another paper.

When her brother came to stand to look over her shoulder, they read the missive together. Katie gasped as she read it twice more before she could believe what was written there.

To Lyndon Flynn, Flynn's Copper Mining Company, Copper Peak, Montana Territory. Results of investigation into Katharine St. Pierre. No information found. Following information might be of interest.

Katrina Theodora Dubois, born May 5, 1863. Mother Rayna Dubois. Father Theodore Flynn. First child of Dubois. Younger brother Ethan Lemieux born September 25, 1872. Father Rene Lemieux. Rayna Dubois died 1872. Children disappeared along with uncle named Elijah Dubois. No further information in New Orleans.

"Uncle?" She shook her head as she watched her brother walk to the bar to refill his glass. "I never guessed Eli was our uncle."

"Not your only one," he said grimly. "Look at the name of your father. Theodore Flynn. That's

Flynn's brother. Your dear 'daddy,' Katie, was actually your uncle. I would guess it was not accidental that Eli chose to come to Copper Peak to prey on Flynn."

Ethan spoke into the silence that had settled on the room. "Eli was talking about coming into a great deal of money. The settlement, he called it."

"He didn't tell me!" gasped Katie. She wished so many questions were not being answered at once. Her head felt as if it could spin off at any moment and disappear into some nether world.

"He swore me to secrecy, because he said he wanted to surprise you, K.T."

"He did," she said mournfully. She was glad of Jonah's arm around her waist, for she feared that her numb feet would refuse to hold her up. Trying to maintain her composure, she asked, "So what now?"

Jonah flung out his hand. "This is yours, honey."

With a wry expression, she said, "No court will award this house and the mine to me. Somehow the story of my role as—"

"You *are* his only living relative, Katie. This is your legacy from a man who hated us both."

"I'm not sure I want it."

"I don't think you have much choice." Jonah sat with her on the settee and drew her to lean against him. Wrapping his arms around her shoulders, he felt her hands rise to rest on his wrists. "What you want to do with it is up to you. Whatever you decide, I will support you totally."

She closed her eyes and savored the rapture of being in his arms again. The familiar scents of sweaty horse and wet wool brought to mind the many years of riding the mountains in search for prey. That world would be denied to her if she chose a respectful life as the owner of Flynn's Copper Mining Company.

"I want to be with you, Jonah," she whispered. "I'm so sorry. You were right, and I was wrong."

Chuckling, he kissed her cheek quickly. "I never thought to hear you speak those words, my love."

"I haven't been wrong before now!" she retorted in the same light spirit.

"No?"

"No! I guessed you were the bandit. I dealt with Flynn so competently that he never suspected I was other than Katie St. Pierre until Les betrayed me. I—"

His palm clamped over her mouth as he commanded, "Enough! I accede to your record, but no more gloating."

Peeling his fingers from her lips, she turned to put her hand against his cheek. It took little urging for him to lower his mouth to meet hers. At its touch, she knew it did not matter what life she chose. The love tested by betrayal and death would grow stronger whatever they decided to do. They had dared to fight the devil haunting their lives and won a love beyond their dreams.